Forced to
b

AT THE
BILLIONAIRE'S
BIDDING

Complete your collection with
all three books!

In June: *At the Prince's Pleasure*
In July: *At the Tycoon's Command*

AT THE
BILLIONAIRE'S
BIDDING

EMMA
DARCY

MELANIE
MILBURNE

SHARON
KENDRICK

All the characters in this book have no existence outside the imagination
of the author, and have no relation whatsoever to anyone bearing the
same name or names. They are not even distantly inspired by any
individual known or unknown to the author, and all the incidents are
pure invention.

M&B™ and M&B™ with the Rose Device
are trademarks of the publisher.
Harlequin Mills & Boon Limited, Eton House,
18-24 Paradise Road, Richmond, Surrey TW9 1SR

AT THE BILLIONAIRE'S BIDDING
© by Harlequin Books S.A. 2009

The Bedroom Surrender © Emma Darcy 2003
The Greek's Bridal Bargain © Melanie Milburne 2005
The Billionaire Bodyguard © Sharon Kendrick 2004

ISBN: 978 0 263 87521 8

024-0809

Harlequin Mills & Boon policy is to use papers that are
natural, renewable and recyclable products and made from
wood grown in sustainable forests. The logging and
manufacturing processes conform to the legal environmental
regulations of the country of origin.

Printed and bound in Spain
by Litografia Rosés S.A., Barcelona

The Bedroom Surrender

EMMA DARCY

Initially a French/English teacher, **Emma Darcy** changed careers to computer programming before the happy demands of marriage and motherhood. Very much a people person, and always interested in relationships, she finds the world of romance fiction a thrilling one and the challenge of creating her own cast of characters very addictive.

CHAPTER ONE

THE large group of local children surging into the foyer of the hotel caught Adam Cazell's attention first—something of a curiosity, given that this was the Raffles Hotel Le Royal, a mecca for wealthy tourists in Phnom Penh, and it was the cocktail hour. Adam paused on his way to the famous Elephant Bar to meet up with the rest of his party, amused by the chirpy excitement of the children, all dressed in long black pants and white tunics, regardless of gender.

Then he saw the woman who was shepherding them forward. *She* brought Adam to an absolute standstill, the sheer exquisite beauty of her catching the breath in his throat, punching his heart, wiping everything else from his mind.

Pale perfect skin, gleaming like pearl shell.

Long, liquid, shiny black hair, falling to below her waist.

Exotic eyes, black velvet, thickly fringed with long silky lashes, their almond shape tilting slightly up at the corners.

Finely arched brows that winged up at the ends, as well, accentuating the fine cast of her angled cheekbones.

A straight elegant nose, the slight flare of her nostrils balancing the lush sensuality of the sexiest mouth

5

Adam had ever seen, full pink-red lips, stunningly delineated by texture, not by cosmetic gloss. She wore no make-up that he could see.

A natural work of art.

Not Cambodian like the children.

She was tall, slender, innately graceful, and what country she called home, what mixture of genes had created her, Adam could not even begin to guess. All he knew was he'd never seen anyone like her. She had no peer amongst all the beautiful women who'd sought his acquaintance, and being one of the few billionaires in the prime of his life, he'd met legions of them.

With all his concentrated brain-power, he willed her to look at him.

She didn't.

She spoke to the children who gave her their rapt attention as though she were some goddess, commanding their reverent obeisance.

'Good heavens!' The surprised voice of his current companion, Tahlia Leaman, jangled in his ears as she hooked her arm around his. 'Fancy seeing Rosalie James here!'

He'd left Tahlia in the bathroom, blow-drying her long blond hair—a tedious activity that always tried his patience. He glanced quickly at her now to see if she was looking at the woman with the children.

No doubt about where her gaze was trained. She raised her other arm in a wave. 'Rosalie! Hi!'

The greeting evoked a frown, a quick look—the lustrous dark gaze skimming right past Adam—a rueful little smile, a nod of acknowledgment to Tahlia, and that was it, the briefest of interruptions to her communication with the children.

'Must be doing her children's charity thing,' Tahlia commented, hugging Adam's arm. 'Come on, darling. The others are probably already waiting for us in the bar.'

It piqued him, not to be at least *noticed* by the woman. In most company he stood out as a big man, well over six feet tall, broad-shouldered, powerful physique, with a face most women considered attractive, wearing well for its thirty-eight years. A good head of hair, too, though the dark brown was liberally streaked with grey, adding to his somewhat distinguished persona. He wasn't accustomed to being passed over by anyone!

'Who *is* Rosalie James?' he demanded of Tahlia, wanting some definitive tag on her.

It earned an incredulous look. 'You don't know?'

'I wouldn't ask if I knew,' he said tersely, wanting information not gushy nonsense.

Tahlia rolled her eyes. 'Only the queen of the catwalk for all the influential designers in Europe and the U.S.—the one model they all vie for to show off their star creations. The rest of us aren't even in the running if Rosalie James is available.'

'Is that a bitchy comment?'

Tahlia grimaced. 'The plain truth. I can't even be bitchy about her, though she does get the plum jobs. When she's not modelling, she works her butt off for orphaned kids and I suspect most of what she earns gets funnelled to them, too. You rarely ever see her on the social circuit. She's not into partying.' Tahlia slanted him a knowing look. 'Not your kind of woman, Adam.'

'No,' he agreed.

And they walked on to the bar.

But the image of Rosalie James lingered in his mind, indelibly printed there, a rarity that both annoyed and intrigued him. Why would such a beautiful woman spend all her leisure time do-gooding, not to mention pouring all she earned into it? What drove her?

Adam knew he was a born achiever. Building up successful businesses had always given him a buzz, though he grew bored with them once they were flying high. His latest challenge was getting a new airline off the ground and he was aiming to organise cheap flights to South-East Asia, scouting the possibilities while ostensibly on this pleasure trip.

To his mind, Cambodia had a lot to offer tourists. Here in Phnom Penh, the Royal Palace and the Silver Pagoda with its fabulous Buddhas—one encrusted with over nine thousand diamonds, another in Baccarat crystal—held so many unbelievable treasures, it was mind-boggling. And seeing Angkor Wat today—that amazing complex of temples built in the twelfth century—definitely one of the wonders of the world, well worth the trip.

He'd brought a few of his company executives and their women with him, and when he and Tahlia arrived in the Elephant Bar, they were there, still raving

over what they'd seen at Angkor Wat. Adam left
Tahlia with them and went to the bar to order drinks.

'A group of children entered the hotel just now,'
he remarked to the barman. 'What are they doing
here?'

'They've come to sing for the tour group having
dinner around the swimming pool this evening. A raf-
fle is being held out there, the proceeds to go to their
orphanage. Their little concert is by way of a thank-
you. Miss James organised it.'

'You know this Miss James?'

The barman nodded and smiled. 'The kids call her
the angel. Sings like one, too. She does a lot of good
here for the orphans.'

Adam frowned. *The angel.* He hadn't seen her as
some kind of ethereal being. Her impact on him had
been very physical. Sensual. Sexual. Which made it
all the more frustrating that she hadn't been aware of
his presence. No recognition of who he was, either.
Not even when she had acknowledged Tahlia's call
had she bothered to show any curiosity about her fel-
low model's escort.

What kind of woman didn't notice such things?

Most of the women he knew were like butterflies,
instinctively seeking the sweet nectar of money. Like
Tahlia, a top-line model herself, happy to be along
for the ride for as long as it lasted. He wasn't particularly cynical about his wealth being a powerful
drawcard, regarding it as the natural order of things.
He enjoyed having the best-looking women in the

world in his company, just as they enjoyed the high life he could provide.

It was something he took so much for granted that one more beautiful woman shouldn't have mattered one way or another. Except...being ignored had got under his skin, especially being ignored when he'd wanted to impress as strongly as he'd been impressed. A passing vexation, he told himself. Rosalie James lived on a different planet to the one he occupied. Pursuing her would be absurd. Non-productive. Clearly in her world, do-gooding had priority over... sinful pleasures.

He tried to block her out of his mind, chatting to his executives about the viability of establishing a Saturn Airline service to Cambodia. But when they moved from the bar to go to the dining room, he heard the singing begin. Her voice—it had to be hers—was delivering the verse of a very melodic song in a clear pure tone, perfect pitch...*angelic.*

None of the recording artists he'd signed for Saturn Records in years gone by had ever come close to having a voice like that. It sent a shiver down his spine. Rosalie James could have been a star in the music world. Still could. With her looks, her talent...

Then the children came in on the chorus, singing with more gusto than musicality, belting out their words at the top of their voices, almost drowning hers out.

Forget her, Adam savagely told himself.

He'd sold off the record company to fund the airline.

There was absolutely no profit in forcing an acquaintance with Rosalie James, either on a personal or business level.

Six months later Adam Cazell saw her again.

And was once more transfixed by her beauty.

He was at the Met in New York. It was the opening night of Puccini's Turandot. Adam was not a big fan of opera but he'd been hooked into attending this premiere—the proceeds to go to charity—by his latest lady, Sacha Rivken, who loved glittery theatrical events that promised lots of celebrities in the limelight. Their affair was new enough for it still to be a pleasure to indulge her.

Along with a festive party of jet-setting friends, they were seated in a corner box of the Grand Tier level of the famous Metropolitan Opera House, enjoying the buzzing atmosphere of a big night out. Sacha had positioned herself and Adam on the curve of the corner so she could more easily spot the most *watchable* people entering the two central boxes which directly faced the stage.

The far box was filled first. Sacha was speculating over who might occupy the adjoining box when the awaited party arrived and a jolt of recognition hit him.

Rosalie James…leading her companions into the front row of seats.

The liquid black hair was coiled around the top of her head, baring a long, pale, swanlike neck, around which hung a fabulous necklace of rubies and diamonds.

No sexless white tunic and black pants tonight. She wore a figure-hugging gown of dark red velvet—breasts, waist, hips, every feminine curve lovingly delineated to breathtaking effect. Little shoulder-cap sleeves swept into a low, heart-shaped neckline that revealed a tantalising hint of cleavage. Her carriage was regal. She looked regal. If she'd worn a tiara, she would have had people wondering what royal family had spawned her.

As she took the end seat, she smiled up at the man about to settle beside her—a big man, his physique every bit a match for Adam's, tall, powerfully built, his face showing a similar mature age, silver strands sprinkled through his chestnut hair, and he was smiling back at her as though they were sharing some very warm, intimate moment.

Never in his life had Adam experienced jealousy, yet a violent black wave of it instantly crashed through him. If her escort could have been mentally zapped into irretrievable atoms, it would have been done in those few out of control seconds. She had given *him* space in her life—a man of the same physical mould as himself—and Adam felt cheated, wronged, every muscle in his body clenching in aggressive anger at this trick of Fate.

'Oh! It's Rosalie James!' Sacha hissed exuberantly, delighted to have recognised the enigmatic top-line model. 'And she's wearing the show-stopper from this season's Bellavanti collection. I bet it's on loan for this premiere, getting more spotlight for the designer. And look at that necklace! On loan from Bergoff, for sure. Must be worth a fortune!'

Not money spent on herself then, Adam swiftly reasoned, nor gifts from a lover, which was a matter of some relief though he didn't stop to examine the cause of this relief. 'Who's the guy with her?' he grated out, wanting some firm identification, a name that could tell him more about her choice.

'Don't know. Quite a hunk, though. Very impressive.'

Which caused Adam's jaw to tighten further.

'James...is she related to the tenor who's making his debut here tonight?' the one opera buff in their party inquired.

Adam flicked open the glossy program he'd bought earlier. The starring tenor's name was Zuang Chi James. 'She's not Chinese,' he pointed out sardonically.

'You haven't read his bio, Adam,' came the faintly mocking reply. 'Zuang Chi was born in China but he was smuggled out to Australia by his family who wanted him to have the chance to develop his voice. He was officially adopted by a previous Australian ambassador to China and his wife, Edward and Hilary James. They found him teachers at the Sydney Conservatorium of Music where he won a scholarship to...'

'Hey! Rosalie James is an Australian, too,' Sacha chimed in excitedly. 'You could be right about a connection.'

Australian? Was that her nationality? Richard

stared at her, thinking there could be few more English names than Edward and Hilary, but Rosalie James didn't look English-Australian. And the guy with the reddish hair next to her looked more like a huge marauding Scot. Her slim, elegant hand was swallowed up in his as the lights dimmed.

Adam suffered through the first act of the opera which was utterly meaningless to him. He couldn't get his mind off Rosalie James and her escort, both of whom looked utterly enthralled by the action on the stage. She didn't once glance in the direction of his box, his seat. Every time Zuang Chi James sang, she leaned forward, her body finely tensed, her focus entirely on the tenor as though she did have some extra personal interest in his performance. Was he her adopted brother? He certainly won the most applause from her.

But it *was* his debut at the Met, surely a milestone in any operatic singer's career, and even Adam conceded he had a magnificent voice. Those facts alone could be eliciting her interest. After all, she sang like an angel herself, though without the resonant power of a trained classical singer. Finally, Adam remembered the proceeds from tonight's premiere were to go to a charity.

That was why Rosalie James was here.

Do-gooding.

Probably most of the people in her box were connected to the charity, directors of the board or committed fund-raisers. Except she was altogether too cosy with the big man beside her for Adam to dismiss him as a charitable connection. The all too obvious rapport between them was like a thorn in his side, constantly irritating.

He was glad when the opera ended.

Supper at the Four Seasons was more his style.

Three months later their paths crossed again.

Unplanned.

Unexpected.

With the same stunning impact as before, but with one big difference. This time Adam was not accompanied by a woman. And Rosalie James was on her own.

It was a Sunday, midsummer in England. Adam left his London residence, looking forward to the pleasure of driving his Aston Martin into the country and collecting his daughter from Davenport Hall where she had spent the first week of her school holidays with her best friend, who happened to be the niece of the Earl of Stanthorpe.

Adam's ex-wife was delighted with that connection to the British upper class. Sending their daughter to Roedean was pure status snobbery on Sarah's part— a ridiculous reason in Adam's mind, but it wasn't a big enough issue to argue over. Besides, Cate seemed happy there, didn't complain about anything.

She'd just turned thirteen, his one and only child from his one and only marriage, and a very bright spark, indeed. He was proud of her, always enjoyed her company when she spent time with him. They had fun together, the kind of adventurous fun her mother had never appreciated—going places, experiencing new things.

To Sarah, there was no place like England and she wasn't happy anywhere else, a fact she made plain by divorcing him three years after they were married. She didn't want to spend her life gallivanting around the world with him. She was now married to a member of parliament and was the perfect politician's wife, do-gooding with the best of them for public brownie points.

Adam wished her well. There was no acrimony between them. The divorce settlement had been more than generous and he still paid for whatever Sarah wanted for Cate. Money, he'd found, bought a lot of harmony. He could have their daughter with him whenever he wanted. Having made time off from business commitments for Cate's summer holidays, it somewhat niggled him that she had chosen to spend the first week of it with her best friend. Didn't she have enough of Celeste's company at school? Or was Davenport Hall a big attraction?

Having been invited there for lunch to meet Celeste's family before whisking Cate away, Adam took particular notice of the place when he arrived, driving slowly through the gateway and down a long avenue of massive trees, their branches intertwining overhead to form a sun-dappled tunnel. He had the eerie feeling of being drawn into some time warp.

Cate had told him the hall was over four hundred years old and the thickness of the tree trunks suggested they were of the same age, yet the leaves were a light pretty green showing a bright continuance of life. At the end of the avenue the driveway circled around a massive stone fountain, water splashing and tumbling in endless cascades, a sparkling pleasure. Beyond it stood an impressive mansion, three storeys high, much of its walls covered by ivy.

The impression of solidity and permanence was strong. This had been the home of the Earls of Stanthorpe for half a millennium. Adam had no need of deep roots himself, but he could feel its attraction here, the sense of security that undoubtedly came with nothing ever changing. Did this place have some special magic to it that appealed to Cate? Or was she being over-influenced by Sarah's values?

He was greeted at the front door by an old butler who'd probably served the family for decades. Having identified himself, Adam was ushered into a huge hallway, a wide strip of rich red carpet bisecting a floor of black and white tiles, a gallery of portraits on the walls, obviously depicting generations of earls. Adam instantly thought he wouldn't want to carry the weight of all this heritage on his shoulders, tying him to the one place for life.

Yet when he was shown into a drawing room of magnificent proportions and furnished with rich elegance, he could understand the tug of possessions that made their own seductive claim. There were three groupings of sofas and chairs and tables, one directly in front of a massive marble fireplace. But no fire was lit or needed. Sunshine streamed through a bank of six windows at one end of the room where a man and woman rose from another sitting area, smiling their welcome.

'Mr. Adam Cazell, m'lord,' the butler announced.

The Earl of Stanthorpe was tall and lean, but with none of the rather effete air Adam associated with aristocracy. He had dark intelligent eyes and a strong grip to his hand. 'Hugh Davenport,' he said, inviting informality. 'A pleasure to meet Cate's father. This is my wife, Rebel.'

Curious name for a lady of the establishment, and she was certainly a distinctive one—a mass of curly black hair tumbling to her shoulders, bright hazel eyes, an unusual angular jawline, a warm, winning smile of perfect white teeth.

Adam smiled back at her as he retrieved his hand from the Earl's and offered it to his hostess. 'How do you do?' A silly greeting, he'd always thought, but it seemed appropriate on this occasion.

'I trust you had a pleasant trip down from London, Mr. Cazell?'

'Adam.'

'Thank you.' Her smile widened to a grin. 'I've learned to be a bit cautious about jumping in with first names here in England. I'm from Australia and old habits die hard.'

Rather intriguing to find a dyed-in-the-wool English earl married to an Australian. Was he a *rebel,* too?

'Please join us,' she went on, gesturing to a nearby armchair. 'The children are out walking the dogs but they should be back any minute.'

She'd barely finished speaking when Cate burst into the room, throwing the double doors to it wide open. 'Hi, Dad! Saw your car coming up the drive,' she breathlessly informed.

Celeste was right on Cate's heels, along with a couple of Yorkshire terriers. 'We ran but you got here first, Mr. Cazell. Oh, do shut up, Fluffy and Buffy!' This to the dogs who were yapping at Adam—a stranger on their territory.

Two small boys raced in past the girls and the dogs, coming to an abrupt and rather shy halt at seeing Cate's father, eyeing him up and down before the older one—possibly all of five—commented with considerable awe, 'He's as big as Uncle Zachary, Mum.'

Rebel laughed at the remark.

Then in strolled Rosalie James.

She looked directly at him.

And all Adam's instincts transmitted a wild belief that the time warp in the tunnel of trees had been spiralling him towards this moment.

CHAPTER TWO

SO THIS was Adam Cazell…Cate's father…

As her nephew had just said, as big as Zachary Lee, but what of his heart? From listening to his daughter, Rosalie had formed the strong impression that Adam Cazell didn't give enough of it to Cate, whose discontent with her home life was all too evident. Celeste thought her best friend's father was *fabulous,* but that had more to do with her image of him as a daring billionaire businessman with enormous buying power.

A colourful man, Rosalie thought, if viewed from the perspective of his flamboyant achievements, but close up…

Then the big man's gaze locked onto hers, jolting her with an emanation of power that squeezed her heart and sent a weird shiver down her spine. Silver grey eyes…like bullets…tearing through defences she had raised a long, long time ago. She stared back at him, helpless to do anything else, feeling his aggression weakening every bone in her body.

Hugh rescued her, moving to draw the boys forward and introduce them. 'These are my sons, Geoffrey and Malcolm.'

It forced Adam Cazell to look at them and say something appropriate, giving Rosalie enough recovery time to be more on guard when her introduction came.

'And this is Rebel's sister, Rosalie James.'

Politeness demanded she touch his hand. He seized complete possession of hers, strong fingers wrapping around it, pressing a hot imprint that felt like a claim on her entire body—his for the taking.

Resistance burned in her mind.

Nobody took her. Nobody!

'Her sister?' The assault of his eyes was briefly halted by a flicker of surprise at the relationship. He glanced at Rebel, then back to Rosalie, frowning.

'No likeness,' she dryly interpreted.

Celeste piped up. 'Everyone in Rebel's family was adopted, Mr. Cazell. From all over the world. Rebel is the English one...'

'And you?' he asked Rosalie, his eyes as sharp as steel knives.

Every instinct screamed to deny him any private information. She sensed he would maul it unmercifully. 'My life is my own, Mr. Cazell,' she said with quiet dignity.

'Adam,' he insisted.

She denied him the familiarity. Give this man an inch and he'd take a mile, and Rosalie was not about to travel his road which she'd already judged to be totally centred on what he wanted. She tore her gaze from his to send a quelling message to her chatterbox niece.

'Let's give Cate the chance to talk to her father,

Celeste. She hasn't seen him for…how long has it been, Cate?'

It was a deliberate barb, aimed at hitting some paternal guilt. Frustratingly, his daughter defused it. 'Oh, Dad will get around to me in his own good time,' she answered off-handedly.

Surprisingly Adam Cazell laughed, released Rosalie's hand and swung towards his daughter, spreading his arms invitingly. 'I could do with a hug, Catie mine.'

Her young face lit up with joy in the openly affectionate invitation. She flew at him and he lifted her up and whirled her around. 'Dad, I'm not a little kid anymore,' she protested, mindful of her dignity in this company but loving his uninhibited pleasure in her nonetheless.

He set her down with a look of helpless dismay. 'The terrible teens,' he moaned. 'You're only one small step into it. Does everything have to change?'

She huffed an exasperated sigh at him. 'You have to face the fact I'm growing up.'

'Well, you can teach me about it over the holidays,' he said with grand generosity.

'Sure.' Her mouth twisted. 'A few weeks to pack it all in.'

The irony floated right past him. Or he chose to ignore it, smiling to dispel the slightly sour note. 'So what have you two been doing this past week?' A twinkling look at Celeste. 'Shall we sit down and you can regale me with teenage girl things?'

Quite a charmer, Rosalie thought, watching Celeste's eager response to the invitation. They all moved to the lounge setting near the windows. With the confidence of a charismatic king, Adam Cazell proceeded to court his daughter and the family whose guest she still was until after lunch.

Rosalie had chosen an armchair slightly apart from the rest of them, determined on observing rather than participating. She knew he was aware of her detachment and would undoubtedly try to breach it sooner or later, which would put her on her mettle again, but she felt safe enough to watch him for a while, and he was quite compellingly watchable.

The charm tempered an innate forcefulness that obviously fuelled everything he tackled, explaining why he succeeded in whatever he undertook in the business world. And he was attractive, as well. Not in any pretty playboy sense. His face was too rugged to be called classically handsome but its strong lines and angles had a very male appeal that Rosalie judged would automatically evoke a positive response in both men and women. Besides which, the rather unruly waves of his dark hair softened the craggy look, adding to his charm, making him appear approachable.

The boys certainly weren't frightened of him.

More fascinated.

As they'd been by Zachary Lee.

The comparison niggled at Rosalie's sense of rightness. Adam Cazell might have the same formidable height and breadth of chest and shoulder as her big brother, promising a strength that would be easy to lean on, but she was sure he was much more a taker by nature than a giver.

She rubbed at the hand he had taken, wanting to erase the lingering sense of his invasive power. He noticed the action and she instantly stopped it, not wanting him to have the satisfaction of knowing he'd left his *touch* on her.

She wasn't sure if it was sex or ego driving him where she was concerned—maybe both. She'd been targeted by too many wealthy and influential men not to recognise that Adam Cazell fancied acquiring her, which, of course, was for the purpose of public show and sex on call until the gloss wore off and desire waned.

Usually such attention was water off a duck's back to Rosalie. But there was something more intense, more personal, more threatening about Adam Cazell. As much as she wanted to dismiss him, it was like he'd burrowed under her skin and she couldn't pry him out. Maybe if she watched him long enough, the disturbing effect of the man would fade.

Oddly enough, his daughter had made a strong impression on her, too. Cate was very bright, older than her years in reading people and where he stood with them. The occasional flash of cynicism in some of her comments had disturbed Rosalie, revealing knowledge bred by disappointment or disillusionment. Cate had grown armour she shouldn't need to have at thirteen.

But a privileged background didn't guarantee a happy upbringing. Celeste, who still looked angelic with her beautiful fair hair and big blue eyes, had been characterised by Hugh as 'an evil seed,' a monstrous child—expelled from one school after another for outrageous behaviour—before Rebel came into their lives and turned everything around for them. Rebel had seen Hugh's orphaned niece as a lost child in desperate need of rescue and had barged straight into proving to Hugh how wrong he was in his reading of the situation.

Rosalie didn't see Cate Cazell as being in need of rescue. She was a survivor, that one, probably with as strong a will as her father. She'd inherited his dark wavy hair, and the shape of his face—the high wide brow and the sharply delineated chisel chin, but her mouth was softer and her eyes were a warmer grey with a ring of amber around the irises. She was tall, too, though with a much more slender frame than her father. Rosalie imagined she'd be very striking when she grew up.

But for now, the girl did crave more of her father's time and attention. And should have it, Rosalie thought, remembering how much it had meant to her to have Zachary Lee caring about her every thought and feeling, loving her, protecting her, making her feel safe and secure. Not alone.

Yes…that was how Cate felt…too much alone. Her family consisted of a socialising mother, too busy aiding and abetting her political husband's career to actually listen to her daughter, a stepfather who was never *there* for her, a father who flew into and out of her life, handing out oodles of ice-cream, but not staying around long enough to realise that sweets weren't enough. No wonder Cate liked being with Celeste's family!

'Rosalie...'

His voice sliding into her private reverie, kicking her heart into a faster beat...the silver bullet eyes trained on her again, commanding her attention.

'I just remembered where I last saw you,' he said with a musing little smile designed to tease her interest.

Modelling put her in the public eye. It was not remarkable that she had been seen somewhere by Adam Cazell, possibly accompanying one of his girlfriends to a fashion show. Was this another attempt to dig into her life?

'The premiere of Turandot at the Met in New York,' he went on, surprising her with the venue named.

'You were there?' Rebel leapt in delightedly. 'You heard Zuang Chi sing?'

He nodded. 'A magnificent voice.'

'He's our brother,' Rebel claimed with pride. 'We were all there for his premiere. The whole family. It was a marvellous night, wasn't it, Rosalie?'

'Yes.'

She hadn't seen Adam Cazell at the opera and didn't like the feeling he had watched her without her knowing. Though she had been more or less on public exhibit that night, paid to wear the dress and necklace for others to see and covet.

He leaned forward on his sofa like a big cat about to pounce. 'Just how many are in your family, Rebel?'

She laughed. 'Fourteen of us. Plus husbands and wives and our wonderful parents. We filled a whole box at the Met, didn't we, darling?' She smiled at Hugh in fond recollection.

'We certainly did. Marvellous night,' he echoed.

Adam nodded in agreement. 'I'm sorry I didn't make your acquaintance at the time. Must confess I only noticed Rosalie.' His gaze sliced back to her, a wry little smile on his lips. 'You were singularly spectacular.'

She returned his smile. 'I was on parade.'

'And the red-haired man you were with?'

'Zachary Lee,' Rebel happily supplied. 'Our *big* brother.'

Satisfaction glinted in his eyes.

A possible competitor dismissed, Rosalie interpreted, thinking he had certainly noticed her escort, probably sizing him up and wondering how *attached* they were.

'None of us are blood relations,' she stated, feeling a strong urge to put a spoke in his wheel. 'That's why we don't look alike.'

'Uncle Zachary is the American one,' Celeste informed him.

'And the one we all look up to,' Rosalie quickly slid in, not wanting Celeste to list off their multinational family, which she was clearly on the verge of doing. A change of subject was urgently needed. 'Do you often attend the opera, Adam?' she inquired.

'No.'

'It was a premiere,' his daughter commented before he could add more. 'Daddy's girlfriends lu-u-uv premieres.'

'Oh, come on, Catie,' he chided good-naturedly. 'I've taken you to a few, too. The Harry Potter film, the...'

'Okay, okay.' She held up her hands in mock defence. 'He's far more into pop music, Rosalie. You know...Saturn Records before he sold it off? He didn't do classical stuff.'

'Which doesn't mean I can't enjoy it.' Slightly more snappish on that reply.

'I've never heard you play it,' Cate argued.

'You're not with me all the time.'

Big blunder.

Cate's face tightened. 'You're right, Dad. What do I get? Fifteen percent if I'm lucky? For all I know you could be playing opera all the time you don't have me with you.' She flashed a gritty look of apology at Rosalie. 'Sorry. Shouldn't have butted in. I can't *swear* my father doesn't like classical music.'

'Never a good idea to speak for others,' Rosalie tossed back with a sympathetic shrug.

Adam Cazell erased the frown evoked by Cate's

rather biting mockery, his sharply penetrating gaze targeting Rosalie again. 'Actually, a good voice attracts my attention regardless of what is being sung.'

'Then you must have enjoyed listening to Zuang Chi,' she replied, wondering if and how he would respond to his daughter's cry for more attention from him.

'To you, as well.'

'Me?' What did he mean? Had she lost the thread of this conversation while thinking about Cate.

His eyes burned into hers. 'I heard you sing at the Raffles Hotel Le Royal in Phnom Penh. You were leading a choir of orphans.'

Shock jammed her mind for several seconds. She struggled to take in the incredible coincidence of his actually being in the same place when... 'That was...nine months ago.'

'Yes,' he said. 'You have a beautiful singing voice. Very pure in tone.' His mouth quirked. 'If I'd still been running Saturn Records, I might have tried to sign you up.'

'Rosalie's birth mother was a professional singer,' Rebel remarked.

'I'm not interested,' she quickly cut in, shaking her head at her sister. 'You know that.'

Rebel sighed. 'It always seemed like a waste to me. Even Zuang Chi said...'

'No! I don't want to be in that world!' The curt dismissal effectively silenced her sister. She turned back to Adam Cazell who was learning—already knew—too much about her for Rosalie's comfort, digging, digging, digging. She turned the screw. 'What were you doing in Phnom Penh, Adam?'

'Scouting for my airline.'

His eyes mocked her evasive tactics.

Every muscle in her body tensed as she felt his intent to close in on her. Hunter...warrior...he embodied both those images in her mind, and for the first time in many many years, Rosalie felt vulnerable to a man.

Hugh's old butler made a timely entrance, announcing, 'Lunch is about to be served in the dining room, m'lord.'

'Thank you, Brooks.' Hugh stood up. 'Girls, boys, Adam...'

He ushered them out, leaving the two sisters to trail after them, a move that had undoubtedly been orchestrated by some telling look from his wife. Rosalie sometimes wondered if the understanding between them was almost psychic. At least, she was momentarily relieved of Adam Cazell's presence, but Rebel, of course, had something to say, linking arms with her for a confidential little chat.

'He's seriously aware of you, Rosalie. Totally captivated, I'd say,' she murmured.

'Rebel, I don't care to be the ornament on any man's arm.'

'I'm not suggesting you should be. I just think it's more than that. He's really interested.'

'He's a playboy. You've heard Cate rattle off all his girlfriends.'

'Well, maybe you should take off some time to play, too.'

Rosalie frowned at her sister. 'Why are you selling him to me?' Rebel had been a super saleswoman before she'd married Hugh and started a family.

A sigh. 'I'm worried about Cate. You must have caught those touches of bitterness when she was speaking to her father. Maybe you could do some good there, Rosalie.'

'Cate Cazell is not a lost child, Rebel. She's strong enough to fight her own battles with her father. I thought she got in a couple of good jabs today.'

'A parent can brush these things off, telling themselves the child is being moody, difficult. None so blind as those who don't want to see, Rosalie. But you could make him see through your eyes. And he'd listen to you. It's not right that Cate feels... abandoned.'

'I don't want to get involved with him.'

'It needn't be a heavy involvement.'

'He'll come onto me hard and fast. I know he will, given half a chance.'

'But you're so practised at holding men off.'

'He's different.'

'Oh?' Rebel looked fascinated.

Rosalie grimaced. 'Don't look at me like that. I know when something's not safe. I *know*.'

A frown. 'I thought you could handle anything.

Sorry for pressing. It's just…I am worried about Cate. She's entering her teens. If she doesn't get what she needs from her father…'

'She does have a mother.'

'Useless. Too full of her own life. It's Adam she looks to. If he's not there for her…'

'Cate will manage in her own way.'

'No. She'll be at risk. If she feels let down and alone…getting into drugs is a very easy step.'

'Why don't you speak to Adam yourself about this?'

'I'm not the one he wants to win.'

Their private chat ended on that line. They'd entered the dining room and the others were there waiting for them to come and sit down.

Adam Cazell's gaze raked Rosalie from head to foot, making her extremely conscious of the strip of bare skin between her hipster jeans and the waist-length blue and white striped bandeau top she wore, her long hair loose over bare shoulders, her face bare of make-up. She felt her blood heating, her pale skin flushing.

She wanted to scream, 'No! Look elsewhere, Adam Cazell.'

But he wasn't going to.

Cate stood beside him, not impinging on his consciousness one bit. It didn't occur to him that winning his daughter was more important than winning another woman.

Rebel was right.

She did have the power to make him listen to her if he had the ears to hear.

Maybe she could handle the risk...for Catie's sake.

It shouldn't take long to hammer the message home.

CHAPTER THREE

SUNDAY lunch at Davenport Hall was always held in the informal dining room and very much a family affair. Regardless of any guests and despite their young age, the boys sat up at the table with their parents, Geoffrey with an extra cushion on his chair, Malcolm with a booster seat on his. They were only five and three but had been thoroughly coached in good manners, and Celeste at thirteen, was very much the young lady.

It was a lovely, bright, inviting room. The furniture was white, the furnishings yellow, and long windows overlooked a rose garden in full summer bloom. The pristine white cloth on the oval table showed off the centrepiece bowl of yellow rosebuds, and yellow linen serviettes in silver holders added their splash of colour. Rosalie sat between the boys, directly across from Adam Cazell who was flanked by the girls, Rebel and Hugh at the two ends.

Adam looked totally bemused as he watched the boys remove their serviettes from the holders and spread them on their laps. No doubt, in the company he usually kept, little children were segregated from the adults, not part of his world at all. Welcome to a real family, Rosalie thought, and wondered if he'd learn anything from it.

The girls dominated the conversation, telling Adam about their last school term—teachers they liked or disliked, hockey matches, tattle about other girls in their class. He indulged their eager chatter, smiling, laughing, frowning quizzically in all the right places. It seemed effortless on his part—no act—no hint of condescension.

He was charming.

And very, very attractive.

Possibly putting himself out to be so because she was observing him.

He shared flashes of amusement with her but made no concerted attempt to engage her in personal conversation. Biding his time, she thought, probably hoping the happy casual atmosphere at the table would lower her guard enough to let him slide inside it later. Having been on the international model circuit since she was eighteen—eleven years now—Rosalie was too experienced with men of his ilk not to know how they made their moves.

When the first strike didn't produce a warm response, set up more favourable circumstances and try a more subtle approach. Few gave up at the first knock-back. Most of them simply didn't believe it. Why would any woman reject such a prize? Only to increase her value and force a chase. But the chase didn't last long. If the desired result wasn't fast in coming, there was always another beautiful woman for such men. Much better for the ego to be appreciated than feel defeated.

Adam Cazell's next move came after lunch. Coffee had been served in the sitting room. The girls had gone upstairs to complete Cate's packing for her departure. Rebel had taken Malcolm up to the nursery for an afternoon nap. Geoffrey was occupying Hugh's attention.

Adam rose from his chair, saying, 'Would you mind if I went for a stroll in your grounds, Hugh? Stretch my legs before driving back to London.'

'Not at all.' Being the thoughtful host he was, his head instantly swung to Rosalie. 'Will you show Adam around?' A rueful smile. 'I doubt Geoffrey has the legs for two long walks.'

Trapped by courtesy.

A clever manouvre from Adam Cazell.

But she was safe in the grounds of Davenport Hall, Rosalie swiftly reasoned, pushing up from her chair to oblige her brother-in-law's guest. And suddenly the silver-bullet eyes were dancing wickedly at her, jolting her confidence and quickening her pulse.

'Is there a maze we can get lost in?' he tossed at her.

'No. But there's a lake you could drown in,' she flipped back at him.

He laughed, his face crinkling, turning up the wattage of his attraction. Rosalie felt her hands clenching in an instinctive need to fight the power that flowed so strongly from him. She had to make a conscious effort to relax her muscles, pretend she was unaffected.

'We'll go out the back way,' she said, and led out into the hallway where he quickly stepped up beside her.

'Are there canoes?' he asked.

She arched an eyebrow at him. 'Didn't you say you wanted to stretch your legs?'

He grinned. 'Canoeing is very physical. You could sit at the other end while I do all the work.'

'The canoes are all one-seaters.'

'You're dashing my romantic dream. Here I am in an old-world setting, in the company of a beautiful woman...'

'And you have a daughter who doesn't want you to be distracted from her,' Rosalie reminded him.

'Ah! The carer of children's needs. I guess this comes from having been orphaned yourself.'

He could turn on a pin. Of course, he had to have an agile and astute mind to be so successful at what he did, and his focus was all on her at the moment, driving to win. Somehow she had to force a refocussing if she was to achieve anything for Cate.

'A child needs to feel someone cares enough to be there for them. Do you think your daughter feels that, Adam?'

'At last she uses my name,' he lightly mocked. 'But does this mean she's warming to me? No. She's using it to emphasise the point that's important to her.'

His accurate analysis made her respect his brain even more. She slanted him a challenging look. 'You haven't answered me.'

'Nor have you, me, Rosalie James,' he swiftly countered, his eyes stabbing her with that truth.

Tit for tat.

Having walked through the hall, they stepped out into the afternoon sunshine and started down the path that led to the ornamental lake. The lawns on either side of it were a lush green. Banks of rhododendrons lent spectacular colour. Waterlilies added their exotic charm. It was a very English scene, Rosalie thought, and knew Rebel had found her home here with Hugh.

She felt completely rootless, herself. No city or country had any special call on her heart. People, yes, but not a place. She wondered if the jet-setting Adam Cazell considered one place home. According to Cate he had residences in London, New York, Hong Kong, and on a Caribbean island. The latter was probably for some taxation alleviation.

'Do you live here with your sister?' he asked.

'No. Just visiting this past week.'

'Where do you call home?'

Rosalie shrugged. 'Nowhere in particular. There are places I can stay whenever I want to.'

'You must have a base from which you work.'

Trying to pin her down. Wanting to know where he could find her. Rosalie wasn't about to make it easy for him though he was right. She had a base in London, the Mayfair apartment owned by Joel Faber, her sister Tiffany's husband. Joel had insisted any one of the James family could use it whenever they wanted to. He'd appointed her the apartment-sitter, knowing full well where most of her money went and wanting to help her in her mission.

'I don't have many possessions,' she said. 'I have no need of them.'

'Are you telling me they can be kept in a suitcase?' he asked sceptically.

'Just about.' She threw him a taunting look. 'I probably fly around the world as much as you do, Adam Cazell.'

'Which gives us something in common.'

'The difference is, I don't have a daughter who's left alone.'

'Cate is not alone. She has her school, as Celeste does. Her mother and stepfather never leave England. She can be with them, call on them...'

'They have other priorities,' Rosalie cut in, shooting him a look that told him he should know that. 'Just because they're here does not mean they are readily available to her. Any more than you are.'

His mouth twisted sardonically. 'You're accusing me of neglect.'

'I'm telling you how it is for her.'

'You've known my daughter for what...all of one week? A bit presumptuous, don't you think, Rosalie?'

'I'm sure you'd like to believe that. Much easier to dismiss what I'm saying.'

His voice took on an edge of anger as he sought a

reason for her argument. 'She's been playing poor little rich girl to you?'

'No. Cate has too much pride for that.'

'Then why are you attacking me?' His eyes sliced at hers. 'Is this your best form of defence?'

'Defence against what?'

He halted. Since she was committed to being his companion on this walk, it forced her to pause and cast an inquiring glance at him. It was easier to ignore the power of the man while walking side by side but standing still, she immediately felt swamped by the intense energy force he emitted, and his strong air of command was reinforced by the blazing certainty in his eyes.

'That's not worthy of you, Rosalie James.'

Her heart missed a beat then leapt into a wild pounding. 'I beg your pardon?' she prevaricated.

'If you're trading truth, then don't lie about what you're feeling with me. It destroys your credibility.'

He was throwing down his gauntlet. Rosalie threw down hers. 'Okay. You'd like my suitcase in your hall for a while. I prefer to pass on that.'

'You can't put what I want in a suitcase. I don't care if you dress up or not.'

She raised her eyebrows mockingly. 'No ornamental display?'

'Irrelevant.'

'Just the *naked* truth.'

His eyes derided her reading of him. 'That I would like, but not in the limited sense you mean.'

A convulsive little shiver ran down her spine as she felt his purpose to invade far more than her body. Rosalie fiercely argued to herself that she was a curiosity to him, an enigma in his kind of world, and he'd teased himself into wanting to know what made her tick. She didn't stop to examine what she felt towards him because it was too threatening to her peace of mind.

'I don't have time for you, Adam.'

'Make time.'

The sheer magnetism of the man tugged at her. She'd felt nothing like this before with anyone. It was as though he was claiming her, and all her self-protective instincts rose to fight any surrender to his will.

'*You* make time...for your daughter,' she hurled back at him.

It did not hit any discernible mark. 'I do,' he replied, still maintaining an implacable concentration on her. 'I take Cate with me during her school holidays. During term I send her postcards from wherever I am. She can call me on my mobile telephone whenever she likes.'

'She's been *here* for the first week of her summer holidays.'

'Not because I failed to be available. It was her choice.'

'And what does that choice say to you, Adam? What does your daughter get with Celeste's family that she doesn't get with you?'

'Since you're bursting to tell me...tell me.'

Rosalie paused, the challenge ringing in her ears, demanding truths that he could recognise, take on board. He was not as much at fault as she had assumed where Cate was concerned. Her mind flitted through all the silent criticisms she had made, trying to home in on the basic problem.

'She's flaunting it in your face, Adam.'

'What?'

'Secure ground that's not going to change.'

He frowned, grimaced, made a gesture encompassing the grounds around them. 'This is not my life. Any more than it's yours. I can't change who I am.'

'She craves what Celeste has—a place to come home to, being an integral part of a family where children are a blessing not a nuisance to be accommodated.'

'I have never treated Cate as a nuisance.' Vehement denial.

'What of your girlfriends? Cate mentioned a string of them. When you have your daughter with you, do you spend much time with her one on one, or is she an extra?'

Another frown. 'She's never seemed to mind when I've had a companion.'

'What choice does she have but to fit in...if she wants to be with you?'

'I take her wherever she wants to go. We have a lot of fun together.'

'You entertain her.'

'Something wrong with that?' he rumbled as though barely holding back an explosion of frustration with her argument.

'It's froth and bubble, Adam. It doesn't ease the loneliness inside. The sense of being a floating part of your life, not of any prime consideration, is eating away at Cate. If you really care about her, take her somewhere special these holidays—just the two of you—and get to know her as a person. She's thirteen. She needs to feel someone loves her for who she is inside.'

He reined in the anger that had been simmering. His eyes scoured hers, searching for ulterior motives to attach to her diatribe against him. There were none. Rosalie stood her ground, waiting for his response, willing him to give her what she needed.

'Why do you care so much?' he asked gruffly.

'Who will if I don't?'

He shook his head. 'Catie is not your business.'

'Caring for children is my business, Adam.'

'She's not an orphan.'

'She's in need.'

He frowned, but he didn't refute what she'd said, which might or might not be a step forward. His expression hardened and his narrowed eyes flashed a cynical look at her. 'Who knows the person you are inside, Rosalie?'

'My family.'

'All fourteen of your brothers and sisters and the people who adopted you?'

'Some more, some less. Overall we're a very close-knit unit, supportive of each other.'

She was arguing Cate's cause because Rebel had asked it of her, though she was sympathetic to it, as well. Oddly enough, she no longer felt so antagonistic towards Adam Cazell. He was not a bad father. Given the man he was and the life he led, he'd certainly made the effort to be a presence in his daughter's life.

His mouth tilted into a wry little smile as he commented, 'Then you're very fortunate...in your family.'

He turned his head, gazing out over the lake, and she sensed his withdrawal from her. He stood a man apart, strongly self-contained, yet possibly he felt very alone on his pinnacle of singular achievement. She wondered about him, whether he'd had parents who'd made the time to know him, siblings who were brought up with him, sharing. What of his ex-wife, his girlfriends...had they ever touched his heart...his soul?

Observing him wrapped in his own thoughts, she was struck by the idea he'd always walked alone, knew nothing else. A man like him had few peers, and those that were would be in contest with him. That was the nature of the beast. As for the women in his life, had any of them seen past what he could give them? Huge wealth and the power that went with it might have been enough for them.

Perhaps she'd been blinded by it herself in making her judgment of him. Impulsively she stepped closer and touched his arm to bring him back from wherever he'd gone. 'You and Cate could form a wonderful bond if you reached out to her,' she pressed.

His biceps muscle tensed. His gaze fastened on hers, bypassing her plea with a piercing intensity that demanded something far more personal. 'What of us?' he shot out, his other hand lifting to grasp her arm.

It was like an electric jolt zapping through her.

Shocked, immobilised, mind jammed, Rosalie could only stare back at him.

'Why trust Cate with me when *you* haven't taken the time to know *the person I am inside*, Rosalie James?'

The words punched into her heart.

The need pulsing from him took her breath away.

Then something deep and alien to her stirred inside Rosalie, a sexual awakening that she had never expected to experience, a wanting to know this man in every sense, a yearning for the kind of love she knew existed between her sisters and the men they'd married. Yet even as she felt this, panic screamed into her mind, beating up the fearful thought—*it's not safe!*

'Da...ad!' came the exasperated call from his daughter.

His jaw tightened. His eyes bit into hers with ruthless and relentless purpose. 'Don't think I'll walk out of your life, Rosalie. We'll meet again.'

She was left shaken to the core as he released her

arm. Her own hand slid limply from his as he turned to face Cate who'd started down the path towards them and now stood waiting, her arms folded with an air of impatience. Or was it resentment that he'd gone off with yet another woman instead of waiting for her?

She'd seen them touching.

Rosalie struggled to block what Adam had said to her out of her mind...focus on the child who was no longer really a child. Her legs carried her automatically, keeping pace with Adam's. They walked apart, but the sense of an inevitable link with him could not be broken.

They reached Cate.

Adam put an arm around his daughter's shoulders and the stiffness instantly went out of them. He hugged her close, smiling, chatting, and she glowed up at him, loving his attention.

He didn't speak to Rosalie again, not in any personal sense. He said a general goodbye to the family, thanking them for their hospitality. All of them trooped out to watch him and Cate drive away from Davenport Hall, the car moving slowly down the avenue of giant elms, as though being gradually drawn through a tunnel to a different time and place.

Rosalie felt a strange tug on her heart.

Into her mind flashed the thought... *I should be with them.*

But it wasn't her journey, she swiftly told herself.

Then Rebel hooked onto her arm and asked, 'Did you do any good?'

She managed an offhand smile. 'I tried.'

'Then he'll make it work,' her sister said with confidence.

Rosalie didn't comment. Rebel had a way of reading things right and Adam Cazell *was* the kind of man who made things work when he set his mind to it.

We'll meet again.

Was that good or bad?

Impossible to know at this point.

Her only certainty was that somewhere in her future, Adam Cazell would walk back into her life and she would have to deal with it, one way or another.

CHAPTER FOUR

ADAM'S mind was greatly exercised by the enigma of Rosalie James as he drove away from Davenport Hall. He felt pumped up by the certainty that she was attracted to him, even against her will, and that will was very, very strong. But why was she so guarded against him? What was she hiding? And how was he going to pry her secrets into the open where he could deal with them?

Beside him, Cate heaved a deeply felt sigh.

Guilt stabbed into Adam. He should be thinking of her, making appropriate plans to deal with the problem he hadn't known about until Rosalie James had laid it on him.

'Sorry to be leaving or glad to be off and away with me?' he tossed at her lightly.

The only response was a private grimace, no return glance at him. 'I guess I can't blame you,' came the resigned mutter. 'She's very beautiful. Even I keep looking at her when she's anywhere in sight.'

'I take it you're speaking of Rosalie James.'

'Who else?' A dry little taunt. 'I'd have to say she's a class above all the other women you've had.'

'I agree she's different,' he said slowly, resisting

the strong temptation to pump his daughter for information on the woman who so intrigued him.

They'd both spent the past week at Davenport Hall, in a family environment where normal barriers would be down, and Celeste would undoubtedly have satisfied any curiosity Cate had wanted answered about the aunt who was a megastar in the fashion world. But newly alert to what Cate might be thinking and feeling, Adam forced himself to focus on the tone and import of what she was saying.

'Have you disliked the women I've had as companions?' he asked.

She shrugged. 'It's not a matter of whether I like or dislike them, is it? I mean…you never ask me. I just get landed with them.'

'Have you found that difficult?'

She brooded in silence for a while.

They left the village of Milton Prior behind. The Aston Marton ate up the road. Adam had plenty to think about as he drove on, waiting for a reply.

It had never occurred to him to ask his daughter's permission to bring any woman of his choice into their lives. He had needs, too, he argued to himself, and Cate had to accept that. He certainly wasn't about to be celibate for the rest of his life. But maybe he should become more aware of how she related to the company he kept. Perhaps he had been too blasé about doing what he wanted, not considering how much he expected Cate to simply fit in.

'I wouldn't mind Rosalie,' she finally said, somewhat grudgingly.

'So you have minded having the others around,' he concluded.

She rolled her eyes at him. 'They're only there for you. You're not that dumb, Dad. They put up with me to have you.'

'Have any of them been nasty to you?'

'Of course not. They're not dumb, either. Usually they do all sorts of stuff to keep me sweet. After all, I am your daughter.'

The cynical flavour of her words struck a bad chord with Adam. Cate was only just thirteen and already she was standing back and assessing people through jaundiced eyes. It shouldn't be like this. But how could he protect her from it? He was who he was and that wasn't going to change.

'Why wouldn't you mind Rosalie James?'

Again she pondered before answering. 'It's a funny thing about Rosalie,' she said as though musing out loud. 'You'd think she'd be full of herself. You know…with how she looks and who she is. The girls at school would just die if she ever visited. I mean she's really huge on the modelling scene and just so stunningly beautiful for real. It's not make-up or clever photography.'

'So I noticed,' he acknowledged dryly.

'But it's like…' Cate looked earnestly at him, wanting him to understand the picture she was drawing. '…none of that is important to her. She shrugs it off as though it's just something she does because she was lucky enough to be born with those looks. No big deal. And you can tell she gets quickly bored if you ask her about it, because before you know it, she turns the conversation around, and you find you're talking about yourself.'

'Well, that's a good trick to protect your privacy.'

'Mmmh…' She frowned, then shook her head. 'I don't think it's a trick.'

'Why not?'

'Because she really listens. It's like…she sees where you're coming from and understands. If it was a trick, what you told her wouldn't mean anything. It would just float by her. Like it does with Mum.' Her voice took on a disturbing edge of contempt. 'Who pretends to listen but you know her mind is off somewhere else.'

He frowned. 'You've got a communication problem with your mother?'

'Duh…' she drawled, her tone of disrespect seeming to encompass him, as well.

Adam didn't like it. He had to remind himself that respect was earned, not a given, even with one's parents. Hadn't he retreated from his own in his teens, realising the generation gap had become impossible to cross? They hadn't had a clue what he was about. They'd marched to a different drum. The easiest course had been to play to their image of how their son should act, and pursue his own path behind their backs.

It was a sobering thought when linked to his daughter.

Cate gave a derisive little laugh. 'Talking to Mum is like talking to that cockatoo in the TV ad.'

'What TV ad?'

A sigh. 'Of course. You don't have time to watch TV.'

'So tell me about it,' Adam invited, ignoring the point of difference in their lifestyles.

'This woman gets a phone call from a friend who's obviously dumping stuff on her and she doesn't want to listen. So she puts the receiver next to her pet cockatoo who's sitting on a perch, and every so often the cockatoo crows into the receiver, "I know. I know." Then finally, "I know, dear." It's a hoot.'

The mimic of the bird's voice was too much like Sarah's for Adam's comfort. He'd have to speak to his ex-wife about this, warn her she was losing Cate through lack of attention.

'The ad is for chocolate, which the woman proceeds to eat,' she went on. 'Pretty clever, huh? Much more enjoyable to consume than a load of stuff that has nothing to do with your life.'

'Very clever.'

Point taken. And very aptly put, Adam thought, aware that Sarah was very wrapped up in pushing her husband's political career, doing everything possible on the social side to promote it. Cate was an appendage, not a prime focus. Just as she was to him, Adam conceded, but an appendage he did give consideration to. It was the quality of the consideration that was in question here.

He wondered how much of this Rosalie James had listened to. And *heard*. His respect for her went up several notches. It would have taken courage, too, to tackle him as she had with a barrage of unpalatable truths.

Cate gave him a look that carried a shrewd calculation that instantly put Adam on his mettle. 'Did you do a line on her?' she asked.

'Who?'

'Rosalie James.'

He found himself inwardly recoiling from the cynical flavour of the question. There was nothing cynical about the feelings stirred by *this* woman and he didn't want to answer Cate in such crass terms.

'Or do you have someone waiting back in London?' she pushed when he didn't immediately answer, her tone flattening out with disinterest in anyone else.

'No. I'm not involved with anyone at the moment.'

In fact, no one since Sacha, whose attraction had died a quick death after the night at the opera. Same with Tahlia after the night in Phnom Penh. Not that any particular fault lay with either woman. In both instances it had been difficult to get Rosalie James out of his mind.

'Well?' Cate persisted. 'You got her out in the grounds alone.'

No doubt about his capacity to arrange whatever

he wanted. How many times had Cate observed him...*doing a line?* Did she feel like a spectator in his life, not a participant?

'Rosalie wanted to speak to me privately. About you,' he stated, knowing that was the only reason for her accompanying him. Her resistance to what he wanted had been rock-solid. Though possibly he had made some dent in it.

'Me?' Cate was astounded.

'Mmmh...' He threw her a smile. 'She likes you. Very much.'

Her face bloomed with colour. Adam wasn't sure if it was pleasure or embarrassment. She quickly turned her head and gazed out the side window. Her hands fidgeted in her lap.

'What did she say?'

He chose his words with care, wanting to establish a new basis for understanding between them. 'That you're extremely smart and I should learn more about you instead of taking you for granted.' He paused to let this concept sink in before adding, 'It struck me as a good idea. So I thought we might spend these summer holidays on Tortola, just relaxing together and doing whatever we fancy. How does that strike you?'

Her head whipped around, her eyes very bright. 'You mean...just the two of us?'

He smiled. 'Yes. Just the two of us.'

'No friends or executives dropping in?' Disbelief in her voice.

'None. I will have to spend an hour or two each day in the computer room, but apart from that, I'm all yours, Catie. We can go shopping in London tomorrow, buy whatever clothes you need, arm ourselves with some new games to play, books to read, then off to the Caribbean. What say you?'

'Yessss!' she almost yelled with excitement, her hands clapping in pure joy. 'That will be terrific, Dad!'

He laughed, happy to have made her happy. 'We'll have a good time.'

'We sure will.'

'But we definitely need some new games. You always beat me at Scrabble.'

'That's because you don't take long enough to think what might score more than the first word you see in your letters.'

'Uh-huh! Then be warned. I shall *think* in future.'

Cate laughed and bubbled with plans.

Rosalie James was forgotten.

But not by Adam.

There wasn't going to be another woman in his life.

Until *she* accepted that position.

CHAPTER FIVE

ROSALIE was organising her packing for the next trip when the telephone rang. She picked up the receiver without any thought of who might be calling, her mind still occupied with the job ahead of her—what was required for it, how much time it would take.

'Rosalie James,' she rattled out automatically.

'Adam Cazell.'

The deep timbre of his voice rolled through her heart like a drum, heralding something momentous. Shock held her rigid and speechless. It was almost a month since their meeting at Davenport Hall. She'd been to Thailand and back, mostly succeeding in shutting him and his daughter out of her mind.

But the shockwave still hitting her now wasn't from just hearing his voice. It was feeling his presence at the other end of the line, reaching out and seizing her whole consciousness, obliterating everything else. The sense of being under siege was instant and overwhelming.

'I want to thank you for the very good advice you gave me the last time we met,' he said warmly, triggering a flood of heat that unsettled her further.

She took a deep breath and fought for calm composure. 'How did you get this number, Adam?' she asked, doing her best to project coolness.

'From your sister,' he answered easily.

'Rebel gave it to you?'

'Any reason why she shouldn't?'

Celeste and Cate...best friends...the personal connection. Rebel probably hadn't thought the rule of privacy applied in this case.

'I did mention how much I appreciated your help with Cate,' he went on. 'And that is absolutely genuine, Rosalie.'

It pricked her interest. 'You've built up a closer rapport with her?'

'It's been a rewarding few weeks.'

'I'm glad to hear it.'

'I thought you might like to come and see for yourself.'

Another meeting. Of course this was his motive for calling. Cate was a complete side issue. He was attacking on a subtle front, planning to segue into her life again through his daughter, and despite knowing this, perhaps because of it, the tug to meet them both again was strong.

Except it wouldn't stop there.

Adam Cazell would mount a campaign to draw her into his life, and she might very well lose herself to this man. And where would she be then? She didn't want to be *owned* by anyone. Personal control was important to her. The freedom to do what she wanted when she could plan it was important to her.

'Cate and I are on Tortola, Rosalie,' he informed, breaking into her fevered thoughts. 'It's one of the British Virgin Islands in the Caribbean. I have a villa here.'

Far away, she thought in relief. He wasn't about to knock on her door, compelling a decision that threw her into conflict with all she'd been up until now.

'Cate and I have spent the past few weeks just lazing around together. We've talked a lot. We'd both like you to come and visit us. Stay a week. Relax and enjoy yourself.'

It was a very seductive invitation…a week on a Caribbean island. She'd never heard of Tortola. It couldn't be one of the more touristy islands. A private retreat, she thought. No paparazzi taking photographs, stirring gossip. She shouldn't feel so tempted. It wasn't possible anyway.

'Thank you, but I have a professional commitment, Adam. I'm flying to New York tomorrow morning to do a photo shoot.'

'How long will that take?'

'A few days,' she answered evasively, resisting the sense of being pinned down.

'It's not far from New York to Tortola. I can have my private plane standing by to fly you down. All you need do is call the Saturn Company office in New York, give your name, and arrangements will be made to transport you here as soon as your work is done.'

Her heart fluttered at the pressure being applied. The urge to go and have done with Adam Cazell in a limited time-frame and out of the public eye, warred with the fear of being trapped in a situation from which there'd be no easy escape.

'I promise you that coming here would not commit you to anything you don't want, Rosalie,' he said in a gentler tone, subtly persuasive. 'Cate can be a chaperone. Is that *safe* enough for you?'

Nothing felt safe with him. 'I barely know you, Adam,' she temporised.

'But you know Cate. Knew her better than I did,' he reminded her. 'And I'm not about to do anything to harm the understanding I've reached with my daughter.'

'Surely she'd prefer to have you to herself.'

'Cate is as much behind this invitation as I am,' came the swift reply.

'I don't think I believe that.'

'Come and find out for yourself.'

Again the strong tug.

'She likes you,' he went on, beating at her resolve to stay clear of the danger he posed. 'And I want to know you, Rosalie. I think you want to know me, too.'

Her stomach contracted. All the muscles around the centre of her sexuality tightened. She did want to know how it would be as a woman with *this* man. And she wanted to know why he affected her so...so uncontrollably. Perhaps, in knowing she could better deal with it.

'Why not give us this opportune time together?' he pressed.

Why not?

A few days of his company might settle this problem with him once and for all. Yet something very basic in her rebelled against surrendering to his will.

'I'll think about it,' she said. 'A short visit to Tortola may fit in. It may not.'

'I won't go away, Rosalie,' he said softly, insidiously.

It was more a statement of fact than a threat. Was he so sure of having invaded her life to such a deep extent she couldn't drive him out? How could he know that she felt him hovering in her consciousness, waiting for entry, pressing for entry?

'No. I don't expect you will, Adam Cazell,' she conceded. 'But letting you in takes some thinking about. Please don't use this telephone number again without my personal permission.'

A small silence, loaded with the tension of him trying to read her mind. Then, 'I'm sorry if you consider this call an unwelcome intrusion. It wasn't meant to be.'

'I prefer to decide whose calls are welcome and whose aren't. Don't use my sister, Adam. Or anyone else in my family.'

'Agreed.'

'Thank you for the invitation. I *will* think about it.'

She hung up, ending the call before he could say anything else, satisfied that she had won some control over the situation. She needed to feel that with him. Especially with him. Because he wasn't going to go away and she had to deal with the disturbance he caused.

Adam heard the click, closing off the verbal connection, leaving him pondering a level of resistance he was not familiar with. Though he had anticipated it with her, couching the invitation in terms that should have won the result he wanted. And maybe it still would. She hadn't said no. The choice had been left open.

As he slowly replaced the receiver, Adam felt his body clenching with a desire so fierce that if Rosalie James had been standing in front of him, he would have charged into carrying her off to the closest bed where she'd have to admit to feeling the same compulsion to explore everything between them. Whatever was getting in the way of their coming together had to be smashed.

Or changed, he corrected with more sober thought. He knew in his bones that force would not achieve anything with Rosalie James, except to drive her further away from him. She might have a large family to support her in times of emotional need, but for the most part she pursued her own course alone and Adam guessed she didn't want the ties of a relationship with a man. He wondered if she'd ever been with any man.

Teasing thought…to be the first.

Though knowing her was far more the goal he had in mind. He'd get there, he told himself. If not here on Tortola, somewhere else.

He strolled out to the wide verandah that overlooked the cove. The emerald water glistened in the afternoon sunshine…beautiful, serene…a world away from the hustle and bustle of New York, the pressures of work, the perfect place to unwind, relax. She couldn't help but let her guard down here, Adam thought, willing her to make that choice.

'So is she coming?' Cate asked, pausing in setting out the game they'd agreed on playing, looking at him with bright, interested eyes.

'I don't know,' he answered honestly. 'She has a photo shoot in New York. She might fly down after that. Depends on how she feels, I guess.'

Cate shook her head at him. 'You're losing your touch, Dad.'

He shook his head back at her. 'I didn't expect Rosalie James to come running.'

'Mmmh…that makes her different, too. I bet you haven't had a girlfriend yet who hasn't grabbed at the chance.'

True enough.

Adam settled himself at the table where the game board and train cards had been laid out. They both enjoyed Union Pacific. It required strategy as well as luck to win, and Cate was a ferocious competitor, looking for every chance to block his progress.

'Disappointing though,' she added on a sigh.

'I think Rosalie James has her own agenda, Cate. She has to decide if she wants to include us in it or not.'

She gave him a calculating look. 'You could help her with the save the children stuff. Give her free tickets on your airline.'

'I wouldn't even suggest it to her.' He was absolutely certain she would freeze him out in no time flat if he tried that tactic.

'Might be a winning move.'

'No. Some people can't be bought, Cate. Rosalie James is one of them.'

She nodded. 'I think you're right. I wouldn't like her if she could be. You know, Mum mixes with a lot of people who are angling for something. They're not *real* friends.'

'I'm sure your mother knows that, too. They're called useful contacts in the political world.'

'I don't like it, Dad. It's all so...' She screwed up her nose in distaste. '...false.'

'Nothing we can do about it, Catie. That's how it works.'

Sarah should be explaining this, he thought, mitigating the impact of Cate's view of her mother's life by spending quality time with her, listening, straightening things out. When they returned to London he'd have to set up a meeting with his ex-wife, make her understand what was going on.

'I guess so,' Cate conceded dispiritedly.

'Come on. Let's play.'

'Okay.' She shrugged off her discontent and gave him a brilliant smile. 'Maybe Rosalie will come. That would be good, wouldn't it?'

'Yes, it would be good but we can't count on it.' No use feeding hope that might build to more disappointment. 'It's her choice.'

And that was a truth he might have to grapple with himself if Rosalie James continued to evade him. But if it was the last thing he did, he'd find out why.

Rosalie forced herself to finish packing for the New York trip. But her mind kept drifting to Tortola. She hovered at her clothes cupboard. A swimming costume? Some light casual gear? Just in case she decided...

It was crazy letting Adam Cazell get to her like this. From everything Cate had said he was a dyed-in-the-wool playboy and she hated the idea of being so...so drawn to such a man. The next woman in a queue—that was all she'd be to him. More of a challenge than most, which undoubtedly stoked his desire. Why was she even thinking of allowing it to happen?

Because...part of her wanted the experience and once it was over and done with, maybe she'd be able to get on with her life and not have to think about him anymore. Everyone said passion didn't last. And it wasn't really giving in to him. It would be a case of mutual consent...if she went to Tortola.

But she didn't feel *safe* about it.

If only Rebel hadn't given Adam her telephone

number…and why had she? It was an understood thing between them that it not be given out without first checking that it was okay with her. Better still to get a return number that Rosalie could ring herself if she wanted to.

She snatched up the receiver from her bedside table and dialled Davenport Hall. As it happened, her sister answered the call and Rosalie flew into attack mode. 'Why did you give Adam Cazell this number, Rebel?'

'What's wrong?' Instant concern.

'You know how I feel about my privacy.'

'I thought you'd want to hear that your advice to Adam about Cate had borne fruit.'

'You could have told me so yourself.'

'Rosalie…it seemed only right that you hear it from him. He was very appreciative, grateful…'

'This has nothing to do with Cate. He wants *me*, Rebel. And you know it. You told me so.'

'Did he ask you to meet him?'

'Yes, he did.'

'If you said no, I'm sure Adam Cazell will respect that decision.'

'He'll keep asking. I know he will.'

'Why are you afraid of him, Rosalie? He's not going to stalk you. He might well keep asking but you can always say no.'

She dragged in a deep breath, quelling the panic that had crept into her voice. 'You shouldn't have given him this number.'

A deep sigh. 'No, I guess I shouldn't and I'm sorry

it's upset you. The truth is…I like him. And while he has certainly been a playboy, some men don't know what they're missing until they find it. I think you would be safe with him.'

That was a huge statement. It momentarily took Rosalie's breath away. Then she rushed back into speech. 'You don't know what you're saying. Adam Cazell and I…we're very different people.'

'I thought the same thing about Hugh when we first met.'

'Rebel, you know where I come from.'

'Yes, and I can't help thinking it's shaped your whole life. And that's not right, Rosalie. There's more to being a woman than working as you do. Not that I have any criticism of what you achieve. I think it's wonderful that you care for and help so many children. But it's too…selfless.'

'It's not. It's the most rewarding thing I can do.'

'Okay. I won't argue with you on that. It's your life, your decision. I'm sorry I did the wrong thing for you. My only excuse is…I hoped it might be right.'

'Okay. Just please don't do it again.'

'The fortress gates are shut,' came the dry rejoinder. 'But I still think it's a shame you're leaving Adam Cazell out in the cold. At least, think about giving him a chance. He might be good for you.'

More to being a woman…

Good for you…

Safe with him...

Rebel's words kept whirling through her mind long into the night.

She didn't know what was true.

CHAPTER SIX

ADAM could not remember ever being so gripped with nervous tension as he watched the small Saturn plane touch down on Beef Island and head down the runway towards him. He had not heard personally from Rosalie James, but she was on board. Confirmation that she was on her way to Tortola had come through this morning. How long she would stay was not given. Which undoubtedly meant it would depend on what happened with him. And Cate.

They stood together, ready to welcome her. Cate had been bubbling with plans all morning—where they should go, what they should show Rosalie while she was here, choosing the guest suite she would have at the villa, making sure it looked welcoming with bowls of flowers in the bedroom and bathroom.

It was very clear to Adam that his daughter had made up her mind that if he had to be attached to a girlfriend, Rosalie James was her choice and she intended to do everything possible to encourage the relationship. The question was...would a happy Cate have the same pull on Rosalie as one who needed attention? Probably not in any long-term sense. She was a woman with a mission.

This was time out for her. Adam couldn't fool himself otherwise. But obviously she had decided to give something of herself to him or she wouldn't have come. So at least this visit was a start. To her it might also be an end. Adam was very aware that he couldn't assume it would comprise anything more than a visit, but he was determined on pushing it as far as he could. In every sense.

'I wonder what she'll be wearing,' Cate said somewhat breathlessly as the plane came to a halt.

'Doesn't matter,' Adam muttered, his gaze fastened on the door that would soon be opened.

'But she is a top model, Dad. And coming straight from a photo shoot. I bet she's got a whole stack of glamorous clothes with her.'

'People who travel a lot, travel lightly. My guess is she'll only bring one suitcase.'

'Bet you're wrong.'

'We'll see.'

His heart kicked into a faster beat as the door opened and the exit steps moved down. She emerged, wearing a floppy white hat and dark glasses that successfully hid any facial expression. But the rest of her looked surprisingly young—vulnerable, Adam instantly thought—and very feminine, dressed in a white off the shoulder peasant blouse with ruffles down the bodice, a black and white polka dot skirt with a frilled hem, and a wide red belt curving around her hips, accentuating her small waist.

'Wow! That's very *in!*' Cate declared admiringly.

But not glamorous. No intent to knock his eyes out.

This was a softer, more accessible Rosalie James. He couldn't even call the dark glasses and hat some form of protective armour against him. The heat and glaring sunlight justified wearing both.

Adam's tension eased as anticipation soared. The spring of confidence was in his step as he strode forward to greet her, a broad smile beaming his pleasure in her arrival. Cate quickly matched pace with him, as eager as he was to get this situation working well.

Having disembarked from the plane, Rosalie stayed by the steps, waiting for the flight attendant to bring out her luggage. She carried a compact black handbag, only big enough to contain a wallet, passport, some make-up, possibly a small hairbrush. As she looked up at the guy now descending the steps Adam saw that her long black hair was loose but encircled at the back of her neck by a red scrunchie.

'You're right, Dad. Only one suitcase and it's not big,' Cate observed. 'Does this mean she won't be staying long?'

'More clothes can always be bought if need be,' he murmured, refusing to accept any limitation where Rosalie James was concerned.

She was here.

The advantage was his.

He wasn't about to let it slip.

Rosalie was a mass of jangling nerves. She'd been reasonably calm on the flight, having made the decision to come and feel her way through whatever developed between Adam Cazell and herself. She had no idea whether it would be good for her or not, but she'd reasoned it would at least get rid of the torment of wondering. But the moment she'd emerged from the plane and saw him waiting for her, the sheer physical impact of the man had instantly assaulted her courage.

He emitted too much power.

It wasn't safe.

How was she going to control this...this experiment?

Would she feel free to walk away afterwards?

She tore her gaze from him and fastened it on his daughter—her lifeline out of trouble if she felt she couldn't go through with Rebel's advice to lay herself open to being a woman with Adam Cazell. Looking at Cate eased the panic in her mind.

The young teenager was wearing a cute outfit— white Capri pants and a white midriff top printed with red cherries, a quirky red hat jammed over her short dark waves. The wide grin on her face promised she was happy about Rosalie's visit, looking forward to sympathetic female company.

The flight attendant brought down the bag she'd repacked days ago in case she did decide to take up Adam Cazell's invitation after she'd finished the photo shoot in New York. It contained enough coordinating garments to cover a week on a Caribbean island, but now a week felt too long. A host of fearful *what ifs* crowded her mind as she thanked the attendant for his services and fought for the composure to face Adam Cazell with a smile. After all, she had come here of her own free will.

'Welcome to Tortola.'

His deep voice seemed to reverberate through her. The silver grey eyes simmered with pleasure as she took the offered hand and managed to say, 'Thank you. It all looks spectacularly beautiful from the air.'

'Our cove is especially pretty,' Cate leapt in. 'The water is a lovely emerald green and you can walk straight down to it from Dad's villa.'

'Sounds wonderful!' Rosalie enthused, thankful that Adam released her hand so she could take his daughter's. 'I don't think I need to ask how you are, Cate. You look like you've been having the time of your life.'

She laughed and squeezed Rosalie's hand as her eyes twinkled up at her father. 'I've been smartening Dad up on lots of things.'

'Didn't know I was so dim until she cut loose on me,' he rolled out with mock concern.

Cate punched his arm. 'I never said you were dim.'

He grinned at Rosalie. 'She shouldn't have told me why I always lost at *Scrabble.* I've won the last three games straight.' He picked up her sui ase and gestured towards the four-wheel drive je n which was obviously their island transport. 'Let's get out of the sun before it fries our brains.'

She walked between the two of them, Cate dominating the conversation with her plan for the afternoon. Since it was already after midday, they'd drive along the coast to Road Town, stop at a restaurant on the harbour, have lunch, then perhaps stroll around the colourful Main Street shops if Rosalie felt like it before taking the Ridge Road over to Cane Garden Bay and along the coast again to where their villa was situated.

'I'm happy for you to take me anywhere on the island, Cate,' Rosalie promised her, pleased to find no sign of disgruntlement in the girl.

Perhaps Adam Cazell had spoken the truth when he'd said the invitation was as much from his daughter as it was from him. Certainly Cate didn't seem to be harbouring any resentment about losing out on a continued exclusive twosome with her father. In fact, she eagerly claimed most of Rosalie's attention, playing tourist guide as they drove to Road Town, chatting on about all they'd done here in the past month, asking about the photo shoot and other modelling engagements coming up in the near future.

For the most part Adam listened, adding the occasional comment but apparently content to let his daughter entertain their guest. It was the same at lunch—wonderful seafood accompanied by tropical fruit drinks—promoting the lazy, relaxed mood of being on holiday, nothing expected of her. The point was reached where she could look at the man who'd brought her here without feeling threatened by his overwhelming maleness.

He was good with Cate. Very good. The affectionate teasing between them reminded her of the ease she always felt with Zachary Lee—nothing hidden, complete understanding. Both of them big men. Was that part of why she found Adam Cazell so attractive physically? Enormous strength was probably linked in her subconscious mind to the ability to protect—a deeply rooted appeal for her. But strength had to be trusted, as well. It could hurt.

Still, she sensed no harm in him. An underlying purpose, waiting patiently for the right time—yes— but the realisation there was to be no haste about connecting more intimately with her made it easy to enjoy being a tourist for a while. And the shops Cate led them into after lunch had much of the unique local colour of the region to offer; fascinating handicrafts, some stunning art from watercolours to sculpture, wonderful island sundresses and shirts.

She even felt brave enough to tease Adam. 'So this is where you bought your gorgeous shirt.' It was printed with red and pink hibiscus flowers, teamed with white slacks.

He laughed. 'Goes with the territory.'

'Makes you look…slightly less formidable.'

'I don't want you to think of me as formidable at all.'

She shook her head. 'I don't believe clothes make the man.'

'Nor the woman,' he quickly returned, the silver bullet eyes shafting that point home, causing her heart to skip at the reminder that this was not just a superficial attraction between them. She sensed there was something innate in both of them tugging to be known, shared, experienced to the full.

It was right to have come, she decided.

Though it didn't make the journey with him any more predictable or less frightening. And Rosalie inwardly recoiled from the idea of giving all of herself. There were some places in her life she kept blocked off. Best that they remain so. The sharing with Adam Cazell could not cross that line. She wouldn't let it.

When they finally arrived at the villa, having driven over the central mountainous spine of the island to the other side, it became obvious that 'our cove' was precisely that, the whole area facing onto it owned by Adam, ensuring a private tropical paradise.

The villa itself was an amazing piece of architecture, a series of pavilions linked by walkways over artificial ponds and artfully designed gardens. There was an inviting array of open areas for viewing the beach and the glorious shades of the sea. The furniture was mostly made of cane, the furnishings all in bright cheerful colours. The whole place generated a sense of pleasurable relaxation.

She was introduced to a cook and three maids who came in daily to look after everything. Two gardeners in the grounds waved to her as Adam indicated she was his guest. Cate showed her to a spacious guest suite that provided her with every modern convenience. Luxury on a grand scale, she thought, yet none of it was an assault on the environment, more a harmonious fitting in to what was here. And no doubt the employment required from the local inhabitants was appreciated by them.

Did Adam Cazell pay them well? She hoped so. Any form of exploitation of native people was anathema to her. She would not model for any dress designer who employed cheap Chinese labour working in oppressive sweatshops. People were people all over the world, though far too often the country of their birth condemned them to a life that had more to do with survival than getting any pleasure from it.

The heat of the afternoon was alleviated by a breeze wafting from the sea. Large overhead fans circulated it more effectively. Rosalie unpacked, undressed, took a shower, then rested on the queen size bed, needing some quiet time to herself. She'd come a long way today. And she'd be going even further tonight...with Adam Cazell.

Best it be done quickly, she told herself, and not think too much about it. She didn't want him thinking too much, either, trying to draw more from her than she was willing to reveal. Her own lack of sexual experience wouldn't matter. The driving force would come from him. All she had to do was surrender to the feelings he stirred, ride them instead of holding back...just let it happen.

A knock on the door woke her. 'It's getting on for dinner time, Ms. James,' a voice called out, the West Indian timbre of it denoting one of the maids. 'Will you be joining Mr. Cazell and Miss Cate, or would you like something in your suite?'

'No. I'll join the others for dinner. Thank you,' she called back.

'We'll be serving it on the front verandah, Ms. James, at seven o'clock.'

'Thank you.'

The light was considerably less brighter now. Must be close to sunset, Rosalie thought, hurrying so as not to miss it from the verandah overlooking the cove. She'd already planned what to wear. Designed for seduction, she thought ironically, knowing no seduction was required. But the outfit did signal her willingness to enter a sexual relationship. She had no doubt Adam Cazell was adept at reading such signals.

A nervous little shiver ran down her spine as she fastened the sarong skirt around her waist. No panties. She might baulk at undressing, the sheer vulnerability of being uncovered striking too many frightening chords. The faster this deed was done, the less she would have to keep her courage steadfast.

The matching top was gathered into a halter neckline and tied at the back. No bra. The filmy material, printed in soft greens and browns, was lined with a flesh coloured fabric. Her nakedness underneath it was not obvious, but accessibility was. It felt strange, knowing she'd be acting on what the clothes promised. Always before they'd been just clothes draped on her body.

She brushed her hair and left it falling loose down

her almost bare back. Some pink-brown lipstick to accentuate her mouth, a touch of green to lend depth to her eyes, and her make-up was done. She slipped her feet into minimal sandals, one strap decorated with green and amber glass beads.

Her pulse quickened as she left her private suite and took the walkway to the main living areas. This was a journey that had to be taken, she kept telling herself. As Rebel said, she was a woman, and there was no denying Adam Cazell had awakened a sexuality that was suddenly craving a sense of fulfilment. Fear had to be suppressed. Her whole adult life had been aimed at helping children who desperately needed help. Now…tonight…she was determined on doing something for herself.

Right or wrong…she would do it…and deal with afterwards…afterwards.

Adam stood near the edge of the verandah, watching the changing shades of colour in sky and sea as the sun started dipping below the horizon. He was also harnessing enough discipline to play the relaxed host this evening, not giving Rosalie any cause to shy away from him. If he could get her to stay in his company after Cate left them, he'd know she was willing to try a relationship with him. It was essential to move slowly, win ground bit by bit, assume nothing.

'I led Rosalie into the best shop for clothes,' Cate remarked, 'but she wasn't interested in buying any.'

He turned to smile ruefully at his over-keen daughter who was seated at the table, flipping through the magazine she'd bought in town. 'That's not why she's here,' he said matter-of-factly.

'Well, she's not all over you like a rash, Dad,' came the pertinent observation.

'We agreed that Rosalie James was different, Cate,' he reminded her.

She frowned. 'I think you're being too laid back. If you want her to be your girlfriend, she has to know it.'

'She knows it. It's a matter of her *choosing*. And I have to respect that or she'll be flying out of here.'

It felt odd to be discussing the situation with his thirteen-year-old daughter, yet he liked the understanding they were forging, the honesty between them. He actually felt less alone, as he knew she did, as well. The trick was to gather Rosalie James into their togetherness, make her feel at home with them.

'People can be persuaded into choices,' Cate pointed out with a wise look.

'If they want to be,' he cautioned.

'She wouldn't have come if she didn't *want* to be. I'll disappear after dinner. Watch cable TV in my bedroom. You might not have bags of time, you know. I think you'd better start persuading.'

'I appreciate your thoughtfulness,'

Her grin acknowledged the calculation behind it. 'All in a good cause.'

She went back to perusing the magazine, just as

Adam spotted Rosalie coming along the walkway from the guest wing. The sight of her took his breath away. She moved like an island girl; loose-limbed, hips swaying, subtly flaunting her femininity yet with a grace that seemed entirely natural. Her long hair swayed too, a shiny curtain of black silk falling to her waist.

But for the creamy colour of her skin, she looked like an island girl, dark hair, dark eyes, exotically dressed in a sarong-style skirt with a halter top that seemed to shift to the movement of breasts that were free of any constriction. The greens and browns of the soft fabric projected a sensual earthiness.

This was not the angel of Phnom Penh. Nor the regal presence at the opera. This was the woman she meant to be here.

Tonight!

Adam's heart started rocketing around his chest.

No persuasion needed.

Though he instantly realised the clock on this visit was ticking down even faster than he had anticipated and somehow…every muscle in his groin was tightening…somehow he had to gain a longer hold on her—a strong hold so she couldn't slip away from him.

Rosalie James had decided.

But the end game had to be his.

CHAPTER SEVEN

THE table was cleared apart from a large platter containing a variety of cheeses, crackers and slices of tropical fruit to be idly picked at whenever tempted. Cate had gone to her room to watch some television program she liked. The maids had been dismissed for the night. Rosalie and Adam were finally alone together, sipping from small glasses of Tokay which seemed to complement the rich balminess of the evening.

An almost full moon, a host of bright stars in the sky, the sound of the sea booming onto an outer reef, flares spotlighting the tropical garden, seductive food and wine, absolute privacy...nothing could be more romantic, Rosalie thought appreciatively, the mixture of primitive splendour and sophisticated luxury appealing to all the senses. Certainly it lulled her nervous fear over what was to come. Which, of course, had been Adam Cazell's design.

He looked sexy, too, his loose, collar-less, gauzy white shirt fastened only by a couple of buttons at the front, the breadth of his muscular shoulders and chest very visible. His white cotton trousers had a drawstring waistline—provocatively casual. One tug...the flick of a thumb on those two buttons...

Rosalie took a deep breath and wrenched her mind off thinking how he might look completely nude. 'Do you come here often, Adam?' she asked.

He shrugged. 'Whenever I feel like a break from the merry-go-round of business and people. I've found it the perfect place to unwind and shed pressures.'

'Is it your favourite place?'

A whimsical smile. 'For what it offers, yes. But other places provide different pleasures. I'm a traveller, Rosalie. Like you.' His eyes pinned hers, silently punctuating the similarity, tugging on that chord in her heart that responded to him, insidiously suggesting there was more to this attraction than sexual chemistry.

It meant nothing, she swiftly told herself, and made the point, 'I don't travel for pleasure, Adam.'

'I know,' he said softly. 'You travel for people. What were you doing in Thailand?'

She frowned, wondering how much he knew about her work with children. He'd seen her with the choir of orphans in Phnom Penh. Was there any harm in telling him more?

'You told Cate over dinner that you'd been there recently,' he reminded her.

'I was visiting my brother, Joseph. He runs a school for orphans in Bangkok. Joseph was one himself before our parents adopted him.'

'Joseph from Thailand, Zuang Chi from China, Rebel, the English one, Zachary Lee from America...

tell me the others in this remarkable family of yours. Rebel mentioned there were fourteen of you and Celeste said you came from all over the world.'

It was a natural enough curiosity, given that he already knew of the family, yet Rosalie knew he was homing in on her—who she was, where she had come from. What would he make of her origin if she revealed that to him? She felt reluctant to give up anything that was intensely private to her, yet she was proud of the James family and how the lives of so many children had been turned around, demonstrating how love and the right care could nurture such wonderfully positive outcomes.

'Tiffany Makana is from Fiji. Tiffany is the only one of us who was a baby when adopted. She was left on a church doorstep. Carol Tay was the oldest one adopted. She and her son, Alan, came from Vietnam. Suzanne Griffith is from Canada. Tom is a native Australian, an aborigine. All of them and Zachary Lee are settled in Australia.'

'That's nine accounted for,' Adam prompted.

'Muhammad and Leah are from India. Both of them are back there now. Muhammad is a doctor and Leah is a nurse, working in Calcutta. Shasti is from Ethiopia. She's in Africa, working for Unicef. Kim came from Korea and is now based in Hong Kong.'

'And you?'

'I was brought out of the Philippines.'

'But you're not a native of that country,' he said with certainty.

'I was born there. My mother was half Filippino, half American.'

'Your father?'

She shrugged. 'I don't know his heritage. I do know he was stationed at a U.S. base near Manila and he must have been tall.'

'You don't remember him?'

'No.'

'No photos?'

'They weren't married, Adam,' she said dryly. 'My mother was illegitimate and so was I. There was no family to take me in when she died.'

'How old were you then?'

'Seven.'

'You went into an orphanage?'

'There are many homeless children in the Philippines. I prefer not to talk about that part of my life.'

His eyes bored into hers, speculation simmering. She blocked it off by demanding knowledge of him. 'Tell me about your family.'

'There's only Cate. My parents are dead. I was an only child. I guess my background could be called privileged in the sense that I wanted for nothing and was sent to good schools.' His mouth quirked into a wry little smile. 'My parents were proud of me in a distant kind of way, but basically I was a cuckoo in their nest and they didn't know what to make of me.'

A cuckoo in the nest...a very evocative statement, recalling that moment by the lake at Davenport Hall when she'd sensed his aloneness. 'So you've climbed to the top of your mountain on your own,' she said, intrigued by the strength of will that had taken him there.

'I've had good people working with me. Just as you've had the James family to support what you want to do, Rosalie.' His eyes locked onto hers with meaningful purpose. 'But the drive comes from within, fuelled by needs that demand we keep going because there's no end to what can be achieved. Isn't that so?'

Her heart jiggled alarmingly as he linked them to a truth she couldn't deny. He was closing in on the person she was, moving to a level that had nothing to do with the sexual one she had accepted. Action was needed, prompting him into pursuing what she *was* offering.

'Perhaps that applies to me and my work with children. There are always more to be helped,' she conceded. 'But you, Adam, surely you could sit on your laurels now. What comes after a global airline?'

She rose from her chair, gesturing to the view as she moved to the edge of the verandah and looked out on the tropical night. 'You could simply enjoy this,' she tossed back at him.

'I do enjoy it. But it's not enough.' He pushed out of his chair and strolled slowly towards her. 'There is no *place* that would be enough. You don't even think of putting down roots, do you, Rosalie?'

'I was talking about you,' she quickly protested.

His eyes gleamed a mocking challenge. 'And I'm pointing out how alike we are. It doesn't matter how many places we leave our suitcases in. You live inside yourself, just as I do.'

'Everyone does that,' she argued, feeling he was weaving a net around her, inexorably coupling her with him.

'Most people get attached to things. Their country. Their community. Their home. Such things give meaning to their existence. Roots...'

He let the word linger, taunting her attempt to evade the links he was forging between them. Rosalie remained silent, every muscle in her body tensing at his nearness. He had to touch her soon. Any moment now. That was the prime reason for inviting her here, wasn't it? All this talking was confusing the issue.

He took her hand, engulfing it with the warmth and strength of his. 'Let's go for a walk together.'

A walk?

He drew her off the verandah and onto the path that led down to the beach before Rosalie found wits enough to query his purpose. 'This is not what I expected from you,' she blurted out.

'Something wrong with a friendly walk?' he lilted at her.

'We aren't...friends.' She shot him a heated look, intensely aware of the physical link of their hands and knowing—*knowing*—there'd been a sexual current running between them all through dinner. 'Don't pretend it's friendship you want from me, Adam.'

'Lovers can also be friends, Rosalie. Especially when they have much in common.'

'Are you friends with all your previous lovers?'

'There've been none like you.'

'Oh, come on!' she protested, savagely dismissing the hook he was throwing out before it sank in and affected her. 'You've probably said that to all of them. And why not? Everyone's different. But don't expect me to believe it means something special.'

'So you use my playboy reputation against me to deride my sincerity,' he mocked. 'It doesn't change what I feel with you, Rosalie. And it is unique in my experience.'

'Fine!' she clipped out, impatient with flattery, with charm, with anything he used to delay the inevitable.

'Why are you so determined to deny it?'

She tried to quell the turbulence he stirred inside her, tried to think straight. 'It won't change anything, Adam. And I wish you'd stop trying to tie me to you in some way.' She halted, stubbornly refusing to be led down paths she was not prepared to take. 'This is a mistake. I'm going back.'

Before she could begin her retreat he stepped in front of her, wheeling to face her, lifting her hand to his shoulder, leaving it there to wind his arms around her in an imprisoning embrace.

'You think sex will make it go away, Rosalie?' he challenged, his eyes glittering with a ferocity of feeling that wrapped around her heart and squeezed it unmercifully. 'Is that why you came? Expecting to burn it off with a brief encounter?'

Her mind screamed yes, yet somehow he shamed her into seeking other answers, ending up in helpless confusion. And there was the heat of his body seeping into hers, arousing an acute awareness of the hard muscularity of his chest, his thighs, and the powerful aggression that demanded she surrender to it. She couldn't think. A flood of strange feelings were swamping her.

'You couldn't be more wrong, thinking the wanting is only physical,' he fiercely asserted. 'But let's test it, shall we? See how forgettable I am for you?'

She could only stare at him, too churned up to say anything. He lifted a hand to her face, his thumb tilting her chin, fingers dragging at the skin on her cheek as though wanting to claw through it to her inner self. His eyes blazed into hers, torches searing her soul, behind them a marauding will, determined on finding all that was hidden to him. A tremor shook her entire body as his mouth descended on hers.

Would he draw her secrets from her?

Would she ever be herself again?

Too late to reject him now. Too late...

He attacked with passion, forcing her lips apart, invading so quickly and with such explosive sensation, Rosalie was too stunned by the wild storm of response rushing through her to do anything but succumb to it. She clung to him, her hands instinctively linking behind his neck, holding on as he kissed her again and again, a tempestuous onslaught that was incredibly exciting.

Adam's head was spinning with the compelling urge to take her, have her. His body was raging with the need to do it now. But he knew it was what she wanted—over and done with—and he fought his own craving, instinctively clutching at the greater need to implant himself so deeply in her consciousness, he would always hold a place there. Be damned if he would let her root him out!

He wrenched his mouth from hers and took a long deep breath. Her eyes opened, unfocused, swimming as though she was caught in a whirlpool and the current was stronger than she had believed it could be. Adam was instantly reminded of the vulnerability he had sensed earlier today. Was this her first time? Had she never known passion with a man?

What should he do? What would be best for her? Ride the tide while she was still caught up in it or slow it down to a pace where she would be conscious of every move escalating to another level and another. Speed could shut fear out, but what memory of it would she have afterwards?

He had to make the memory stick. A blur was no good to him. He dropped a softer kiss on her mouth, his lips grazing sensually over hers, his tongue gliding teasingly over the sensitive inner tissues. He felt a convulsive little shiver run down her spine, her breasts lift and fall in a silent sigh.

'Walk with me, Rosalie,' he commanded, though his voice was no more than a gentle murmur.

She made no reply but there was no resistance in her body as he tucked her close to him, the silk river of her hair flowing over the arm he held around her waist. She leaned into his support as they walked and he knew she was shaken, unsure of where they were going but trusting his lead, accepting that what had been started was to be finished where he chose.

It didn't matter to her but it did to him. A night to remember, he kept telling himself, steering her across the lawn to where a flowering frangipani tree lent its exotic scent to the night air. Under its leafy branches were two sun-loungers facing the sea, but he didn't want to use them, not for making love to this woman. He moved her out of the shade, into the moonlight, close to the beach, where the floral scent mixed with the fresh salty smell of the sea and they could see the waves lapping the sand and the stars shining brightly above the horizon.

It felt right...a primitive setting for a primal act... his senses acutely alert to the fundamental nature of what had to be achieved here...a union that would bind her to him so deeply it could span the inevitable separations and endure in a space of its own.

He didn't question the need that centred exclusively on this woman. He trusted the gut instinct that told him unequivocally she was worth more than all the rest, and if he lost her, there would be an emptiness in his life that could never be filled. It flashed into his mind that there was one bond that would seal a future togetherness—a bond that he suddenly wanted so much it spilled into speech.

'Have you ever thought of having a child of your own, Rosalie?'

A child of her own…

Rosalie's stomach clenched at this further diversion from what she needed to happen. Her mind had been swirling with the sense of time and place—him at the centre of it—the tremulous feeling of being drawn into a web of natural forces that belonged to this moment, making it feel right for her to accept they were part of it, merging with it.

'There are too many children,' she cried in protest, the child she'd been too indelible a memory for her to see beyond it.

'Perhaps so,' he murmured, turning them both to face each other, his hands on her waist, his eyes focused intently on hers. 'Yet why deny what is natural to you…natural to *us?*' he went on, his deep voice resonating with a seductive power that vibrated through her. 'The sea, the earth, the air…you can smell it all around you, the birth and growth and re-cycling of life.'

'But we can choose what we do,' she broke in, and in a wild demonstration of the choice she had made, she reached out and deliberately undid the buttons on his shirt, baring his chest, placing her palms on the taut hot flesh underneath the flimsy fabric.

'Yes,' he agreed, scooping in a quick breath, his eyes glittering at the daring move. 'And I'll take the chance you've given me.'

There was none, she thought fiercely. She was *safe* from any *chance* happening tonight. If he was saying he wasn't about to use protection, it didn't matter. She didn't need it. Her fertile cycle was five days away. A new life would not be seeded on Tortola. She would be gone before any danger of pregnancy could occur. But she wouldn't tell him this. Let him think whatever he wanted as long as…

Her breath was trapped in her chest as his hands undid the ties at the back of her halter top. The bodice fell forward, leaving her breasts naked, their tip-tilted peaks tightening at the sudden exposure to the night air and his burning gaze.

In all her parading down the catwalk in see-through creations, she had never felt self-conscious about displaying her body. It simply showed off every aspect of how the clothes looked. But this was different. It was personal. And she could feel her flesh tingling with pinpricks of heat as he seemed to examine every contour, circles within circles.

Her breath finally whooshed from her lungs as he tossed the garment on the grass and stripped off his shirt, letting it fall behind him. His muscular strength was immediately evident, causing a little shiver of apprehension to run down her spine. He was such a big man. Would he be gentle with her?

Too late to worry about that now.

He had the physical fitness of a long-term survivor, and the build to support it. The mind, too—sharp, clever, far ranging. If she were to have a child by him...no, don't think it. Don't go there! Being with him like this was a giant step for her. Everything inside her quivered as he pulled the drawstring on his pants and stepped out of this clothing, fully naked and so aggressively male, fear instantly seized her mind.

She fought it. She had come here to know what it was like. Decision made. He was her choice. She forced her hands to undo the sarong, toss it aside with a bravado she didn't feel. His gaze raked her from head to foot and back again, a visual assault that had every muscle in her body clenching.

'The perfectly constructed woman,' he said with a wisp of a smile. 'No doubt you've been told that innumerable times. But you weren't made for strutting clothes. That's an artificial thing. Totally meaningless.'

He moved closer. Her heart broke into a wild fluttering as he ran his fingers lightly over her shoulders, down her arms. He lifted her hands to his shoulders, then traced her underarms with the same tantalising brush of his fingertips, the feather-light caress continuing down to her waist, her hips, thighs, raising trails of prickling heat as though his touch was infiltrating her bloodstream and it was responding with eager leaps and bounds.

'This body was made to mate with a man,' he murmured, his gaze holding hers with mesmerising intensity. His hands spread over her stomach and glided up to cup her breasts. 'And these were made to suckle a child.' His thumbs fanned her hardened nipples, making them ache for a more satisfying contact. 'This is what life is about, Rosalie...our coming together just as nature intended.'

She savagely blocked that claim out of her mind. This was nothing but a physical connection and she wouldn't let it be turned into more. His arms pulled her into an embrace that sent shockwaves of sensation from every point of contact. This was it, she thought in a frenzied flow of fear and excitement.

'Come with me,' he commanded, his voice suddenly harsh with an urgency he carried into a kiss that seemed violently invasive, yet instantly stirring a fierce passion to commit herself to an equal plundering of his mouth, silencing all the talk, wanting only action.

But he spoke anyway, silently, insidiously reaching into the woman he said she was, lifting her up, her long hair coiled around his hand, arching her back so that he could take her breasts in his mouth, one by one, swirling his clever, knowing tongue around her nipples, kissing them with a deep rhythmic tug that sent arcs of piercing pleasure through her body... terrible, wonderful pleasure that awoke every long-suppressed female instinct inside her, bringing them to screaming wanton life.

Then he laid her on the soft grass and trailed kisses across her stomach as though wooing the woman within, or warming the womb into which he'd spill his seed, and his hands were easing the passage to it, caressing her inner thighs, parting the intimate folds of her sex, promising what was to come with softly sliding fingers.

And her body was craving it, convulsively welcoming each subtly tantalising invasion. But her inner focus changed, became confused as he moved his mouth lower and found a far more intensely sexual target, generating waves of exquisitely excruciating pleasure that she could hardly bear.

She felt herself writhing, arching, her whole body violently out of control. Her hands were scrabbling through his hair, pulling, pressing, blindly seeking some course that would answer the tumultuous need within. And finally he answered it, lifting himself over her, knowing she was open to him, open and waiting tremulously, wanting the ultimate fulfilment of all he could give her, and she sighed with intense relief as she felt him push into her, felt her inner muscles contract around him, felt the glorious fullness moving slowly onward, meeting the resistance of her virginity, pausing.

Even in that brief moment of panic she couldn't bear the thought of him stopping. If there was pain, there was pain. She didn't care. She dug her fingernails into his back, crying out, 'Do it! Do it!' the savage urgency of her desire for him to finish what he'd started overriding any hesitation by either of them.

He surged through the thin barrier—only the slightest sense of tearing, swiftly soothed by the fierce satisfaction of feeling him move past it, going deeper, deeper, filling the empty ache, replacing it with an ecstatic sense of completion.

It didn't hurt. They fitted. And he drove that amazing knowledge into her consciousness again and again, slowly, quickly, a wildly addictive rhythmic beat, mating with her, she thought on a sharp wave of new understanding, and she was helpless to do anything but take him into herself, discovering dark untravelled roads of emotion, deep inner needs clawing at the closed gates in her mind, forcing them open, exulting in being open to him and whatever he forged with her, climbing for an endless time, reaching a taut agony of pleasure, a piercing, awesome place that burst into incredibly sweet ripples that released a swift, brilliant sense of melting together, merging...

And as she lay enthralled by the changes he'd wrought in her by this act of mating, still held by him, she could not stop herself from wondering about the new life they might have made if it had been the right time, and felt a desire for it she would never have conceded before.

The absolute completion, she thought, and realised for the first time, what Rebel meant about being a woman…with a man who made her feel she wanted all this with him…all there could be between them… because of how it felt together.

And none of it—none of it—was forgettable.

CHAPTER EIGHT

ADAM didn't want to think. He just wanted to hold on to her, fill his senses with everything about her, her warm musky scent, the satin smoothness of her skin, the silky spill of her hair, the soft rise and fall of her breasts on his chest as she breathed her contentment to be with him like this, her head on his shoulder, their legs in an intimate splice.

Yet thoughts kept darting in and out of his mind, all of them related to her choosing him to take her virginity. How big a thing was that? Had she simply decided it was time and she could use him to do it? Have the experience he offered, no strings attached?

Everything she'd said tonight pointed to an acceptance of a brief encounter only. But was that defensive? Maybe she was afraid to feel too much. She was drawn to him, possibly against her will, fighting to reduce the attraction to dismissible limits. Did she realise now that some things were too strong to be rationalised away? What was she feeling this minute?

Her first time!

He hadn't even asked... 'Are you okay, Rosalie?' The words burst from his lips in jolting concern that he hadn't considered any physical distress. She'd pushed him, gone with him, but whether out of driven desire or determination…had the pleasure outweighed the pain? He knew she had climaxed.

Impatient for an answer, he rolled her onto her back and propped himself up to watch her face, read her expression. 'Why didn't you tell me it was your first time?'

She sighed, shook her head slightly, as though denying it, or denying it any importance, perhaps wishing he hadn't realised.

'Rosalie…' He gently stroked her cheek, forcing the dark liquid eyes to look directly into his. '…I'm not a fool.'

She took a deep breath and admitted, 'I didn't want it to change anything. I wanted you to take me as you would any other woman.'

'You're not any other woman.'

Her mouth quirked into a wry little smile. 'I've heard it said all cats are the same in the dark.'

'Only by people of no discrimination.'

'But it is the same…the same act.'

'No. It's different with every person. It relates very closely to how you feel about them. It wasn't just chance that you chose me for this,' he said with sudden certainty.

She seemed to struggle for a reply. 'Rebel said… I'd be safe with you.'

'Safe…' It was a strange word to use, so strange Adam knew intuitively it was important, possibly a key to all her reactions to him. He filed it away in his mind, plus the fact that she had discussed her decision with her sister, revealing her sense of vulnerability about it.

'Did I hurt you, Rosalie?' he asked softly, feeling a wave of tenderness as he comprehended the bravery that had brought her this far with him.

'No. It was…' Her face broke into a brilliant smile. '…amazing, Adam.'

The way she spoke his name gave him an enormous thrill. It felt like an acknowledgment of him as someone very special. Her first lover. Her *only* lover, he fiercely vowed.

'Thank you,' she added huskily, reaching up to stroke his cheek. 'It was more…than I'd ever allowed it could be.'

And would be more still, Adam determined, recognising an awed wonderment in her touch, in her voice, in her eyes. But he had to take care of this beginning first, wash away any blood, ease any sense of rawness, make her want him again. And again. Her 'Thank you' was warning enough there was a clock ticking in her head and it had to be stopped.

He rose to his feet and drew her up with him. 'Let's walk on down to the sea,' he said, wrapping his hand around hers and leading off, aware that the docility emanating from her now might soon be gone. He had to seize every advantage she surrendered to him.

Rosalie could hardly believe she was doing this… walking naked with a man who was equally naked. It was strangely liberating, as though everything else in their lives had been shucked off and there were only the two of them in a world of their own. Like Adam and Eve. She smiled at the whimsical thought. Could the Garden of Eden have been like this?

She looked up at the stars, felt the granules of sand crunching under her feet and a gentle breeze wafting over her skin, smelled the salt from the sea and the scent of exotic blooms, and revelled in a sense of unspoiled innocence, a clean sheet upon which anything could be written, a shiny new beginning.

My birth as a woman, she thought, glancing at the man who had brought her here, wondering if he had knowingly set this scene for her, aware of its magical appeal and sensitive to how it would feel.

He caught her glance. 'Yes?'

But she already knew the answer, remembering what he'd spoken of beforehand, words she hadn't wanted to hear. 'It's a fantasy,' she said in a rush of understanding how clever he was.

'No. It's real. Everything around us...you...me... it's all real, Rosalie.' His smile was very white in the moonlight. 'Why not just live the moment?'

So seductive...living the moment. They walked into a softly dying wave that frothed around her feet. There was only a gentle swell in the bay. She could hear the boom of the sea breaking on the reef beyond it. His hand tightened around hers as they moved on, though there was no danger of her falling or being swept away from him. The water was like a warm caress on her legs, the sand underfoot quite firm.

Sight, sound, smell, touch...easy to immerse herself in these physical realities, easy to accept their influence on her emotions. Let go of everything else, she told herself, and just be a woman with a man for this one night, *live the moment*—a magical moment in time—without any reference to the past or future.

She'd been conscious of a stickiness between her thighs but whatever it was—some bleeding, a residue of their sexual intimacy—the water washed it away. Adam saw her touching herself there and halted, his face flashing concern.

'Are you sore?'

She laughed away a wave of shyness at his sharp observation. 'I said it was amazing, Adam. I wasn't expecting...what you did.'

He grinned, relieved to think she was remembering the pleasure he'd given her. 'There are many other things I'd like to do with you,' he said wickedly.

'I want to swim.' She wriggled her fingers against his grasp, reacting to a sudden sense of entrapment, a feeling he wasn't going to let her go.

He did, instantly releasing her hand. 'Then we'll swim together.'

She didn't mind that idea.

Sharing was fine.

Imprisonment was not.

They were already waist-deep and they both dove forward, swimming towards the centre of the bay,

Adam matching his pace to hers. It was invigorating and blissful, feeling the water streaming past her naked body, her hair floating completely weightless.

She'd never done this before…another first… imbuing her with an even deeper sense of being at one with totally primitive elements, free of all care from the strictures of society and the career that demanded perfect grooming.

She grinned at the thought of seaweed hair horrifying the designers who employed her, and the photographers with their finicky vision of perfection.

'What's amusing you?' Adam asked.

They'd slid into a lazy sidestroke and he was watching her, perhaps checking if she was tiring. She stopped swimming and trod water, curious to know how he viewed her. Was the glamour she portrayed as a model part of her attraction for him?

'This is not the woman you saw at the opera in New York,' she stated provocatively.

He grinned. 'I like it better with your armour off.'

She cocked her head, considering his answer. 'More…touchable?'

'More reachable.'

With a quick manouvre, he took her hands and linked them behind his neck, then kicked out underneath her, bringing her buoyant body up to float above his as he started a slow backstroke, taking her with him towards the beach.

'I don't need to be towed,' she told him, though she didn't mind. In fact, it made her feel happily aware of how strong he was, and using that strength to give her an easy ride through the water.

'Just keeping you safe,' he answered.

Safe...

Physically she did feel safe with him now. The fear she'd attached to having any sexual activity was gone. He'd shown her how incredibly marvellous it could be with the right man, a man who knew how to give pleasure instead of...her mind shied away from the brutal activities she'd seen as a child.

It need not be like that.

It should not be like that.

Zachary Lee had told her, assured her, but right up until this night with Adam the barrier of fear had held back any real belief in what anyone had said. Even now it seemed strange that she could feel this big man moving beneath her, his naked sex rolling over her stomach as he swam, and not find it the least bit scary.

She liked it. Liked the brush of her breasts against his chest, too. And the drift of her thighs touching his. It was...deliciously sensual.

He stopped swimming. 'We can stand here,' he said, proving it by whooshing upright.

Her legs immediately sank, her feet hitting his, already firmly planted on the sandy bed. The surface of the water lapped her shoulders. Her arms instinctively lifted higher, winding themselves around his neck for support. Or maybe clinging on to the closeness because it felt so good.

Adam smiled at her. 'They called you an angel in

Phnom Penh. You looked like a queen in New York. Right now you sparkle like some mythical siren from the sea.'

'Luring men to their deaths?'

He laughed. 'Give me the kiss of life instead.'

She stared at his mouth, thinking she had never initiated a kiss. Except for kisses of greeting or affection, strictly on the cheek. He bent his head to make it easy for her lips to meet his, prompting the urge to experiment, to do it slowly, knowingly, assessingly, so she would remember exactly how it was and what she felt from it.

'Then let me do the kissing,' she said, her gaze flicking up to his in appeal, not wanting him to take control this time.

'As you wish,' he murmured, his eyes gleaming with a soft indulgence that sent a wave of warmth racing through her.

She touched her lips to his, a light rubbing that produced an electric tingling. Her tongue automatically licked out to soothe the effect and tasted salt, obviously from the sea water. His lips parted as she licked further, and tentatively she slid her tongue into the seductive heat of his mouth, moving it over his palate, a gentle, teasing invasion that felt daringly exciting. And slowly, his tongue began to tango with hers, inciting her into quick, darting movements that felt like a spurting fountain of delicious sensation.

Her heart quickened its beat, seeming to thunder in her ears, throb in her temples. Her head swam with a kind of intoxicating pleasure. One of her hands raked through his hair, curling around his scalp to grasp him more tightly to her. She felt his hands curve around her bottom, hoisting her higher so that their faces were level. She had to break the kiss to gulp in air.

'Wrap your legs around my hips, Rosalie,' he whispered urgently.

Yes, that was better. Very satisfying. And he was kissing her now, but she didn't mind him taking over because he knew how to make it even more exciting. Then she felt the insertion of himself between her thighs and gasped in shock that he could think of doing it in the water.

'Is this okay with you?' he quickly asked.

She looked at him, saw that he cared for her, and felt a wild elation at merging so intimately with him here. 'Yes,' she almost sang, throwing her head back and laughing at the stars in the brilliant night sky.

He pressed a trail of kisses down her long neck, found the pulse at the base of her throat and heated her blood with sizzling excitement as he plunged himself deep inside her, jolting her again with the incredible pleasure of feeling him there. And she tightened the lock of her legs around him, exulting in the sense of having this man in her hold, enveloping him, owning him.

Always she'd thought men had the power, power she had to skirt or somehow turn to her own use when possible, evade when it threatened her, but the realisation burst like a thunderclap that there was a different truth, especially with sex...the power of a woman to take a man like this, have him inside her because that was what she wanted and where he wanted to be. And it felt good. It felt great.

She swayed from side to side, loving the sensation of him being so deeply implanted within her. Then he moved her into a rocking motion that was even more delicious. And she kissed him with a spontaneity that just welled up in her and spilled into a joyous, uninhibited passion to experience all this wonderful man could give her, teach her, show her.

They stayed entwined like that for a long time, stoking the intense pleasure of being so intimately connected, revelling in it, savouring it, finally driving it to that shattering peak beyond which they fell into a blissful languor, content to simply feel the water floating around them.

Adam carried her out of it, her head resting contentedly on his shoulder. He carried her right up the beach to the villa garden and laid her on a lounger under a tree, lifting her long wet hair over the back rest to let it dry.

He broke off a large spray of creamy flowers from the tree and stretched out on the adjacent lounger, turning on his side to face her, smiling as he plucked the flowers from the spray and rubbed them gently over her skin, wiping away all the droplets of water and leaving the sweet scent of frangipani from the satin-soft petals.

Impulsively she took what remained of the spray

to do the same to him, pushing him onto his back and commanding him to lie still. She found it quite entrancing, touching him like this, tracing the delineation of his muscles, his magnificent physique completely bared to her wanderings over it.

She even caressed his inner thighs and the sexual components that had previously struck fear in her. No fear now. More a tender curiosity, and an awe in the masculinity that stirred so much that was female in her.

'Keep doing that and you'll arouse me again,' Adam growled.

She flashed him a teasing smile. 'Perhaps I want to see.'

'Then you make love to me, Rosalie,' he gruffly invited.

Make love?

How did one make love to a man?

She remembered what he'd done in giving intense pleasure to her, and not knowing if it would be at all the same for him, she twirled a flower over one of his nipples, then leaned over and drew the small nub into her mouth, copying his kiss and caresses.

She heard his sharply indrawn breath, felt the quick rise of tension in his body and felt a burst of elation in her success. Instinctively her hand glided down his stomach to stroke him as he'd stroked her, and she found it intensely exciting to feel him strengthening to full arousal under her touch.

She moved to his other nipple, tugging, licking,

thrilled by his response as she felt the hardness grow tighter, tighter, yet the skin at the top remained soft and clearly very sensitive for when she rolled her thumb over it, Adam's breathing became very quick and shallow. Then she remembered the terribly intimate kissing that had felt so incredibly exquisite and she moved down to take him in her mouth and...

She'd barely done so when Adam jackknifed up from the lounger, lifting her to straddle him, positioning them both so she sank onto his erection, and once again knew the fantastic feeling of taking him inside her. She slid forward, propping her hands on his shoulders, and found a rhythm of her own, which he made more intensely exciting by stroking her breasts, her stomach, her hips, wonderful circling caresses that sensitised her whole body, turning her into a wantonly sensual creature that gloried in every touch and movement.

And she could see the pleasure in his eyes, feel it coursing through his body, knew he felt all that she felt, and when they'd both driven it to exhilarating heights and finally brought it down to a gloriously humming contentment, she lay encompassed in his arms, dreamily looking up at a faraway heaven and knew what people meant when they spoke of heaven on earth.

It could not be better than this.

Complete and utter peace and happiness.

CHAPTER NINE

CATE had already started breakfast when Adam strolled out to the verandah where they invariably ate their meals. One of the maids had told him Miss James had not yet emerged from the guest suite. He had wanted Rosalie to share his bed but she had refused, insisting on sleeping alone in her own quarters. Which made him wonder if she was intent on filing last night away as a *fantasy*.

He shook his head over that damned insidious word, wishing she hadn't used it. Surely he'd given her enough effective reality to show her what they could have together in a continuing relationship. Yet still she had chosen to separate from him. The reason for it kept exercising his mind.

Because that was her unshakable intention—a brief connection, then separation? Or because she simply wasn't used to sleeping with a man, waking up to him, facing him the morning after?

He felt very much on edge until he could see her again and assess the outcome of their intimacy.

'Hi, Dad!'

He forced a smile for his daughter who was subjecting him to a blast of bright curiosity.

'So is it a good morning or not?' she pounced before he could even return her greeting.

'Looks good to me,' he drawled, viewing the sparkling water of the bay.

'I'm not talking about the weather,' Cate shot at him in exasperation. 'I *was* expecting to see you and Rosalie come to breakfast together.'

He shrugged. 'Possibly she's still asleep.'

'You don't *know?*'

'I don't think she'd appreciate my going to her suite to check,' he answered dryly.

Cate huffed and shook her head knowingly at him. 'You must be slipping, Dad. I thought for sure it was on last night.'

He frowned at her rather crass view of his relationships with women, though he couldn't deny sex had been the driving force behind most of them. Certainly there'd never been a case of separate bedrooms under the same roof before.

'I did tell you Rosalie was different, Cate,' he said shortly, moving to pour himself a glass of pineapple juice.

A worried look gathered on her brow. 'She didn't actually turn you down, did she? I mean…you've still got a chance with her?'

'First and foremost Rosalie James is our guest. We'll *all* do what she wants.'

It was a curt reproval, possibly unfair given his daughter's personal interest in this affair, but he didn't want to discuss the situation with her, especially when he didn't have a firm handle on it himself.

He settled in his usual chair at the table and sipped the juice. Cate attacked her bowl of cereal again, her discontent over his failure to win the woman of her choice clouding her face. It reflected his own discontent. Not that he was about to concede failure. Rosalie had certainly been happy having sex with him—one very positive factor—but the parting had rattled his confidence in sealing a deeper, more lasting bond.

'You can't always order what you want, Cate,' he wryly observed.

'But what can she have against you?' came the instant argument. 'You're rich. You could give her anything. You've got sort of macho good looks. And for an older guy, you're in great shape. Even the girls at school think you're sexy.'

'Sex isn't everything. Neither is wealth,' he sliced back, not liking her thinking in those terms. She was barely thirteen. Had he been a bad example to her? Or was this just the silly stuff young girls carried on about? 'Has your mother talked to you about boys?'

She huffed and glared derision at him. 'I'm not a baby, Dad.'

'No, but you do need to learn to place a value on yourself, and that has more to do with the person you are inside than what any boy has to offer in the way of sexiness or what he can buy you.'

She cogitated this for several moments, then asked,

'Is that the difference? The value Rosalie places on the person she is inside?'

'In the long run, yes,' he answered with certainty.

'But she did come. That means something, doesn't it?' She paused, then said hopefully, 'A trial run?'

'Perhaps,' he said non-committally, too acutely aware that the trial might have run its course last night if Rosalie's only aim was to experience sex with a man.

'So what do we do today? I could leave you together, cycle over to...'

'No. Let's just carry on normally. Okay?'

She grimaced. 'Won't give you many opportunities to be alone with her.'

He shook his head. 'I don't want you to feel pushed aside anymore. You and I, Cate...we're a team.'

Her eyes lit with delight in this further proof of his commitment to her and Adam realised anew how little time he had given her over the years. One summer vacation together didn't make up for it, and he wasn't about to erode what ground he had established with his daughter by concentrating entirely on Rosalie. Besides which, it would probably be the worst move he could make in her eyes, too. It was Cate's welfare that had spurred her into accepting his company in the first place.

'Well, I guess you know what you're doing, Dad,' she said happily, and with a shrug at his supposedly superior experience, she went back to eating her cereal.

The problem was, he didn't. He could only feel his way forward with Rosalie James. She didn't fit into any easy to categorise personality—still a mystery to him. He now knew she'd been born in the Philippines, of mixed parentage, orphaned at seven, and rescued from what he surmised to be wretched circumstances by some member of the James family.

She'd grown up in a caring, supportive household, climbed the modelling ladder to international stardom, used her earnings and all her spare time to help needy orphans, and up until last night, steered clear of any intimate relationship with a man.

Because she hadn't felt *safe* with them?

Sexually safe?

This would suggest some earlier traumatic experience, perhaps even as far back as when she was a homeless child. *I prefer not to talk about that part of my life.* Though she hadn't been raped. Her virginity repudiated any possibility of that.

Perhaps her talk of being *safe* with him related to trust.

Trust that he was an inherently decent person who wouldn't do anything to hurt her?

Trust that she could have sex with him without fear of any consequences she didn't want?

A playboy...

Except he wasn't playing with her. His priorities had been completely altered by Rosalie James. He was very, very serious about wanting her as a partner, not a temporary fling that barely touched his life. She had to be sensing that by now. But would she let herself respond to what they could have together, or was the determination—the need?—to be free and unencumbered completely unassailable?

The sound of footsteps instantly broke his private reverie and drew his gaze to the walkway from the guest house. His heart kicked with a buzz of aggressive adrenalin as he spotted Rosalie strolling towards the open living area that led out to the verandah.

She wore the same black and white polka dot skirt she had arrived in, the same sandals, a different white top—sleeveless and form-fitting, with a floppy frill gracing a V-neckline—but this latter garment did nothing to erase the ominous feeling that these were her travelling clothes.

Was she done with him? Satisfied that Cate was getting the parental attention she was missing before? Every muscle in Adam's body tensed in fighting mode. He would not accept a decision to leave, yet he couldn't force her to stay. He desperately needed a means of persuasion.

Rosalie's inner tension increased a hundredfold as Adam rose from the chair at the table on the verandah. He wore only a pair of white shorts which left so much of his physique bared to her view, it was impossible to push the memories of all her intimate contact with him into a manageable space in her mind. They flooded out, totally wrecking the discipline she had tried to impose upon the feelings he'd stirred in her.

Then he hit her with a smile that caused her heart to turn over—a smile reflecting *his* memory of the private sharing of themselves in a flash of pleasure that drove a tide of heat through her entire body.

'Good morning,' he said, while she struggled for the composure needed to deliver her decision to leave Tortola today.

The journey of discovery was over, she'd told herself in her private suite. Adam Cazell had done her a great favour in showing her there was another side to sex that held nothing negative at all. In fact, it was more wonderful than she could ever have imagined. But she had also realised it could become a terrible distraction if she let herself think about it too much. There were other more important things in her life than pursuing selfish pleasure.

'Hi!' came a greeting from Cate at the other end of the table, diverting Rosalie's attention to Adam's daughter who was also smiling pleasure in her presence. 'Sleep well?'

'Yes, thank you.'

She managed a responding smile even as she was struck by the realisation that she hadn't been considering how the girl might feel about an abruptly broken visit. Cate had put a lot into making her welcome yesterday, and the young teenager began pressing more hospitality onto her now.

'Dad hasn't eaten yet. I was just about to ask our

cook to get started on lashings of bacon and eggs. Would you like some, too?'

Rosalie hesitated, tempted by what would be a decadent breakfast for her. Modelling demanded she be always watchful of her weight but it was so long since she had indulged herself with such foods, she suddenly felt a strong yen for them.

'Could the eggs be poached?'

'Absolutely fat free,' Cate promised with a grin, and skipped off, heading for the kitchen.

'Juice?' Adam asked, moving to a sideboard where a jug of it sat beside a group of glasses. 'It's pineapple.'

'Lovely. Thank you,' she answered, totally in two minds about what she should do now. Disappointing Cate would not be good, though she did have her father with her.

'Cate is becoming very conscious of her figure. Terrified of developing puppy fat,' Adam remarked as he set the filled glass of juice on the table and pulled out a chair for her. 'The fashion industry has a lot to answer for,' he dryly added. 'I'm counting on you to give my daughter a balanced view of what is healthy eating. As a mere male, I'm not considered an authority on these important issues, but she'll listen to you.'

'Well, being overweight can become a blight on a girl's life,' Rosalie answered lightly, grateful for any line of conversation that excluded last night.

'On a boy's, too.' He settled back onto his own

chair, his eyes engaging hers as he pursued the topic. 'But it's mostly girls who go down the path of anorexia.'

Rosalie frowned over what was a very serious issue, indeed, and Adam's daughter was, as Rebel put it, in an *at risk* situation where she might be drawn to something she could control, something she thought might make her more attractive to the people whose opinion meant something to her, or simply draw more notice to herself.

'Are you concerned that Cate might fall victim to that kind of psychological problem?' she asked seriously.

'It's about control, isn't it? Right now I feel she's too controlled about what she eats. And too thin for her height.'

'She's at an age of quick growth. I'd call her more slender than thin, Adam. And I thought she ate with a normally healthy appetite yesterday.' But being so conscious of Adam, had she really noticed?

'No French fries with her fish at lunch. Which she picked at. And nibbled a bit of salad,' he informed her, demonstrating keen observation of his daughter's diet. 'Same last night. No sweets or cheese. A small bowl of bran flakes with skim milk for breakfast. She'll probably fiddle with a slice of melon while we eat ours.'

'It's not enough.'

'My thoughts exactly. Will you speak to her about it, Rosalie?'

She nodded, thinking how perverse it was that a girl who had every food available to her would choose to starve herself when there were so many starving children who'd fight over scraps from garbage bins.

'Have you told her mother, Adam?'

'I will. I've only noticed it since we've been here. But knowing Sarah, she'll only scold, not take the time to lay out a good pattern to follow. Cate admires you. Whatever you say is more likely to get through to her.'

'Okay. I'll try.'

'Thank you. After breakfast I usually go to my computer room to check on business for an hour or so. You won't mind if I leave you with her?'

She shook her head. 'Makes it easy for me to lead into it.'

He smiled, his eyes warming with very personal appreciation. 'I'm glad you're here, Rosalie. Everything about you feels good.'

She found herself smiling back, thinking the same of him, and not just in a sexual sense. He wasn't crowding her physically. Hadn't even touched her while seeing her seated. And this appeal for her help with Cate meant he both trusted and respected her as a friend to his daughter. And very possibly a needed friend.

Which reminded her that he'd linked Cate to his invitation to Tortola and she had seen that primarily as a subterfuge to get her here, perhaps wrongly so.

In fact, it was she who had pushed for and initiated what had happened last night. Adam might have intended talking about his daughter when he'd suggested the walk in the garden—a friendly walk. She'd only been thinking of herself and her need…to *use* him for what she wanted.

Shame curled through her as she recalled her claim they could only be lovers, not friends. And despite her emphatic dismissal of any other involvement, he had been a very generous and considerate lover to her. To leave both him and Cate flat now would be incredibly mean and wrong. She couldn't go today.

'I hope I can do some good,' she said with heartfelt sincerity.

'You have the power,' he returned with a wry twist, leaving her feeling he meant far more than any influence she could wield with his daughter.

'Bacon and eggs coming up in five minutes!' Cate announced, swinging attention back to her as she took her place at the table again. 'I told cook to do your bacon in the microwave, Rosalie. It should come out nice and crispy. No grease. One of the girls at school tipped us off on that trick.'

'Common practice in the U.S.,' Rosalie commented, smiling at her, then breaking s aight into the subject of diet.

Adam sat back and let it all flow, feeling an intense sense of relief. Not for Cate's sake. It was true enough he was concerned about this dieting fad of hers, but it would have been easy enough to line up some expert nutritionist in London to set her straight on healthy eating. He thanked his lucky stars that he'd hit some sympathetic chord in Rosalie that had won more time from her.

She would stay today.

He watched her reaching out to Cate, projecting keen interest in the answers his daughter gave to questions about her friends at school, what kind of meals were served there, what they liked and disliked, how attuned the girls were to fashion and how much importance they placed on it. She was plumbing background information to give her an understanding of exactly where Cate was coming from, yet doing it in such a warm friendly way, Cate was basking in the personal attention.

And the simple truth was…Rosalie James cared.

There was no pretence in this.

She genuinely cared about his daughter.

Adam wondered what he had to do to draw the same caring to himself. Did he seem totally self-sufficient to her? Not in need of her company or craving to share more than a sexual connection?

I'm here, too, he thought, barely quelling a violent urge to impress that on her. He had to go slowly, use the time he'd won to put her in a comfort zone that made staying here more desirable than going. Whatever fears she had about associating with him any longer had to be erased, or at least soothed.

Tonight she would be his again.

Though his instincts warned him to let her think she was in control.

He smiled to himself. He didn't believe either of them were in control of the effect they had on each other. The difference was he wanted to explore it while she wanted to escape it. But the power of it was so strong...

And Rosalie had chosen to stay another night.

CHAPTER TEN

THE fourth night and the last night…

No going back on this decision, Rosalie told herself, though there was no absolute necessity for her to leave. She just felt herself getting in deeper and deeper with the Cazells. Their attractive company and the seductive ambience of the island seemed to be playing havoc with her usually strong sense of purpose.

She no longer had any *reason* for staying here and prolonging her visit was pure self-indulgence, which wasn't like her. Not like her at all. And it gave her an uneasy sense there'd be a price to be paid later— a bigger price every day she stayed. Nothing really came free. As it was, she wasn't sure how she was going to handle the attachment she now felt to both Adam and his daughter. She hadn't planned to get so involved with them, hadn't wanted either of them to tug at her heart.

She should have left after the first night.

Or at least the second.

Yet here they now were at Cappoon's Bay where a huge island party was being held around the Beach Shack, a ramshackle tin structure right in the surf. It was the night of the full moon and everyone was having a great time, eating, drinking, dancing to a metal band, living for the fun of the moment and certainly not thinking of tomorrow.

And the plain truth was, Rosalie couldn't remember ever feeling quite so relaxed and happy to do nothing, just being alive and enjoying it. She and Adam were sharing a rug on the sand, a hamper of drinks and snacks on hand for ready refreshment. Cate was in line for a Bomba dance further down the beach, joining in the hilarity and clapping of the closer spectators. It was another intoxicatingly beautiful night on Tortola.

But it had to be the last one. She had finally made an independent stand today and Adam had made the arrangements for her departure tomorrow, so it was counter-productive to start wishing the pleasure she'd known here could be stretched out indefinitely. Besides, Adam and Cate would be heading back to London themselves at the end of the week.

'Can't you stay until then?' Cate had pleaded.

'I'm expected in Paris to get ready for the pret-a-porter fashion shows,' Rosalie had excused, instinctively avoiding the extra intimacy of departing the island together, like a family going home from vacation.

They weren't a family. Yet there had been times when she'd felt a strong sense of belonging, especially with the man who was sitting beside her. It wasn't only the physical intimacy generating that feeling, either. Sometimes he simply looked at her and it seemed he knew her through and through, as though they had lived a whole life together and there were no secrets between them. Which was ridiculous. And disturbing.

Only Zachary Lee had ever looked at her like that, understanding without need for any spoken words. But her big brother did have a knowledge of her that Adam Cazell didn't. Or was Adam gifted with amazing intuition? Certainly as a lover he was sensitive to every nuance of her response to him.

She moved her gaze from the spectacle of the party revels, fastening it on the profile of the man who had made her feel so much pleasure in being a woman. Pleasure in simply being with him, too. She liked him—liked looking at him, talking to him, even touching him, feeling his very male strength. Rebel had been right. She was safe with him. But she wasn't safe from the emotions he stirred.

'You don't *have* to leave, do you, Rosalie?' he said quietly, breaking the comfortable silence between them. 'You're choosing to go.' He turned his head, his eyes scouring hers for the reason. 'Would you mind telling me why?'

'I stayed longer than I meant to, Adam,' she excused, not really capable of explaining the confused sense of losing some critical part of whom she'd been before coming here.

'I know.' His mouth curled into a wry smile. 'You came to have a need fulfilled and a question answered. That only took one night.'

Again she felt a squirming wave of shame at her initial intention to use him for her own satisfaction. 'I thought you'd be getting what you wanted, too.'

'An itch soothed?' he mocked, his eyes deriding this shallow view of him.

'You didn't really know me as a person,' she argued.

'I knew that I wanted to know you. Mind, heart and soul, Rosalie. Not just your body.' His gaze drifted down to travel over the feminine curves he now knew so intimately. 'Which is very beautiful,' he added softly, then lifted his gaze to hers again. 'But I've known others who were also beautiful in their own way. That was not the experience I sought from you. I think we have much more to give each other.'

She felt a rush of panic at the claim he was making on her mind and heart and soul. It was one thing to trust him with her body, quite another to entwine herself so deeply with him that her ability to act on her own was compromised because she'd be missing him all the time.

'Adam, this has been a kind of idyllic time. And I thank you for it.'

'But you want it contained here.'

'Yes,' she said, immensely relieved that he understood.

'Because you think it will be different once we're back in the world?'

'It can't be the same. There'll be other demands on us. You know that, Adam.'

'Our time together would obviously be considerably limited, but to me that would make it even more special.'

'And what if I'm not around when you want me around?' She raised a deliberately challenging eyebrow. 'You're a man who's used to getting what you want, Adam. How soon before you step in and interfere with my life because you're frustrated with the situation?'

He shook his head. 'I'm well aware that I'd always come second to your work, Rosalie, and if I tried to come first I'd lose you. I thought we could both make some reasonable accommodations.'

'Can't you see I don't fit?' she flashed at him from the inner angst he was stirring. 'I'm not a party person. I'd only want...'

She stopped, appalled that she had almost admitted the still churning desire to prolong this relationship beyond what was sensible or even practical, given her commitment to other things. More important things, she fiercely told herself. Adam didn't need saving but countless children did.

'You'd only want what we've had here,' he finished for her.

'It's not possible,' she stated emphatically, wishing she hadn't conceded anything.

'The place doesn't matter, Rosalie. It's how we

spend the time together. And I assure you I wouldn't want to waste it on a social whirl with other people.'

'Please...stop!' Her eyes begged for relief from being pressed. 'I have a mission. You don't fit into it, Adam.'

His gaze burned with a steady intensity. 'I could. If you'd allow me to...'

'No! Whatever you did would only be for me and I don't want to feel beholden to you.'

'I give to a lot of charities. None of them feel beholden to me.'

'It's just money. You're not personally involved with them.'

'But money buys equipment that helps. I could supply whatever you thought was needed in your orphanages. You could tell me about it...'

'And then I'd be dependent on you,' she cried.

'Is that so terrible?'

'Let me go, Adam. Just let me go.'

It was a desperate, tortured plea. She wrenched her gaze from his and stared blindly out to sea, drawing her legs up on the rug and hugging them, subconsciously making herself smaller so she didn't feel so exposed to him and his attack on a decision that had to be right. All these years of commitment to rescuing children in need held more meaning to her than any one on one relationship.

He fell silent but the silence was no relief. It tore at nerves already stressed by having to fight his strong attraction. It raised tormenting doubts in her mind. She hated the idea of leaving him feeling *used* by her.

But she had given him something of herself. More than she'd given any other person. And it wasn't as though it hadn't been a mutual desire being pursued. And satisfied. There was no reason to feel this burden of guilt, as though she had denied him some further right to her.

'What about Cate, Rosalie?' he asked. 'She thinks you're her friend. Are you cutting her off, too?'

It sounded callous, brutal, but there was only so much of her to go around. 'I hope I've made some positive difference to her life, Adam. It's all I can do.'

'All you *choose* to do,' he sliced back at her with a sudden savagery that cut her to the quick.

The tension inside her erupted. Words flew from her mouth, exploding from the sealed compartments in her brain and powering through the emotional pressure he was laying on her.

'I didn't *choose* a father who didn't care to know me or look after me. I didn't *choose* a mother who was little more than a prostitute, whose death gave some of her lowlife companions the idea of using me for their dirty profit. I didn't *choose* to be kidnapped and locked up in a house where children were supplied to rich, foreign paedophiles...'

'Paedophiles!'

His shock fed some weird satisfaction inside her, driving her on. 'I didn't *choose* to witness what happened to some of those children, but there was no escape from it, and I knew my turn was coming. The evil men who ran that place talked about me as a prize who'd fetch a very high price and they were keeping me for one particular client...'

'You were only seven!'

'There were some there younger,' she hurled at him. 'Some who died from their injuries. And if Zachary Lee hadn't been an investigative journalist at the time, hadn't broken that wicked ring wide open and rescued me...'

The fierce torrent of words died in a shuddering sigh. She clamped her mouth shut and closed her eyes, wanting to block out the memories that had burst from her with so much explosive force. She'd never told anyone this. Of course, the James family knew. They all knew about each other. But no one else. Never anyone else. And why she'd told Adam now...she shook her head. Some deep clawing need for him to understand? To let her go...

'There are other children out there...in similar circumstances,' she choked out over the huge lump forming in her throat.

'It's okay, Rosalie,' he said gently. 'I see where you're coming from. I see where you have to go.'

'Cate has you.'

'Yes. She has me.' He heaved a deep sigh and murmured, 'And who am I to clip an angel's wings?'

The silence was not so stressful this time though it held a weight of sadness that Rosalie sensed was shared by both of them. They sat apart, and she felt his loneliness as much as she felt her own. It hurt. They had been so close the last few days. But there was a bigger picture than just the two of them and a greater hurt that needed to be prevented...at all costs. How could she think of limiting her aid and taking what this man offered?

Would he be a helpmate to her?

Could she trust him not to interfere, not to pressure her into doing less and less?

Wouldn't the heart-tearing anguish she felt now just be repeated again and again and again if she tried to continue a relationship with him?

Better that it be stopped now. The decision was made. Adam had accepted it. Tomorrow she would leave and get on with her own life.

Adam slowly and painfully came to the conclusion there was nothing he could do or say to alter Rosalie's decision. Her life was built from her experience as a child and her memories—his jaw clenched as he envisaged the images that were stamped so traumatically on her mind—could never be erased or even diminished. She would live with them forever.

He felt incredibly privileged that she had chosen him—of all the men she could have had—to show her that sex could be an act of loving, not hurting, that it could be about giving pleasure, not taking it with brutal disregard for the other person. He hoped...no, he knew she had that understanding now, and at least it would have contributed some measure of good to balance against the bad.

But letting her go…

Just the thought of losing her was gut-wrenching. Everything within him wanted to fight to keep her, if only partially in his life. He could and would help her in her mission, but getting her to accept that…now wasn't the time. With the realisation of what he was dealing with—no mystery anymore—he knew he had to give her the space she was demanding, the freedom to act according to her conscience.

Maybe it was his own need arguing that the connection between them was too strong for a clean cut to be possible. Maybe Rosalie could put him and everything they'd shared behind her. He just couldn't bring himself to believe it. Destiny had a strange way of working. He was convinced they had been meant to meet, that he was the one man for her, she the woman for him, and they *would* meet again because this was not enough. Not for either of them.

There was still some time left here. With a sense of intense urgency, Adam searched his mind for how best to break this silence and reach out to her again, bring her back to him for this one last night on Tortola. The way she was sitting—her body language alone told him she was in deep retreat, probably from the shock of having opened up to him, spilling out what was terribly private and personal.

Had she ever confided her background to anyone else?

No. Adam felt an absolute certainty on that point. It would only be the strength of their connection that had released those secrets and she hadn't connected like this with anyone else. He had to regain and re-inforce the bond she had felt with him.

'Thank you for telling me, Rosalie,' he said quietly.

She sat like a stone statue, staring blindly out to sea.

'You have my solemn promise that no one else will ever get knowledge of that part of your life from me. It's safe.'

She sighed and moved her head slightly to flash him a sadly ironic smile. 'Safe,' she repeated, her dark eyes filled with a darkness he couldn't read. He sensed pain. 'I didn't even think of…of possible gossip.'

'You don't have to. It won't happen.'

'I guess…I guess…I have to trust you.'

'You can. And you have trusted me, Rosalie, with far more than what you were driven to speak. The gift of yourself was…is…something I will always value very deeply. And that, too, is an absolutely private thing, belonging only to us.'

Her eyes shone with the welling moistness of tears. 'Thank you, Adam,' she said huskily.

'Take my hand.'

He held it out to her and after a moment's hesitation she unfolded her arms, reached out and surrendered her hand to his, letting him reforge the physical link between them. It felt fragile, uncertain, yet there was trust implicit in it, belief that he meant her no harm and would do whatever was in his power to ensure none came to her through him.

'After you're gone tomorrow, I'll explain to Cate that your involvement with both of us was a gift of caring about our relationship and how it should be. I'll put it in perspective for her so she'll understand it wasn't intended to be…something lasting.'

Though it was, Adam thought, and felt Rosalie's fingers tighten around his, an instinctive, anguished protest against separation, revealing the torn nature of past needs and current desires.

'I'd…I'd appreciate that. Tell her I'm sorry…if I raised expectations…I can't fulfil.'

He nodded, running his thumb over the underside of her wrist, feeling the agitated leap of her pulse. 'So let's set this aside now, Rosalie, and make our last evening here a happy one together. Okay?'

A tautly held breath whooshed out. Her shoulders slumped in relief. She flashed him a grateful smile. 'That would be good.'

Rosalie hoped she gave no sign of any underlying stress while the party on the beach raged on. Cate ducked back and forth from the dancing, picking up cans of diet Coke and regaling them with the wild and funny antics she'd seen or engaged in, her high spirits infectious enough to make Rosalie laugh at her reports.

Between his daughter's haphazard visits for liquid

refreshment, Adam did his best to entertain her with his own amusing commentary on island activities. He recounted the odd English influences that the native population had adopted as right and proper, the anomalies like driving on the left of the road in American vehicles designed to be driven on the right, the bandaged people who were occasionally seen shopping in Road Town, clients of a very secluded clinic on the island where very discreet facelifts were done.

It passed the time easily enough until Cate was ready to go home. The trip back to the villa seemed all too short. The *family* part of the night was over with Cate declaring she was totally laid waste and heading straight for bed. Which left Rosalie alone with Adam, acutely conscious of how she had spent every other night here with him, desperately wanting the intimacy they'd shared yet feeling hopelessly awkward about it, having virtually ended any hope of a continuance.

Adam was holding her hand again but it was more a friendly link, not a sexual one. Maybe she had killed his desire for her, telling him about the horror of her childhood. Or maybe he felt she had already removed herself from any deeper physical closeness with him. She started wriggling her fingers free of his hold, wanting to bolt to her bedroom because she simply couldn't face more talk.

He turned to her, recapturing her hand, grasping the other and lifting them both to rest palms open on his chest, holding them there, forcing her to feel the heat of his body and the pounding of his heart.

'Rosalie…'

She shot a pained gaze up to his and her own heart instantly kicked into a thunderous beat. There was no mistaking the naked wanting in his eyes, the intensity of the appeal he put into words.

'Will you be with me…give me…tonight? All night?'

She had left him to go to her own suite every other night, wary of giving him the idea she was committed to an ongoing affair, needing to keep some integral part of herself to herself, away from the enthralment of how he made her feel with him. But he knew it was the end now. They both did. There was nothing dishonest or misleading about staying with him. And she wanted one last beautiful memory to take with her.

'Yes. Yes, I will, Adam,' she promised him in a soft, yearning whisper.

He enfolded her in his arms and the warm comfort of his embrace soothed the ache inside her. Her hands slid up around his neck and buried themselves in his thick, wavy hair, revelling in touching him again. Their lips met in a kiss that melted any sense of lone-liness, that breathed new life into the magic of being with this man.

Then with his arm curled around her shoulders, hugging her to his side, they walked to his suite where they undressed each other in a slow, silent ceremony, savouring every sensual pleasure given and taken.

'This isn't sex, Rosalie,' Adam murmured as he took her in his arms again and pressed soft, tender kisses to her temples, her eyelids, her nose. 'It's making love.'

And she understood that truth as his mouth claimed hers and her body instinctively strained to get as close to his as possible, because she didn't just *like* Adam Cazell. She *loved* all that he was and she wanted him to feel it, to let him know he wasn't just *an experience* to her. It was the one parting gift she could give and she gave it unreservedly, transmitting it in every touch, every response, her whole body attuned to loving…mind, heart and soul.

And when he was deep inside her, paused there for them both to revel in the sense of absolute union, she looked at him, her eyes filled with all the blissful emotion he stirred, and whispered, 'You'll always be part of me, Adam.'

'And you, me,' he answered.

It was a truth she took with her when she flew away from Tortola the next morning. It was a truth that haunted her in the days, weeks, months that followed. Regardless of how busy she made herself, regardless of her mission to save children who needed saving…

Adam Cazell could not be forgotten.

CHAPTER ELEVEN

ROSALIE had just returned to the Mayfair apartment and was sorting through the games she'd bought when the telephone rang. They were all games she'd played with Cate and Adam on Tortola and she'd been particularly impressed with the Rummikub one—a form of gin rummy played with tiles. She was planning another trip to Cambodia and thought the children in the orphanage would really enjoy something novel to play with.

'Hi! Rosalie James,' she announced into the receiver, not even wondering who the caller was, her mind lingering on memories of balmy afternoons on the villa verandah and the kind of *family* fun she'd shared over board games, Cate fiercely competitive with her father, but sweetly helpful to Rosalie who wasn't familiar with the rules.

'It's Rebel. I haven't seen you for ages and ages.'

Not since the day she'd met Adam Cazell at Davenport Hall.

'I've hardly been here,' Rosalie quickly excused.

'Come down to lunch tomorrow. It's the last day of Celeste's half-term break and she'd love to see you, too.'

Celeste was Cate's best friend. Was this a ruse to

set up a meeting? Rosalie sharply recalled her sister's persuasive part in pressing an involvement with the Cazells.

'Did Celeste bring anyone home with her?' she asked cautiously.

'No. It's just family. And I won't inflict other visitors on you,' she dryly added, well aware of Rosalie's anti-social attitude. 'Okay?'

The swift rise of tension abated. 'Okay. It will be good to see the boys, too.'

'I'll send the Rolls for you. Nine o'clock?'

'Fine.'

A family day... Rosalie gave herself a stern mental shake as she put the receiver down. She had always enjoyed being at Davenport Hall and it was stupid to avoid going there just because it would inevitably be a reminder of what she had turned away from. There was a plethora of reminders anyway, even the games she'd bought.

And in several telephone calls since her visit to Tortola, Rebel had only once mentioned Adam Cazell, rather tentatively asking if he had made a nuisance of himself since she'd given him the Mayfair number. Rosalie had assured her sister he'd been very much the gentleman, not pestering her at all, and she apologised for having been testy about Rebel's judgment of him. He had, indeed, been *safe*.

There'd been no gossip linking them together. Adam had made no attempt whatsoever to change the decision she'd made. There'd been no deliberate contact, nor any *accidental* meeting. The only thing he'd done was to press a business card on her before they parted, insisting that she keep it in case she ever wanted to call him for any reason whatsoever.

However, it did cross her mind now that Cate might have told Celeste about her visit to Tortola, and if Rebel was nursing that information…was the invitation to lunch an opportunity to probe?

Rosalie felt her nerves tightening up again and heaved a deep sigh to relax them. So what if the subject of Adam did come up? She could deflect it quickly enough and her sister wouldn't tread too heavily on sensitive ground.

As it turned out, neither Celeste nor Rebel mentioned the Cazells. Rosalie was warmly welcomed at Davenport Hall. They were all delighted to see her. Geoffrey and Malcolm instantly demanded she play with them, and after a very congenial morning tea, they carted her off to their playroom where Daddy had set out a wonderful Grand Prix race track. She was given a remote control to race the blue car against the red car and the green car. Geoffrey had to show her not to go too fast around the corners so the car would not zip off the track.

Over lunch, Celeste peppered her with questions over fashion matters, particularly the pret-a-porter shows in Paris, explaining that the girls at school would want to know what Rosalie thought would be the most popular new trends for the coming winter.

Reminded strongly of Cate's obsession about being

thin, Rosalie hoped Adam's daughter was following a better balanced eating plan now. She noticed Celeste did not hesitate to eat a slice of strawberry cheesecake for dessert, but her adopted niece had a very sensible mother in Rebel, one who would instantly crack down on unhealthy fads where her children were concerned.

The question slipped out before Rosalie realised what she was saying. 'How is your friend, Cate Cazell?'

'Cate? She's great! Scored the winning goal in our last hockey match,' Celeste answered with glee.

'Well, good for her!' The relief of not having opened up a potentially personal landmine encouraged her to satisfy the need to know more. 'I thought she was…unhappy within herself…when she was here at the beginning of the summer vacation,' she remarked, her eyes questioning.

Celeste shrugged. 'Cate had a thing about her parents not really caring about her. That seems to be all sorted out now.'

'I'm glad to hear it.' Somehow she couldn't stop herself from asking, 'Is she with her father for this school break?'

'No. He's in Hong Kong. But she had a whole lot of stuff planned with her mother so she was happy about being with her in London.'

'That's good.'

Celeste turned to Hugh, asking what time he wanted to drive her back to Roedean and Rosalie silently and painfully reflected that it had been stupid to feel a sense of belonging with the Cazells. Adam was half a world away, going about his business as usual. Cate had a mother who was obviously giving more attention to satisfying her daughter's needs. The part Rosalie had played in their lives was done.

And why that should make her feel depressed she didn't know. She had chosen to be alone. It was easier to do what she did independently of others. No strings attached. Nothing owed to anyone.

She should be pleased that she had accomplished some good, at least for Cate. Adam had certainly shown himself to be a more caring and observant father on the island, and...what was his ex-wife's name? Married to the British MP, Gerald Mayberry. Sarah...yes, that was it. Sarah had apparently been enlightened on her parental responsibility by Adam.

So there was nothing to feel down about.

Nevertheless, when Rebel asked her to stay on and keep her company while Hugh returned Celeste to school, Rosalie was quick to oblige, relieved to put off going home to a lonely apartment. Her sister was always bright and cheerful, and any conversation was better than silence right now.

Though when she was roped into bathing the boys, ready for bed, she found her mind roving back to what Adam had said about having a child of her own. Geoffrey and Malcolm were such darlings and Rebel adored them. When Rosalie had queried her about having brought *more* children into the world, her sister had declared she was bringing up her boys to have a social conscience, and the world certainly needed more people who had that.

'What happens when you die, Rosalie?' had come the challenging counter. 'Who will carry on your work? We've been so lucky to be part of the James family. Don't you think what was done for us should never be lost?'

Continuance…

It was important.

There just hadn't been a man who'd ever given Rosalie pause to consider marriage and family for herself. And there was no point in linking Adam to that idea now. Too late….

Once the boys were put to bed, Rebel linked arms with her as they strolled downstairs again. Her eyes twinkled triumphant pleasure as she said, 'You see? Whatever you said to Adam Cazell about Cate did make a difference. She's not at risk anymore.'

'I hope not.'

'What about you, Rosalie? Still happy to whizz around the world, doing good where you can?'

'It's rewarding.'

Her sister sighed. 'Well, I do think you should have given Adam Cazell a chance. I liked him.'

'Mmmh…'

'Okay, okay, I promised not to push anyone at you and I won't. Let's go to the TV room and watch the news while we're waiting for Hugh. He shouldn't be too late for dinner.'

They settled in armchairs, Rebel having poured them both small glasses of sherry as pre-dinner drinks. The television provided a focus that precluded any need to make conversation. Rosalie rarely drank much alcohol but she was contemplating drowning out her thoughts tonight. No worries about drink-driving. Hugh's chauffeur would see her safely home when it was time to go and she could fall asleep in the Rolls.

The news commentary was a meaningless blur until Rebel gasped, 'Oh, my God!'

The screen was showing the wreckage of an expensive car. 'What?' Rosalie queried.

'Listen!' came the urgent command.

'...member of parliament, and his wife, Sarah, were rushed to hospital but both were declared dead on arrival. Mrs Mayberry's daughter was returned to her school earlier this evening and is waiting for her father, well-known British billionaire, Adam Cazell, to return from Hong Kong...'

'Cate!' Rosalie leapt to her feet, the sherry spilling over the glass in her agitation. 'She must know her mother's dead and she has no one with her.'

'The headmistress would have taken her under her wing. I hope she's not seeing this. Look at the car...' Rebel was shaking her head in appalled horror.

Rosalie spun on her, shouting to break through the shock. 'She's just lost her mother. *Her mother,* Rebel! Remember how that feels? Do you think a headmistress can give her what she needs? And it's almost a

fourteen hour flight from Hong Kong. It will be tomorrow morning before Adam can get to her.'

Rebel looked bewildered. 'But what can we do?
We're not relatives, Rosalie.'

'We're friends. We're sympathetic friends. She
likes it here. We can go and get her. Cate has to be
with people who care. Who'll look after her...'

Rebel was on her feet. She whipped the glass from
Rosalie's wildly gesticulating hand, set it down, then
grabbed her upper arms. 'Listen up! We have no
right...'

'Adam will give me the right.' She tore herself out
of Rebel's grasp and driven by unshakable purpose,
headed for the sitting room where she'd left her handbag. 'I'll call him. Call him now.'

Her sister followed, crying out what she obviously
thought was sensible logic. 'How on earth do you
think you can contact him in Hong Kong? Or in flight
if he's already on his way home?'

'Adam gave me a number and said I could reach
him on it anywhere, anytime, for any reason.' She
was already hunting through her wallet for his card.
'Cate shouldn't be left on her own tonight.'

'Rosalie...you barely know the man.'

'I know him.' She flashed a hard, impatient look
at her sister. 'You said I should give him a chance
and I did. It was good. I spent days with him and
Cate on a Caribbean island...'

Rebel's mouth dropped open in shock.

'…and I can't stand back and do nothing when Adam isn't here for her.'

'Right!' The dropped jaw clicked back into place though her eyes still looked dazed. 'Call him then. I'm with you.'

Rosalie whipped out the card and carried it to the great entrance hall where the closest telephone was situated. She dialled the number, determined purpose thumping through her heart, not even pausing to consider she was re-forging a connection with the Cazells, remembering only too vividly how frightened and lost and empty she'd felt when told her mother was dead. No one had taken her hand or hugged her to make her feel safe. She'd been left alone…

'Adam Cazell…'

His voice was curt, tense, the pent-up need for fast action coursing through it, just as it was coursing through her.

'It's Rosalie, Adam.'

'Rosalie…' The pained yearning in his voice struck deep chords, reawakening the hurt of parting, the ache of not being with him.

'I'm at Davenport Hall,' she said quickly. 'I want to go and get Cate and bring her here, be with her until you come. She may need me, Adam.'

'Yes.' Intense relief. 'I spoke to her earlier. She's totally distraught, Rosalie.' A deeply scooped in breath, then gruffly, 'Thank you for thinking of her.'

Her stomach contracted. She was thinking of him, too, wanting the togetherness they'd known, needing contact, being part of him. Even so, she fiercely concentrated her mind on what had to be done. 'Will you call the headmistress, clear the way?'

'At once.'

'Are you still in Hong Kong?'

'No. I left as soon as word reached me. I'm in flight to London.'

'Come here when you land. It will be more private for both of you.'

He was a very public figure. Cate's stepfather had also been one. There'd be reporters. She didn't care for herself. Comforting Cate and protecting her from the media was far more important.

'Yes.' No need to spell it out to Adam. He knew. His voice was furred with intense gratitude. 'Thank you. And thank Rebel and Hugh for me.'

'I will.'

'Rosalie…' Just the way he said her name tugged on her heart so strongly, a lump of emotion welled up her throat. 'It's a big help…knowing you'll be with Catie.'

The emotion conveyed in calling his daughter Catie rather than Cate brought tears to her eyes. She struggled to speak, heard Adam taking another deep breath and tried it herself.

'I'll call her,' he said more firmly. 'Tell her you're coming. It will mean a lot to her.'

She knew it meant a lot to him, as well, knew the line she'd drawn on Tortola had been crossed and there'd be no going back to separate lives. But she couldn't think about that now. This was a time for fast and effective action. And compassion. She swallowed hard, clearing her throat to speak.

'I'll set off now.' She swallowed again but her last heartfelt words were a bare whisper. 'Take care, Adam.'

Tears blurred her eyes as she set the receiver down. She turned blindly to Rebel who'd stood by transfixed, listening to the one-sided conversation with Adam. 'Will you call your chauffeur…to bring the Rolls around?' Rosalie choked out.

Rebel snapped into purposeful action. 'Of course. And I'll call Hugh on his car 'phone. He can backtrack, be there to lead you straight to Cate when we arrive. Being the Earl of Stanthorpe can be very handy to cut through fuss and give us a smooth passage. Oh, and tell Mrs. Tomkins and Brooks what we're about. They can watch over the boys. And a room needs to be prepared for Cate. For Adam, too, if he wants to stay.'

She pounced on the telephone and Rosalie rushed off to carry out her instructions, grateful that her sister now had her mind set on practicalities. The housekeeper and butler of Davenport Hall were quick to take in the emergency and respond to it. Within ten minutes she and Rebel were in the back seat of the Rolls-Royce and on their way to Roedean.

The first half hour of the trip to Sussex was travelled in silence. Rosalie appreciated the uninterrupted time to recollect her composure and focus her thoughts on how Cate would be feeling, having spent these past few days with her mother, saying goodbye to her without any warning it would be a final goodbye.

Rebel stirred, turning a sympathetic face to her. 'Do you want to talk about your relationship with the Cazells, Rosalie?' she asked softly.

'No.' It was too personal, too intimate, too private, and she didn't know where it was going. She grimaced an apology for the bluntly negative reply. 'It will work itself out...one way or another, Rebel.'

A nod of acknowledgment, then silence again.

Rosalie was remembering the words she'd spoken to Adam on their last night together—*You'll always be a part of me*—and his reply—*And you, me.*

Half a world might be separating them but the physical distance was irrelevant. The passage of time since Tortola meant nothing, either. When she'd been speaking to him on the 'phone, it had felt exactly the same—minds, hearts, souls touching in a unison that went beyond any rational understanding. There'd been no need to explain anything. And in that tacit acceptance of what they shared lay some future path.

But that had to wait.

Reaching Cate came first.

CHAPTER TWELVE

ROSALIE had no hesitation in walking into the head-mistress's sitting room where Cate was waiting for her. She'd been warned that Adam's daughter was in deep shock. The girl had not spoken except to her father. Food offered had not been eaten. No tears had been shed.

This had been reported to Mr. Cazell when he'd called to direct that custody of his daughter be given to Rosalie James. He had not wanted Cate to be disturbed or treated by a doctor. She was to go with Ms. James who would look after her for him at the Earl of Stanthorpe's residence.

So much trust was riding on her shoulders but Rosalie didn't flinch from it. She closed the door quietly behind her, knowing Rebel would now be organising their departure from Roedean, having a word to Celeste, packing Cate's clothes, taking her bag down. Her sister would ride with Hugh in his car, Rosalie and Cate to ride together in the Rolls. Her only task was to reach past the block Cate was subconsciously using to shut out what was unbearable.

She was sitting by a window, staring blindly out into the night. Darkness was better than light to a traumatised mind. It hid what couldn't be looked at.

Rosalie knew this from her work with rescued children who were too frightened to accept that they *were* rescued.

But she believed trust had been established between herself and Cate, and the rapport they'd shared in the past would no more have been lost than it had been between her and Adam. As she crossed the room she picked up a chair and placed it at right angles to Cate's so it wasn't directly confrontational, but close enough to reach out to her. The girl did not acknowledge her, not by glance or word, even when she sat down next to her.

'Cate, it's Rosalie,' she announced quietly. 'I'm sorry about your mother. I know you were with her these past few days, and I hope they were good days for you.'

The girl's jaw tightened. Her throat moved in a convulsive swallow.

'I hope it was the best time ever,' Rosalie gently pressed.

Cate's head jerked around, her eyes filled with pain. 'She's dead. I'll never see her again.'

'I know.' She reached out and took one of the suddenly clenched fists from the girl's lap, stroking to ease the fighting tension. 'I know you'll only have memories of your mother now, and they'll never fill what you need from her, but you do know that she loved you and wanted to give you the best of everything. That's a memory you must keep alive because it's very precious and it's the one expression of your love for her that you can put into practice by striving to be the best person you can be—a daughter she'd be proud to have given birth to.'

Tears welled into her eyes. 'I didn't say it, Rosalie. I didn't say I loved her.'

'Your smile, your laughter, the happiness in your eyes, your kiss goodbye…all those things told your mother that you loved her. She knew, Cate. Believe me. She didn't need the words to tell her so.'

'She listened to me this time. She really did. But I didn't tell her how much it meant to…to…' Her voice choked on a sob.

'To feel you were a real part of her life?' Rosalie finished sympathetically, then shook her head. 'It would have meant a lot to her, too, being a real part of yours. Sometimes we busy ourselves with so many outside interests, the one special bond we should value most gets pushed aside. But it's not lost. It's too strong a bond to be lost. And when it comes first, it's wonderful for both of you, Cate. That doesn't have to be said. It just is.'

Tears were rolling down her cheeks but she looked directly at Rosalie and asked, 'Do you feel a bond with me and Daddy?'

The answer welled straight from her heart. 'Yes. And I'm here for you, Cate. To hold you safe for your father while he's flying back to you.' She took her other hand and pressed gently. 'Will you come to Davenport Hall with me?'

She nodded.

Rosalie stood and drew Cate to her feet. The girl wobbled slightly and Rosalie dropped her hands and drew her into a tight hug, feeling the slight body sag against hers and arms flying around her waist to hold on. She softly stroked her hair and back, imparting all the comfort she could as Cate wept on her shoulder.

Eventually the heaving sobs eased into shuddering little sighs. 'Does Daddy know I'll be at Davenport Hall?' came the woebegone question.

'Yes. He'll come straight there from the airport, Cate.'

Another deep sigh, then, 'I'm okay to go now, Rosalie.'

There was no delay in their departure from the school. Hugh and the headmistress saw them into the Rolls. Rebel was standing by Hugh's Jaguar, waiting to take off ahead of them. She gave the thumbs up sign, a silent assurance that everything would be ready when they arrived.

Once they were on their way, Rosalie encouraged Cate to recount the whole half-term break with her mother, knowing that talking would be the best release for pent-up feelings and she'd be able to ease any lingering sense of guilt that inevitably came with the thought of *if only...*

The sudden bereavement was bad enough. The sense of being cheated of all the years ahead was hard to come to terms with. But there really was no cause for guilt to weave its insidious way through Cate's emotions and Rosalie kept focusing on the positive things that had happened during the half-term break, trying to make Cate feel glad that she'd had the chance to get close to her mother again.

By the time they arrived at Davenport Hall Rosalie knew that exhaustion had set in. Rebel led them up to the bedroom suite that had been prepared for Cate, who was too worn out to even attempt to eat anything. A mug of hot chocolate was all she could manage. Rosalie tucked her into bed and sat by her, holding her hand. They still talked, but only in a piecemeal fashion...random thoughts, comforting assurances. Eventually Cate went to sleep.

Rebel had moved a big winged armchair and foot-stool close to the bed, along with cushions and a rug so that Rosalie could make herself comfortable. A nearby traymobile held flasks of soup and hot choc-olate, as well as a supply of buttered bread rolls and freshly cooked muffins. Rosalie looked at it all but she had no appetite for anything. She settled herself in the armchair, intent on keeping watch over Cate for the night.

Adam would come in the morning.

She didn't let herself think beyond that.

It was for Cate, Adam kept telling himself. He must not read anything more into Rosalie's act of compas-sion. Somehow she'd heard he was in Hong Kong and she'd thought instantly of his daughter being alone and in need.

God knew how many traumatised children she'd helped over the years. He was deeply grateful that she'd been here to give Cate her hand and heart through this horror of Sarah's death. To press her for what *he* wanted...wrong time, wrong place, wrong everything. It couldn't be done.

Yet it had been months—long empty months— since Tortola and this was his first chance to...no, it couldn't be done!

Adam had this fixed firmly in his mind when he finally arrived at Davenport Hall. One of his company limousines was being chauffered for his convenience and as soon as it was brought to a halt, he was out, having instructed the driver to wait until further notice.

Even as he hurried up the steps one of the great entrance doors to the hall was opened by the butler. The elderly man gave him a grave nod. 'Good morning, sir.'

'Good morning,' Adam automatically returned. It was only seven-thirty but obviously someone had been posted to watch for his arrival so he could be fast-forwarded to his daughter. It cemented his impression of the Davenports as kind, generous people.

Rebel was standing just inside the great entrance hall. 'Adam,' she greeted quickly. 'You made good time.'

'The advantage of owning an airline.'

'Brooks, please take care of Mr. Cazell's chauffeur.'

'Certainly, m'lady.'

She hooked her arm around Adam's and led him down the hall to the grand staircase at the end of it as she delivered information. 'Cate is still asleep. Rosalie has sat beside her all night in case she needed soothing but the sleep has been deep and peaceful. The two of them talked for a long time so I think the talking eased Cate's mind.' She flashed him a sympathetic look. 'I am sorry about her mother, Adam. Such a dreadful end to a life.'

'The worst possible time,' he returned with a grimace. 'I'd spoken to Sarah about Cate's need for more of her attention and from what Cate told me, her mother was giving it. Which makes the loss even more acute. I deeply appreciate your having her here. Very good of you.'

'Hugh and I were only too pleased to have the opportunity to help. Rosalie...' She paused, looked at him with eyes that both searched and appealed. '...she's a very special person, Adam.'

Was it a warning?

'I know,' he said quietly. 'The most special person I've ever known.'

The assurance of his feeling for her sister seemed to both satisfy and vex. 'No meddling,' she muttered under her breath as they started up the stairs.

Of course she had to be curious about their association, Adam thought. He wondered how much Rosalie had told her to explain involving herself with his daughter. Minimal information, he decided. What

they'd shared would be kept very private, but there
was no denying a bond between them. Which gave
him some hope for the future.

'There's an in-house communication system on the
bedside table in Cate's room,' Rebel went on matter-
of-factly. 'Please call for any service you'd like. Do
you need some refreshment brought up to you now?
Coffee, tea…?'

'No. I'll wait until Cate wakes. Thank you, Rebel.'

'You and Cate are welcome to stay at Davenport
Hall as long as you like. Please don't feel you have
to hurry off.'

'Thank you again for your kind hospitality, but
we'll go when Cate is ready. I think she'll want to be
home with me in London.'

'Yes. When it comes right down to it, there's no
running away from what has to be faced,' she sadly
remarked. 'It's feeling loved and cared for that helps
turn the corner.'

It made him wonder what Rebel—another child
adopted into the James family—had come from?
Which brought him back to Rosalie's mission. No
doubt her sister supported it, yet he sensed she supported his cause in pursuing a relationship with
Rosalie, too. Perhaps an ally, if one was of any use.

They reached the corridor on the first upper floor.
Rebel steered him to the left and they walked almost
to the end of a long wing, halting at a door which
had been left slightly ajar so there'd be no noise with
opening or closing. 'They're in here. I'll leave you to

it, Adam,' Rebel murmured, withdrawing her arm and turning back the way they'd come.

Adam braced himself for a meeting he had been convinced would happen, but not in these circumstances. Every muscle in his body was gripped with tension as he forced the necessary discipline into his mind. Rosalie was here for Cate, he recited, but his heart was thundering in his chest, not in tune with that dictate, beating a savage belief that she was here for him, too. He tried to ignore it, pushing himself into action, his hand reaching out to open the door wide enough for him to enter.

The room was dark, curtains drawn, but the opening door let in enough light for him to see this wasn't merely a bedroom, but a very large guest suite; armchairs grouped on either side of a fireplace, a writing-desk set in front of a window, table and chairs, a bookcase, television set...

He took a deep breath and stepped inside. A huge four-poster bed hit his gaze—Cate's head, motionless on the pillows. And there was Rosalie, rising from an armchair beside the bed, her face very pale, tired, but her dark velvet eyes locking onto his, beaming a silent, forceful message not to move or speak.

He didn't even breathe as he watched her come to him, unable to stop himself from feasting on every detail of her...the spill of her silky black hair over her shoulders, the dark plum coloured sweater that hugged the curves of her breasts and accentuated her small waist, the black slacks that encased her long, beautiful legs. She gestured for him to step back into the corridor and he just managed to recollect himself enough to do so and focus his mind on Cate again.

'How is she?' he asked as soon as Rosalie had pulled the door almost closed behind them.

'Better for talking through her thoughts and feelings with me, Adam, but please understand she'll cling to you today, and you must give her a strong sense of security with you. Don't go out anywhere and leave her, not for anything. She'll be afraid of losing you, too. It's not a fear you can reason with and it won't go away quickly.'

Her advice made instant sense to him. 'Understood,' he said, responding to the urgent intensity in her voice, her eyes. 'Thank you for all you've done, Rosalie.'

A ghost of a smile as the urgency faded. 'Thank you for trusting me.'

He'd trust her with his life. And Cate's.

Maybe she sensed the fierce wave of emotion flooding through him, or saw it in his eyes. She stepped away from him, nodding to the door, 'You'd better go in now, Adam.'

Instinctively his hand reached out to her. 'Don't go before we leave.' The words burst from his need to say much more.

'I won't,' she softly assured him. 'I'll be in the sitting room.'

Huge relief. 'Thank you.'

She nodded again and turned to go.

He didn't want to watch her walking away from him.

He stepped back into the room where Cate would see him the moment she awoke.

CHAPTER THIRTEEN

CATE leaned forward from the back seat of the limousine, looking past Adam to Rosalie who'd stood back for the chauffeur to shut their door. 'Tomorrow...you promise?' she checked anxiously.

'I promise,' came the firm assurance.

Adam's frustration was considerably eased by that promise as the limousine moved slowly around the large stone fountain and headed down the avenue that took them away from Davenport Hall. It didn't matter that she was only coming for a simple afternoon tea, pressed into it by Cate's plea for help on what to wear for her mother's funeral. It was another chance to be with her, a chance to talk of other things.

She had refused his invitation to dine with them tonight. 'As a thank you,' he had insisted. She'd shaken her head and answered, 'Not appropriate, Adam,' and her eyes had known what he really wanted.

Whether she wanted it, too, had been impossible to gauge. He'd been fighting to contain the rampant desire to just sweep her into his embrace and kiss her into submission. That, too, had been impossible...in front of Cate.

But tomorrow he'd make some time alone with her.

He would speak, regardless of the decision she'd made on Tortola, press for a change of mind, offer her everything at his disposal to give, anything as long as he could persuade her to take some place in his life.

'Remember what you said about Rosalie on Tortola, Dad? That we had to let her go because a lot of children in terrible circumstances depended on her?'

He winced at the reminder. 'Yes, I remember.'

There'd been no other choice then.

Maybe there still wasn't, but given half a chance he'd test her decision to the limits. They belonged together. And right now his body was in total rebellion against accepting another long separation.

He was sorry Sarah was dead. Especially sorry for Cate. Yet the base truth was, he'd moved past any love he'd felt for his ex-wife a long time ago. It was Rosalie who consumed the centre of his universe. Everything else was peripheral.

'Last night when Rosalie came for me...' Cate looked at him hopefully. 'She said she felt a bond with us, Dad.'

'Yes. That much is true.' He sighed and threw her a rueful little smile. 'But it doesn't mean she will stay with us, Cate. Don't count on it, sweetheart.'

This drew a frown. 'She makes me feel...I don't know. It just feels good with her.'

'It's how she makes me feel, too. And probably all

the children she helps. In Phnom Penh, they call her the angel.'

'The angel,' Cate repeated wistfully. She turned her head, staring out the side window, thinking her own thoughts.

Adam was fiercely thinking Rosalie was just as human as he was, enjoying the pleasure of their intimacy, revelling in it. She couldn't have forgotten how it was for them. He wouldn't let her forget.

After a while, Cate muttered, 'I guess angels know everything.' She turned pained eyes to him. 'She said Mummy did love me.'

'Of course she did.' He reached over and squeezed her hand. 'I love you, too.'

A big sigh. 'I wish…it could have always been like this half-term break with her. I was mean and cranky before…when she was too busy to bother with my things.'

'It's okay. Don't beat yourself up about it. Your mother understood that she'd been…neglecting you, Cate. She wanted to make it up to you.'

'Rosalie said…'

'Yes?'

She frowned, trying to get it right. 'It was about the special bond getting pushed aside because of other things. But it was never lost. It was always there…'

You'll always be a part of me.

'…and it was wonderful when it came first.'

Yes!

Hope soared through Adam's heart.

Tomorrow...

Afternoon tea... Rosalie's heart was in a helpless twist. Having given her word to Cate, she had to get through the couple of hours she'd be expected to stay, but seeing Adam again, feeling the sheer sexual magnetism of the man, the tug of his mind on hers...it just made the ache for him so much worse.

She could have been with him last night, could have shared the amazing intimacy that still haunted the dark hours before she went to sleep. And her dreams. His invitation had not been only for dinner. If she'd said yes, she might have said yes to much more, and then would come the temptation to fall into a part-time relationship with him, which would completely muddy the clear course she had mapped out for her life.

No more than a couple of hours, she determined as the limousine Adam had sent for her drew up outside his residence in Knightsbridge. It was a three storey building, facing a very pretty, enclosed park just across the street. Only a few blocks from Harrods, she thought, should Cate's clothes not be suitable for her mother's funeral. A quick shopping trip, afternoon tea in the food hall...it was a way out of being in Adam's company.

Unless he insisted on going with them.

And then she'd be alone with him while Cate tried on clothes.

The chauffeur opened the passenger door. With a

sigh of resignation, Rosalie braced herself to do her best for Cate while holding Adam's strong attraction at bay for the duration of this one unavoidable visit. She stepped out, crossed the sidewalk, and started mounting the steps to the front porch.

The front door was opened before she even reached it. Rosalie tensed, but it was not Adam facing her but Cate, obviously impatient for her arrival, wearing hipster jeans and a cropped sweater striped in dark blue and green, and looking relieved to see Rosalie.

'You're here!' came the unnecessary statement, conveying an uncertainty that was undoubtedly a reaction from having her mother ripped from her life.

Rosalie instantly focused her mind on giving the needed reassurance. She smiled. 'It wasn't far to come from Mayfair and riding in that huge limousine feels like riding in an armoured tank.'

It won a grin. 'It does kind of shut you away from the rest of the world, but it's a lot more cushy than a tank.'

'True. One is spoiled for comfort.'

Rosalie maintained the smile while stepping past Cate and pausing for her to close the door, but being inside Adam's home put her on edge, making it difficult to keep her facial muscles relaxed. Her mind was at war with the impulse to take everything in, know more about him, which would inevitably increase the colour and substance of memories that were already too vivid. She had to concentrate on Cate.

'Dad took me over to Mum's place this morning. I got the clothes she bought for me and a whole lot of other stuff I wanted to keep.' Her grimace told Rosalie it had been a stressful experience even before Cate added, 'I don't want to go back there.'

Too full of ghosts right now. 'You may want to later, Cate,' she said gently, hugging the girl's shoulders. 'Sometimes, it's good to revisit a place where a very memorable part of your life has happened, *after* you've moved on from it. You see it as…just a place…and you know the people you shared it with have moved on, too.'

'I guess…' she muttered, and heaved a deep sigh. 'I kept seeing Mum everywhere. I mean…not really seeing her but…'

'All her touches around the house.'

'Yeah…' Another sigh. 'Anyhow, I just shoved everything into bags so my room here is a bit of a mess at the moment.'

'Plenty of time to sort it out, Cate.'

'Mmmh…' She gestured to an opened door. 'Dad's in here.'

Rosalie surreptitiously took a deep breath as she entered the room, hoping to calm her nerves and give her brain a clearing shot of oxygen. Adam stood in front of a gas fire set in a black marble surround, above which was a spectacular Drysdale painting—a stark red-brown scene of the Australian Outback. Her peripheral vision picked up black leather sofas with geometrically patterned cushions in bright colours, but *he* completely dominated his surroundings.

A big man exuding power, not only from his impressive physique which was casually clothed in black jeans and a dark maroon shirt, but from his strongly boned, rugged-handsome face and the silver grey eyes that were so laser sharp with intelligence.

The intensity of his gaze instantly stripped Rosalie of any armour against the intimacy she had known with this man. The yearning to have it again flooded through her, an embarrassing heat that was mostly hidden by her black pantsuit and white blouse, but not even desperate willpower could diminish the warm tingle in her cheeks.

'It's good to have you here, Rosalie,' he said, making the statement feel very, very personal.

'Cate asked for my advice,' she returned, desperately trying to get herself back on an even keel.

He nodded. 'I'm glad she'll have the benefit of it.' He shifted his terribly unsettling gaze to his daughter. 'Cate, why don't you go up and try on what you think might be suitable out of the clothes you brought home, then come down and show both of us?'

'Okay,' she agreed.

Which spurred Rosalie into offering a safer option. 'Would you like me to come with you? Help select...'

'No, no...' She backed off, hands fluttering up in protest. 'You can hardly move in my room, it's such a mess. I'll do what Dad said.'

Leaving Rosalie alone with him.

The moment Cate was gone, Adam started towards her. She stood like a mesmerised dummy, her heart rocketing around her chest, feeling determined purpose engulfing her, seeing the glitter of reckless and uncontrollable desire in his eyes.

He plucked her handbag from her clutch, tossed it on the nearest sofa, took her hands, lifting them and pressing hot kisses onto their palms, then placing them on his shoulders, leaving them there as his arms encircled her, scooping her hard against him. His chest heaved under the soft press of her breasts. For a moment his head tilted back, chin jutting in an aggressive lift, then his gaze swept down, capturing hers in violent challenge.

'I've thought of holding you like this too many times. I need the reality of you, Rosalie. It's a need that claws at me night and day and won't let go because I know you're out there somewhere…and I want you.'

The passionate outburst, the strong hot imprint of his body on hers…both were direct and powerful hits on the need she felt for him. The mission that had driven her life was forgotten as his mouth crashed down on hers, and everything within her gloried in a wild sense of rightness as she welcor ed him in to her inner self, kissing him back, revei ing in the riotous sensations that claimed her mind and swirled through her body.

'You can't deny this! You can't!' he muttered fiercely as he broke the kiss to draw breath. His hand clamped around her head, pressed it onto his shoulder, his fingers clawing her hair as though desperate to reach into her brain. His lips were brushing her ear as he hoarsely whispered, 'We belong together. Say it! Admit it!'

She didn't want to say anything. She just wanted to savour the feel of him while she could. She closed her eyes and breathed in the scent of him, moved her face closer to his throat, tasted him.

'No!' She felt the word explode from him. He jerked away, stepped back, grabbing her upper arms, forcing her to look at him. 'I won't let you take what you want and leave me again. Understand this, Rosalie. You and I were made for each other. In far more than the sexual sense.'

Made for each other? The words bounced around her brain, not connecting to any overall certainty at all. Sexually, yes. The screaming need in her body attested to that truth…if there was such a truth *as being made for each other.* Her physical response to him was overwhelmingly positive. And the sense of belonging together was terribly strong. But there were other things…important things…that claimed her, too.

Her eyes begged mitigation from the accusation of *taking* him. 'I didn't start this, Adam.'

'Yes, you did, Rosalie. You called me.'

'Because you couldn't be there for Cate.'

'So you stood in for me. Because you and I are one.'

'No. Because...'

'Your mind and heart were instantly locked to mine and Cate's, Rosalie. A bond that no one else shares...has ever shared.'

'She needed someone who could help. That's what I do, Adam,' she pleaded.

'You called because you couldn't *not* call me. What flows between us is so strong...'

'I knew how she'd be,' Rosalie answered wildly, trying to fight off the assault of his willing her to accept more than she could let herself accept. Her memory supplied a host of children needing the same kind of help.

'And me. You knew how I'd be, too,' he threw back at her. 'Wanting you there for both of us.'

The passion in his voice made her temples throb. 'What are you asking of me?' she blurted out, her mind buckling under the pressure pouring from his.

'To let us into your life. Be part of it.'

'You are.'

'In spirit. But it can be much more than that, Rosalie. Partners, in every sense of the word.'

'You mean...living with you.'

'Yes.'

The idea of committing herself to an ongoing relationship with him brought a rush of panic. She wouldn't be free to do what she had to do. 'Adam, I'm booked on a flight to Cambodia tomorrow. The children in the orphanages are expecting me.'

'I wouldn't try to stop your work. I'd support it in every way I could.'

'You don't know...'

'I'll learn.' He released her upper arms and cupped her face, fingers dragging at her skin, reinforcing the urgent intensity in his eyes. 'All the resources at my disposal can be yours, too, Rosalie. Fly on my airline. It won't cost you anything. I'll set up another Saturn company to recruit and pay people who'd like to be involved in your mission. If saving children is your life's work, bring me into it. Share it with me. I'm here for you.'

The bombardment of offers had her mind reeling. 'You haven't thought this through,' she answered weakly.

'I've thought of little else since you left Tortola.'

'It's too much.'

'No. It will never be enough. But together we could make more of a difference, Rosalie.'

Was that true? Or was it all dependent on...his pleasure? 'What if you don't get enough of what you want from me?'

'You think I could cut you off? Cut everything off?' He shook his head, his eyes mocking any possibility of that eventuality. Then he spoke the words she had spoken to him, injecting them with a powerhouse of emotion that ravaged her heart. 'You'll always be part of me. Always. And any part you give me of yourself...it won't be enough...I know it...but it will be better than nothing. And that I also know.'

She wasn't sure. She felt helplessly torn.

'So what I'm offering you now will not be taken away,' he asserted. 'It will not be used as barter for more of your time. It's a gift...in exchange for the gift of having you in my life for at least some of the time.'

Coming home to him...in between trips and modelling assignments...having his support in what she had to do...would it be blind self-indulgence to say *yes?* She wanted to be with him, wanted it so much...but if she gave in to all she felt for him, would she start letting the really important things slide?

'The children have to come first,' she recited frantically. 'They need me.'

'Rosalie...'

Cate's voice, wobbling over her name!

She wrenched herself out of Adam's grasp, instinctively spinning around to deal with the distress she'd heard, alarm beating at her heart over what Adam's daughter might have been listening to, heightening her emotional fragility.

Cate was in the doorway. She wore the same clothes as before—possibly not even having gone to her bedroom to change. Tears were rolling down her cheeks as she shook her head at Rosalie, crying, 'Can't you see?'

Rosalie lifted her hands in automatic appeal for some mutual understanding.

Cate's hands also lifted as she stepped forward, her

whole body leaning into her own appeal. 'Daddy and I…we need you, too,' she choked out, her tear-wet eyes begging for that naked truth to be taken into consideration.

No, it was too much…too much for Rosalie to take on. This was emotional chaos…engulfing her…a net of entrapment closing her into a place that wasn't hers. Cate needed her mother…her mother was gone…it was transference. She had her father. And Adam…he had stood alone before. He could again. There was no *ultimate* need. It wasn't a life and death issue as it was so often with the children. The children…

'I'm sorry…sorry. I can do no more. I have to go.' The words spilled out in taut little jerks. Escape now was paramount. Her heart felt as though it was breaking under the pressure these people were laying on it. 'My bag…' She didn't have it. There, on the sofa. Grab it. Go. Don't look at them again. Don't stop.

'Rosalie…'

Adam calling to her, his deep voice thrumming in her ears, raising goose bumps on her skin, tugging inexorably on the intimate bond that had been forged between them. She'd rushed blindly past Cate, reached the doorway into the front hall, but somehow her feet wouldn't move any further. He was calling to that part of her he owned…that no one else had ever owned.

She looked back.

Anguish in his eyes, burning into her soul.

'Forgive me,' she cried, knowing that his accusation was true.

She *had* started it. Selfishly...wantonly...recklessly...going to Tortola...getting too deeply involved...

He shook his head. 'There's nothing to forgive.'

'Yes, there is,' she replied in an agony of guilt.

But there was no blaming her for anything in his eyes. He looked at her as though he knew everything about her, understood everything about her, and there was not only an absolute acceptance of who she was and what she did but something more, something that caressed and warmed her mangled heart and flowed into the dark places of her soul, making them lighter.

'Nothing to forgive,' he repeated, then softly added, 'I love you.'

CHAPTER FOURTEEN

THEY came...flying in to Tortola from all around the world...every member of the James family. Because it was Rosalie—Rosalie from the Phillipines—who was getting married, and none of them had ever believed she would. They wanted to meet this man who'd won her heart. They wanted to feel sure he was right for her, all that she needed him to be.

It was totally irrelevant that Adam Cazell was a billionaire businessman whose Saturn Companies encompassed global interests. Rosalie was the special one. They knew her as strongly determined, dedicated to her mission, but each and every one of them was aware of her past and the vulnerability of a heart that gave without ever counting the cost to herself. They needed to assure themselves that Adam Cazell was also a giver, not a taker.

Zuang Chi, despite being the star of a much acclaimed operatic tour in Europe, left his role to his understudy. Muhammad and Leah made arrangements for their patients in Calcutta to be cared for by other doctors and nurses. In Hong Kong, Kim set aside the complex legal task of making citizens of refugees. Shasti informed the UNICEF people in Africa she was temporarily needed elsewhere—an important family affair. Zachary Lee, negotiating on a television program in Los Angeles passed the negotiation on to an assistant.

In Australia, Joel Faber, Tiffany Makana's husband, organised the travel arrangements for those of the family living there, also ensuring that Carol and Alan Tay's tourism business in Haven Bay would be looked after while they were away. Suzanne Griffith and her husband, Leith Carew, flew from the Barossa Valley in South Australia, leaving their vineyards in the able hands of Leith's father and collecting Tom from Alice Springs on their way to Brisbane to join the others for the big trip.

Joseph, in Thailand, promised the orphans in his school lots of photographs of Rosalie's wedding and used the special ticket Adam Cazell had sent him to fly free on any Saturn plane. Breaking their tour of South America, Edward and Hilary James, who had gathered so many lost children into a family, made their own way to Tortola to see their adopted daughter married... Rosalie, at last finding the love *she* most needed...they hoped.

Rebel and Hugh brought Celeste with them—still Cate's best friend—and were special guests at Adam's villa on Tortola. Rebel was to be Rosalie's matron of honour at the wedding, Hugh, Adam's best man. It was at Davenport Hall, on Christmas Eve, that this marriage had been proposed and agreed to. Neither of them had any doubts that a pledge based on a very special love had been made.

Nevertheless, Rebel understood that the family would have to see it for themselves.

Rosalie was...Rosalie.

So they all came to Tortola, arriving on many different flights. Transport was waiting for them. Private villas had been rented to accommodate them, people employed to see to their every need. Adam was as keen to meet the remarkable James family as they were to meet him, curious to see the influence of their supportive network in play. He held open house at his villa for any one or all of them to drop in whenever they wanted to, prior to the big day of the wedding.

Celeste had told Cate the stories behind each adoption into the family, actually going so far as to advise her, 'You should get Rosalie to adopt you, like Rebel did me. Then legally you're one of them, too. You'll want to be once you meet them. The whole family is amazing!'

Cate was over the moon anyway, so delighted that Rosalie was going to marry her father that it wouldn't have mattered what the James family was like, but she was intrigued and impressed by them; Leah so graceful and feminine in her beautiful saris, Shasti stunningly regal wearing a turban and Ethiopian robes, Tom, the aboriginal Australian, with all the dignity of his ancient race.

Adam was very conscious of them making their assessment of him and how he behaved towards their sister. Their observation was subtle. So was the probing about future plans. It felt like fine tentacles of caring weaving through everything they said, touching lightly on him, more sensing for truth than testing for it. Gradually what reservations they'd held gave way to warm approval and Adam felt himself being drawn into what he thought of as their charmed circle, a place where what they were all about was understood as right for each person.

'How was it for you when you met them?' he asked Hugh when they had some time alone together.

They were sitting on the verandah overlooking the cove, enjoying the sea breeze and a relaxing drink. Most of the family had left after a very long luncheon. Rebel was going over tomorrow's wedding ceremony with Edward and Hilary. Cate and Celeste had raced off for a swim. Rosalie was strolling along the beach with Zachary Lee, the big brother who had once incited intense jealousy in Adam, but who now had his deepest gratitude for having saved Rosalie.

Hugh slanted him a sympathetic smile. 'Overwhelming, at first. They're such positive people. It's like…nothing can defeat them. They made me feel ashamed of what I'd been and determined to become a better man.' He heaved a rueful sigh, then added, 'But most of all I felt privileged that Rebel had chosen to marry me.'

Privileged…yes. Adam nodded. 'We're both very fortunate men, Hugh.'

'You have the harder road with Rosalie. Rebel was content to make her home with me.'

'We don't have to be in the one place. That's not

how it is for us. It's knowing we can come home to each other. Always.'

Hugh looked somewhat bemused. 'That's almost exactly what Rebel said. Right from the time she saw the two of you together at Davenport Hall, she figured if there was any man for Rosalie, you were it. That's why she gave you the Mayfair telephone number.'

'Is that so?' Adam grinned, recalling how he thought he'd manipulated Rebel into giving it. 'Smart woman, your wife.'

'Mmmh…used to be a super sales person. Did her best to sell you to Rosalie, too, but she honestly thought the fortress gates had remained shut. Came as a big surprise when she found out Rosalie had opened them to you.'

The fortress gates…it was an evocative phrase.

She had let him in. But it was only love that kept the gates open, that made her feel safe with him. Adam silently vowed he would never give her reason to doubt his love, that it would be reaffirmed whenever he saw the slightest need in her to have it reaffirmed. He wanted Rosalie to feel safe with him for the rest of their lives.

They walked along the water's edge where the sand was firm, their bare feet catching the occasional swirl of froth from the gentle waves. Of all her brothers and sisters, Rosalie was most comfortable with Zachary Lee. She'd trusted him before she'd trusted anyone else.

'This is a beautiful place,' he remarked appreciatively.

'Yes. It's where I first came to know and trust
Adam.'

'Were you frightened?'

'Yes and no. I felt…a compulsion…to be with him
like that…even though the idea was scary. Then I just
wanted him more and more. He made me feel safe
with him, Zachary.'

'Yes. I can see that is so.'

They smiled at each other, their understanding encompassing more than could be put into words.

'Adam is like you in a lot of ways. Big…'

Laughter bubbled up from his huge barrel chest.
His eyes merrily teased her. 'I didn't know you'd
peeked at me in the raw.'

She thumped him, then laughed as heat rushed into
her cheeks. 'I meant big in his mind and heart. But I
have to admit I love his body, too.'

'Good!' His eyes softened as he added, 'Then your
world is now in better balance, Rosalie. As all of us
have wanted it to be for you.'

She frowned. 'Was I so wrong, Zachary?'

'No. Not wrong. Just…incomplete. And now
Adam fills the place you'd blanked out of your life.'

Blanked out…the realisation dawned on her that
she had done precisely that—put up a barrier that precluded any man from getting close to her, denying
that the woman inside her had any use for one.

Until Adam, who'd stirred both need and desire,

awakening the woman she'd blanked out, giving her his love.

Asking nothing.

Just giving.

Giving as she had given hundreds of times to children who had *blanked out,* because it was needed, and only when Adam gave her his love had she known that she needed it, too...needed it from him.

A big man...as big as her dearest brother, Zachary Lee, who had rescued her. Adam had rescued her, too. From the loneliness she had thought was an inevitable outcome from the path she had chosen. But it wasn't so. Adam had shown her how it could be. How it was now. Together. Sharing everything.

Except...she suddenly thought of something else she'd blanked out of her life—something Adam had asked her about on their first night here. A child of her own. She'd denied any possibility of it, but now...not a child of her own but one created from their love for each other. His child, too.

She smiled.

Continuance.

As Rebel said, passing on the love to help make the world a better place.

'Is that a private smile or one you can share?' Zachary Lee asked teasingly.

She grinned happily at him. 'This one belongs to Adam. I'll share it with him tonight.'

'The wedding is not until tomorrow,' came the arch reminder.

She laughed. 'Adam wanted to have it made legal. As his wife I'd always have direct access to anything he owned. He wanted me to feel secure about that. But the bond between us…it doesn't need any reinforcement, Zachary.'

'So we're just celebrating it, are we?'

'Yes.'

'Well, it gives us the chance to feel happy for you. And we are, Rosalie. All of us.'

It was a glorious morning. Perfect, Adam thought. Nature at its best. A more fitting showcase for the bride of his heart than any cathedral in the world. Which she could have had if she'd wanted it, along with a designer wedding dress dripping with diamonds. But such things didn't matter to Rosalie. She'd wanted to be married here, on the island, out in the open and with only the family present.

No formal clothes. Most of the men were dressed in similar clothes to himself and Hugh—brightly patterned, open-necked, floral shirts and white trousers. The women were just as colourful, told to wear whatever they pleased and felt comfortable in. He'd seen Cate and Celeste in matching turquoise sarongs, dashing around to get *their* music set up for the wedding.

'Does Rosalie know about this?' he'd asked.

'It's a surprise, Dad,' Cate had declared excitedly.

'And absolutely right,' Celeste had assured him.

It was time now. The family had gathered under the shade of a big mango tree. A local wedding celebrant was waiting beside Adam and Hugh. Cate and Celeste had taken up a poised position on the edge of the verandah, both of them carrying baskets.

The hi-fi speakers they'd set up suddenly burst into sound. It was an old Abba song—*Take a Chance On Me*—and the two girls danced off the verandah steps and literally bopped down the makeshift aisle to the cheerful beat of the music, happily hurling flower petals from their baskets in all directions. Their exuberance made everyone smile. And Rebel, trailing after them in a royal blue sarong and with a huge grin on her face, wasn't above doing a few joyful dance steps herself.

Chances indeed taken, Adam thought, and here they were, celebrating the outcome.

The music ended. The girls joined the family gathering. Rebel took her place near the marriage celebrant. All heads were turned to the verandah as Rosalie made her appearance, flanked by Edward— the only father she'd known—and Zuang Chi, who had offered to sing a song for his sister and the man she'd chosen to marry.

Adam felt his heart swell at this first sight of his bride. He'd seen her in many roles, dressed like a queen or with the simplicity of a peasant. Today she looked as ethereal as a vestal virgin and as earthy as an island princess, incredibly beautiful, and glowing with an incandescent smile aimed straight at him.

She wore a filmy white sarong tied over one shoulder. Her long glorious hair swept down over the other shoulder, falling to her waist. A garland of frangipani flowers circled her head. She carried a spray of them in one hand. As she stepped off the verandah, the rippling drape of the sarong parted to show bare legs, and he saw that her feet were bare, too.

As though she was coming to him with nothing but herself.

It was more than enough for Adam.

This woman, whom he cherished beyond anything he'd ever held dear, was about to become his wife.

Rosalie felt Adam's love pouring out to her as she walked towards him. Behind her, she heard Zuang Chi's magnificent voice lift into the song, *There for me,* and she knew it was true of Adam. She hoped he knew it was true of her, too, that she would always do her best to answer his needs.

They did belong together. She was certain of it now. Adam...the first man...the only man for her...mind, heart and soul reaching out...mating forever.

He held out his hand to her.

She placed hers into it, knowing she was safe with him.

Always.

She looked into his eyes, and the need to say the words that expressed all she felt for him welled up and spilled from her lips...

'I love you.'

The Greek's
Bridal Bargain

MELANIE MILBURNE

Melanie Milburne says: "I am married to a surgeon, Steve, and have two gorgeous sons, Paul and Phil. I live in Hobart, Tasmania, where I enjoy an active life as a long-distance runner and a nationally ranked top ten Master's swimmer. I also have a Master's Degree in Education, but my children totally turned me off the idea of teaching! When not running or swimming I write, and when I'm not doing all of the above I'm reading. And if someone could invent a way for me to read during a four-kilometre swim I'd be even happier!"

CHAPTER ONE

'PLEASE don't go in there, Bryony,' Glenys Mercer told her daughter tremulously. 'Your father has an important…er… visitor with him.'

Bryony's hand fell away from the doorknob of the main study as she turned to look at her mother, standing in the great hulking shadow of the grandfather clock that had kept time at the Mercer country estate for six generations.

'Who is it?' she asked.

Her mother's drawn features seemed to visibly age before Bryony's clear blue gaze.

'I'm not sure your father would like me to tell you.' Glenys Mercer twisted her thin hands together. 'You know how he is about those sorts of things.'

Bryony did know.

She moved closer to her mother, her light footsteps on the polished floorboards echoing throughout the huge foyer, reminding her yet again of the emptiness of the grand old house since her brother's death.

Ever since Austin had died almost ten years ago the house had seemed to grieve along with the rest of the family. Every window, room, corner and shadowed doorway held a memory of a young man's life cut short, even the creaking of the staircase every time she went up or down seemed to her to be crying out for the tread of his steps, not hers.

'What's going on, Mum?' she asked, her voice dropping to an undertone.

Glenys couldn't hold her daughter's questioning gaze

and turned away to inspect the intricately carved woodwork on the banister.

'Mum?'

'Please, Bryony, don't make a fuss. My nerves will never stand it.'

Bryony suppressed a heartfelt sigh. Her mother's nerves were something else she knew all about.

There was a sound behind her and she turned to see her father come out of the study, his usually florid face pale.

'Bryony…I thought I heard you come in.' He wiped his receding hairline with a scrunched-up handkerchief, the action of his hand jerky and uncoordinated.

'Is something wrong?' She took a step towards him but came up short when a tall figure appeared in the study doorway just behind him.

Cold dread leaked into every cell of her body as she met the dark unreadable gaze of Kane Kaproulias, her dead brother's sworn enemy.

She opened and closed her mouth but couldn't locate her voice. Her fingertips went numb, her legs trembled and her heart hammered behind the wall of her chest as her eyes took in his forbidding presence.

He was much taller than she remembered, but then, she thought, ten years was a long time.

His brown-black eyes even seemed darker than they had been before, the straight brows above them giving his arresting features a touch of haughtiness.

Her eyes automatically dipped to his mouth as they had done every time since the day she'd put that jagged scar on his top lip.

It was still there…

'Hello, Bryony.'

His deep velvet voice shocked her out of her private reverie bringing her startled gaze up to meet his compelling one.

She cleared her throat and tested her voice, annoyed that it came out husky and tentative instead of clear and forthright. 'Hello... Kane.'

Owen Mercer stuffed his handkerchief into his pocket and faced his daughter. 'Kane has something he wishes to discuss with you. Your mother and I will be in the green sitting room if you should need us.'

Bryony frowned as her parents shuffled away down the great hall like insects trying to escape the final spurt of poison from someone holding a spray can above their heads. Her father's words seemed to contain some sort of veiled warning, as if he didn't trust the man standing silently just behind her not to do her some sort of injury while he had her all to himself.

She turned back to face Kane once more, her expression guarded, her tone clearly unwelcoming. 'What brings you to Mercyfields, Kane?'

Kane held the study door open and indicated with a slight movement of his dark head for her to go in before him.

His silence unsettled her but she was determined not to show how much. Schooling her features into cool impassivity, she stepped through, trying not to notice the musky spiciness of his aftershave or the expensive cut of his business suit as she made her way past his imposing frame.

The Mercyfields housekeeper's bastard son had certainly turned some sort of professional corner, she reflected. There was no trace of the gangling youth of her childhood now. He looked like a man well used to getting his own way, certainly not one who took orders from others.

She crossed what seemed an entire hectare of Persian carpet to take a seat on the wing chair near the window overlooking the lake. In an effort to maintain her composure she slung one long slim leg over the other and inspected the pointed toe of her shoe as she gave her ankle a twirl.

She knew he was watching her.

She could feel the pressure of his dark gaze on her body as if he had reached out and touched her. She was well used to male appraisals, but somehow whenever Kane Kaproulias looked at her she felt as if every layer of her clothing was slipping away from her, leaving her vulnerable and exposed to his all-encompassing dark eyes.

She sat back in the chair and regarded him with a cool impersonal stare.

He held her look without speaking. She knew it was some sort of test to see who would be the first to look away, but as much as she wanted to escape that brooding mysterious gaze she held on, not even allowing herself to blink.

His eyes went to her mouth and lingered there.

Bryony felt an almost irresistible urge to run her tongue over the parchment of her lips but fought against the impulse with every fibre of her being. So great was the effort to appear unaffected by his disturbing presence she began to feel the hammer-blows of a tension headache gathering at her temples, and her resentment towards him went up another notch.

Finally she could stand it no longer.

She got agitatedly to her feet and, crossing her arms over her chest, faced him determinedly.

'OK. Let's skip the weather and the current cricket score and get right down to why you are here.'

He held her defiant glare for another pulsing pause. 'I thought it was time I paid the Mercer family a visit.'

'I can't imagine why. You're not exactly on the Christmas card list any more.'

His mouth thinned in what she recalled was his version of a smile. 'No, I imagine not.'

She forced her eyes away from the jagged edge of his scar, surprised at how it still affected her to see it after all this time.

He looked fit and strong, as if he was no stranger to hard physical exercise, and his skin was tanned, but then, she reminded herself, his maternal Greek heritage had always given him somewhat of an advantage in the summer sun. Standing before him now, her creamy skin seemed so pale in spite of the intolerably hot weather they'd been having since Christmas four weeks ago.

'How is your mother?' she felt compelled to ask out of common politeness.

'She's dead.'

Bryony blinked at his bluntness. 'I…I'm sorry…I hadn't heard…'

His eyes glittered with hard cynicism. 'No, I expect the passing of a long-term servant wouldn't quite make it to the Mercer breakfast table, let alone as a topic for discussion over lunch or dinner.'

The bitterness of his words stung her as he clearly intended it to. As much as she hated admitting it, he was very probably right. Her parents would never discuss servants as if they were real people. She'd grown up with their attitudes, had even demonstrated similar ones herself, but as she had grown older had shied away from maintaining such outdated snobbery.

Not that she was going to let *him* know that.

No, let him think her the spoilt brat heiress of the Mercer millions.

She sent him an imperious look over one shoulder as she wandered back to her chair, taking her time to arrange her skirt over her knees.

'So—' she inspected her neatly French-manicured nails before lifting her blue gaze back to his '—what do you do these days, Kane? I don't suppose you've followed in your mother's footsteps and clean up other people's messes for a living?'

She knew she sounded exactly like the shallow socialite

he'd always considered her to be; she could even see the slight curl of his damaged lip as if he was satisfied his opinion had been justified by her crass words.

'You suppose right.' He leant back against her father's antique desk with the sort of indolence she'd come to always associate with him. 'You could say I'm in shipping.'

'How very Greek of you,' she observed with undisguised sarcasm.

His dark eyes challenged hers, a flicker of anger lighting them from behind. 'I am just as much an Australian citizen as you are, Bryony. I've never even been to Greece, nor do I speak any more than a few words of the language.'

'How can you be sure of your true heritage?' she asked. 'I thought you didn't know who your father was?'

It was a nasty taunt, and one she wasn't proud of, but his manner had increasingly unnerved her to the point of reckless rudeness.

She watched as he reined in his anger, the white edge of his scar standing out as his mouth tightened.

'I can see you still like to play dirty,' he said.

She shifted her gaze back to the unfathomable depths of his. 'When pressed to do so, yes.'

'Let's hope you can cope with the consequences if such a need arises in the very near future.'

Bryony couldn't hold back a small frown at his coolly delivered statement. There was something about his demeanour that alerted her to the strange undercurrents she'd felt swirling about her ever since she'd driven down from Sydney that morning.

'Why are you here?' she asked. 'What possible reason could you have to be here?'

'I have several reasons.'

'Let's start with number one.' She set her chin at an imperious angle even though inside she was trembling with an unnamed fear.

He crossed one ankle over the other, his action drawing her eyes to his long muscled thighs.

She tore her gaze away and forced herself to hold his Sphinx-like stare.

'Number one is—' He paused for a mere fraction of a second, but it was long enough for another flutter of unease to feather along the lining of her stomach. 'I now own Mercyfields.'

Her eyes widened in alarm. 'W-what did you say?'

Kane ignored her question and continued with implacable calm, 'Number two is I also own Mercer Freight Enterprises.'

She swallowed her rising panic with difficulty. 'I-I don't believe you.'

Again he ignored her strangled comment. 'I also own the harbourside apartment and the yacht.' He paused as he gave her an inscrutable look before adding, 'However, I have decided to allow your father to keep his Mercedes and Jaguar; I have enough cars of my own.'

'How very magnanimous of you,' she managed to quip caustically. 'Is there anything else in the Mercer household you think you now own?'

He smiled a hateful smile that chilled her already tingling flesh.

'I don't just think I own the Mercer package, Bryony— I *do* own it.'

He reached for a sheaf of papers that was lying on her father's desk behind him and handed them to her. She took them with fingers that felt like wet cotton wool, her tortured gaze slipping to where her father's signature should have been but very clearly wasn't.

Each document was the same.

The new owner of everything to do with the Mercer millions was now Mr Kane Leonidas Kaproulias. The houses, the business, the investments, the yacht...

She let the papers flutter to the floor as she stood up on watery legs. 'I don't understand…how did this happen? My father would never let things get to this state! He'd rather die than see you take everything.'

The loathsome smile was back. 'Actually, he was quite agreeable to it all in the end.'

'I don't believe you. You must be blackmailing him or something, for he would never allow you to—' She stopped as she thought about her father's recent behaviour. Always a stressed-out control freak, he'd definitely worsened of late. Christmas had been a tense affair, his constant harping on at her had seen her make up an excuse to leave a couple of days early, even though she'd felt guilty at leaving her mother.

Had Kane set him up to destroy him?

He certainly had all the motives one would need to implement such a plan, for even though her father had sponsored Kane's private academy education as a goodwill gesture he'd still treated him appallingly during the time he'd lived on the estate, when his mother had been employed to do the cleaning.

And not just her father. Her brother, Austin, had been relentless in his bullying at times, not to mention her own reprehensible behaviour, which still made her cringe with shame whenever she allowed herself to think about it…

'I wouldn't exactly describe it as blackmail.' He cut across her thoughts. 'Suffice it to say I persuaded him to consider his somewhat limited options. And, as I expected him to, he took the easy way out.'

'The easy way?' She gave him an incredulous look. 'You call handing over several million dollars worth of assets the easy way out?'

'It is when you're facing a lengthy term in prison.'

She stared at him speechlessly, her heart ramming

against her sternum until she was sure it was going to jump out and land at his feet.

'Prison?'

'Jail, the slammer, penitentiary, crim-coop, calaboose...'

'I know what a bloody prison is, for God's sake,' she snapped. 'What I don't understand is why my father deserves to go there. What's he supposedly done? Forgotten your birthday?'

'Now that would indeed be a crime, considering my number five reason for being here.'

She mentally backtracked: one was the Mercyfields estate, two was the business, three was the yacht, four the city apartment...

'What are you talking about? You've got it all; what more is there?' she asked.

'I'm surprised you haven't guessed by now. It is, after all, the one thing I've wanted ever since the day my mother and I walked through the Mercyfields gate.'

'Revenge...' She almost whispered the word, so deep was her panic. 'You're after revenge...'

His dark eyes never once left her face. 'Now, what form do you think that revenge might take, sweet Bryony?'

She injected her look with as much venom as she could. 'I have no idea how the mind of a sociopath works; I'm afraid you'll have to tell me.'

He laughed, a deep rumble of amusement that sent ice through her veins. 'How ironic you see me in that way.'

'How else could I see you?' she asked. 'You were sent from Mercyfields with a criminal record for damage to property and unspeakable cruelty to animals, or have you forgotten about Mrs Bromley's spaniel?'

His eyes hardened as they burned down into hers. 'I did not commit that particular crime. The property damage, however, was an unfortunate outburst of temper on my part and I took full responsibility for it.'

She gave a derisive snort. 'So you've grown a halo over the last ten years, have you? What a pity I can't see it.'

'You only see what you want to see,' he said with bitterness. 'But there will come a time when you'll have to face the brutal reality of the truth.'

'I find it highly entertaining to hear you mention the word truth as if you and it are regular acquaintances,' she tossed back. 'So tell me, Kane. What instrument of torture do you have planned? I take it I'm the one who has to pay the price, otherwise why would I be summoned to appear?'

'Your father has an unfortunate habit of ordering people about, but I hope that he will soon see the error of his ways. I thought it in your best interests for you to be here this afternoon. I did not ask him to summon you.'

'Can we get straight to the point of this?' she asked with increasing impatience. 'I'm getting a little tired of all the word games.'

Kane drew in a breath as he studied her incensed features. She thought the worst of him and for now that suited him. He couldn't afford to let her find out his real motives in coming here today.

He'd waited a long time for a chance to confront Owen Mercer. Ten years of working unspeakable hours to climb up from the depths he'd been tossed into. Rage had simmered in his blood for the last decade as he'd waited for the opportunity to strike back.

Austin Mercer had met his destiny and, as much as Kane knew the family still grieved their loss, he didn't feel a microgram of regret that the only male Mercer heir was now dead and buried.

Kane's mother, Sophia, on the other hand, had died before he could provide her with the things he'd so wanted to give her in return for all the sacrifices she'd made.

All the filthy sacrifices Owen Mercer had made her make.

He watched Bryony's struggle to keep cool under pressure and privately admired her for it. Her father had caved in like the cowardly bully he was, but Bryony was a fighter and he still had the scar to prove it.

She was even more beautiful as a young woman than she'd been as a teenager. Her figure was slim and she moved with the easy grace of someone well trained in the art of classical ballet. Her silky blonde hair was long, drawn back into a single clip at the back of her neck, her eyes an azure, mesmerizing blue. Her mouth was full and tended towards a petulant sneer, but he knew that was probably because she considered him totally beneath her, not worthy of the million-dollar smile she flashed at other men.

But he was patient. He'd waited this long; he could wait a little longer…

Bryony found Kane's scrutiny increasingly disturbing but stood her ground, waiting for him to speak. She reassured herself that he couldn't possibly do any worse than he'd already done. If it were indeed true that he now owned everything she would have to move out of the city apartment, but there were plenty of other places she could rent instead.

Her work as a ballet teacher brought in a reasonable income, but she still had to be careful financially, mostly because she found it hard to charge the going rate when children from less fortunate backgrounds fell behind in their fees.

She knew she could always supplement her income some other way, although she had no intention of asking for her father's help. She suppressed a tiny bubble of what threatened to be hysterical laughter as she even considered taking up house cleaning.

'Would you care to share the joke?' Kane asked.

She stared up at him, uncertain of what to make of his expression. 'No, actually, it wasn't even funny.'

'Not much in life is, is it?' he asked.

She compressed her lips by way of reply. He of all people knew how much she'd idolized her older brother—yes, life wasn't all that much fun any more.

'I have made a deal with your father,' he announced after another one of his nerve-tightening pauses.

'Oh?' She hoped she sounded uninterested.

'I'm giving him the chance to escape the harrowing experience of the judicial system.'

'Why would you do that?' She frowned. 'Especially since…' She didn't finish the sentence. She still remembered the shame and disgrace Sophia Kaproulias had gone through when her son had been charged with wilful damage. The local paper had got wind of it, calling Kane Kaproulias an ungrateful rebel who had turned on the benefactor who'd paid for his private education.

The hand of the law had fallen hard on him and she was glad it had. She'd heard he'd spent some time behind bars but had got out early due to good behaviour.

Somehow good behaviour and Kane Kaproulias didn't sit all that well together in her opinion, especially now, with him watching like a hawk did before it made its final swoop.

'Your father would not survive a month in prison,' Kane said. 'Your mother wouldn't even make it past the first day.'

'*My mother?*' She looked up at him in sudden consternation. 'What has my mother got to do with any of this?'

'Your mother would be implicated in aiding and abetting a criminal,' he informed her impersonally. 'And, since I now own and control the family fortune, no decent lawyer would defend their case.'

'You're making this up…you have to be…'

'I'm afraid not, Bryony. Your father has been doing some rather shady deals over the past few years. I got wind of it and decided it was time to make him face the music, so to speak.'

'With you as principal conductor, I suppose?' Her look was arctic.

'But of course.'

She took a prickly breath. 'So what is my role in all this? You can hardly implicate me. I don't have anything to do with the family business; I never have.'

'That's true; however, you do have rather an important role to play now. For unless you play it both your parents will leave Mercyfields in the back of a police van as I did ten years ago.'

It was hard to maintain her composure as a vision of her fragile mother came to mind. She felt the drum beat of fear pounding deep in her stomach, sending shockwaves all the way to her brain as she tried to imagine what he had planned for her.

What sort of sick revenge would he require to appease his bitterness over the past?

There was only one thing she thought of that would truly rock her to the core of her being, but surely he wouldn't be thinking along those lines...

He straightened from his leaning position against her father's desk and strode with loose-limbed grace to where she was sitting on the edge of the wing chair, her crossed leg trembling just ever so slightly as he drew nearer.

She looked up at his face and for the first time realised she had seriously underestimated him. There was a hint of ruthlessness in his glittering eyes, as if he couldn't wait to tell her of what he had in store for her but was deliberately making her wait to draw out the agony of her suspense for his own enjoyment.

She was close to losing her head and sensed he knew it. Her mouth was dry, her hands damp and her neck and shoulders so tense she could feel a muscle spasm begin in the middle of her back, beating in time with her increasing headache.

She got to her feet, then wished she hadn't as it brought her far too close to the wall of his body, her thighs almost touching his.

She shrank back but one of his hands came out and held her by the elbow, making escape impossible.

'Get your filthy hands off me.' She hissed the words at him with aristocratic hauteur.

His nostrils flared and she felt the unmistakable tightening of his grasp for endless seconds before he finally let her arm go.

She fought to keep her breathing under some sort of control but the feel of his long fingers on her had set off a host of strange electric sensations throughout her body. She felt frightened of him but drawn to him all at the same time, making her feel confused and disoriented.

'In time you will get used to having me touch you, Bryony,' he said. 'You may, in fact, eventually crave it.'

'I wouldn't have you touch me for all the money in the world,' she told him with stiff pride.

'What about for all the money in the Mercer family vault?' he asked.

'W-what are you talking about?'

He gave her an unfathomable look. 'You see, that is my plan for you, Bryony. Your parents will maintain their freedom and, as I'm feeling generous, a certain level of financial support, but on one condition and one condition only.'

She gave one tiny nervous swallow before she could stop herself. 'Which is?' she asked, not really wanting to know the answer, somehow sensing it wasn't going to be what she wanted to hear.

And she was right.

It wasn't.

'I want you to be my wife.'

CHAPTER TWO

BRYONY knew she was giving a very good imitation of a stranded fish, with her mouth opening and closing in shock, but there was little she could do to stop it.

'You're a whole two months early for April Fool's day,' she said when she could find her voice.

'This is not a joke, Bryony.'

'You surely don't expect me to take this seriously?'

'If you want your parents to avoid the weight of the law, then yes, I do.'

'This has got to be some sort of sick joke!' she insisted. 'It has to be!'

'No.'

His one word answer upset her more than if he'd rattled off an entire dictionary of words at her.

Her long stunned silence came to a jarring end when he announced with implacable calm, 'You will be my wife within a fortnight or both of your parents will be staring at the four walls of a cell.'

'You definitely need a little work on the proposal, Kane.' Her tone was deliberately dry to disguise her distress. 'It makes one wonder how you approached the whole issue of dating over the last few years. What did you do? Drag the nearest woman off by the hair?'

'No, I never found I had to resort to such tactics.'

'What did you do? Pay them?'

'Careful, Bryony,' he warned her silkily. 'It wouldn't be wise to test my control too much. I might be tempted to walk away with the lot and let your parents face a judge and jury all on their own.'

19

She wished she had the courage to call his bluff, but as her father's business affairs were so unknown to her it made her realize she was at a distinct disadvantage.

'I can't imagine why you would want to marry me.' She injected her tone with icy disdain. 'We have nothing in common.'

'I take it you're referring to the fact that you have what your family likes to think of as blue blood while mine is, shall we say, a little contaminated?'

'Your entire brain is seriously contaminated if you think I would ever agree to be your wife. I wouldn't even agree to be your neighbour, much less live with you in a relationship such as marriage.'

'It's understandable you'd find the notion of marriage to me a little distasteful, but in time you may come to see it as justice well served.'

'My parents would never allow such a marriage to take place,' she said with somewhat shaky conviction. 'It would break their hearts to have their only daughter marry the illegitimate son of one of their previous housekeepers.'

'Your parents have expressed their distress but wisely realize what's at stake. They've given their permission, not that I needed it, of course. I would have gone ahead without it anyway.'

'Aren't you forgetting something?' She gave him a scornful glare. 'Isn't the bride supposed to accept the proposal?'

'You have no choice other than to accept.'

'Well, here's news for you, Kane Kaproulias. I do *not* accept your outrageous proposal. You'd have to have me drugged and hogtied to get me within a bell's toll of a church to marry you.'

'I wasn't thinking along the lines of a church wedding.'

She stamped her foot on the carpet at her feet. 'There is *not* going to be any sort of wedding!'

He continued calmly, as if she hadn't just screeched at him. 'It will be a civil ceremony with the minimum of guests.'

'The last thing I'd call you is civil,' she tossed back. 'You're acting like a primitive jerk issuing these stupid commands like some sort of dictator.'

'I can be very civil when I need to be, Bryony, but if my buttons are pressed a little too often I'm afraid you might find me less than urbane.'

'I find you less than human! What were you thinking, coming back here after all this time waving property deeds around and insisting on extracting revenge when you were the one in the wrong in the first place? You are seriously unhinged if you think for one moment I'd commit myself to a man I loathe with every breath in my body.'

'I shall enjoy teaching you to respect me. I've been waiting a long time to do so.'

'How could I possibly respect you?' she threw at him coldly. 'You're the very last man on earth I would ever respect. You're nothing, do you hear me? Nothing but a piece of—'

She didn't get time to finish her stinging insult. He was suddenly towering over her, both of his hands on her upper arms, hauling her up against his hard body, the contact of his flesh on hers knocking all the air out of her lungs.

His head came down, blocking out the fading afternoon sunlight as his mouth came crashing down to hers.

She began to struggle but as soon as his tongue drove through the cleft of her lips she felt herself melt as if he'd turned a switch inside her body from off to on. Sizzling heat coursed through her as his mouth commandeered hers with a mastery she knew was his particular speciality. After all, it had been him who had taught her long ago how truly devastatingly tempting a fiery kiss could be.

She felt the stirring of his body against her stomach,

making her legs go weak with unexpected longing. She couldn't understand her response to him, much less do anything to stop it. Need clawed at her insides, making her kiss him back without the restraint she'd intended on executing.

She felt the ridge of his scar as he shifted position, felt too the rasp of male skin in the dip between her chin and mouth, making her sink even further into his pulsing heat.

He dropped his hold and stepped back from her, his movement so unexpected and sudden she actually swayed on her feet.

It took her at least six precious seconds to gather herself enough to glare at him while she wiped her mouth with the back of her hand as if to remove the taste and feel of him from her lips.

'Don't you ever try that again,' she ground out furiously, more angry with herself than him. 'Who do you think you are?'

'I am your fiancé until the week after next,' he said smoothly. 'After that you will wear my ring and receive my body without complaint.'

'I hope you've got ready access to a large supply of stupefying drugs,' she bit out. 'For I can't imagine any other way you're going to get me to agree to sleep with you.'

The edge of his mouth lifted in a twisted smile. 'Such dramatics I suppose are to be expected from someone who has had their own way all her life. Marriage to me will be the making of you, Bryony. I guarantee it.'

'You're assuming, of course, that I'm going to agree to this preposterous plan.'

'I'm not just assuming—I'm counting on it. Any doubts you may harbour at this point will soon be swept away with just one conversation with your father.' He walked to the door and held it open for her. 'Why not go to him now and get it over with?'

She hesitated, somehow sensing that once she walked through that door she was going to be entering a completely different stage of her life.

He elevated one dark brow at her as he waited for her to move past, his action seeming to mock her indecision, igniting her fury anew.

She drew in a breath and, stiffening her spine, stalked past him with her head in the air, giving him her best imitation of affronted aristocratic pride.

She sensed his self-satisfied smile as she moved past and, clenching her teeth, strode away down the hall, her footsteps echoing with an agitated syncopated beat.

Her parents were in the green sitting room, her father standing at the window staring out over the view of the extensive gardens, her mother sitting in a frozen position on one of the linen covered sofas, her hands tied into two tight knots in her lap.

Bryony closed the door behind her with a little click that made her mother instantly flinch and her father turn around to face her.

'What the hell is going on?' she asked.

Her mother began to sob brokenly.

'Shut up, Glenys.' Owen Mercer threw his wife a disparaging glance. 'It's too late for hysterics; it won't change anything now.'

Bryony hated the way her father always dismissed her mother but, as much as she wanted to berate him for doing it now, she was here for other reasons and didn't want to be distracted from them.

'Is it true?' She addressed him squarely. 'Does Kane Kaproulias now own everything?'

She saw her father's Adam's apple move up and down in his throat and the fine beads of perspiration clinging precariously to his fleshy upper lip.

'Yes…it's true.'

She blinked at him in shock. 'But...but how? How did such a thing happen?'

Her father seemed to be having some difficulty in meeting her eyes.

'I made a few mistakes,' he began awkwardly. 'None of them serious, but over time they started to bank up behind me.'

'What banked up behind you?'

'Debts...'

'What sort of debts?'

He told her a sum and she sank to the nearest sofa. 'Oh, my God.'

'Kane heard about it and swooped in for the kill. There was nothing I could do to stop him.'

Her mind was racing with the effort of finding a way out of their predicament but all she could see was her future mapped out for her as if written in her blood on the wall.

Kane had come after her.

She was the one he had chosen to pay the price.

'He's offered us a solution to our problems,' her father said into the silence.

'Oh, really?' She gave him a cold look. 'I don't suppose you've agreed to his tidy little solution, have you?'

'Darling...' her mother began.

'I told you to keep out of this, Glenys,' Owen barked at her before turning back to Bryony. 'He's a rich man. I might have asked for someone a little less...er...primitive, but his wealth will more than make up for that.'

'You think that money means anything to me?' she asked. 'Don't you realize what you've done? You've sold me like some medieval bride!'

'You could do a lot worse.'

'I'd like to know how.' She sprang off the sofa in agitation. 'I hate him! He's a criminal, or have you forgotten that little detail?'

'We all make mistakes, Bryony…'

'I can't believe I'm hearing this!' she gasped. 'You were the one to send him off to whatever correction facility he went to. How can you allow him to step in and carry me off like some sort of caveman?'

'You're being hysterical just like your mother.'

'*I'm* being hysterical? This whole farce is hysterical! I will not marry him and that's my final word.' She spun away and stomped to the door and had her hand out to turn the knob when her father spoke, instantly freezing her to the spot.

'He has information about me that will send both your mother and I to prison for the rest of our lives.'

Bryony turned around slowly, as if by prolonging the moment she might find her life had turned back to what it had once been, not the theatrical drama that was facing her now.

No such luck.

The look on her father's face was nothing short of desperate and her mother was bent over double on the sofa, the sounds of her distress muffled but no less disturbing.

'What did you do?' she asked when she could move her stiff lips into gear. 'Kill someone?'

His eyes skittered away from hers. 'I won't distress you with the details.'

'I think under the current circumstances I can handle it,' she informed him drily. 'My shockometer has already blown a fuse this afternoon so one more hit shouldn't make much difference.'

'I don't wish your mother to be upset.'

'You've made it your lifetime's work to make her upset so I can't see why you're feeling so solicitous now.'

'I won't be spoken to like that, young lady,' Owen growled at her darkly.

'I'm not a child you can smack into obedience,' she

flashed at him, recalling all the times he had as if they were yesterday. 'I'm twenty-seven years old so you can hardly resort to such brutality now.'

'You deserve Kaproulias as your husband,' her father snarled at her. 'You need someone cruel and calculating to bring you to heel.'

She didn't think she had hated her father more than at that point in her entire life.

She knew Austin had been his favourite child. She had never come first in his affections and had barely managed to scrape in second. His work was his life and he'd brandished his wealth about with self-indulgent pride. She would have walked away long ago and never looked back except for her mother...

'So my fate is sealed.' She flicked a glance towards the bowed figure on the sofa, her heart sinking all over again at the sight of her mother's brokenness.

'It's the only way out,' Owen said. 'You owe us this. You're a Mercer and we must always stand together.'

'What a pity you didn't consider that when you went on your little gambling spree.' She sent him a disdainful look. 'I'm assuming that's where most of the money has gone?'

He didn't bother denying it. 'I was on a winning streak, my numbers were up and then it all changed.'

Oh, how it had changed, she thought with increasing despair.

'Kaproulias is being quite generous,' her father continued. 'He's paying for your mother and me to go on a trip to get out of the line of fire. There are people after me...'

As far as she was concerned they were welcome to him but she couldn't bear the thought of her mother suffering any more grief. In spite of her father's mean-spirited nature, she knew her mother still loved him desperately.

Bryony couldn't imagine ever allowing herself to love

someone so unguardedly. Her heart was untouched and, as far as she was concerned, it was going to stay that way.

She left the harrowing spectre of her parents' financial demise to the confines of the green sitting room and made her way towards the stairs.

'I wish to discuss the details of our marriage with you.' Kane's deep voice sounded from behind her.

She sucked in an angry breath and turned on her heel to look at him, wishing she'd made it up four or five steps so she could at least have given her craning neck a rest.

Had he really been that tall all those years ago?

She was a good five foot seven, could even stretch it to ten in some of her heels, but he still towered over her, making her feel small and insignificant.

'I thought you would have taken the hint by now and left,' she said. 'I don't have anything to say to you.'

'We have a wedding to arrange.'

'It seems to me it's already been arranged—' she sent him a withering look '—by you.'

'I want your input on one or two details.'

'You've made all the decisions so far, so feel free to make the rest. I don't give a toss.'

'Do you not wish to know where we will live?'

She hadn't given it a thought. So much had happened in the last hour; she was still reeling from the staggering blow she'd received, her brain more or less paralysed by a combination of fear and sick resignation.

Marriage to Kane Kaproulias was quite clearly inescapable. While she would have happily left her father to the pack of wolves currently after his blood, her mother was another thing entirely. Even if Bryony had to wed Lucifer himself it would be preferable to watching her mother destroyed.

She would not—could not let that happen.

'Mercyfields is out of the question,' she said, carefully

avoiding his eyes. 'I need to be close to my work in the city.'

'You won't need to work once you are my wife, or at least not in that capacity.'

She frowned at his statement. 'Of course I must work. I love my job.'

'I don't mind if you have a job as long as you run my home for me according to my standards.'

Her jaw dropped open. 'What did you say?'

His mouth tilted in a self-satisfied little smile. 'I want you to be a proper wife. You will keep our home clean and tidy as well as cook on the occasions we don't dine out.'

She couldn't believe her ears. She felt like shaking her head to make sure she wasn't going deaf and misinterpreting what he'd said.

'You want me to do *housework*?'

'But of course.'

'I don't *do* housework,' she stated emphatically.

'All wives do housework.'

'Not in this century they don't.'

'I don't expect you to do everything, of course—' he folded his arms casually '—or at least no more than your family demanded of my mother.'

She was starting to put the pieces together in her head and it wasn't looking pretty. Kane was out for blood for the way her family had supposedly treated his mother, but she could hardly recall ever speaking to the woman in the whole time she'd occupied one of the servants' cottages at the back of the estate.

Sophia Kaproulias had been a quiet and seemingly diligent worker, but Bryony hadn't been encouraged to mix with the household or grounds staff, especially when a rumour had started going around about the housekeeper's promiscuous behaviour with someone on the estate.

Besides, she'd been at boarding school most of the year

and during holidays at Mercyfields she'd pointedly avoided the housekeeper in case she came into contact with Kane who'd always seemed to her to be rather sullen.

She refused to think about the one occasion she had come into closer contact with him…

'You're totally sick.' She clenched her hands into fists by her sides.

'On the contrary, I'm in the peak of fitness and health,' he returned as he held her infuriated gaze with ease.

She fought against the temptation to run her eyes over his tautly muscled form as he stood before her. She could sense the strength of his body, and imagined each and every muscle had been honed to perfection by a strict and disciplined approach at some state-of-the-art well-appointed gym.

She sucked in her post-Christmas tummy and gave him a glowering stare. 'You think you've got it all worked out, haven't you? Mr Nobody makes the big time and lands himself a trophy wife. But you're in for a surprise, for I refuse to be any man's slave in any room of the house.'

Kane watched as her eyes flashed with hatred and couldn't help wondering how passionate she'd be in bed. His body grew hard just thinking about it, speculating on how many men there had been before him.

She had the sort of mouth that begged to be kissed, the softness of her bottom lip jutting in sulkiness, tempting him so much he had to push his hands into the pockets of his trousers to stop himself from reaching for her again.

'I don't need a slave, I need a wife.'

'You don't need a wife; in my opinion you're in desperate need of a behavioural psychologist.'

He laughed at her, the rich deep sound surprising her into silence.

She stood immobile at the foot of the huge staircase,

staring up into his eyes while the grandfather clock kept solid time in the background.

One second…two seconds…three…four…five…

'I have to get back to the city,' he said, jolting her out of her stasis. 'I'll contact you at the city apartment to inform you of the arrangements.'

She watched as he made his way to the front door of her family home as if he owned the place, realizing with a sickening little lurch of her stomach that he now did.

And not just the house…

Bryony waited until the sound of his car driving over the crushed limestone driveway faded into the distance, the crunch of displaced stones reminding her of the impact he'd had on her in the space of little more than an hour.

How was she to cope with extended periods of time in his presence, much less marry him?

Marriage to anyone was anathema to her, let alone to someone whom she hated.

How had her father got them into this? And if her mother had known something of it, why hadn't she thought to warn her?

Too agitated to stay within the house but for some strange reason unwilling to leave by the same exit Kane had just used, she turned and made her way out through one of the rear doors into the gardens.

She stood and breathed in the scent of sun-warmed roses, their heady fragrance a welcome relief from the cold and formal atmosphere of the house.

A light afternoon breeze shivered over the surface of the lake in the distance, its fringe of weeping willows offering Bryony a solace she found hard to resist. She walked across the verdant expanse of well-manicured lawn, her light footsteps cushioned by the lushness of fastidiously clipped growth, and headed for the shade of the arc of willows on the far side of the lake.

It was much cooler near the water.

She sat on one of the large rocks and, slipping off her shoes, dangled her toes in the cool dark depths, watching as the bowing branches moved on the surface like feathery fingertips as the eddy of disturbed water reached them.

She hadn't been to this dark secluded spot for ten years.

Even the gardeners didn't come this far. Their work was to make the exposed parts of Mercyfields appear perfect at all times. Under here, where the pendulous branches of the willows shielded the house from view, was of no interest to them.

She breathed in the earthy smell of the damp bank, the fragile lace of maidenhair fern shifting faintly as the warm breath of the breeze moved through the shady sanctuary, and her thoughts drifted just like the water she'd disturbed...

It had been one of those unbearably hot afternoons the countryside of New South Wales was famous for, the smell of eucalyptus-tinged smoke lingering in the sultry air, the clouds overhead gathering in wrathful grey clusters as if deciding whether or not to take out their rage on the earth below.

She'd come down to the lake to bathe in private, for even though the large kidney-shaped swimming pool lay near the wisteria walk at the rear of the house she hadn't wanted to be observed, preferring the secluded shade of her favourite hideaway.

At seventeen she'd been conscious of the weight she'd gained during her final term. An injury to her knee, her anxiety over exams and the stodgy diet ordered by Madame Celeste had taken its toll on her normally svelte figure. She hadn't been able to dance for eight weeks and it showed.

She'd slipped into the cool embrace of the dark water

and sighed with pleasure, her limbs feeling like silky ribbons released after months of being tightly coiled. She'd swum back and forth beneath the shield of the hanging arms of the willows, glad to be finally free of the constraints of the school term.

She'd lain on her back and looked up through the canopy, the dapple of sunlight speckling along her wet body as if someone had dropped a handful of gold-dust over her.

Smiling at her overactive imagination, she'd begun stroking backwards, her arms slicing through the water, gradually gathering speed as she'd pretended she was in the final heat of the Olympic fifty metre backstroke, she was in front…she was going to win… *Thump*!

Bryony had gagged on the mouthful of water she'd swallowed before turning around to see what she'd run into, expecting to find a fallen log or even a partially submerged rock.

She had not expected to see Kane Kaproulias standing waist-deep in the water with his nose streaming blood…

'Oh, my God!' she gasped while her feet searched vainly for a foothold in the slippery mud.

'Did I hurt you?' he asked as his hands came out to her shoulders to steady her.

Bryony felt her feet sink into the velvet mud, offering her a stability she badly needed once Kane's warm brown work-roughened hands touched the creamy skin of her shoulders.

She stared up at him, fighting for breath, suddenly conscious of the tight cling of her Lycra bathing suit which, in her current physical shape, was at least two sizes too small.

'No…' she said a little breathlessly, 'you didn't hurt me at all but look what I did to your nose.'

'It's nothing.' He let her go and rinsed his face in the water.

'I didn't know anyone was here, otherwise I would have—'

'It's just a nosebleed, Bryony, it won't kill me.'

She found it hard not to stare at his face. She hadn't seen him for months. During her last holiday he'd been working part-time on a neighbour's property, only coming home occasionally to see his mother. She'd heard he was saving up enough money to put himself through a university course but she had never asked him what he'd intended studying.

He looked much fitter and stronger than the last time she'd seen him. At twenty-two he was only a year older than her brother but somehow he seemed to be so much more mature.

Austin was boisterous and loud, as were most of his friends who often spent time at Mercyfields during their university vacations, their numerous boyish pranks in stark contrast to Kane's silent brooding presence. She suspected his surly demeanour was an inbuilt part of his personality and not just a reaction to being labelled the cleaning lady's son.

She couldn't imagine what her father would say if he could see her now, standing in the water with Kane, his broad smooth chest glistening with droplets of moisture as he looked down at her with eyes darker than the mud beneath her curling toes.

'Do you usually swim here?' he asked.

'I…no…not usually.'

'You shouldn't come here, especially not alone.'

She didn't care for the quiet authority in his tone. She was the daughter of the house, he was the servant's son—he had no right to tell her what to do.

She tilted her chin at him. 'Why not? It's my lake, not yours.'

The look he gave her was hard to decipher given the

shady nook they were in, but she suspected he was sneering at her behind the screen of his dark lashes.

'If you hurt yourself no one would find you.'

'How could I hurt myself? I'm a good swimmer.'

'You're a very careless swimmer.' He gave his nose another wipe with the back of his hand. 'Instead of me it could have been a rock you hit. You could have easily knocked yourself out and drowned.'

'It's none of your business what I do,' she said, annoyed that he was right but unwilling to admit it. 'If I want to swim here I will and nothing you say or do can stop me.'

Bryony became increasingly aware of the pulsing silence. The shadows danced like wraiths around them, the water where his blood had spilled lapping gently against her thighs like a caress, heightening her awareness of his physical closeness in the most intimate and primal way.

The sunlight shifted, revealing more of his face to her, and she was relieved to see that his nose had more or less stopped bleeding. But then she gave a tiny involuntary shiver as she saw his eyes slide down to the overflow of her breasts, her tight bathing suit doing an inadequate job of keeping them contained with any sort of decency.

She crossed her arms and glared at him. 'I'll tell my brother you have insulted me by leering at me like that.'

His gaze lingered another full ten seconds before he lifted it to meet her flashing one. 'Do you imagine I am afraid of that spineless little jerk?'

She was incensed by his attitude towards the older brother she adored. 'You will be when I tell him you've touched me under the willows of the lake.'

He didn't say a word, just stood watching her steadily, which somehow made her even angrier.

'Do you think he won't defend his sister from the filthy hands of the cleaning lady's son?' she added spitefully.

'He very probably will,' he answered after another long

cicadas-beating-in-the-background pause. 'So in that case I'd better make sure that what's coming to me is well and truly warranted.'

She was still trying to make sense of his coolly delivered words when he reached for her, his strong arms coming around her, pulling her out of the sucking mud and up against his hard body. His mouth came down, his lips warm and firm as they explored the soft surface of hers.

Bryony had never been kissed before and wasn't quite sure how to react. Part of her insisted she pull away at once, but the lure of finding out what a real man's kiss tasted like won. She closed her eyes and gave in with a soft sigh of pleasure at the feel of his mouth discovering the moistness of hers with a determined probe of his tongue. She could taste the metallic saltiness of his blood where it had come into contact with his mouth and a new and totally alluring sensation unfurled low in her belly, making her cling to him unashamedly.

He suddenly pulled away from her with a jerky movement that made her lose her footing. She went sprawling backwards, landing ungainly on her bottom in the mud, the murky water lapping her chin as she glared up at him in outrage at being released without warning.

He offered her a hand at the same time as her other hand came upon a rock under the water, her fingers curling around it as he hauled her inelegantly to her feet.

It was his smile that made her do it.

Without really thinking of the consequences, she raised her hand and smashed the rock in her tightly clenched fist against that sneering mouth...

CHAPTER THREE

BRYONY blinked herself back out of the past and stared down at the now still surface of the lake, surprised the water wasn't still red even after ten long years.

She hadn't thought an injury could bleed so much.

She hadn't thought she'd been capable of such a despicable action.

She hadn't thought he'd wait for ten long years to have his revenge…

She drove back to the city that night, unable to stay a minute longer now she'd disturbed the vault of her memory. Her parents hadn't questioned her decision to leave. Her father hadn't even bothered to say goodbye but her mother had more than made up for it by standing on the marble steps at the double front door, tears streaming down her face as she'd waved her off.

Bryony turned on the music system and hoped the heavy strains of a Mahler Symphony would distract her from what lay ahead, but even as she pulled into the garage of the apartment block two hours later she knew there was no escaping her nemesis.

Fate had written the script of her life ten years ago and now it was finally time for her to take her place on the stage…

By the time Bryony arrived at the studio on Monday, Pauline LeFray, her teaching partner, had already finished her warm-up stretches.

Pauline wiped her hands on a small towel, her brow furrowing at the look on her partner's beautiful face.

'What's going on?'

Bryony slipped off her wraparound skirt and reached for the barre, easing herself into her pre-teaching routine.

'It would take me a decade to tell you,' she said, stretching her calves.

Pauline glanced at the clock on the wall. 'We've got ten minutes until the five-year-olds arrive. Want to quickly summarise?'

Bryony eased her hamstrings into action as she met her friend's interested gaze. 'I'm getting married.'

'Married?' Pauline gasped.

Bryony lifted her right leg to the barre and bent her head to her knee, staring at the wooden floorboards below as she spoke. 'Married as in wedlock, matrimony...' *Jail,* she added silently.

'This is a bit sudden, isn't it?' Pauline asked. 'I mean...I didn't know you were even seeing anyone. *Have* you been seeing someone?'

Bryony changed legs and repeated the exercise, again staring at the floor. 'No.'

Pauline's frown deepened. 'You're not making a whole lot of sense, Bry. You haven't had a date in years and now you tell me you're getting married. Call me thick if you like, but how does that work? You're not doing some crazy mail-order or Internet hook-up thing, are you?'

I wish, Bryony thought. Better to marry a perfect stranger than someone you couldn't bear to look at because...

'It's nothing like that,' she answered as she straightened. 'I know it's sudden but he's someone from my...past and we just hit it off, so to speak.'

'Hit it off?'

Bryony gave her a false smile and hoped it would pass for pre-wedded joy. 'He's tall, dark and handsome and disgustingly rich.'

'Rich?' Pauline stared at her. 'You don't do rich, remember? The last guy you dated, what was it…three years ago, didn't even have a job!'

'I've changed my mind.'

'Hello?' Pauline waved her arms in the air at her. 'It's me—Pauline. You can't seriously expect me to believe you are attracted to a guy because of the size of his wallet.'

'OK, so it's not his wallet I'm attracted to.' Bryony avoided her friend's eyes in the wall-to-wall mirror as she stretched her arms.

'Now you've got me even more worried. What else did this guy show you apart from his wallet? Don't tell me you've finally done the deed?'

Bryony felt a trickle of warmth leak into her belly at the thought of Kane's body possessing hers and in spite of the air-conditioning of the studio her whole body grew hot.

'Have you?' Pauline probed when she didn't answer.

Bryony turned around and reached for her towel. 'Not yet.'

'Not yet? What do you mean, not yet? If you're going to marry him, don't you think you should check out if everything's in good working order?'

'I'm perfectly healthy and—'

'Not you, dummy.' Pauline rolled her eyes. *'Him.* He might be a complete dud for all you know. Would you buy a car without taking it for a run first? It's the same with men. Take it from someone who knows about these things. If he's not good in bed the relationship is dead.'

Bryony considered telling her the truth about her relationship with Kane but decided against it at the last minute. It was too complicated to explain, even to a close friend. It was better to let Pauline think it was a match made in heaven rather than reveal the true hell of her situation.

'We've only just become engaged,' she said instead. 'It's all happened so fast but I'm sure we'll…er…get around to it.'

'Yeah, well see that you do,' Pauline advised as the outer door opened and ten little girls traipsed in dressed in tiny tutus and ballet slippers.

Bryony plastered a welcoming smile on her face as she faced the girls and hoped that by the end of the afternoon Pauline wouldn't return to the topic of her sex life.

She didn't have a sex life and, marriage or no marriage, she wasn't going to have one if she could help it.

It was three days until Kane contacted her.

She knew it was him even before she picked up the receiver on her bedroom extension.

'Hello, Bryony.'

'Who is it?' she asked, pretending not to recognise that unmistakable deep velvety voice.

'You know who it is.'

'How am I supposed to know who it is if you don't identify yourself? Didn't your mother ever tell you it's polite to announce your identity when you call someone?'

'My mother taught me many things,' he said, 'and I intend to act on all of them.'

She wasn't sure she wanted him to elucidate on just exactly what he meant so she changed the subject.

'Why did you call?'

'I think it's time we went out on a date.'

'A date?' She frowned. 'Save yourself the time and bother, Kane. You don't need to wine and dine me; you've paid for me already, remember?'

'As you wish.'

She knew it was inconsistent of her to be disappointed by his ready agreement but she just was.

'I guess we can discuss the wedding arrangements just as easily over the telephone as we can over a dinner table somewhere,' he continued. 'I've decided we'll have the ceremony conducted at Mercyfields overlooking the lake.'

Her hand around the receiver tightened until her knuckles went completely white.

'Your mother will appreciate you being married at your home,' he added when she didn't speak.

'It's no longer my home,' she pointed out somewhat sourly. 'It's yours.'

'It will belong to both of us. Your parents' things will be moved out while we're on our honeymoon.'

'Honeymoon?' she choked.

'That's what newly married couples usually do, is it not?'

'Yes…but…'

'I've arranged a week on a private beach on the south coast.'

'The south coast?'

'You do know where that is, don't you?' he drawled.

'Of course I do, but I—'

'It will be slightly cooler there than the city but the water is warm and the beach long and lonely.'

'You sound like a travel journal,' she said with a touch of scorn.

His rumble of laughter sent a shiver over the surface of her skin.

'I like to get away from the hustle and bustle of high city life,' he said. 'I go there quite a lot. It's just about the only place you can still have the beach to yourself, no jet-skis, no crowds, just the sound of the waves beating along the shore.'

Bryony could almost smell the sea-spray. She loved the beach but it had been months since she'd felt the sand between her toes.

'Your parents will leave for a month-long cruise of the Pacific Islands the day after our wedding,' he informed her, apparently undeterred by her lack of response. 'Until I settle all his debts over the next few weeks, your father needs to keep his head down. Your mother, quite frankly, needs a holiday.'

It was difficult not to voice her agreement but somehow she managed to remain silent.

'It will take me the best part of that month to sort out the mess your father has made,' he went on. 'I have to wait until I get clearance of some international funds to relieve the situation.'

That did get her attention.

'International funds? What international funds?'

'I recently inherited my maternal grandfather's estate in Greece. I have to wait until the bank clears the funds to access them.'

Bryony's forehead creased in a frown. His maternal grandfather had been wealthy? It didn't make sense. Why then had his mother worked her fingers to the bone cleaning?

'I thought you didn't know any of your relatives.'

'I don't, nor do I wish to. They didn't help my mother when she most needed it so I don't see why I should pay them any attention now.'

'But surely if your grandfather left you his entire estate you must feel some sort of obligation to go and see the rest of the family and—'

'My grandfather's money is nothing more than guilt money. I've made my own fortune without it.'

'Then why are you using it to sort out my father's debts?'

'You're not listening, Bryony,' he chided her. 'I told you, my grandfather's money is guilt money. I think it's highly appropriate if I use it to dig your father out of the hole he dug for himself.'

Guilt money.

Her stomach churned as she thought about it.

'Exactly whose guilt are we talking about here?' she asked.

'I think you know whose guilt we're talking about,' he answered.

She took a breath and hoped he didn't hear the way it snagged in her throat.

'What sort of outfit should I wear to the ceremony?' she asked for the want of something to say to steer the subject away from the topic of guilt.

'It's a wedding, Bryony. Your mother will expect you to look like a bride.'

He really knew how to press her buttons. Her mother had been planning her wedding since she'd been five, her enthusiasm undaunted by her daughter's flat refusal to select herself a groom.

'I don't look good in white,' she said. 'It's not my colour.'

'Wear cream, then.'

'Shouldn't I be wearing black?' she asked. 'After all, isn't this the end of my life as I now know it?'

'Quite frankly, I don't care what you wear,' he said with the first sign of impatience in his tone she'd heard. 'Your job is to appear at the right time, say the right words and do what you're told. If you don't your father and mother will be cruising the exercise yard of whatever correctional facility they're sent to instead of the Pacific Islands.'

Bryony stared at the buzzing receiver in her hand as he ended the call with an abruptness that left her feeling somehow deflated.

Her mother rang the next morning and arranged a time to meet her in the city to select the wedding finery. Bryony had to give herself a mental shake once or twice to remind herself that this wasn't going to be a normal wedding in any shape or form, because her mother was quite clearly on a mission and had been waiting years to execute it.

'I don't want a huge bouquet,' Bryony insisted in the florist's shop.

'You must have a big bouquet,' Glenys said, thrusting yet another design under her nose. 'This is the most important day of your life; you have to have everything perfect.'

Bryony stared down at the various floral arrangements in the brochure in front of her and wondered what had ever been perfect in her parents' marriage. Her mother continually danced around her father's demands, subsuming her own needs into the satisfaction of his. What was perfect about that?

'I'll have the roses,' she told the hovering assistant. 'Cream, not white.'

They left the florist to do yet another round of the bridal boutiques as she had been unable to find anything that suited her colouring or her figure.

'I need to go on a diet,' she lamented at the fifth boutique, her hands pushing against her tummy where the satin of the gown she was trying on was showing too much detail of her Christmas indulgences.

'You worry too much about your figure,' her mother remonstrated as she eyed the gown. 'I was at least ten pounds heavier than you when I got married.'

'At least you were marrying the man of your choice,' Bryony said.

There was a funny little silence.

Bryony twirled around to face her mother, the rustle of the garment she was wearing the only sound in the changing room.

Glenys bent to the hem of the gown, fussing over some little detail which Bryony hadn't noticed.

'Mum?'

'Yes, darling?' Glenys straightened and gave her an absent look.

Bryony rolled her lips together and, taking a breath, took one of her mother's thin hands in hers, the tendons on the back reminding her of the struts of an umbrella.

'You do want me to marry Kane, don't you?'

Glenys gave her a watery smile. 'I know you don't think much of him but he's doing us all a favour by marrying you.'

'You make me sound like some sort of white elephant you can't wait to get rid of,' Bryony said indignantly.

'I don't mean to, darling, but your father has…' She inserted a little choked sob. 'Your father hasn't been the same since Austin…left us.'

Bryony felt like screaming with frustration.

Why couldn't anyone in her family say the words?

Austin had *died*.

He hadn't passed away.

He hadn't left.

He'd *died*.

She sighed and, reaching out, gave her mother a consoling hug, catching sight of herself in the mirror opposite, the outfit she was wearing making her look like a meringue without the cream and strawberries.

'I hate this dress.' She released her mother and began stripping off the gown. 'I want something simple and elegant. Is there nowhere in Sydney where I can find what I want?'

She found it in Paddington.

It was cream, it was long and voluminous, it was elegant—it was perfect.

Even if her groom wasn't.

He rang that night as if he'd somehow sensed she'd found what she was looking for.

'Hello?'

'Hello, Bryony.'

She pursed her lips sourly. 'Who is it?'

'You know who I am, so stop playing games.'

'I'm not playing games. I just wish you'd identify yourself when you call.'

'Don't you have caller ID?'

'I still like to know who is speaking. Numbers mean nothing to me.'

'You're definitely your father's daughter then.'

She frowned. 'What do you mean?'

She heard the rustle of papers before he spoke. 'Your father has made the most God-awful mess of things. There are creditors breathing down my neck as we speak.'

She wasn't sure how to respond. Should she thank him for what he was doing, even though he was taking away her freedom by doing it?

'I had no idea…'

'No, I imagine not,' he said. 'Are you doing anything right now?'

She tried to think of something that could be legitimately occupying her time at seven-fifteen in the evening but she'd already washed her hair that morning.

'No…'

'Good,' he said. 'I'll pick you up in fifteen minutes.'

'But—'

The receiver buzzed in her hand for the second time in twenty-four hours. She put it back in its cradle and stared at her reflection in the mirror, wondering why it was that her mouth suddenly felt the urge to smile.

Bryony opened the door fourteen minutes and twenty-one seconds later to find Kane standing there dressed in a black dinner suit, his thick hair still showing the grooves of a recent comb.

'Ready?'

She nodded, not sure what to expect but resigned to go along with whatever he had planned.

'I have tickets,' he said once they were in his silver Porsche.

'What for?'

He gave her a quick inscrutable glance as he turned over the engine, 'The ballet.'

She turned back to the front of the car and hustled her thoughts together.

The ballet?

He was taking her to *the ballet*?

She toyed with the catch on her evening purse. 'I didn't have you pegged as a ballet man.'

'I like a good dance as much as the next man.'

She had to force herself not to look his way. 'I must admit I can't quite imagine you prancing around in a leotard.'

His laughter washed over her like a soft rain shower.

'No, but I can definitely imagine you doing it. I've seen you many times.'

She swivelled her head to look at him. 'You've *seen* me? Where?'

Kane expertly manoeuvred the car into a tight space between a Fiat and a Volvo a short walking distance from the Opera House.

'At Mercyfields in the ballroom.'

She sat back in her seat in shock.

He'd *seen* her?

He'd seen her pretending to be the next bright star of the ballet world, when all the time her knee was telling her it was time to quit her dream of professional dancing.

'I hope you liked what you saw,' she said, then wished she'd phrased it a little better.

'Oh, I did.' He wrenched on the handbrake. 'It was quite a revelation.'

She could just imagine. A leotard was so unforgiving at the best of times, let alone when an injury had set one to the sidelines for weeks on end. Her brain fizzed with the many possible viewing opportunities he might have taken advantage of.

'Come on,' he said, opening her door for her. 'I don't want to miss the first half.'

The first half made her cry, not that she let on.

She sat silently in her seat at the Opera House and bit down on her bottom lip to control the distinct wobbling of her chin at the sights and sounds in front of her.

She'd been to the ballet countless times but for some strange inexplicable reason seeing *Cinderella* with Kane sitting so close beside her unravelled her normally tightly controlled emotions.

During the interval she spent an inordinate time in the powder room, and when she came out to the raised eyebrow question on his face she muttered something disparaging about the discrepancy between male architects' designs and female needs and returned to her seat with her head well down.

She barely made it through the rest of the performance.

She knew most of the cast and watched in a combination of awe and envy at what they were doing, wondering if there would be a time when she would be able to let her dreams go without a pang of deep regret.

The applause was deafening and she joined in with it enthusiastically, knowing how much it elevated a performer's confidence.

The curtain came down on the stage like eyelashes closing over eyes and she felt Kane stir beside her, his strongly muscled suit-clad arm brushing the bare skin of hers.

'Thank you.' She rose to her feet and gave a discreet sniff. 'I really enjoyed it.'

He unfolded his tall body from the seat and looked down at her, his brow creasing into a small frown. 'Why are you crying?'

She turned away from his intense scrutiny. 'I'm not crying. It's somebody's perfume that's set me off. I have allergies…I'm allergic to some scents…' She blew her nose inelegantly and stuffed the tissue up her sleeve. 'It's the cross I have to bear for having a sensitive nose.'

'I hope my choice of aftershave doesn't affect you,' he said, holding her back with a hand on her hip so that someone could squeeze past them.

She felt the full imprint of his warm hand through her dress and felt her skin lift in response to his soft touch.

'Oh, no,' she said without thinking. 'I really like your…I mean I don't think it's that…I'm just sensitive, that's all.'

'Come on.' He took her arm once the aisle was clear. 'I don't know about you, but after watching all that exercise I'm starving.'

Bryony spooned another mouthful of blueberry cheesecake into her mouth and promised herself that tomorrow her diet would start in earnest.

Kane was sitting opposite with a barely touched summer pudding on his plate, his eyes steady on her.

She dipped her spoon into the creamy denseness of her dessert and holding it in front of her mouth, asked, 'Since when did you start subscribing to the ballet?'

He stirred the long black coffee the waiter had placed in front of him a few moments ago.

'I don't subscribe regularly but I do enjoy certain performances.'

She scooped up another spoonful of pure sin and asked, 'Do you have a favourite performance?'

'Not really,' he answered, picking up his cup and raising it to his lips. 'What about you?'

She looked down at the two remaining blueberries on her plate and began chasing them with her spoon, thinking about how she should answer. Should she say *Cinderella*? What about *Swan Lake*? But then there was *Petroucha* and *Prince Igor*...

'I love the whole atmosphere of ballet,' she said at last. 'I love the training and the discipline, the costumes and the emotions one has to engage in order to perform.'

He placed his teaspoon on the saucer of his coffee cup. 'So you have to feel something to dance?'

'Oh, yes.' She gave up on the last blueberry and looked across at him. 'You have to *be* the character, feel the things they would be feeling, just like an actor does on stage or in the movies.'

'You must miss it terribly,' he commented.

'Yes...' She stared at the lonely blueberry and sighed. 'I do.'

'Tell me about your dance studio.' He set his cup back down.

She toyed with the edge of the tablecloth. 'I teach classical ballet five afternoons a week.'

'How many students do you have?'

'I share the workload with my partner, Pauline, and two junior teachers, but the total enrolment stands at about one hundred and fifty students.'

'That's a lot of little girls in tutus.' He reached for his coffee once more.

'Yes...'

'So tell me—' he leaned forward in his seat to rest his wrists on the table '—does every little girl dream of being a ballerina?'

She found his dark eyes totally mesmerizing.

'Not just girls,' she said. 'We have several boys as well.'

'It must be difficult for them,' he said, 'being so outside the square, so to speak.'

'We try to make them feel comfortable. We have one who is absolutely brilliant, very focused and determined. I think he'll make it.'

'Not many do?'

She shook her head and looked back down at her plate. 'Not many girls, let alone boys. It's not always about pure talent. It's a combination of physical ability and luck and a certain level of skill.'

'What stopped you?'

She gave him a rueful grimace before she squashed the hapless blueberry with the back of her spoon.

'I have a dicky knee, as they say in the business.'

'Have you seen someone about it?' he asked.

She pushed the purple mess of her plate away. 'I've seen the best money can buy and he said the same as all the rest. Take up swimming instead.'

'Did you tell him you do a mean backstroke?'

Her eyes went to his. 'No…I didn't tell him that.'

He picked up his coffee and took a sip, looking at her over the rim of his cup. 'I would if I were you. It might make him feel a whole lot better about taking your dancing away from you.'

No one had ever mentioned to her how difficult it must have been to relinquish her dream of professional dancing. How ironic that it was Kane Kaproulias who had done so first.

'I haven't swum in years,' she said, unable to stop her eyes from going to the white-ridged scar on his top lip.

He waited until her eyes made their uncertain way back to his. 'Neither have I,' he said and, turning away from her, signalled to the waiter for the bill.

CHAPTER FOUR

BRYONY fell into step beside him as they made their way back to his car, unable to stop thinking about the evening they'd just spent together.

Together.

What an intimate word to be using when referring to someone like Kane Kaproulias!

He activated the central locking and opened her door for her, waiting until she was inside and belted up before closing the door and making his way around to the driver's door.

She watched his progression from under the screen of her lashes, her eyes taking in his tautly muscled form and the easy grace with which he moved.

He looked across at her as he clipped on his seatbelt, his dark eyes dipping briefly to her chest as if he couldn't help himself.

'I was thinking we could have a nightcap or another coffee somewhere. I've narrowed it down to my place or yours, but I'm open to other suggestions.'

Bryony felt a sudden desire to see where she was going to reside.

'Your place will be fine.'

'My place it is,' he said and fired the engine with a roar.

His place was nothing like she'd imagined.

Somehow she had thought his residence would be along the lines of the tackily overdone opulence of recently acquired wealth, but when he pulled into the driveway of his Edgecliff house she was surprised to see that it was of

51

modest proportions with just the right amount of prestige to make it stand only slightly apart from its neighbours.

She walked with him to the front door, the fragrance of jasmine and honeysuckle wafting through the warm evening air as he turned his key in the lock.

The black and white tiles of the foyer welcomed her as she stepped inside, the sweeping staircase winding upwards elegantly, nothing like the menacing dark wood coil of Mercyfields.

'The kitchen is this way,' he said, moving towards a door off the hall. 'And, if you need it, the bathroom is the first on the left.'

She chose the bathroom, not because she particularly needed it, but more because she wanted to gather herself for a few precious moments.

She stared at her reflection in the gilt-edged mirror and wondered how she was going to negotiate the next few moves.

Kane was all politeness now, but what would happen when he had a circle of gold around her finger?

She was scripted as his trophy wife, the spoils of war, so to speak. He had waited a long time to claim her, no doubt planning every move of his revenge in fastidious detail...

She gave a little shiver and bent her head to wash her hands, but as she dried them on the soft towel provided she couldn't help wondering who it was who kept his house in perfect order.

Nothing was out of place. Not a used dish or glass, not a speck of dust anywhere. The mirror in front of her was spotless. Would he expect her to keep it that way? Or had his threats been made simply to prove a point about the way in which his mother had been treated during her time as their housekeeper? But how could she tell for sure?

He was waiting for her in the kitchen, a tray set out with

coffee steaming in two cups, a liqueur bottle with two shot glasses and chocolate.

Her eyes went straight to the chocolate, her mouth watering at the thought of allowing a square of its forbidden pleasure past the rigid shield of her lips.

Remember Christmas, she told herself.

'No, thank you,' she said as he offered her the mouth-watering squares.

'Dieting?' He raised one brow at her, his mouth tilted in mild amusement.

'Always.' Her tone was rueful as she took the cup of coffee off the tray he was holding.

He didn't respond, which somehow irritated her. Why couldn't he have reassured her by saying she didn't need to diet? Most men would have, but then she remembered... He wasn't exactly like most men. He didn't issue empty compliments; neither did he speak unless he had something worthwhile to say.

'How long have you lived here?' she asked over the rim of her cup.

'Close to three years.'

Three years.

He'd been living *this* close for three years? Her apartment was a few minutes away in Watsons Bay. She'd probably passed him on the road many times without knowing it, had maybe even walked past him on the street. It gave her a funny feeling to think of them being within such close proximity without her knowing it, especially as her awareness of him was so acute when he was in the same room as her, much less when he was touching her...

'Where were you living before?' she asked to fill the sudden silence.

'Here and there,' he said, stirring his coffee.

She took a sip of her coffee and wondered why he was being so evasive.

'I understand you've found a dress for our wedding,' he said.

She stared at him. 'How did you know that?'

He gave a could-mean-anything shrug.

She narrowed her gaze. 'Have you been speaking to my mother?'

'Do you have a problem with that?'

'Yes, I do have a problem with that,' she said through tight lips.

Who did he think he was, calling her mother and quite possibly upsetting her? It wasn't as if he were a real son-in-law-to-be. He was their enemy, he'd deliberately set out to destroy them and his marriage to her was the final blow in his dastardly enterprise.

'Don't you think it might appear strange to other people if I never speak to either of your parents?' he asked.

'I think people will think it even stranger if you do,' she told him. 'You've taken everything away from them, including me. I think that more or less warrants a cold war, don't you?'

'There will be no cold war, as you call it,' he insisted. 'Nor will anyone outside your family know our marriage is anything other than a genuine love match.'

'*Love?*' she spat in indignation. 'How dare you insult me by using that word when referring to our situation?'

'What are you going to do about it, Bryony?' He held her glittering gaze and drawled with deliberate insolence, 'It's not as if you can call on your cowardly brother any more to settle the score for you.'

She flinched as if he'd struck her, so hurtful were his words. She couldn't find her voice, and the anger she needed so badly to defend her dead brother was inexplicably out of reach, replaced by a sudden and uncontrollable urge to cry.

She caught her lip to stop it from trembling, the saltiness

of blood informing her she was doing considerable damage to her mouth in an effort to maintain her fragile composure.

She put down the cup she was holding and, turning away, reached for her evening purse where she'd placed it on the bench.

'I have to go…' she mumbled, almost stumbling over her feet in her haste to leave. 'I'll get a cab.'

'Bryony.'

Kane's deep voice commanded her to turn back to face him.

She slowly turned and aimed her gaze at a point to the left of his shoulder so she didn't have to witness the satisfaction on his hateful face that he'd finally made her crack emotionally.

'I—I want to go home.' She did her best to inject some steely determination into her tone but her voice wobbled dangerously.

'I'll take you home in a minute.'

'I want to go now.'

There was a lengthy uncomfortable silence which Bryony suspected was a deliberate ploy on his part to get her pride to drop to rock bottom where he wanted it—at his feet.

But, to her surprise, he gave a long deep sigh and reached for his keys. 'Come on, then.'

She'd expected a fight and had been so busily preparing herself for it that his ready acquiescence shifted her completely off course. She followed him out to his car in a wooden silence, the sheen of tears filming her eyes making it difficult for her to negotiate the path.

She felt his hand at her elbow as she almost stumbled, his touch light but protective, and even though her pride insisted she pull out of his hold, for some reason she didn't.

A few minutes later Kane pulled up in front of her apartment, but even before he could get out of the driver's door she'd opened hers and, with her head down, walked stiffly towards the entrance of the building without bothering to say goodnight.

Kane let out another sigh and waited until he was sure she was safely inside the building before reversing out of the car park with a squeal of rubber on the road that he was sure could be heard on the opposite side of the harbour.

Bryony worked her way through the week with an energy fuelled by her simmering rage at how Kane had crushed her so ruthlessly, promising herself she'd have her own revenge as soon as she could orchestrate it.

She ignored the phone when it rang and deleted any messages without listening to them, and when the security intercom sounded at the apartment she glared at it without responding.

Her last class on Friday evening was a private lesson with a young teenager who was on a slow path to rehabilitation after a serious horse-riding accident. Ella Denby hadn't regained her confidence and needed lots of encouragement from Bryony to keep rebuilding her skills.

'OK, now let's take it really slowly,' Bryony said as the young girl stood in front of the mirror with her. 'Try the first position…great.' She smiled encouragingly and continued, 'And the second…good, now here comes the more difficult one as it requires a little more balance, position three.'

Ella's right arm curved upwards while the other was just below shoulder height, her legs crossed at the ankles, her posture almost perfect except for a tiny wobble when she pointed her toes.

'Good, Ella, now try position four.'

Ella reversed the pose and the wobble was hardly noticeable this time.

Bryony caught her young student's smile in the reflection of the mirror and returned it with a brilliant one of her own.

'See? I knew you could do it! Now, let's finish off with the fifth and…' Her words trailed off as she met another pair of eyes in the mirror.

Kane was standing at the back of the studio, his hands in his trouser pockets, his dark gaze trained on her.

'Excuse me, Ella.' She touched the young girl's shoulder briefly. 'I won't be a minute.'

Even though she wore track pants over the top she was still conscious of her close-fitting leotard as she crossed the floor, conscious too of her lack of height in her ballet slippers as she came to stand in front of him.

'Do you mind?' she demanded in an undertone. 'Can't you see I'm in the middle of a lesson?'

Kane looked down at her without speaking.

Bryony checked over her shoulder to see if Ella was watching before turning back to him, leaning closer to whisper, 'I said: do you mind?'

He took his hands out of his trouser pockets and reached for her, pulling her into his chest and covering her startled mouth with his.

It was a brief hard kiss but no less distracting than any of his others.

He let her go and she wobbled, not unlike her young student, as she stepped backwards, her eyes flashing with instant fury.

'If you don't leave immediately, I will—' Her harsh whisper was interrupted by the sound of Pauline's voice calling out from the staff room door a few metres away.

'So *this* is the man of your dreams!' She came over and held out her hand to Kane. 'I'm Pauline LeFray, Bryony's teaching partner.'

'Kane Kaproulias.' He smiled and took her hand in his.

'It's a pleasure to meet you at last. Bryony has told me all about you.'

Liar! She'd only mentioned her name once, Bryony seethed as he dished out his particularly lethal brand of charm, watching in disgust as Pauline almost melted into a pool at his feet.

'I think it's so terribly romantic, you sweeping her off her feet like that,' Pauline gushed.

'She deserves it,' Kane said, his dark eyes gleaming.

Bryony sent him a fulminating glare over the top of Pauline's head, infuriated at his double meaning, knowing he was doing it deliberately just to goad her.

Pauline turned to face her. 'I'll take over with Ella if you two lovebirds want to fly off.'

'No, I—'

'Oh, would you?' Kane cut Bryony off with a grateful thousand watt smile towards Pauline. 'I haven't seen Bryony for a while and I'm getting rather impatient to be alone with her. You know how it is.'

'I do indeed.' Pauline beamed up at him in approval. 'Take her away and paint the town.' She flapped her fingers up and down in a little wave and left them to go to Ella, who was standing back at the barre trying to do a complicated stretch.

Bryony turned a vitriolic look his way and, tossing her head, went towards the staff room, informing him as she stalked off, 'I have to get changed.'

'Don't be too long, *agape mou*,' he called after her.

She turned at the door to look back at him, forcing her mouth into an overly sweet smile that didn't match the anger sparkling in her eyes.

'I won't be too long…*honeybunch*.' She blew him a kiss across the surface of her palm before she closed the staff room door behind her with a sharp little click.

Bryony let out her breath as she leant against the back

of the door, her fists clenched in fury at the way he had so cleverly manipulated the situation to force her into going out with him. She could just imagine him the other side of the door busily congratulating himself on yet another clever manoevre executed to serve his ends.

She stuffed her leotard into a bag and pushed her feet into her shoes, not even bothering to tidy her long hair which had begun to slip from the high pony-tail she'd arranged earlier. She ignored her cosmetics and, snatching up her purse, went out to the studio, rearranging her out-raged expression into one of pre-nuptial bliss entirely for Pauline's and Ella's sake.

It was a pity they weren't even watching, which meant Kane got the full benefit of her smile which annoyed her no end.

'Shall we go?' He took her hand and, shouldering open the door, led her outside.

The warmth of the early evening hit her like a hot wet towel as soon as they stepped out of the building, the high humidity in the atmosphere instantly making her blouse be-gin to stick to her back.

She walked beside him, incredibly conscious of his hand swallowing hers. She couldn't stop thinking of that very same hand and its twin on her body, touching her…

She pulled out of his hold in agitation and stared furi-ously at the pedestrian lights as if willing them to change so she didn't have to stand beside him for any longer than necessary.

'Where would you like to go?' he asked.

'Home, preferably alone,' she said, striding out as the lights changed.

He caught her in half a stride and took her hand again, this time making sure she couldn't slip out of his grasp.

'You're crushing my fingers,' she snapped at him irri-tably.

'You're crushing my ego,' he returned.

She flicked him a glance, blowing a loose strand of long blonde hair out of her face as she did so.

'I'm sure it will make a complete recovery and come bouncing back bigger than ever.'

He threw back his head and laughed.

She sent him another caustic look but the edges of her mouth had already begun to twitch slightly and she eventually had to give in to the urge to smile. She turned her head away so he wouldn't see it but it was too late.

'Do you know that's probably the first genuine smile you've ever given me?'

Her smile faded as she considered his comment.

Had she *never* smiled at him?

She'd known him for much of her teenage life; how had it happened that she had not once considered him worthy of a smile?

'I hope you made the most of it,' she said tightly. 'It won't happen again.'

'Don't bet on it, *agape mou*,' he drawled.

'I wish you would stop calling me that.'

'You'd better get used to it, for in a matter of a week we'll be husband and wife. Such name-calling comes with the territory of the newly wedded.'

'The only names I want to call you are socially unacceptable,' she said.

'I don't care what you call me, Bryony, as long as you call me to bed.'

'*Dinner,*' she informed him coldly, her cheeks heating. 'That's how that saying goes—call me to dinner, not bed.'

His smile was playful and totally disarming, so totally disarming that she had to look away immediately and pretend she hadn't seen it.

Careful, she warned herself. Don't let your guard slip around such charm. Don't mess with him.

Kane took her to a small restaurant a short walk from the studio, the dimly lit interior suiting her need to keep her expressive face out of his reading zone.

Bryony examined the menu wishing she could have the fettuccine carbonara but her quick mental tally of the calories put her off.

'I'll have the green salad, no dressing.' She closed the menu firmly.

Kane studied her for a long moment and then as the waiter approached informed him, 'I'll have the Porterhouse steak with forrestierre sauce and my fiancée will have the fettuccine carbonara.'

'But—' Bryony opened her mouth to protest but the waiter had already gone. She swivelled back to scowl at Kane, who was sitting as if butter wouldn't melt in his mouth, and then thought with resentment that if it did his hard body wouldn't suffer the consequences as hers would.

'Do you know how much cream is in that dish?' she asked.

'You can afford a little indulgence now and again.'

'I think I can be trusted to order my own meals,' she said. 'I have to watch my figure, every dancer does.'

'I'll watch it for you,' he said and then let his eyes do exactly that by sliding over her lazily, lingering on the swell of her breasts.

'Stop it!' she hissed at him furiously, conscious of the other diners in the tiny restaurant. 'What will people think?'

'They'll think I can't wait to get you home and into bed, that's what they'll think.'

She felt hot all over at his words. Her face flamed and her spine felt as if someone had just set a blowtorch to it, melting it like warmed honey.

'You know I don't want to sleep with you,' she bit out.

'I'm confident I can get you to change your mind.'

'Your arrogance is misplaced for I won't be changing my mind.'

'You should run that by the rest of your body before you go backing yourself into such a tight corner.' His eyes dipped back to the pointed peaks of her breasts where her nipples were clearly outlined. 'Could be the rest of you might not agree.'

She sent him a withering look and crossed her arms. 'It's cold in here.'

The edge of his mouth lifted sceptically. 'It's close to thirty degrees. Mario warned me when I booked that the air-conditioning was playing up.'

'You booked?' She stared at him. 'You were that confident I'd come?'

He lifted his wineglass. 'You're a pushover, Bryony.' Winking at her, he tossed the contents down his throat. He put the glass back down and added, 'I promise you, I will always make you come.'

She stared at him in a combination of outrage at his *double entendre* and fear that he would actually fulfill his promise.

She couldn't hold his gaze, even in the dim lighting.

'You're going to be very disappointed.' She addressed the tablecloth rather than face the burning glitter of his dark eyes.

'I don't think so.'

'Could we please talk about something else?' she asked in desperation.

'If you like.'

She gnawed at her lip for a moment, hunting her brain for a suitable topic but before she could come up with something he leaned towards her and spoke in an undertone. 'I think I should warn you there's a woman making her way to our table to speak to me. Someone I used to date.'

'Why are you telling me? Do you think I'm the least bit interested in who you've managed to bribe into your bed in the past?'

He sat back in his seat and refilled his glass from the bottle on the table. 'I just thought it would be polite to warn you.'

'Well, you can take your version of politeness and stick it where—'

'Kane!' a husky feminine voice cooed just before a waft of heady, cloyingly cheap perfume hit Bryony's flaring nostrils.

Bryony turned her head to see a blonde sashay up to the table, leaning her glorious cleavage down so Kane could have an exclusive view as she purred at him, 'You naughty man. You haven't called me in ages.'

'I've been otherwise engaged.'

The brassy blonde totally ignored the real blonde sitting in silent fury at the table and continued in a breathy voice, 'Well, you know my number if you're ever at a loose end.'

'I haven't forgotten it,' he said with a little smile.

Bryony felt like slapping it from his face and had to thrust her hands in her lap to stop herself from giving in to the temptation.

She sat silently seething at the disgusting little tableau being acted out in front of her, furious with him for allowing it to continue but equally annoyed with herself for even giving a damn.

Of course he would have slept around.

He was thirty-one years old.

He was a man, wasn't he?

Wasn't it imprinted in their genes to spread themselves as far and wide as they could?

'I'll be seeing you.' The woman blew him a kiss that ruffled the flowers on the table with her nicotine-scented breath. 'Don't do anything I wouldn't do, will you?'

'You have my word on that, Luna,' he said.

Luna?

What was she, some kind of planet orbiting around him? Bryony gave a disgusted little snort as the woman made her way back to her noisy table of equally cosmetically and surgically enhanced revellers.

'I did try to warn you,' he said.

'I'm not sure any type of warning would have been enough.' She slanted a disparaging glance his way.

'It was just sex.'

She rolled her eyes. 'When is it anything else?'

'Good point,' he acceded and refilled his glass.

'All I can say is you're definitely marrying up.'

'Am I?' One dark brow rose over his eye like a question mark.

She opened her mouth to sling another stinging retort his way but the waiter appeared with their meals, the creamy garlicky fragrance of her fettuccine distracting her from her mission.

'Enjoy.' The waiter beamed as he sidled away.

Bryony picked up her fork and, giving Kane one last resentful glare, dug her fork into the steaming dish in front of her without a single pang of guilt.

After dinner was over Kane walked her back to her car where it was parked behind the studio, waiting until she was safely inside before hunkering down to speak to her through the still open door.

'Want to have some fun with me on the weekend?'

She tried not to stare into the depths of his brown-black eyes. 'I'm…busy.'

'How busy?'

'*Very* busy.'

'Doing what?'

She thought for a moment. 'I have to babysit my neighbour's diabetic cat.'

He chuckled and got to his feet, his hand on the door to stop her from closing it. 'Can't you think of a better excuse than that?'

She turned over the engine and reached for the door handle. 'I have to mop the floors.'

'And that's going to take you all weekend?'

'I do it with my tongue.'

The look he sent her was pure temptation but she resolutely pulled the door shut, turning her head to the road ahead.

She gunned the engine and took off with a little squeal of brakes but it was several blocks before she could erase the vision of his slanted smile and even longer to stop her stomach tilting at the thought of being tied to him in marriage.

CHAPTER FIVE

As soon as Monday morning arrived Bryony felt as if she was on an out of control rollercoaster heading towards the weekend where the wedding loomed like a disaster just waiting to happen. There was nothing she could do to stop it. The invitations were out, the flowers ordered, the cake made, the dress hanging in her wardrobe.

Pauline was effusive in her praise of her choice of groom when she arrived at the studio. Bryony didn't have the heart to tell he wasn't exactly *her* choice of bridegroom…

'So *handsome!*' Pauline clasped her hands together theatrically. 'And that *scar!* Has he told you how he came by it? Isn't it intriguing?'

Bryony felt sick.

'He's *so* gorgeous!' Pauline continued. 'No wonder you fell for him so quickly. God, I would have dived into his bed even if it was filled with great white sharks.'

Bryony couldn't help laughing. 'You're seriously nuts, do you know that?'

'He's nuts about you,' Pauline said, folding her arms across her chest. 'That's as plain as that scar on his face.'

Bryony wished she wouldn't keep referring to *that* scar.

'He got it in a fight,' she said, hoping to deflate her partner's bubble of admiration.

No such luck.

'I thought as much,' Pauline said, admiration colouring her tone. 'What was he doing? Defending some girl's honour?'

'I…I'm not exactly sure of the details…'

Pauline gave a deep dreamy sigh. 'I wish I could find someone like him to defend me…'

'Women can defend themselves,' Bryony felt it necessary to point out. 'Anyway, fighting is so…primitive.'

'Give me a primitive man any day over one of those meterosexuals who think you've committed a heinous sin for borrowing their razor.'

Bryony didn't answer.

Her mind was far too busy with a vision of Kane's razor sliding up from her ankle to her thigh and beyond…

Her mother phoned that evening, her tone lighter than Bryony had heard it in years.

'Darling, I just had to tell you,' Glenys said somewhat breathlessly. 'Kane has settled all your father's debts. He phoned a few minutes ago. Isn't that nice?'

Nice? What was nice about blackmailing her into marriage?

'Yes,' she said instead, inwardly seething. 'He's nothing if not nice.'

'I'm so glad you think so,' her mother said. 'I mean…I did hope you would feel some sort of gratitude for what he's done for us…'

'Believe me, Mum, I'm extremely grateful,' she said, trying to keep the sarcasm out of her tone.

'I'm very relieved, darling, because I didn't like to think of you marrying him when you hated him so much.' There was a delicately timed pause. 'You don't hate him any more, do you?'

Bryony found it difficult to answer with any degree of honesty. On one hand she hated him with every bone in her body, but then…

'I'm not sure what I feel about him.' She went for the middle ground.

'He's a good man,' her mother said. 'One sort of knows these things.'

Bryony frowned. If her mother thought he was such an angel, why had she been complicit with her father in putting him behind bars ten years ago? None of it made any sense. Was there something they weren't telling her?

'Yes,' she said by way of answer to her mother. 'One does.' But she didn't believe it for a second.

The day of the wedding was mostly fine but a storm loomed overhead in steel-grey clouds that frowned down upon the perfectly trimmed and tended gardens of Mercyfields like disapproving eyes on a scandalous scene.

Bryony put the finishing touches to her face and hair and wished it would pour with rain to ease the tense atmosphere.

'You look beautiful—' her mother sniffed as she stood back to look at her '—radiant, in fact.'

Radiant with rage, Bryony thought sourly as she flicked her veil over her face.

'I'm ready,' she lied and turned to the door.

'I'm so proud of you...' her mother gulped and picked up her train. 'So very, very proud of you.'

Bryony blinked back the sudden tears, hating Kane all over again for putting her through this.

He was waiting for her at the end of the wisteria walk, his gaze unwavering as she approached with steps that were deliberately out of time with the music of the string quartet.

What did she care? He was marrying her for all the wrong reasons. She was not going to be a submissive dutiful wife, no matter what amount of money he flashed around.

She met his dark mysterious gaze as she took her place beside him, her chin going up a fraction as the celebrant addressed the gathered guests.

'We are gathered here to…'

*To force a woman against her will to marry a man she loathes…*Bryony's imagination went off at a tangent, wondering what the assembled guests would say if she told them the bitter truth.

'If anyone here has any reason why this couple should not be joined in holy matrimony, let them now speak or for ever hold their peace,' the celebrant continued in an authoritative tone.

Bryony wished she had the courage to tell the small crowd the real story—that he'd forced her into marriage by holding her parents' freedom to ransom. What would Great-Aunt Ruby, who was mopping up her tears, think then? And what about Uncle Arthur, who was smiling at her like a Cheshire cat who had got both the cream and the canary and two mice thrown in as an entrée? Not to mention Pauline, who was sobbing into a handkerchief, doing her best imitation of a romance addict who couldn't wait for the happy ending.

There wasn't going to be a happy ending.

Bryony knew it as certainly as the clouds gathered overhead in growing disapproval.

'You may kiss the bride.'

She was jolted out of her automated responses by the lowering of Kane's head as his mouth came towards hers. She braced herself for the impact of his warm lips, but in the end she realised there was nothing she could have done to reduce the effect on her senses as his mouth covered hers.

She forgot about the host of witnesses.

She forgot about the fact that she was supposed to hate him.

She forgot that she had resolved not to respond to him in any shape or form, having to concede that in the end it was his shape and form that was very likely going to be her downfall.

He was all male.

All hard, irresistible male as he held her against him, his large hands on her hips, his fingers splayed possessively, making her shiver with reaction as he brought her even closer.

She felt every imprint of his body on hers, his long rock-hard thighs brushing hers and the tantalizing hint of his growing arousal pressing against her stomach reminding her of what was to come.

She pulled out of his hold and gave him a forced little smile, hoping the guests couldn't see the flutter of panic reflected in her eyes.

The guests applauded their passage back down the wisteria walk and Bryony stretched her stiff smile even further as she met each and every indulgent eye.

None of this was real.

It couldn't be!

She was married to a man she'd hated since childhood.

A servant's son no less.

She caught her father's gaze and tried to hold it but he shifted his eyes away as if he couldn't bear to see the sight of her walking arm in arm with his dead son's enemy.

Her mother was mopping up tears as usual but she was smiling through them, which to Bryony was somewhat of a consolation.

'Smile, Mrs Kaproulias,' a voice said from the crowd and a camera flashed in her face, and another and another.

Bryony faced the cameras, her tight smile making her face ache with the effort.

It was going to be a long afternoon…

The first flash of lightning came about five p.m., just as the last of the guests were leaving. The catering staff were quietly and competently packing up in the background while Bryony stood by Kane's side, trying not to panic at the thought of being alone with him once the Mercedes carried her parents out of the Mercyfields gates for the last time.

It was all arranged.

Her parents were leaving on the cruise the very next morning after staying at the city apartment overnight, where they would return to live once their vacation was over.

Mercyfields now belonged to Kane Kaproulias—her husband.

The dust stirred up by her parents' departure was soon settled by the first droplets of rain, the sweet earthy smell of dry ground receiving moisture filling Bryony's nostrils as she stood on the veranda under the scented arras of the jasmine clinging from the second floor balcony.

Kane leaned forward so his lower arms were resting on the veranda rail beside her, his dark gaze looking out towards the hills where the lightning was playing.

'Looks like it's going to be a big one,' he observed.

'It might pass us by,' she said.

'I could feel it coming on all day.' He brushed a fly away from his face and turned his head to look at her. 'Couldn't you?'

His face was on a level with hers, his dark eyes so close she could see the heavy fringe of his lashes as they lowered slightly to squint against the angle of sunlight.

Her eyes slipped to his mouth, almost of their own volition, and she felt the most inexplicable urge to reach out and trace the ridge of his scar with her fingertip, to explore its contours for herself.

A slash of lightning threw its green-tinged light across the veranda, closely followed by the predatory growl of thunder, but she didn't even flinch. She was too absorbed in looking at him, wondering when he was going to...

'You like storms?' he asked.

Bryony watched the movement of his lips as he spoke, a flutter of something indefinable passing over the floor of her belly.

'Yes…' Her eyes went back to his. 'Do you?'

He turned his head to look out over the fields, breathing in the scent of dampened dust, closing his eyes for a moment as if committing it to memory.

She took the moment to study his features, the slightly Roman nose, the lean chiselled jaw, the dark shadow of masculine growth in spite of his morning shave and the mouth that smiled so fleetingly.

What was he thinking?

Was he busily congratulating himself on finally having acquired Mercyfields?

Was he thinking of his mother working long hours to provide for him?

Or was he thinking of the bride he'd bought? And how he would soon possess her?

Kane pushed himself away from the rail and turned to look down at her. 'I'm going to have a drink to celebrate.'

'You'll understand when I don't join you?' Bryony's tone was deliberately sarcastic in an effort to keep her distance.

He held her hardened look for a moment. 'Don't you want to drink to our future?'

'I think I'll give it a miss, if you don't mind.'

'Fine.' He strode towards the open French doors. 'I'll see you later. I have some things to see to.'

She stared fixedly at the reflection of the angry clouds on the surface of the lake, wondering if what happened on the first day of a marriage was any indication of what would happen throughout its duration.

Was their union always going to a battle between two bitter parties, each vying for the upper hand?

The lightning split the sky into jagged pieces, the roar

of thunder so close now that the old house seemed to almost shudder behind her in fear.

Acting entirely on impulse, Bryony stepped down from the veranda and, lifting her creamy voluminous skirts about her ankles, tiptoed through the gathering puddles on the driveway to the huge lawn beyond the rose garden.

She kicked off her shoes and, lifting her face to the splutter of warm rain, pirouetted three times, her gown billowing around her like creamy rose petals thrown up by a playful breeze.

The rain anointed her face as the lightning rent the sky, the drum roll of thunder booming in her ears, but still she danced.

She was on earth's stage with the orchestra of nature accompanying her in a performance which spoke of regret and loss in each and every twirl of her body and poignant point of her toes.

She danced for her brother, whom she still missed so much, thinking of his life cut short by a stupid accident that should never have happened.

She danced for the loss of her freedom, envisaging a bleak future married to a man who saw her as a battle trophy instead of someone he could come to love.

She danced for Kane's mother, Sophia, who hadn't seen her son rise to the heights in her lifetime, but had spent hers in menial work to bring about his success. How she must be smiling down on him now, the proud new owner of Mercyfields.

She would have kept on dancing but the storm was receding, the strains fading away just like dying applause.

She picked up her shoes in one hand and, gathering her muddy skirts in the other, made her way back to the house through the storm-ravaged rose garden where the soft petals lay just like the used confetti on the lawn overlooking the lake where the official photographs had been taken.

Kane was leaning in the doorway as she came back up the steps, his brooding expression reminding her of the sky moments earlier.

'You could have been struck by lightning,' he growled at her.

'I did try, but it just wouldn't co-operate.' She flicked her wet hair back off her face in a defiant gesture. 'So you're stuck with me after all. What a pity you couldn't have Mercyfields without the excess baggage of me.'

'Mercyfields means nothing to me.'

'No, I know it doesn't.' She glared at him resentfully. 'You just wanted it to prove a point. You had to wrench it away from my father—the man, who I might remind you, paid for your education out of the generosity of his heart. You wouldn't even be the person you are today without his help.'

'No—' he gave her an unreadable look, his tone cryptic '—I certainly wouldn't be.'

'Are you happy now?' she continued bitterly. 'You've finally achieved what you set out to do, to bring the Mercer family to your particular form of rough justice. What a pity Austin wasn't here to make your sick pleasure all the greater.'

'You think it's sick of me to want to see justice done?' His tone turned harsh and embittered. 'I'll tell you what I think is sick. Your brother wasn't the angel you think he was, nor indeed is your father. Your refusal to see the truth about them is what I would call sick.'

She was incensed by his callously flung words. She was under no illusions about her father, but Austin was something else.

He had no right to malign him.

No right at all.

'Who are *you* to call my brother to account?' she spat. 'You, the son of our promiscuous cleaning lady?'

She shouldn't have said it but it was out before she could stop it. She saw the flare of anger in his eyes, his features darkening with the effort of keeping it under some sort of control.

'What exactly do you mean by promiscuous?' His eyes ran over her like burning coals, scorching her from head to foot.

'I…' She swallowed and began to step backwards but his hand snaked out and held her fast.

'I asked you a question, Bryony.' His eyes glittered dangerously.

Fear widened her eyes as his fingers bit into the flesh of her arm, but her pride demanded she stand her ground and not cower as she had done so many times with her father in the past.

'Your mother was sleeping with someone on the Mercyfields estate,' she said, tilting her chin arrogantly. 'Everyone knew about it.'

He gave her a narrow-eyed look. 'Do you know who it was?'

She moistened her dry lips before answering. 'No. No one would tell me. I…I think it was one of the gardeners.'

He let her arm go and turned away.

Bryony stared at his stiff back and wondered if he'd known about it before now. If not, she could just imagine the shock he must be feeling and she immediately felt ashamed.

'I'm…I'm sorry…' she said. 'I thought you already knew.'

He swung around to face her once more, his scarred lip even more noticeable as his mouth stretched into a sneer.

'Oh, I knew all right.'

She wasn't sure how to interpret his tone.

'Did you know who she was…seeing?' she asked.

It seemed a very long time before he answered.

'Leave it. What does it matter now, anyway? She's dead.' He turned away and gripped the railing with tight hands, looking out across the gardens with sightless empty eyes.

Bryony's brow creased as she watched him.

'How did she die?' she asked after another long silence.

She heard him take what sounded like a painful breath, but his voice when he spoke was stripped of all discernible emotion. 'Suicide.'

Suicide? Coldness crept along her skin in spite of the still warm evening air.

'I'm sorry…'

'Don't be.' He turned to look at her. 'You weren't the one to drive her to it.'

She couldn't look away from the deep sadness in his gaze; it struck at the heart of her to see such raw suffering, having been through the process of grief herself.

'How long ago did…it happen?' she asked.

'Not long enough for me to forgive the person responsible.'

'Suicide creates a lot of guilt in those left behind,' she offered as comfort, not entirely sure if it was adequate but feeling the need to do so all the same.

'But unfortunately not in the people most to blame.'

'You shouldn't blame yourself…'

'I don't.'

She blinked at his forthright statement. 'Then who do you blame?'

His eyes shifted away from hers and she knew without him even saying it that the subject was now closed.

'We have an early start in the morning,' he informed her impersonally. 'Why don't you have a bath and go to bed and I'll wake you at first light?'

She stared at him in confusion. Didn't he want her to…?

She opened and closed her mouth, hunting her brain for

the right way to express herself, when he gave her a small smile touched by ruefulness.

'You think I would be such a brute as that, Bryony?' he asked.

'I...' What could she say? Yes, she thought him ruthless enough to insist on consummating their marriage, but then...

'I know you think I just crept out of the primeval soup, but let me assure you I have no interest in sleeping with you this evening,' he said.

She stared at him for a moment, the ambiguity of her feelings confusing her. She'd been expecting relief to course through her at the unexpected reprieve but instead she felt out of sorts and strangely let down.

'I see.' She lowered her eyes as she hitched up her muddy gown with a hand that wasn't quite steady.

Kane reached out and tipped up her chin with one long tanned finger, his eyes instantly reminding her of the lake and the secrets lying amongst its dark murky depths.

She held her breath as his mouth came closer, the warm caress of his breath on her face causing her lashes to flutter downwards. She felt the soft brush of his lips over hers, the dryness of her mouth making his scarred top lip cling to hers momentarily as he lifted his mouth away from hers.

She opened her eyes and felt the full heat of his gaze and, before she could stop herself, she lifted her index finger to his mouth, gently tracing the white edge of his scar.

He stood very still but she could feel the deep thud of his heart where her other hand had crept to press against his chest.

'I should have said this a long time ago...' she began awkwardly, her cheeks filling with heat.

'You don't need to.' His voice was low and rough.

'I—I do.'

'It was a decade ago,' he said. 'You were just a kid.'

She felt the sting of tears at the back of her eyes for what he must have suffered and yet, as far as she knew, he'd told no one...

'Why did you tell everyone you'd tripped over?' she asked, her voice catching slightly. 'Why didn't you tell them the truth?'

'For what gain?' he asked. 'I goaded you and you hit back. As far as I was concerned, it was over.'

But it hadn't been over.

He'd come back for her, just as he had come back for Mercyfields.

'Besides,' he added, 'I didn't want my pride dented any further. Can you imagine the ribbing I would've got if everyone had known you'd hit me with a rock?'

She bit her lip in distress. 'There was so much blood...'

'It wasn't a pretty sight,' he agreed.

'You had every right to report it...I deserved to be...'

'Don't beat yourself up about it, Bryony.' He eased himself away from her. 'One would be extremely lucky to get through life without a scar or two. Mine is a little more visible than most, but there are a lot of people out there with bigger scars than this, the only difference being they're on the inside where they do a whole lot more damage.'

She could well believe it. Didn't she have wounds of her own lying festering where no healing hand could reach?

'Sleep well.' He flicked her cheek with one long finger before moving down the steps of the veranda and into the creeping shadows of the evening.

Bryony stared after him until she could no longer distinguish his tall form from the trees he'd walked towards.

The lake in the distance gleamed with the golden glow of the setting summer sun, the long fingers of fading light reaching as far they could across the surface, as if intent on peeling away what secrets lay there undisclosed...

CHAPTER SIX

BRYONY ignored the clawfoot bath and had a quick shower instead, climbing into bed soon after, not expecting to sleep a wink, but when she woke to the sound of the birds stirring in the gum trees fringing the gardens she realised just how exhausted she must have been.

She was out of bed and dressed before Kane tapped on the door.

'Time to get up, Bryony.'

'I'm up,' she called back and straightened the bed before reaching for the bag she'd packed the previous day.

Kane had the car running outside, the boot open ready to receive her luggage, his brow lifting ironically at the sight of her modest bag.

'Not taking the kitchen sink this time?'

She shook her head.

He shut the boot and once she was settled took his place behind the wheel and turned the car on to the long sinuous driveway leading out to the road.

Bryony maintained the silence even though a hundred questions were chasing each other around her head.

Why had he left her in peace last night?

Wasn't his possession of her part of his detailed plan for revenge?

And, if he wasn't intending to sleep with her, why was he taking her on a honeymoon?

Or was he deliberately stretching out her torture by prolonging her anticipation of his possession, knowing how much she dreaded it?

She drank in the view as they moved further down the

coast, the sweeping views delighting her even as her trepidation grew at what lay ahead.

Kane drove with his usual quiet competence, sending an
idle comment her way once or twice, but largely seeming
to be disinclined to talk at length.

Bryony's resentment grew with every minute of silence.
She couldn't help thinking he was doing it deliberately to
increase her tension by not even bothering to put her at
ease with casual conversation.

After another hour of silence he turned left and headed
the car along a dusty road which seemed to Bryony to be
leading nowhere. She flicked him a glance but he seemed
to be preoccupied with negotiating the numerous potholes
in the road.

The car thumped over another and she chanced a quick
glance his way. 'Where are we going?'

He slowed down to bump over the next dip in the rough
gravel. 'It's not far now; wait till you see the view.'

She sat back in her seat, trying not to wince as the car
lumbered over another chasm in the road.

He was right about the view, she decided a few minutes
later.

The azure blue of the sea stretched out as far as the
horizon, a speck of a rocky island floating in the distance,
the white fringe of sand of a long beach below the cliff top
breathtaking to say the very least.

'It's…beautiful…'

'It gets better.' He unfolded himself from the car and
came around to her side but she was already out, breathing
in the salty air.

'How did you find this place?' She turned towards him,
her eyes alight with undisguised pleasure.

'It's not exactly off the map,' he said, which didn't really
answer her question.

She decided not to pursue it and drank in the view

instead. 'I love the sound of the sea...it sounds so... powerful.'

The boom and crash of waves below gave credence to her words. She wandered over to the cliff face to look out to sea. Then, turning around to face him once more, she saw for the first time the cottage perched on a higher shelf of the cliff. It was cleverly disguised from the road, adding to the whole feeling of seclusion.

'Wow...' She let out her breath on a note of pure wonder.

He came to stand beside her, their bags in his hands. 'You like it?'

'I love it!' She sent him a quick glance and scuttled up the rough path to get a closer look.

Kane followed at a distance, his own enthusiasm for the place taking a back seat to hers. He gave a soft smile as he saw her scamper off to investigate the view from the upper level, her long hair escaping its tight pony-tail, her cheeks pink from the sea breeze as she lifted her face to the bright glare of the sun.

He unlocked the cottage and she followed him in, her face still aglow.

'I can't believe such a paradise still exists!' she enthused. 'There's no one around for miles.'

'No,' he agreed. 'I prefer it that way.'

She looked at him but he was gazing out to sea, his eyes narrowed against the sunlight spilling through the large windows.

'Come here,' he said, and without taking his eyes off the ocean, held out an arm for her to join him.

She hesitated for the briefest moment before slipping underneath his shoulder, his arm drawing her close as he directed her vision to a speck out to sea.

'See that?' he asked, pointing into the distance.

Bryony peered to where his finger was directed. 'What is it? A boat?'

'No, watch…there—did you see them?'

She watched in wonder as a pod of dolphins surfaced, their gleaming backs clearly visible where the sun caught the smooth perfection of their silvery skin.

'Dolphins!' she gasped, unconsciously slipping her arm around his waist as she peered into the distance.

'They'll come in closer to shore in a day or two,' he said, glancing down at her.

'Will they?' She looked up at him in amazement. 'How close?'

'Close enough to swim with them.'

'Really?'

He nodded, looking out to sea again. 'I've swum with them lots of times.'

'Oh, wow…I've always wanted to do that…'

'Then you will,' he said, releasing her. 'I'll organize some lunch for us. Why don't you go and check out the pathway to the beach? I'll give you a shout when I have things ready.'

'Are you sure?'

He waved her away. 'But take care on the path down the cliff; the gravel is slippery in spots.'

Bryony made her way through the coastal vegetation to where a well-worn path led down the cliff to the beach. It was, as he'd said, unstable in spots, but she clung to the grass roots as she negotiated her way d wn to the icing sugar softness of the sand below.

She kicked off her sneakers and sank her toes into the sand, relishing the feeling of freedom as the minutiae of tiny particles sifted over her feet.

The water sparkled with invitation, the lace of foam reaching her toes as each wave crashed into the shore. The water was warmer than she'd been expecting and, glancing over her shoulder to the cottage on the cliff, she made sure Kane wasn't anywhere near the windows as she stripped down to her underwear, throwing her clothes to one side before plunging into the spewing waves.

She struck out through the wash to where the waves were forming, letting each one swell over her, lifting her up and lowering her in a gentle rocking motion.

She bobbed about for a while before catching a wave back to the shore, laughing as it spilled her out of its force amongst the crushed shells in the shallows.

She scrambled to her feet and went back in, looking for an even bigger wave to ride, undaunted by the roar of the surf as it gouged at the sand.

She came down the face of the next swollen wave, her legs almost folding over her head as it threw her towards the shore, her exhilarated laughter echoing along the stretch of lonely beach.

She pulled herself upright and, swinging her hair back out of her eyes, saw Kane standing on the fringe of white sand, watching her.

She hadn't noticed him coming down the path and wished she'd been more attentive. Her lacy underwear was hardly the sort of attire she wanted to face him in, but the water was making her shiver by now and she had no choice but to make her way back to where she'd carelessly flung her clothes.

She avoided his eyes as she bent down to retrieve her cotton casuals, knowing her underwear was probably no less revealing than the red and white bikini she had in her bag at the cottage, but feeling self-conscious all the same.

'You looked like you were enjoying yourself,' he observed.

She buttoned the waistband of her trousers before responding. 'I was. I haven't been to the beach in ages.'

Kane's eyes ran over her lightly, taking in her seaweed

adorned hair and the radiant glow the physical exertion had put in her cheeks. 'You should do it more often.'

'I know.' A tiny sigh escaped as she wrung out her hair. 'I just never seem to get the time. Besides…it's no fun by yourself.'

He gave her a long and intent look. 'You haven't dated regularly?'

She hesitated over her reply.

She didn't want to sound like some desperate and dateless soon-to-be thirty-year-old woman, but neither did she want to pretend she had the sort of lifestyle that saw her flitting from man to man in search of the perfect lover.

'Now and again.' She took the middle ground in the end. 'I guess I'm what's known as ''hard to please''.'

'It's understandable,' he said.

She looked at him, pushing the wet slick of her hair over one shoulder. 'Why do you say that?'

He gave one of his non-committal shrugs. 'Just a guess.'

She shoved her feet into her shoes and made her way to the path to avoid having to respond.

She knew he thought her a spoilt heiress with too much money and not enough morals, but she had deliberately avoided emotional entanglements for the simple reason that she didn't want to end up like her mother. Of course now the irony of her situation was particularly galling. Here she was, tied to a man who hated everything to do with her and her family.

The lunch he'd set out was simple but exactly what she needed—fresh crusty bread, cheese, a small salad and chilled white wine.

She took the glass he handed her and lifted it to her mouth, her taste buds singing as the crisp passionfruit and gooseberry flavours burst over her tongue.

'Mmm…this is nice.'

'It's local,' he informed her, picking up his glass. 'There are vineyards in the neighbouring hinterland.'

She sat at the table and laid her napkin over her lap. 'How did you arrange for all this food to be here?'

He took his seat and handed her the bread. 'I have some friends who look after this place for me.'

'This is your place?'

He took a sip of wine before answering. 'I bought the property a few years ago. I built the house last year.'

She sat in a stunned silence. '*You* built the house?'

'You find the notion of me doing so difficult to believe?'

'No…it's just I…' She wasn't sure what she thought. 'How did you make your money?'

'The usual way.'

'Luck?'

'Only someone from your sort of background would assume that,' he said. 'No, it was sheer hard work and lots of it.'

'What sort of work?'

'The sort you and your family have always viewed with undisguised disdain—physical labour.'

She took another sip of wine as she collected her thoughts. Bitterness had crept back into his tone and, while she could hardly blame him considering her father's snobbery of the past, she wanted the softer, more reachable Kane back. Although he'd done his best to hide it, she'd seen a glimpse of a different man other than the one sitting opposite her now and she realised with a pang, that she wanted to see more.

'I guess someone has to do it,' she said. 'But how did you rise to the sort of heights you've achieved?'

'The construction company I worked for was going into receivership so I made a bid for it with the help of a friend who gave me the necessary financial leg-up. I worked during the day, studied at night and paid him back with interest within a year of taking over the business.'

'What are you planning to do with my father's company?'

He gave her a brittle look as he reached for his wine. 'I'm going to sell it.'

She felt the ruthless purpose in his blunt statement, wondering what else he had planned for the rest of his newly acquired assets.

'And Mercyfields?' she asked. 'Do you intend to sell that too?'

'Not yet.'

She wasn't sure if she felt relieved or disappointed.

On one hand the thought of her family home being sold to the highest bidder appalled her, but on the other hand why would he keep an estate that had witnessed his repeated degradations as a youth by members of her family, including her?

'I thought you said Mercyfields meant nothing to you,' she said. 'Why keep it?'

'Quite frankly I loathe the place.' There was no mistaking the astringency of his tone. 'But I have things I want to do there first.'

'Such as?'

He gave her one of his inscrutable looks. 'Exorcise a few ghosts, that sort of thing.'

She felt a shiver of apprehension scuttle over her flesh.

'Austin's ashes are there...' She swallowed painfully. 'We spread them after...the year after you left.'

'I didn't *leave*, Bryony.' His dark eyes glittered. 'I was evicted.'

'You deserved it,' she said, remembering it all as if it had been last week, not ten years ago...

It had been a couple of weeks after she'd encountered him at the lake. During that time she'd avoided him meticulously, but in spite of her attempts to keep him at a distance she'd come out of the breakfast room one day a few months before Austin had died to find Kane waiting outside her father's study. His customary indolent pose had irritated her, so too had the way his dark eyes ran over her lazily.

She could still recall the contemptuous curl of his damaged lip, red and inflamed where infection had struck, intensifying the already considerable damage she'd caused.

She'd caught her breath, wondering if he was finally going to spill the beans on her despicable actions. She'd been waiting for the axe to fall for a fortnight, knowing he was probably delaying doing so to prolong her torture.

Was that why he was standing outside her father's study now?

She'd felt sick with the thought of what would happen if her father was told. Although bigoted and racist and at times even aggressive himself, she had known her father would not tolerate her demonstrating such violence and what the punishment would be if he ever found out—he would take it out on her mother.

'Hello, Bryony,' Kane drawled. 'I haven't seen much of you lately. Where have you been hiding?'

'I haven't been hiding,' she bit out and made to brush past.

An iron fist came down on her arm, the tanned work-roughened fingers almost cruel in their grasp.

Bryony's eyes met his above their joined bodies, the burning intensity of his brown-black gaze frightening her as much as it drew her towards him like a moth to a light too hot to touch. She felt the pull of his body, the heat radiating towards her, the male scent of him a combination of exercise and musky maleness that sent her senses into acute awareness. Her reaction to him shamed her, frightened her…secretly terrified her.

'Let me go, Kane.'

She knew he wasn't going to obey her command, and for years later often wondered what would have happened if her brother hadn't come into the hall at that point.

'Let her go,' Austin commanded.

Kane's eyes flashed with hatred so intense it totally unnerved her, but he let her arm go and stepped backwards.

'What are you doing in the house, you filthy scum?' Austin sneered at him nastily.

'I have an appointment to see your father.' On the surface Kane's tone was polite but his physical manner was all surly insolence. 'I have something I wish to discuss with him.'

Bryony's eyes went to his in nervous appeal but the quick glance he slanted her was bitter and unbending. She moistened her dry mouth, her hands twisting into knots in front of her churning stomach.

'What do you want to see him about?' Austin asked with his usual haughtiness.

There was a nerve-tightening pause.

Bryony felt her breath stall as Kane's dark eyes met hers for a heart-stopping second before moving away to address her brother.

'A private matter.'

She felt the ice water of fear spill into her veins. This was it…he was going to tell her father…

'A private matter, eh?' Austin's grey eyes glinted with derision. 'I wonder what sort of issue could have to be so private between you and my father.'

Kane didn't answer, for just then the study door opened and Owen Mercer stepped out, a heavy scowl on his face.

'What's all this noise out here?' His glance flicked over the little tableau. 'Bryony, I've told you before not to mix with the staff. Go to your room.'

'But I—' she began, but her father cut her off with a warning look from beneath his heavy brows.

'Bryony wasn't intentionally with me, Mr Mercer,' Kane said. 'She was just walking past.'

'He was touching her,' Austin put in with cold clarity. 'God knows what would have happened if I hadn't come along.'

Bryony stared at her brother in alarm. What did she think he was doing? Surely he knew how their father would react to such information?

'I thought I told you to go upstairs.' Owen turned his florid expression her way.

With a momentary hesitation which she knew would annoy her father immensely, she stepped away and turned towards the stairs.

She heard her father dismiss Austin before the study door was closed as Kane met him in private.

She had never been told what had been discussed during that meeting, and her embarrassment for her role in what had led up to it had kept her questions unasked.

All she knew was that within an hour of being dismissed from his meeting with her father Kane had driven one of the gardener's tractors up and down the huge lawn overlooking the lake, the vicious teeth of the plough on the back tearing at the soft lush grass in a criss-cross of savage bites that had taken months and thousands of dollars to restore.

As if that wasn't enough, he had then driven the tractor through the rose garden, tearing at decades of priceless bushes before parking it in the shallow end of the swimming pool.

Sophia Kaproulias had been summarily dismissed from her job within minutes of her son being escorted from the estate by two burly police officers.

Bryony had watched from her bedroom window as his

wrists were restrained by handcuffs before being shoved towards the waiting police van.

Just as he was getting in Kane had turned his gaze towards the house, his sweeping look coming to rest on Bryony standing in the frame of her window.

She'd watched, her breath tightening her chest as he'd gathered some moisture in his mouth before spitting it viciously to the ground at his feet.

It still chilled her to think of the silent purpose in that single action.

It had been a warning…

Bryony could feel Kane's tension as he sat opposite her at the cottage table, as if he too had just travelled back in time.

'You know you deserved it,' she repeated. 'You caused thousands of dollars of damage, not to mention the grief and suffering you caused Mrs Bromley when you callously ran over her dog.'

He jaw tightened as he held her accusing look. 'I'm afraid if you want to find a scapegoat for that particular crime you have no need to look any further than from within your own family.'

'For God's sake, Kane! Nero was found in the middle of the savaged lawn with tyre tracks over his back! How can you sit there and say you didn't do it?'

'I told you before, I did not kill that dog.'

Bryony felt confused, torn between wanting to believe him incapable of such a despicable act of cruelty but equally unwilling to lay the blame on someone much closer to home.

'I suppose you expect me to believe someone else ran over the dog and planted his dead body so you would get the blame?' she asked.

His mouth twisted as he pushed himself away from the

table, the action sending a shock wave through the wine in her glass.

'Believe what you like,' he said roughly. 'See if I give a damn.' He turned for the door and it slammed behind him, making her flinch.

She stared at the still shivering wine and put her hand on top of the glass to steady it, her brow furrowing in bewilderment.

What was she supposed to think?

Although he'd always been taciturn and a touch surly she had never considered him the sort of person who would treat an animal with such heartlessness, but how could she be sure?

Did she really know him?

He'd stepped out of the past, taking ruthless control of everything marked with the Mercer name and, as far as she could see, her parents had let him do so without so much as a fight.

She had been the one to take the full brunt of his revenge, a revenge that he had planned meticulously.

She cleared away the barely touched food and once the plates and glasses were in the dishwasher wandered through the house.

It was beautifully crafted, the timbers of Tasmanian celery top pine and myrtle featuring throughout. She trailed her hand over the smooth surface of the railing on the mezzanine level, marvelling at Kane's skill in bringing raw timber to such perfection.

She looked out towards the ocean rolling in and sighed. Would she ever know the full story?

Austin wasn't around any more for her to ask about his version of events. It didn't seem possible that the older brother she'd adored all her life could be party to what had gone on. She knew he and Kane had been at loggerheads most of the time during their youth and, although that didn't really excuse her brother's boorish behaviour towards him, she knew it had been well modelled by their father. Austin had simply adopted the same attitude from an early age and, to some degree, to her everlasting shame, so had she.

Bryony made her way back down the path to the beach, hoping the afternoon sea breeze would blow away her low spirits. She wandered along the water's edge, stopping now and again to inspect a shell before continuing past a pair of sooty oyster catchers who were inspecting the waterline with interest.

A small flock of white-fronted terns carved the air a few metres in front of her, their wings moving in perfect unison as they circled back around as she passed.

It was the first time in her life that she'd walked on a totally deserted beach, the experience filling her with a sense of quiet awe.

It made her wonder about Kane's need for solitude. Was he trying to escape the shame of his past by surrounding himself with the fragility of untouched, as yet unspoilt nature?

There was so much she didn't know about him, but how could she draw closer? Wouldn't it be disloyal to Austin's memory for her to develop feelings for the man who had made it his life's mission over the last ten years to destroy her family?

She turned her face to the stiffening breeze and wished she could erase the night of his accident from her memory for ever, but in moments like these when her guard was down it all came flooding back.

She'd been home on mid-term break, lying in her bed, her thoughts drifting preparatory to sleep when she'd heard a car pull up at the front of Mercyfields. Wondering who was calling at that late hour, she'd peered out of her bedroom window to see two police officers approaching the front door, their hats in their hands as a mark of respect.

She'd heard her mother's bloodcurdling scream a few moments later and from that point Bryony's life had gone into a tailspin from which she had yet to recover. She'd switched on to automatic to get through the trauma of funeral arrangements and the identification of Austin's poor crushed body.

The inquest findings had indicated speed and alcohol were involved, but her parents had insisted he was innocent. She had let them think what they liked for their grief was so palpable she knew it would serve no purpose adding to it with details that could in no way change the final outcome.

Austin was dead.

Nothing and no one could bring him back.

The least she could do in honour of his memory was to keep Kane Kaproulias at a safe distance.

Her heart depended on it...

CHAPTER SEVEN

BRYONY was almost back to the cliff path when she saw something lying in the shallows about halfway along the beach in the opposite direction to which she'd walked.

She shielded her eyes from the slanting glare of the sun to see if she could make out what it was, but before she could identify it she heard the thud of rapid footsteps running through the sand behind her.

She swung around to see Kane sprinting towards her and in one of his hands a lethal-looking knife glinted dangerously.

She shrank away as he approached but he ran on past, calling out to her over his shoulder. 'It's one of the dolphins. I think it must be hurt.'

It took her but a second or two to get her legs into gear and, ignoring the protests of her knee, she ran behind him, coming to a heavily panting halt two hundred metres or so later.

It was indeed one of the dolphins.

It was lying on its side in the frothy shallows, one lustrous eye staring at her in unblinking pain.

'Oh, my God!' She sank to her knees, stroking her hand gently along the muscled skin of its neck. 'What's wrong with you, baby?'

Kane was examining the other side, his expression as he faced her murderous with rage.

'Fishing line.' He swore once, quite savagely, and she realised it was the first time she'd ever heard him do so.

'Fishing line?' She stared at him over the top of the dolphin's back.

He nodded grimly. 'We'll have to roll him over so I can get to it. It's embedded in his other flipper.'

'Won't we hurt him by moving him?'

'He'll die if we don't; he's halfway there already.'

Bryony watched in anguish as the dolphin rolled its eye at her as if giving credence to Kane's gruff statement.

'Put your arms under here.' He directed her as she joined him on the other side of the dolphin. 'Make sure your nails don't scratch him, and push.'

She dug her feet into the sand and did as he commanded but the dolphin was a fully grown adult and heavy, not to mention terribly slippery.

'Come on, Bryony, one more try,' he said. 'Here we go—one, two, *three…*'

The silvery body shifted slightly but the movement had distressed the poor creature, who began to struggle, his tail threshing about, sending a spray of water all over them both.

'And again, *agape mou,*' Kane directed as he shook the dripping water out of his eyes, his hands still braced against the dolphin's body. 'We can do it, I know we can…now *push…*'

She gave an almighty push, wondering why she was feeling so touched by his endearment when previously she'd berated him for addressing her so.

The dolphin moved at the same time as her knee gave way, but she gritted her teeth and kept pushing till he was safely turned over. Her breathing was still laboured as she stared down at the tortured flesh of the dolphin's flipper, the nylon of fishing line almost cutting it in two.

'Oh, you poor thing…' she gasped in despair.

'It's all right.' Kane set the knife in position. 'Just try and hold him still for a minute while I get rid of this.'

She wasn't sure she would have much to offer in resistance if the creature decided to move, but as if sensing

Kane was trying to help he lay still as the knife cut through the vicious bite of the line.

Kane straightened and gave her a rueful smile. 'That's the easy part over with, now for the difficult bit.'

'The difficult bit?' She gave him a confused look.

He nodded his head towards the water, now even further from where the dolphin was stranded as the tide ebbed away.

'Oh, no…' Her face fell.

'Oh, yes.' He tossed the knife to the sand past the waterline and positioned himself at the dolphin's tail. 'I'll try and pull him a bit closer but, as I do, can you watch that his damaged flipper doesn't get too traumatized as we go? He's likely to struggle but there's no other way.'

'OK,' she said and took up her position, her bottom lip between her teeth as Kane began to pull.

The dolphin eyed her soulfully before beginning to thrash to dislodge Kane's grasp.

'No, sweetie,' she cooed and stroked its head. 'He's trying to help you. Don't fight against him; you'll only hurt yourself.'

She thought about the words she'd just spoken and wondered if there was a truth in them for her as well as for the beached dolphin. She had done nothing but fight Kane, and it could well be only her who would get hurt in the end.

The dolphin's flipper began to drag along the shelly sand as Kane gave another pull so Bryony got on her knees and, keeping a few inches ahead, dug out a trench to allow it to pass through without catching.

'Good thinking,' Kane said in approval and, gritting his teeth, gave another huge pull. 'Almost there…'

As soon as the dolphin felt the water deepen he began to writhe in earnest. Bryony sat back on her heels, the path she'd dug no longer necessary as the creature began to float, his blowhole closing over as he felt the water finally take his weight.

Kane let the tail go just as the dolphin turned for the bay, the late afternoon sun shining on the rubber-like silver of his back as he swam off.

Kane turned and looked at Bryony sitting in the shallows, her cheeks flushed with effort, her blonde hair like a mermaid's, her beautiful face turned towards the deep blue waters of the sea.

He walked out of the waist deep water to the shallows and, smiling down at her, offered her a hand. 'We did it, Bryony.'

Bryony took his hand but stumbled as she got to her feet as her knee refused to take her weight. He frowned as he steadied her, his arms against her strong but gentle.

'What's wrong? Are you hurt?'

She winced as she tested her knee once more, clutching at his sodden T-shirt for balance. 'I've done something to my knee...it'll be right in a minute.'

'Let me see.' He knelt down carefully and rolled up her cotton trousers, sucking in a sharp breath when he saw the already swollen joint. 'That looks painful.' He straightened to look down at her, concern etched across his darkly handsome features.

'It is.' Her expression twisted ruefully.

'I'll carry you back to the cottage.' He began to put his arms around her.

'No!' She put a hand on his arm to stop him. 'I'm too heavy to haul up that path.'

'Too heavy?' He gave her an amused look before scooping her up in his arms. 'Listen, *agape mou*, the dolphin was heavy. After lugging that thing back into the water, I can tell you, you're going to be an absolute breeze.'

Bryony had to admit as he brought her to the door of the cottage a short time later he was a whole lot stronger than she'd accounted for. The dolphin episode notwithstanding, she knew it couldn't have been easy carrying a child up the awkward path let alone her! And yet he'd kept up an easy level of conversation as they went, his breathing rate not even accelerating while hers, with her body pressed so close to his, was skyrocketing out of control.

He set her down in the bathroom and, making sure she was steady, reached across and turned on the shower.

'Strip off and have a quick shower, then I'll bandage your knee.'

She looked at him in alarm as he turned back to face her once the water temperature was right.

'What's wrong?' he asked.

She compressed her lips for a moment. 'You can leave now…I think I can manage.'

'On that knee?' He frowned at her. 'You'll end up slipping over and doing even more damage. Don't be stupid, do you think I haven't seen a naked woman before?'

'You haven't seen *this* naked woman before,' she said with a touch of pride.

He gave her a challenging look. 'Not yet, but soon.'

Bryony snapped her teeth together, not sure she wanted to rise to that particular bait.

Kane's eyes glinted teasingly as he handed her a big fluffy towel. 'Have your shower in peace. I'll be just outside the door if you need me.'

Her eyes followed him as he went out of the bathroom, her thoughts in tumbling disarray.

The running water called her back and, peeling off her wet clothes, she hobbled under the steaming spray and tried not to think of Kane's dark eyes on her body some time in the future.

Her skin shivered in spite of the warm water, tiny goosebumps of awareness lifting her flesh until she was tingling all over. What was happening to her? Was she so starved of physical affection she had to pine after a man who'd married her for revenge?

She turned off the shower and dried herself roughly, doing her best to force her mind away from the disturbing images it persistently tried to conjure up. Images of her body locked with Kane's in the act of possession, his long hard body moving in time with hers, his mouth smothering the soft gasps of delight bursting from deep within her.

Bryony thrust her arms through the sleeves of the bathrobe she found hanging on the back of the door and, once she was securely covered, called out for Kane to come back in.

He came in bearing a first aid kit and a small stool for her to sit on while he attended to her knee.

He ran his hands over her joint, testing for tender spots with such competent gentleness she couldn't help remarking on it.

'You look like you've done this before.'

He looked up and gave her one of his slanted smiles, his eyes so dark she could barely distinguish the pupils from the irises.

'Once or twice.' He shifted his gaze and undid the cellophane wrapping on the tube of bandage and began winding it around her knee. 'On a construction site there are always issues of safety. First aid training was part of the employment package.'

'You should have been a doctor.' She inspected her neatly bandaged leg.

'I've been told my bedside manner needs work.'

Bryony was absolutely certain there was nothing wrong with his bedside or, for that matter, his *inside* the bed manner, but she wasn't going to tell him that.

'Thanks for bandaging it,' she said instead and, with his help, got off the stool and tested her weight on her leg.

'How does it feel?' he asked.

'Sore, but better for the support, I think.'

'Good.' He scrunched up the cellophane wrapping and placed it in the small bin under the basin before turning back to her. 'Want me to carry you or do you think you can hobble a bit?'

'I'll give hobbling a try.' She took the arm he offered.

They made their way back to the lounge overlooking the view and he helped her on to one of the white linen sofas, pulling over a footstool for her to place her leg on.

'I think it must be time for a drink,' he said. 'What will you have—white wine, champagne or something soft?'

'What are you going to have?' she asked.

'I was thinking along the lines of a cold beer, but don't let that stop you having what you'd like.'

'I'd like champagne but it seems a shame to open it for just one person.'

'I think I can afford it just this once,' he said with a hint of a smile.

'Champagne it is, then.' She found herself smiling back.

'That's two,' he said, looking at her thoughtfully.

'Two what?' She blinked at him in confusion.

'Two genuine smiles,' he said. 'Not bad, considering how long we've known each other.'

She watched him as he fetched their drinks, not sure she had ever known the man she saw in front of her now.

Where was the sullen son of the housekeeper? Where was the young man who had pressed her brother's buttons so much? Where was the man who had cruelly run down their neighbour's much loved spaniel and left it to bleed to death in the middle of the lawn he'd ravaged so callously?

Kane was none of those men—he was someone else entirely, which meant she was in very great danger of being tempted into letting her guard down around him.

He came back over with an effervescent glass of champagne for her, a beer in his other hand.

'Cheers.' He lifted his bottle in a toast. 'Here's to our friend, the dolphin.'

'To the dolphin.' She chinked her glass against the lip of his bottle of beer.

He took the seat to her right and, placing his feet on the coffee table, crossed his ankles. 'You did a great job out there, Bryony.'

'I...I did?' She felt ridiculously pleased by his comment and silently berated herself for it.

'Sure you did. No hysterics, you just got on with the task at hand.'

'He was suffering...'

'Yes, but he's one of the lucky ones.' He took a swig of his beer. 'I've seen too many who haven't made it. It's not exactly what you'd describe as a pleasant sight.' He reached forward to set his bottle down on the coffee table near his crossed ankles, before leaning back with a sigh.

'It's happened before?' she asked. 'With a fishing line?'

'Not just fishing line—nets mainly. The tuna industry has a bad reputation where dolphins are concerned. They often swim over large schools of tuna and, as a result, get trapped in the nets.'

'That's terrible.'

'It's not just tuna-fishing crews.' He leant forward for his beer once more. 'A lot of amateur fishermen throw their snagged lines or bits of rubbish overboard, but as dolphins, and to an even greater degree seals, are very inquisitive marine mammals they often find themselves snared. As you saw from our friend, it can do untold damage, for a youngster particularly, as their body continues to grow around the noose. While a dolphin doesn't use its flippers to swim, they use them to stop and turn. Being disabled leaves them seriously vulnerable.'

'What can be done?'

'Education, lobbying, that sort of thing. But it all takes time, valuable time.'

'You really care about this, don't you?' she asked, watching him closely.

'I don't like seeing the innocent suffer; it all seems so pointless.'

Bryony considered his words, trying to align them with her view of him as a heartlessly cruel man who would stop at nothing to get his way.

None of it seemed to fit.

He was a man of contradictions. He had a heart, but up until this point she had never seen it displayed. She recalled the almost inhuman strength he'd called upon to drag the dolphin to safety. Was that really the same man who had forced her into marriage as an act of revenge?

She took a sip of her champagne and tried to organize her thoughts into some sort of framework where he could be innocent of all charges, but it just wouldn't work.

He had been sent to prison for what he'd done. He'd deliberately sabotaged Mercyfields, killing an innocent animal in the process, all in an attempt to get back at her family.

He was guilty.

He had to be, for if he wasn't…someone else had to be and that she just couldn't bear.

'I'm kind of wondering at this point how your views on animal cruelty fit in with what you did to Mrs Bromley's spaniel.'

He visibly stiffened, his hand around his beer bottle tight, his eyes when they met hers dark with sudden anger. 'How many times do you require me to say I didn't kill that dog?'

'Enough times for me to believe it,' she tossed back.

'You wouldn't believe it even if the bloody dog came back to life to tell you for itself,' he bit out. 'You've had me painted as the villain almost from the first day I walked on to the Mercyfields estate with my mother when I was fourteen.'

'OK, then.' She sent him a challenging look. 'If you didn't do it, who did? Everybody knew that dog came to visit the kitchen for scraps at the same time every day. He was like a part of the family. Gloria Bromley was my mother's nearest neighbour and closest friend.'

His mouth twisted as he reached for his drink. 'Your sainted brother had a dark side. I think he did it to get back at me.'

'You only *think* he did it?' Her tone was cynical. 'Where's your proof?'

'I have no proof. I just think he did it. He was always looking for an opportunity to get me off side with your father. It was exactly the sort of thing he would do.'

'My brother loved animals,' she put in. 'All animals.'

He gave her a disdainful look. 'Your brother's only saving grace was the fact he loved you. Unfortunately your reciprocal love for him blinded you to the real persona he kept hidden from his family. I know for a fact he ordered me to be beaten up after our incident at the lake.'

She stared at him in shock. 'W-what?'

His scarred lip curled. 'Didn't he tell you?'

She shook her head, her stomach turning over.

'I thought he'd relish the chance to reveal to you how he'd taught me a much needed lesson.'

'I don't know what you're talking about.'

'You expect me to believe that?' His eyes were like black diamonds, brittle with bitterness.

'I didn't tell a soul about what…what happened between us.'

'You didn't need to. It seems your brother had his willing spies. Within minutes of our meeting at the lake he was already marshalling his henchmen. He was too cowardly to do it himself, of course; he had to assign four men to beat me to a pulp while he watched on from the sidelines in sick enjoyment.'

Bryony stared at him in abject horror. Could it be true? Could her brother have done such a despicable thing?

'*No...*' Her protest came out on the back of a strangled gasp.

'Why do you think my lip scarred the way it did?' he asked.

She swallowed the lump of nausea in her throat, not trusting herself to answer.

'Go on believing in your angelic brother for as long as you like, but I for one cannot regret his passing. As far as I'm concerned, he was a low-life just like your father who would stop at nothing to achieve his own ends.'

Bryony felt the energy drain from her as if someone had pulled a plug from deep within her body. She couldn't get her head around anything he had told her this evening. She didn't want to believe what he was telling her but the alternative was becoming equally unpalatable.

Someone was innocent.

Someone was guilty.

She had to choose.

'I need some time to think about this...' she said.

'Take all the time you need.' His tone was curt. 'I've waited ten years for the truth to surface; a few more days, weeks or even months won't make much more difference.'

There was so much bitterness in his tone that she felt tempted to put her vote of truth with him, but then she thought of Austin and his devotion to her, the way he'd protected her from their father when things had got out of hand, as they often had. How could she taint her precious memories of him?

Kane's beer bottle was empty as too was his cold distant gaze as he trained it on her. 'I'm going for a walk. Help yourself to whatever food you fancy. I probably won't be back before nightfall.'

Bryony watched in silent anguish as he left the cottage, the screen door snapping shut behind him cutting all contact off with him as surely as his clipped statement.

She sat on the sofa and watched as the lowering sun spread its rays across the water, the long flat horizon stretching as far as the eye could see.

How far from the swathes of manicured lawns and meticulously tended gardens of Mercyfields this wild untamed paradise was. How different the cottage was from the heavily ornate mansion she'd spent most of her childhood in. Kane's cottage was simple and functional but it seemed to her to have an atmosphere of tranquility about it, as if it was here and only here he could truly be himself.

She wasn't sure why he'd brought her here given his embittered views on her family. Why taint the perfection of his sanctuary with her presence, a woman he'd married as a pay-back for past sins?

She knew his anger towards her simmered just beneath the thin veneer of politeness he'd recently maintained; the slightest negative comment from her would lift it to the surface and he would become prickly and defensive all over again.

They had worked so well as a team on the beach rescuing the dolphin, her respect for him going up in leaps and bounds at the humane way in which he'd acted.

She had met few men in her life she felt she could truly respect. Her experiences with her controlling father had made her cautious, and the last thing she'd wanted to do was end up like her poor mother, married to a man who treated her appallingly, her love for him keeping her tied to him in spite of her great unhappiness. But it was becoming more and more clear to her that Kane had certain qualities her father had never possessed. His care and concern over her knee, the gentle way he'd tended to it and how he'd smiled at her and made her comfortable, were actions totally foreign to someone like her father, who viewed any sort of physical ailment as a weakness of both mind and body.

She sighed as she thought about how she'd spoilt the recent and fragile truce between them by mentioning the past; the old ruthless Kane had come back with a vengeance, storming from the cottage with an angry scowl.

The trouble was she wasn't sure she could afford to allow herself to get too close to him once this little spat blew over. He unsettled her in so many ways; her body had recognised it all those years ago and she knew that if she wasn't too careful her mind and heart would rapidly catch up. She was already confused about her see-sawing emotions; they seemed to be changing from one moment to the next.

Would she be able to keep him at a safe emotional distance long enough to prevent herself from falling in love with him...or was it already too late?

Kane walked the length of the lonely beach, relieved to see that the dolphin hadn't re-beached itself in the last hour or so. He was hopeful the injury it had sustained would soon heal in the salt water of the clean blue sea; however, he'd seen too many washed-up bodies in the past to take this particular rescue for granted. The irresponsible cruelty nauseated him, especially as it was so avoidable.

The wind was by now whipping up the surface of the bay into white caps and a lonely gull rose in an arc above his head, its plaintive call barely audible over the sound of the wind-driven surf.

Kane loved the untamed wildness of it all. It answered a need in him so deep and strong he felt it like a pulse in his body.

The constraints of city living were a necessity in order to control the vast empire he'd acquired but as soon as he had an opportunity to escape he took it. The isolation of this particular beach was like no other he'd ever seen. There was no development; even the road was unsealed and unsignposted, which left it well and truly off the tourist trail. It gave him a sense of power to think that this part of paradise was his to keep as it was, beautiful and as yet unspoilt, and he would do everything in his power to keep it that way.

His wealth was something he had never allowed himself to become complacent about, certainly given his youth spent at Mercyfields as the housekeeper's illegitimate son. Never had a day gone by without Austin or Owen Mercer reminding him of his lowly position. It still made his stomach crawl to think of all the things his mother had been made to do and, even though it had taken him ten years to address the balance, he was determined to enjoy every minute of bringing about the justice he knew would allow him to finally move on without the burden of guilt he'd been carrying ever since his mother had taken her own life.

Bryony was the only hiccup in his plan for revenge. It made him a little uneasy how he'd made her believe he'd swept her up into the maelstrom of his revenge, making her think the worst of him, when all the time he was hiding his real motives. There had been no other way; too much was at stake.

He could hardly tell her the real reason he'd insisted on her marrying him. He hadn't been prepared to risk her saying no. She was married to him and he was going to make sure she stayed that way because that was the only way to ensure her safety.

The men after Owen Mercer had nothing to lose; they wanted to get at him in any way possible and Bryony was an easy target. It had taken Kane several hours of tense negotiations to convince them to leave both Glenys and Bryony alone. His only way of keeping them safe had been to take Bryony as his wife. That way no one would touch her, for in doing so they would then have to deal directly with him. He had loved her for too long to stand back and watch someone use her as a way to get back at her father.

It was too late to back out now.

Far too late…

CHAPTER EIGHT

BRYONY limped out to the seaboard deck to watch as the sun began to set, unable to refrain from sighing at the remote beauty of the uninterrupted horizon as the light gradually faded.

The first star appeared and then another. Then, after another half an hour, the inky blackness of the sky was peppered with the peep-holes of a trillion stars. The great sweeping whiteness of the Milky Way spread above her, the twin smudges of the greater and lesser magellanic clouds close by. Never had she seen the sky in such glorious exhibition, it was like being inside an observatory, so brilliant was the display.

She hadn't heard the soft tread of Kane's footsteps coming up from the cliff path until the shadow of his tall figure loomed over her, making her gasp.

'Oh!' She gripped the railing of the deck to steady herself. 'You scared me.'

'Sorry.' His one word was gruff and her brow instantly furrowed. Was he apologizing for disturbing her or for something else? She inspected his features in the soft light coming from the cottage behind them but, as usual, it was hard to know exactly what he was thinking, much less what he was feeling.

She said the first thing that came to her mind. 'Did you see any sign of the dolphin?'

'No.' She heard his faint sigh of relief. 'I guess he's made it back to the rest of the pod.' He turned and leaned his back on the railing to face her, his face less shadowed as the light fell upon its masculine angles and planes. 'How's the knee?'

'Fine.' She tested it and disguised her grimace of pain. 'I'm sure it will be better in a day or two. It usually is.'

'You've had this happen before?'

She gave him a twisted and somewhat sheepish smile. 'Yes, but never from shifting a dolphin.'

'What happened the last time?'

'Well…' She slanted him a little glance of embarrassment before inspecting the night sky once more. 'The last time I hurt it I was doing my best to avoid the bride's bouquet at a wedding.'

'Oh?' There was a wealth of both interest and amusement in his tone.

She turned back to look at him. 'I put in a huge effort to avoid its flight path but it virtually landed in my lap as I stumbled over the leg of a chair.'

The line of his usually hard mouth had softened with a smile and she had to look away, pretending an avid interest in astronomy when all she could think of was the brilliance of his dark eyes and how they threatened to outdo the splendour above her head.

'Is that a satellite?' She pointed to a moving light making its way across the canopy.

He turned and looked upwards. 'Yes, there are hundreds out there.'

'The stars are amazing…' She let the silence of the night take over her paltry attempts to make conversation, her awareness of him increasing with every heartbeat.

After a while she heard him lean back against the railing and, sending a glance his way, saw that his dark gaze was still trained on her.

'You never intended to get married, did you?' he asked.

She pressed her lips together before answering flatly, 'No.'

'Because of your parents?'

'What do you mean?' She looked back up at the Milky Way so as to avoid the penetration of his stare.

She heard the slight rustle of his clothes as he shifted position.

'The way I see it, the only thing keeping your mother tied to your father is guilt.'

Bryony frowned into the darkness. 'My mother loves my father.'

'Poor misguided fool.'

His tone brought her head around, her frown deepening. 'My mother took her wedding vows very seriously. She's…loyal and—'

'She should have left him years ago.'

As much as Bryony was finding the topic of her parents' marriage distinctly uncomfortable, she was intrigued as to why he would consider it his place to even discuss it, particularly with her.

'You seem to me to be a highly unusual person to be an authority on marriage. After all, you had to bribe me into being your bride.'

'I don't deny the circumstances surrounding our marriage are unusual and to some degree regrettable but—'

She rounded on him crossly. '*Unusual? Regrettable?* If you're having seconds thoughts on, what is it, day two of our marriage, can you possibly imagine how I feel?'

'I know you hate being tied to me, but that's the way it is and that's the way it's going to stay for the time being.' His tone had hardened considerably.

'I can have the marriage annulled as soon as we return to Sydney,' she threatened.

The look he gave her was challenging. 'Then perhaps I should make sure that such a claim will be considered null and void.'

She tried to outstare him but felt sure he would see the

sudden and unexpected light of unruly desire in her eyes at his sexily drawled statement. She spun away and stared at Orion's Belt instead, her hands on the rail tight as she fought to control her reaction to him.

'You should be grateful I'm not quite the ruffian you've always assumed me to be. I could have had you from day one and we both know it,' he said into the suddenly stiff silence.

Bryony wanted to deny it but her skin was already tingling in awareness of him standing so close, the fine hairs on her bare arms lifting like antennae.

'You were hungry for me ten years ago,' he continued. 'The only reason you hit out at me was because you were angry at yourself for dallying with someone so beneath you. It wasn't quite what a Mercer should do, was it, Bryony? Allowing the housekeeper's son to kiss you and touch your breasts like some common little tart.'

She turned to defend herself but the dark intensity of his eyes immediately put her off course. The truth was that she still felt the shame of her reaction to his hard body all those years ago. She felt it now, the heat building up inside her looking for a way out. It burned in her breasts, it fired her mouth and it smouldered in her belly, sending a fiery trail to the core of her femininity where she most secretly longed and ached for him to be.

She stared at him for endless seconds as the heady realisation dawned. She didn't want him to think of her the way he thought of her family. She didn't want him to think her an arrogant snob who had always looked down her nose at him. She wanted him to love her as she had grown to love him.

How had it happened? How had her hatred turned to such desperate longing?

It wasn't as if he'd turned on the charm; in fact, he'd done the opposite. He hadn't complimented her nor courted her with flowers and jewellery as other men would have done. Instead he had charged into her life and demanded she marry him on his terms and his terms only.

But even still she had fallen in love with him.

She looked into his dark eyes and swallowed. At what point had her heart betrayed her? Had it been when he'd rescued the dolphin? Or perhaps it had been when he'd tended to her knee, his touch gentle and sure. Or maybe it went back much further than that…maybe it had been in the cool shadows of the lake ten years ago when his mouth had first covered hers.

The irony of it was inescapable. She was in exactly the same position as her mother—the position she'd sworn all her life she would never allow herself to be in—she was in love with a man who didn't love her.

A light playful breeze picked up a strand of Bryony's hair and blew it across her mouth but before she could brush it away Kane's hand reached out and carefully tucked it behind her ear, the brush of his fingers making her quiver with reaction.

'But we're equals now, *agape mou*,' he said, the low tone of his voice stroking her senses into instant overdrive. 'And very soon we will become lovers.'

She ran her tongue over her dry lips and watched in nervous anticipation as he followed the movement with his eyes. His hand moved to cup the side of her face in a caress so unexpectedly gentle her heart felt as if someone had just reached into her chest and squeezed it.

His thumb rolled over her bottom lip, his eyes holding hers in a mesmerizing trance. She saw the raw need reflected in his darker-than-night gaze—felt too the magnetic pull of his body, the heat of it drawing her closer and closer. She lifted her right hand and gently touched the dark shadow forming along his lean jaw, the sound of the soft pads of her fingers moving across his unshaven skin audible in the stillness of the night.

'Do you still hate me, Kane?' She spoke the words before she could stop them, her voice just a whisper of sound.

'Is that important to you, Bryony?' he asked after a small pause.

'I...I don't want you to hate me...' She captured her bottom lip with her teeth, her hand falling back to her side.

Kane used his thumb to gently prise her mouth open so her lip could escape the snag of her teeth, the action so achingly intimate her stomach began to crawl with hot desire.

'You'll make yourself bleed doing that,' he chided her softly.

She tried a little smile but it didn't quite work. Her eyes went back to his mouth, her breath hitching when she saw his head come down, his mouth stopping just above hers, his warm breath feathering against the too sensitive surface of her lips.

'I won't hurt you, Bryony. I want you to know that.'

She closed her eyes on his kiss, the movement of his lips unhurried and exquisitely gentle. Her mouth flowered open as soon as his pressure increased, her stomach hollowing when his tongue searched for and found hers. Heat fired through her limbs as he brought her up against his aroused body, the probe of his erection a stark but heady reminder of his potency and her own melting need. She could feel it between her thighs, the silky moisture triggered by the sensual movement of his mouth on hers and the intimate probe of his slow-moving tongue as it called hers into a primal dance.

After a few breathless minutes he lifted his head a fraction, his eyes burning a pathway to her soul.

'Let's go inside.'

He released her to open the sliding screen door of the

cottage and she stepped through on unsteady legs, her skin shivering in reaction as he slid the door closed behind him.

'Come here.'

His single command made her flesh tingle with the anticipation of his touch and she stepped towards him, her face up-tilted to his, her heart thumping against the wall of her chest at the promise in his eyes.

His lips met hers in a blaze of heat that left no part of her untouched by its intensity. She felt the soft tug of his teeth on her bottom lip and boldly nipped him back, her tongue responding to the thrust of his as it entered her mouth, circling it, commandeering it, conquering it.

His body was hard against hers, making her melt even further as she realised how instant and strong his desire for her was. She wanted the evidence of it imprinted on her tender flesh. She ached to feel the abrasion of his male skin on hers, the bunching of his sculptured muscles as he held her close.

She heard him suck in a harsh breath before his mouth covered hers once more, this time with even less restraint as his rigid control finally slipped out of his grasp. His tongue unfolded over hers, the heat and purpose of his embrace leaving her breathless.

Kane lifted her in his arms, his mouth still locked to hers as he carried her to the bedroom upstairs, each and every one of his footsteps making her feel as if he was taking her closer and closer to the fulfilment she had craved for so long.

He broke his kiss to lay her on the big bed, his dark eyes illuminated with passion as he stood back to haul his shirt from his body.

Bryony couldn't take her eyes off his muscled chest, the sheen of his skin making her want to touch him all over. She reached up her arms towards him and he came down to her, his weight pressing her down into the mattress.

She didn't give him the chance to change his mind. Her fingers went straight to the waistband of his jeans and slid the zip down with a determination fuelled by spiralling desire.

His black briefs were already straining with the extension of his erection and, as she unpeeled them from him, she felt her breath squeeze in the back of her throat at the thought of him possessing her.

She traced the length of him with exploring tentative fingers, the satin smoothness of his skin fascinating her, the tiny pearl of moisture beading on the tip reminding her that he was fighting to contain his release under the ministrations of her hands.

She looked up at him and saw that same battle raging on his face, his expression contorted with desire, his eyes neither open nor closed, his breathing rapid, his whole body tense.

She began to increase the pace of her stroking but he reached for her hand and, pulling it off him, secured it within his against the flattened pillows above her head.

'You don't play fair, *agape mou*.' Kane's warm breath caressed her lips. 'Is this what you really want from me?'

'I think you've always known this is what I've wanted from you.'

He examined her expression closely. 'I thought you said you had no intention of sleeping with me?'

She aimed her gaze at the tanned skin of his chest, her fingertip tracing a circuitous path around one dark nipple. 'I've changed my mind.'

She felt the full heat of his gaze as she lay in his embrace. Her limbs felt useless, as if they were disconnected from the stabilizing ligaments that kept them in place.

'What changed your mind?'

'I don't know...' She circled his other nipple. 'I guess I'm curious about you. You don't seem to be the person I thought you were.' She lifted her eyes back to his. 'I guess the only way I'm going to know the real you is to get close to you.'

Kane bent his head to kiss her, still trying to summon up the strength to set her away from him, but somehow the delicate probe of her tongue searching for his was his final undoing. There was a shy hesitancy about her movements which made them all the harder to resist. The feather-like touch of her hands as they roved over his back made his skin tighten with pleasure and he took control of the kiss with a deep groan against her mouth. He had planned to give her more time, hoping she would come to care for him before committing herself physically, but his self-control had limits and he was well and truly at the end of them now with her lying beneath him.

Bryony could feel every bulge and ridge of him against her, the latent strength of him so apparent that her stomach hollowed as she thought of him driving through her, wondering if she should have told him she wasn't quite the party girl he thought her to be. In the end she decided against telling him for the simple reason that she didn't want him to stop what he was doing.

His mouth had moved from hers to take a slow pathway to her lace-covered breast, his tongue like a hot taper along her sensitive flesh. Her T-shirt went over her head but later she couldn't recall which of them had removed it from her body; their hands seemed to be bumping into each other's in a desperate attempt to remove the final barriers between them.

She felt the heat of his gaze as her breasts were freed from the lacy bra, his lazy appraisal firing her up beyond belief. He made her feel so damn sexy! Just one look from beneath those dark brows and she was smoking inside and out.

He reached out a fingertip and circled one jutting nipple,

his touch so light it felt like a butterfly's wing brushing over her.

'I have wanted to do this for so long.' His tone was husky as he moved his finger to her other breast and feathered over her other nipple.

She writhed beneath his barely there touch, her eyes glazing with need.

'How long?' she managed to ask, her soft mouth releasing the words on a soft gasp of pleasure.

Kane's dark eyes seared hers. 'Too long.'

His answer secretly thrilled her. It made her feel a surge of pure feminine power that she had lit a flame in his body all those years ago which had never quite burned itself out.

He wanted her.

He'd always wanted her.

Yes, he had gone to extraordinary lengths to claim her but she didn't want to think about that now. Caught up in the moment as she was, the last thing she wanted to do was speculate on what exactly had been Kane's intention in marrying her. It was enough for now that he wanted her with a desperation that he was barely keeping contained. She felt it in the press of his large body on hers, the heat of his swollen erection burning against her thigh, the increasing pressure of his mouth as it returned to hers.

He peeled away the lace of her French knickers with a glide of his hand along her thigh, his mouth never once leaving hers. She felt his hand come back up to begin an intimate exploration which left her fighting for air. One long gentle finger divided her, pushing into her secret folds with devastating accuracy, sending sharp spurts of desire all through her quivering flesh. He withdrew his finger to cup her in the palm of his warm hand, his action so restrained she wondered if he sensed her inexperience. Had she been so transparent?

She made room for him between her legs, the feel of him

so close to her making her ache with a yawning emptiness. She felt the intimate nudge of his body before he checked himself with a softly muttered curse.

'What's wrong?' she asked softly, terrified he was going to call a halt.

He gave a rueful grimace and, reaching across her, opened the bedside drawer and removed the foil packet of a condom. She watched as he tore the packet open before sheathing himself, her stomach doing a crazy little somersault at the thought of him moving inside her unexplored tenderness.

He pressed her back down, his mouth just above hers, the mingling of their breaths intensifying the intimacy of the moment.

'I'll take it slowly,' he said softly. 'I don't want to hurt you.'

You could never hurt me, she wanted to say. How had she ever thought he was capable of cruelty? His touch was so poignantly gentle, almost worshipful. The holding back of his undoubtedly superior strength stirred her deeply, making her realise how much she had misjudged him in the past.

'Relax for me, Bryony,' he said against her lips, his turgid length parting her slowly.

How could she relax with her feelings spinning out of control? She wanted him to fill her, to surge into her moistness and claim her as his. He was taking too long; all her nerves were stretched to breaking point in anticipation of his possession, a possession she had craved so long it was like a dull ache in her soul. She wouldn't be complete until he made her his; she knew it as certainly as she knew her love for him would last a lifetime and beyond.

He kissed her softly and, impatient with need, she toyed with his bottom lip with her teeth. He deepened the kiss, crushing her mouth as he drove forwards with carefully measured control.

Bryony felt him begin to stretch her and she forced herself to relax enough to take him further, the sensation of him inside her making her greedy for more and more of his length. She lifted her hips to his and he went even deeper, the harsh groan that escaped from his lips sending a shiver of delight right through her.

She felt him check himself once more, fighting to maintain control as her body tightened around him as if made especially for him. She heard the Greek curse under his breath, as if finally giving in to the lure of her slick body, and he surged forward with one deep thrust that sent a shockwave of delight through every nerve and cell of her body.

He filled her completely, stretching her with increasing urgency as the pressure for release began to build with incessant force. Bryony felt the flicker of it along her inner thighs before it moved to the core of her where it pulsed heavily with every rapid beat of her heart. It was impossible to escape from the maelstrom of feeling his body was evoking in hers. Every nerve in her body seemed to be screaming for release from the delicious tension building within her.

'Let go, Bryony,' Kane urged as he orchestrated his movements to intensify her pleasure. 'Don't hold it back, let yourself go.'

She felt the rolling waves of release wash over her just as the rough surf had done earlier in the day, her high cries of pleasure not unlike the sound of a seabird rising on an up-draught of ocean-warmed air. She could even hear the roar of the sea in the distance and knew she would recall this first wondrous moment of fulfilment each and every time she set eyes on the surf in the future.

Kane waited until she had settled back in his embrace

before taking his own pleasure in four deep thrusts that sent him over the edge and into ecstasy's oblivion.

Bryony felt his deep spasms and secretly delighted in the agonized expression on his face as he finally allowed his control to slip, his deep guttural groan and the contortion of his features telling her more than words could ever do.

He collapsed on top of her, his breathing ragged and uneven. 'You have no idea how long I've waited for this moment.'

She smiled a secret smile. She knew all right, because she'd felt it too. She ran her fingertips up and down his arm, not quite sure she could meet his eyes right at this point.

It was a full minute before he spoke again.

'Look at me, Bryony.'

She lifted her eyes to his after a moment's deliberation. 'Thank you,' she said simply.

'For what?'

'You know what for.'

He reached out a hand and brushed a strand of hair out of her face with such gentleness she felt the wash of tears at the back of her eyes. The pad of his thumb caught one tear as it escaped and, pressing it to his lips, he kissed it before placing it on the soft tremble of hers.

'Did I hurt you?'

She gave a jagged sigh. 'No...not really.'

'I'm so much bigger than you.' His eyes went to her slight body, still trapped beneath the weight of his. 'And you were so inexperienced.'

She felt an inward cringe but hoped he wouldn't pick up on it. 'Was I so obvious?'

He coiled a strand of her hair around his index finger as if thinking about her question. He released the golden strand before he answered. 'I know you were determined to keep it under wraps but there's no shame in being selective over lovers, at least not in this day and age.'

She shifted her gaze to a small dark brown freckle near his left nipple, concentrating on it as if her life depended on it.

'Were you waiting for someone special?' he asked.

She gave what she hoped was an indifferent shrug. 'Not really...I just hadn't got around to it.'

'Too busy licking the floors?'

She felt the colour surge into her cheeks but smiled anyway. 'I don't really do that, you know.'

His answering smile did serious damage to the equilibrium she was trying to maintain.

'No, I sort of guessed that.'

A small silence settled like fine dust between them.

Bryony considered moving out of his loose embrace but was loath to do so. She liked the warmth of his body against hers, the smell of his skin, the feel of his long legs entwined with hers.

She tiptoed her fingertips up the length of his forearm, her eyes following the movement rather than lock with his once more.

'I didn't know it could be so...' She bit her lip momentarily. 'So...enthralling.'

'It depends on who you're with.'

She concentrated even harder on his freckle. 'Is it different with...someone else?'

He tipped up her chin so she had to meet his gaze. 'That was beyond anything I've ever experienced before.'

She couldn't help feeling reassured by his answer and hoped to God it was genuine and not one of the many lies men told to keep the peace.

She lowered her eyes to his mouth, unable to stop herself from staring at his scar. It was like her own personal signature slashed across his mouth and, no matter how many times she looked at it, each and every time she felt her stomach twist anew with shame and regret.

She lifted her fingertip and traced the rough edge, her heart squeezing painfully as she heard his quickly indrawn breath. Slowly she raised her gaze back to his, this time not even bothering to disguise the film of tears in her eyes.

'I wish I could make it go away.' Her voice was barely audible, her mouth trembling as she fought to hold back her emotions. 'I hate myself for what I did to you.'

'Listen, Bryony.' He tipped up her chin once more. 'This scar and I have been through a lot together. I wouldn't get rid of it even if I could.'

'But why?'

'Because every time I look at it I think of you at the lake, the way you felt in my arms. It's a small price to have paid for the memory.'

Bryony wasn't sure if he was teasing her or telling her the truth. His expression gave nothing away and, while his endearment had been delivered casually, it had been exactly that—casual. It didn't necessarily mean a thing. She wanted to convince herself he had loved her for all those years but it seemed too far-fetched to have any basis in reality, especially given the way he'd gone about demanding reparation for her family's part in his past.

She lowered her eyes and, with a barely audible sigh, leant her head against his sweat-slicked chest, her ear pressed to the deep thud of his heart. She closed her eyes as one of his hands began to stroke through the silky strands of her hair, wishing with all of her heart that she could stay like that for ever.

CHAPTER NINE

BRYONY opened her eyes some time later to find Kane's dark gaze trained on her, his arms still around her, his long legs entwined with hers.

She moistened her dry mouth as he moved against her intimately, the hot surge of his flesh against hers sparking a slow steady burn deep inside her.

She sighed as his hand slid up from her waist to shape her breast. His hand stilled its movements, his palm warm as it rested against her soft flesh.

Her thoughts went haywire as he bent his head, his tongue gently laving the tightness of her nipple. She buried her fingers in his dark hair and became lost in the glory of being in his arms, telling herself she would think about the future some other time, for now this was where she wanted to be. Maybe he didn't love her but he certainly desired her, and as long as he continued to do so, surely she had a chance to show him how much her feelings had changed?

She sighed again as he took her mouth beneath his, her slim arms coming around him, holding him to her, the soft tremble of her body against his propelling him to claim her without restraint, his harsh groan as he did so igniting her passion to new heights.

She felt herself being caught up in the rhythm of his deep stroking thrusts until her body sang with delight as every nerve stretched and tightened in search of release.

When he lifted her hips to intensify the contact of his hard body with her softness she tipped over the edge of reason into the free fall of heart-stopping ecstasy, the tremors of her body sending him on his own pathway to paradise. She felt him empty himself, the deep shudders of his large body reverberating along her much smaller one. Such physical closeness was mind-blowing to her. It seemed almost sacred and she wanted to hold the moment to store it away for private reflection.

Kane eased himself away from her and lay with his hand across his eyes, his chest moving up and down as his breathing gradually returned to normal.

Bryony lay in an agony of indecision. Should she tell him of how her feelings had changed or should she pretend things were as they had been before?

She took an unsteady breath and wished she had the courage to nestle up against him for reassurance. Apart from his obvious physical reaction, he seemed so unaffected by what had passed between them while her flesh was still tingling from his touch even as her heart was bursting with emotion.

In an effort to appear as unmoved as he, she eased herself off the bed and reached for a bathrobe with forced casualness, tying the knot at her waist as she turned back to face him.

'I'm going to have a shower,' she announced, releasing the curtain of her hair from the back of the bathrobe.

'Want some company?' His eyes flared with kindling desire.

'I think I'll be much quicker on my own,' she answered somewhat primly.

His deep chuckling laugh sent a riot of sensations through her tingling flesh. 'Have your shower, Bryony. I won't disturb you any more tonight.'

She moved towards the bathroom, not sure she wanted him to see just how deeply disturbed she was by his presence. Her body ached tenderly where he had been, her inner muscles protesting with each step she took.

'Bryony.'

His voice stalled her progression and she turned to look back at him propped up amongst the bank of pillows, his hands behind his head in a self-possessed manner, the thin sheet barely covering his arrant maleness.

'Yes?' Was that her voice, that tiny breathless whisper?

He looked at her thoughtfully without speaking.

Bryony felt her skin rise in goose-pimples at the undisguised heat in his gaze, as if he could see through the towelling fabric of the robe she was wearing. She unconsciously tightened the tie at her waist as his gaze ran over her, lingering on her mouth before returning to her face.

'It was always going to happen, you know.'

She looked at him uncertainly. 'What was?'

'You and me,' he said. 'It was only a matter of time.'

She turned back to the bathroom, unwilling to let him see the raw emotion she was feeling. Would she ever be able to look into those dark eyes without restraint? Would she have to disguise her love for him for years to come, never once revealing how deeply moved she was by his passion? How was she to negotiate such a future?

She turned on the shower and stepped under the spray, the fine hot needles stinging her flesh where a few minutes ago his mouth and hands had lingered. She sucked in a ragged breath as the water ran between her thighs, reminding her anew of his possession and the unerring gentleness of how he'd introduced her to his length. How had she thought him a barbarian for all those years? His touch had been almost reverent as he'd led her to paradise, his patience with her inexperience moving her to tears.

She closed her eyes and tried to envisage a future where they could both have what they wanted but it seemed impossible. Kane had wanted revenge and had sought it ruthlessly, taking everything away from her parents, including her. For her to love him so unreservedly seemed to be somewhat traitorous to Austin's memory and tantamount to treason where her father and mother were concerned. How could she have it both ways? Wouldn't she always have to choose between them and her own happiness?

When she came back to the bedroom Kane appeared to be sleeping, his long body taking up more than his fair share of the bed. Bryony hesitated beside the bed, wondering if he would notice if she slipped off to the spare room.

'Don't even think about it,' he rumbled without even opening his eyes, his hand holding open the sheets for her.

With just the slightest hesitation she eased herself in beside his warm frame, her breath tightening as his arms came around her to draw her into the hard wall of his chest, his long legs entwining with hers.

'Comfy?' His breath tickled the back of her neck as he spoke.

Bryony suppressed a shiver as his palm came to rest on her belly, his fingers splayed possessively against her quivering flesh.

She lay stiffly, not willing to move in case she betrayed her growing need of him. The masculine hair on his chest tickled her, his stirring erection tormented her and his warm breath on her shoulder tantalized her until she could barely think.

'Relax.' His tone held a trace of amusement as he tucked her closer against him. 'You're as stiff as a board.'

Her eyes widened as his hard male presence slipped between her legs, the heat and length of him almost burning her soft skin where it pressed so insistently.

'I could say the very same about you,' she gasped as his fingers moved a fraction lower.

She felt his rumble of laughter all along the sensitive skin of her back where it was pressed up against him.

'Go to sleep, *agape mou*.' His lips kissed the smooth skin of her shoulder. 'I think you've had quite enough of me for one night.'

She closed her eyes and tried to make her muscles relax but it became increasingly impossible to ignore him. Her body began to pulse with need, her legs trembling where he lay between them, his hardness against her softness reminding her of all of the essential differences between them.

She listened as his breathing evened out, holding her own breath in case she alerted him to her unease, unwilling to reveal how much he unsettled her.

Just when she thought she could stand it no more she felt him move behind her, his hands coming to her shoulders, turning her over so she was lying half beneath him, his chest pressing against her tight breasts where they lay aching for his touch beneath the simple cotton of her nightgown.

The moonlight coming in from the windows cast his features in silver, the white line of his scar clearly visible as he looked down at her with eyes smouldering with desire.

'Is this what you're after?' he asked, slipping into her warmth as her legs made room for him between them, her nightgown bunched up around her waist in wanton abandon.

Her choked 'yes' was swallowed by the descent of his mouth and her arms came around his neck to hold him to her as his body delved into hers for the release they both craved. She felt herself climbing towards it, the delicious sensations coursing through her, rising to a crescendo inside her head until she was uncertain where her body ended and his began.

The tumultuous release was a revelation to her; she had never imagined her body to be capable of such intense feelings as she soared to the heights of ecstasy.

His pinnacle of pleasure echoed through her tender flesh, the heat and strength of him as he burst forth demonstrating how tenuous his control had been. It secretly delighted her that she could bring him to such a point. It showed him at his most vulnerable, lost to the sensation of intimate flesh on intimate flesh and skin on skin in the mind-blowing exchange of pleasure.

She nestled against him, her cheek pressed against the wall of his chest where his heart thudded, his arms loose around her but no less possessive.

She felt safe in a way she had never felt before.

She closed her eyes and breathed in the warm scent of his skin, her hands around him, holding him to her, her lips silently mouthing the words she didn't quite have the courage to say out loud: *I love you.*

Kane stared at the moonlight dancing on the ceiling above him, the soft weight of Bryony in his arms a burden he had waited years to bear. His body still throbbed with the echo of pleasure, his heart tightening at the realisation of his need for her to fill his life in every way imaginable.

For years he had scoffed at the notion of love, fighting against being ensnared by such a confining emotion which could only leave him as vulnerable as his mother had been. He'd had affairs that had touched his body but not his heart and he had turned away from them with few regrets.

He glanced down at the sleeping woman in his arms, her soft mouth pressed against his chest, her slight body warm from the intimate embrace of his.

He slid his hand down the smooth silk of her arm, his mouth softening as he recalled the way she had responded to him. He hadn't been expecting innocence but it had delighted him all the same, making him feel as if she had been waiting for him all those years.

He felt her shift against him, her arms tightening around his waist, the soft murmur of something unintelligible leaving the soft shield of her lips as she burrowed even closer.

His hand went to the gloss of her hair, his fingers threading through the silky strands as if willing them to bind her to him.

He heard her sigh as she snuggled against him, her guard well and truly down now she was asleep.

He lowered his chin to the top of her head, closing his eyes as he breathed in the flowery scent of her hair, the fragrance of her skin, the touch of her hands where they lay against him like a soothing balm on the rough edges of his tortured soul…

CHAPTER TEN

BRYONY woke to the sound of the surf pounding the shore, a stiff breeze stirring the waves, the white caps of foam galloping across the surface of the bay like a thousand horses.

She turned from the window as the bedroom door opened, unconsciously clutching the edges of a bathrobe around her naked body as Kane's dark eyes met hers.

'How did you sleep?' he asked.

Bryony found it hard to hold his gaze as a vision of their passion-driven bodies flitted unbidden into her mind. In the cold hard light of morning her actions of the night before seemed totally out of character and inconsistent with her earlier determination to keep well away from him, marriage or no marriage.

It appalled her that she had fallen into his arms so unguardedly, practically confessing her love for him while he was no doubt congratulating himself on finally achieving his despicable ends.

How he must be gloating with victory! He had taken everything off her father and to add to his considerable haul she had unthinkingly given him that which she had offered no other man.

She could see the light of triumph in his eyes as they ran over her possessively and she inwardly seethed.

Shame sharpened her tongue and injured pride brought daggers to her eyes as she faced him.

'It was wrong of you to take advantage of me last night. You know very well I wasn't ready to make that sort of commitment. It was nothing less than barbarous of you.'

His expression instantly tightened, his eyes darkening as they narrowed slightly.

'I only took what was on offer, *agape mou*,' he drawled. 'And, as for not being ready—' his lazy gaze dipped to her pelvis and back '—you were so very wet and—'

'No!' Bryony clamped her hands over her ears so she didn't have to hear her shame spoken out loud. 'That's not true! I didn't want you. I don't want you. I hate you.'

Kane held her defiant glare. 'We are married, Bryony, and now we are lovers. There's no going back.'

'Find yourself another sexual plaything,' she tossed at him heatedly. 'Have all the affairs you like. See if I care.'

'You know you are far more like your mother than you realize,' he said after a telling little pause.

Something in his tone unnerved her, making her autocratic demeanour slip a fraction. 'W-why do you say that?'

'Your mother has consistently turned a blind eye to your father's affairs for years.'

Bryony's mouth fell open and it was a full thirty seconds before she could locate her voice. 'My father's…*affairs*?'

He gave her a scathing look. 'You surely don't expect me to believe you didn't know?'

She gave a convulsive swallow. 'I…I had no idea…'

'Oh, come on now, Bryony.' His tone was now impatient. 'Isn't this taking family loyalty a little too far?'

'I know my father isn't perfect…'

'He's far from perfect, in fact, I'd call him more of a pervert.'

She reared back as if he'd struck her. 'You can't possibly mean that.'

'You should know me well enough by now to know I mean what I say. Anyway, why are you so keen to defend him?'

'He's my father…'

'So, no matter what evidence there is, you will continue

to take his side, even though your gut feeling tells you differently?'

'You know nothing of my feelings.'

'I know you love your mother and at least we have that in common,' he said. 'I loved my own, even though I thought she was a fool to put up with what she did.'

'My mother loves my father…' she stated for the sake of something to say, even though to this day she had never really understood her mother's continued devotion to a man who treated her so appallingly most of the time.

He gave her a long assessing look. 'Your mother hasn't been the only woman to love your father.'

Something in the intensity of his gaze held her transfixed. She felt as if she was on the cusp of something life-changing…as if he were about to dislodge every stable rampart she'd carefully constructed around her life to keep it as secure as possible under the constantly shifting circumstances.

'His…affairs do you mean?' she ventured.

'One in particular springs to mind.'

'Which one?'

He held her gaze for an interminable pause. 'The one he had with my mother.'

The words fell into the room like the boom of a firecracker exploding. Bryony felt herself clutching at the chest of drawers behind her to anchor herself against the shock of his revelation, her thoughts flying around her head, trying to find a foothold to steady herself against the gut-wrenching realisation that what he had just revealed was in all probability true.

But Kane's mother?

'Your…your mother?' she gasped. 'My father had an affair with your mother?'

The look he gave her was filled with hatred but somehow

she knew it wasn't directed at her. 'Your father wanted value for his money and he made damn sure he got it.'

She swallowed the lump of bile in her throat. 'What do you mean?'

His eyes were like burning coals as they held hers. 'Why do you think he offered to pay for me to go to the same private school as your brother?'

Bryony felt as if the floor had moved beneath her so great was her shock. She opened and closed her mouth but no sound came out of her strangled throat.

'He struck up a deal with my mother,' Kane continued grimly. 'He offered to foot my educational bills in return for her sexual favours. My mother agreed to it because she loved me and wanted me to have what she couldn't give me, having been rejected by her family for having a child out of wedlock. She also agreed to it because she believed Owen genuinely loved her. That, of course, was her biggest mistake.'

'How…how long did…they…?' she could barely get the words out, so great was her distress.

'Their affair went on for years. I knew nothing of it until the day you saw me waiting outside your father's study. I decided to find out if the rumour I'd heard was true.'

She stared at him as awareness gradually dawned. 'That's why you wrecked the lawn and the roses, wasn't it?'

'I wanted to put that bloody tractor right through the house but you were inside and…' He cleared his throat and continued, his tone harsher than ever. 'Your father always prided himself on the immaculate condition of the garden and lawn. I guess it was the first thing I thought of in that initial moment of blind fury. I wanted to make that garden as dirty and chopped up as I felt inside for having received the financial benefits of my mother's sacrifices to your father's demands.'

'I...I don't know what to say...' She felt the sting of tears and blinked them back. 'I feel so ashamed...'

'You have no need to be,' he said. 'I sought my revenge against your father and succeeded.'

'Your...your mother's...suicide...' She took an unsteady breath before continuing. 'She did it because of my father, didn't she?'

He gave a single nod. 'When I was taken away by the police she begged him to pay for my bail so I wouldn't have to go to prison. Of course he refused and sacked her both professionally and personally within minutes of my eviction. She took her life a few months later, before I could help her deal with her shame and guilt. I found a journal she'd kept; it filled in the parts I hadn't known about. She was devastated by his rejection, not to mention deeply ashamed of me being incarcerated. She had no money to fight for my case legally, so in the end it all became too much for her.'

Bryony found it difficult to take it all in. Her brain felt as if it had been clamped between two book-ends with great force and her eyes ached with the pressure of welling tears.

'I think I'm starting to see why you demanded marriage,' she said. 'Ravaged lawns and gardens aside, it was the perfect way to twist the knife in my father's gut.'

He didn't respond, which frustrated her no end.

'That is why you did it, wasn't it, Kane? You wanted to rub his nose in the fact that his lover's bastard son had got the lot in the end, including his daughter. It wasn't enough that you'd swept his assets from under him, you had to take me hostage too.'

'I felt it appropriate at the time,' he answered.

'Appropriate?' She all but gaped at him. 'Haven't you ever heard of the saying two wrongs never made a right? You got my father back, my mother too, although I have no idea what she ever did to you to incur your wrath. As for my brother, I realise you both couldn't stand the sight of each other. And, as for me...' She did her best not to let her gaze dip to his mouth but she felt the magnetic pull and finally had to give in to it. She gave a ragged little sigh as she stared at the hard line of his damaged lip. 'I...I just wish you could have left me out of it...'

His hands came back to her shoulders, holding her so she had to look up at him once more.

'I could never have left you out of it. You were part of it from day one.'

Bryony knew tears were tracking twin pathways down her cheeks as she held his forceful gaze but she was beyond disguising her pain.

'You make me sound like some item you've had your eye on in a shop somewhere for years; do you have any idea how that makes me feel?'

'Would you have ever considered entering into a relationship with me without me forcing you into it?' he asked her roughly.

His question surprised her into silence.

She tried to imagine what it might have been like to have met as two adults without the history of their diverse backgrounds coming between them, but it was almost impossible to think of her father ever agreeing to her associating with anyone like Kane. Owen Mercer was unashamedly racist and had always made it clear she was never to date outside the white Anglo-Saxon boundaries he'd laid down. Kane's half-Greek heritage would have caused the first stumbling block and his class the second.

Kane's gaze released hers as he stepped away from her. 'I guess that's my answer then,' he said. 'You're a Mercer after all, born and bred to always believe yourself above the rest of the human race.'

'I don't think like that any more, Kane.' She brushed at her face with her hand. 'I know I was an appalling little bitch to you before, but I'm not like that now; surely you can see that?'

He turned and looked at her, his expression impossible to read. 'What's happened, Bryony? Have you suddenly decided you don't hate me any more now that you know the truth about your father?'

Bryony held herself very still, her breathing coming to a stumbling halt.

'Your father was the same. He couldn't stand the sight of me until I showed him my bank balance. Then he couldn't wait for me to be his son-in-law.' He stepped towards her, tipping up her chin so she had no choice but to meet his diamond-sharp gaze. 'Be sure of one thing. I will have you whether you love me or hate me. It makes no difference to me.'

Bryony pulled away, her heart thudding in reaction to the steely purpose in his tone.

'As far as I can tell, the only emotion you ever allow yourself to feel is hate; you have no room in your life for love, even if by some miracle I had changed my mind,' she said through tight lips.

'If I believed it to be a genuine emotion I would make room for it. I watched my mother prostitute herself for love; is it any wonder I no longer trust the concept?'

'But aren't you asking the same of me that my father asked of your mother?' she demanded. 'You're using me just as he did your mother.'

'I am not using you, Bryony,' he insisted. 'Unlike your father, I have at least given you the security and respectability of marriage. You came to me willingly last night and you will again. You don't want to admit it due to your stubborn Mercer pride, but you want me even though you say you hate me. I knew it ten years ago and so did your brother and your father but they did everything they could to sabotage any chance of a relationship between us.'

'But you only want me out of revenge and spite! What sort of basis for marriage is that? How long do you expect it to continue?'

'I've told you before: our marriage will continue indefinitely, for even now, as a result of our lovemaking last night, you may well be carrying my child.'

Bryony's blood chilled as she recalled the second and third time she'd received his hard male body during the night. She could still feel the sexy silk of him between her legs, the intoxicating scent of their combined passion one of the first things she'd noticed on waking.

Had he planned it? Had he planned to ensnare her even further into his complicated web of revenge by neglecting to use protection in order to tie her to him indefinitely?

The years stretched ahead of her, long lonely years filled with the misery of the emotional emaciation her mother had suffered, the continued cold indifference of her husband turning her life into a wasteland of lost opportunities and unfulfilled dreams while her children watched on in silent tortured anguish.

'I suppose this was all part of your plan?' Her eyes cut to his with bitterness. 'You have orchestrated this so I have no way out.'

'I did not really intend to put you at risk of pregnancy so early in our relationship but last night I could think of nothing but having you in my arms at last.'

From any other man she might have been mollified by such a confession but, coming from Kane, she felt angry instead. He'd made no secret of his desire for her, a desire that had been smouldering for ten long years, steadily stoked by hatred and bitterness until he could finally make his move.

'I don't know how you can sleep at night,' she said. 'You are no better than my father, using people for your own ends with no regard for their feelings.'

'You have indeed a right to be angry, Bryony, but it is misdirected while it is aimed at me. I am not interested in exploiting you for my own ends. I only want what is best for you.'

She threw him a caustic look, her tone dripping with sarcasm. 'I suppose you think I should be grateful for being selected for the highly esteemed position of your wife?'

He didn't answer but she could see the tightening of his lean jaw as if he was trying to be patient with her in the face of her taunt.

She stalked across the room to stand just in front of him, her finger stabbing at his chest, her eyes flashing with fury.

'You might have forced me into marriage but I won't allow you to crush me the way my father did my mother. I would rather kill myself, do you hear me?'

He held her fiery look for so long she began to feel a little foolish standing there, her body far too close to his, the deep thud of his heart pushing against the sensitive pad of her finger.

Just when she thought she could stand it no longer he suddenly cupped her face in his hands and dropped a swift hard kiss to her mouth.

He stepped back from her and left the room without another word, the door swinging shut with a soft click behind him.

Bryony lifted the finger that had read his heartbeat to the trembling curve of her mouth and wondered how she could both love and hate him at the same time.

CHAPTER ELEVEN

THE sun was warm and the breeze light as Bryony made her way down to the beach an hour later. Her knee stood up to the journey, her limp easing off enough so she could walk almost normally once she was off the slope of the cliff path.

She placed her towel on the sand and sat with up-bent knees as she watched the surf, the earlier white caps flattened out now the breeze had dropped.

She could see Kane swimming in the distance, well beyond the breakers, the sun glistening on his back as he made his way along the length of the beach, his easy relaxed style demonstrating his superb physical fitness.

She couldn't help thinking of her brother's slighter build, his tendency for sunburn and his aversion for all things to do with the water as a result. Her father, too, was no fan of regular exercise and now in his sixties was showing the excesses of his earlier years, even the flight of stairs at Mercyfields drawing heavy breaths from his lungs.

Somehow Bryony couldn't imagine Kane ever allowing himself to get out of shape. It was part of his magnetic power; the sculptured muscles and toned limbs spoke of discipline and self-control, something she knew her family had demonstrated very little of over the years.

She squinted against the sunlight as she followed Kane's progress, her heart doing a crazy little lurch as she saw the surface of the water swirling a few metres behind him. She frowned as she got to her feet, shading her eyes from the glare as she tried to make out what was following him as he swam. She caught sight of a dorsal fin and her heart rammed against the wall of her chest in panic. They were on an isolated beach. If he were to be attacked by a shark she hadn't a hope of getting him out of the water and up the cliff path to help and safety.

She cried out to him but he was swimming on with his head down, only turning every fourth stroke or so for air, the swell of the wave between him and the shore interrupting his view of her frantic waving.

She bit her lip as the fin disappeared. She imagined the grey body sneaking up on him, the lethal jaws wide, hungry for blood.

'*No!*' She was running through the waves towards him, throwing her arms about as she shouted at the top of her voice. 'Get out, Kane! Get out of the water! Sharks! *Sharks!*'

It was no good. He was still swimming, totally oblivious to the imminent danger he was in.

Bryony ran through the shallows until she was closer to him and, throwing all caution aside, ploughed ungainly through the waves to deeper water, her lungs almost bursting as she screamed for him to look around.

She trod water for a moment, trying to locate the shark, and didn't see the wave until it was on top of her, rolling her over, the downward pressure of the sheer weight of water as it broke sending her face first to the sandy bottom with an aspiration of water not air trapping her lungs into immobility. She clawed at the sand to anchor herself but another wave followed the previous one and sent her along her nose through the shelly sand.

She was out of air and at least one and a half times her height below the surface, the tumultuous waves still rolling in leaving her little time to scramble to the surface.

Her chest grew tighter and tighter and panic sent white spots of alarm through her line of vision as her body cried out for oxygen.

With a strength she had no idea she possessed she spotted the surface and aimed for it, her limbs feeling like lead weights as the need for air clawed at her. She could see the sunlight on the surface and tried to reach it, but the weight of the water kept dragging at her, pulling her down as if with invisible clutching fingers…

Kane stopped swimming and, as he trod water, flicked the hair out of his eyes and looked towards the towel where Bryony had been sitting. He'd seen her come down to the beach a few minutes earlier, her red and white bikini showing off her figure even though she'd tied a sarong around her waist, no doubt to shield it from his hungry eyes.

She was gone.

He looked right along the shore but she was nowhere in sight. He turned to inspect the water and caught sight of the pod of dolphins as they drew close and circled him.

Even though he'd done it many times before, each time he swam with them he felt like laughing right out loud in sheer joy. Their tentative friendliness thrilled him, especially as their contact with humans was so limited in such an isolated place. He ducked beneath the pod to see if the injured dolphin had rejoined them but in amongst the swirl of silver streamlined bodies he caught sight of flowing blonde hair and pale, lifeless limbs a few metres away.

The hammer blow of dread hit him in the chest as he surfaced and, taking a deep breath of air, he dived back down and scooped Bryony off the sandy bottom and took her to the surface.

'Bryony!' He brushed the hair out of her pallid face as his hand sought her wrist to check her pulse. She wasn't breathing as far as he could tell and, fighting down his fear, he towed her out of the deep water, half carrying, half dragging her to the strip of sand.

He fell on his knees beside her but before he could begin

CPR she gave a gurgling groan and, turning her head, sent the contents of her stomach into his lap.

'Bryony!' He settled her into the recovery position and waited for her to empty the rest of her stomach, the tortured heaving gulps making him wince in empathy.

'All done?' He frowned down at her, his hand at her temple gentle as it brushed a wayward strand of hair away.

She nodded and fell back against the sand. 'Sh-sharks…' she gasped. 'There…were…sharks following you…'

He frowned. 'You came out to warn me of sharks?'

She nodded and wiped at her streaming nose with the back of her shaking hand. 'They…they were following you. I…I had to do something or you would—'

'Dolphins.'

'—be killed and…w-what?' She opened her eyes fully and stared at him.

'Dolphins, Bryony. They were dolphins, not sharks.'

'But…but the fin…it was huge. It was right behind you.'

'I've swum with them heaps of times. They often follow me.'

Bryony felt foolish, pathetic and very, very sick. She shut her eyes and stifled a groan of shame as she thought about her screaming passage through the water, almost killing herself in her attempt to save someone who was in absolutely no danger.

'You were very brave to come into the water if you thought I was being stalked by sharks.'

'I-I had to do something.'

'You could have let them eat me. I'm fully insured, so just think of how wealthy you would be. Mercyfields and my millions; what more could a girl want?'

Bryony opened one eye and glared at him for his insensitivity. 'It might have escaped your notice, but I'm not really feeling up to your sick jokes right now.'

'It's true though, isn't it?' He fielded her icy glare with

a challenging look of his own. 'You didn't have any need to rescue me, certainly given the terms of our relationship. Why did you do it?'

'I had nothing better to do.' She closed her eye and turned away.

'That's not an answer and you know it.'

'I can't stand the sight of blood,' she said. 'I didn't want to have to carry whatever limbs were left over back up that path for the mortician to classify.'

'Charming.'

'You asked for it.'

'Come on.' He got to his feet and offered her his hand. 'We'd better have a rinse off before we go up to the house.'

She took his hand and got to her feet unsteadily, a wave of embarrassment washing over her when her gaze fell upon his thighs, where most of her breakfast had landed.

He saw the pathway of her vision and smiled. 'You can anoint me with whatever bodily fluids you like. I can handle it.'

She spun away from him and strode somewhat shakily to the shallows where she washed her face, all the time conscious of him a few feet away as he performed his own rough ablutions.

They made their way back to her towel in silence. Bryony was relieved. She felt every type of fool for blundering into danger without thinking. The drowning toll was in no need of any bolstering by her but she had truly panicked at the thought of losing him and had acted on impulse instead of clear rational thought.

'Don't be so hard on yourself, Bryony,' Kane said as he pushed open the cottage door for her to go in a few minutes later. 'To tell you the truth, I'm really touched that you put yourself in danger for me. Remarkable when you think about it, considering the depth of your loathing for me.'

She compressed her lips to stop herself from responding to his teasing taunt.

'Maybe you don't hate me as much as you thought,' he added when she didn't speak.

'Don't hold your breath.'

He laughed at her stiffly delivered retort, her previously pale cheeks now bright with heightened colour. 'Now, now, *agape mou*,' he chided. 'Don't be angry at me. I just saved your life.'

She slammed the door on his chuckle of laughter and, turning the shower on full, stepped under it and promptly burst into tears.

Bryony avoided him for the rest of the day. She pretended to be sleeping when he came to her room some time later, not sure she wanted him to see her reddened eyes and blotchy skin.

At six p.m. he knocked on her door again and informed her that he was preparing dinner. She mumbled something in reply and, dragging herself off the bed, sifted through her things and pulled out a sundress and small three-quarter sleeved cardigan for when the evening grew cooler.

She slipped her feet into low sandals and went to the mirror to inspect her face. She grimaced as she saw her reflection. Her eyes were shadowed as well as red-rimmed and her nose was grazed from her trip through the sand. She applied some concealer to it before brushing her lips with lip-gloss. She left her hair loose, hoping it would provide some sort of screen from his penetrating gaze.

He was waiting for her in the lounge, thrusting the paper he'd been reading to one side as he got to his feet.

'How are you feeling?' he asked.

'I'm fine.'

'You slept for ages; I was worried.'

'You had no need to be.'

'All the same you had a nasty shock. It can affect you for hours later.'

'As you can see, I've made a full recovery.'

He came closer and, bending down, inspected her nose. She had nowhere to look but into his eyes and her heart gave a sudden lurch as she saw the flicker of warmth smouldering there.

'Does that hurt?' He touched her nose so softly she wondered if she'd imagined it.

'N-no.'

His eyes held hers for a long moment.

'You've been crying.'

She lowered her eyes. 'No, I haven't.'

'Are you feeling unwell?'

She shook her head without looking up at him.

'Bryony.'

She tried to step away but his hands captured her shoulders, bringing her closer. She was surprised by the warmth of his gaze, the way it softened his features and loosened the tightness of his mouth into a relaxed smile.

'Why do you keep insisting on fighting this?'

'I don't know what you're talking about.' She struggled in his hold but he wouldn't release her.

'You are fighting yourself, Bryony, not me. I know you want me. We want each other and now there is no one to stop us from having what we both want.'

Bryony swallowed. He was right. She did want him. It didn't matter that he had engineered their marriage for his own ends, the truth was she'd always wanted him and his seemingly outrageous proposal had given her the perfect excuse to have him, even if it had been on his terms and his terms only.

She was enslaved by her love for him. She didn't want to think about a future without him. That was why she had put her own life at risk to save him. She just couldn't bear another ten years without him in her life. Ever since the day he had kissed her she had felt connected to him in the most elemental way. For years she'd told herself it was her guilt over the way she had damaged his lip, but deep down she had known it was much more than that.

Kane completed her in a way no one else could. She felt half alive without him, her body craving the weight of his glance, let alone his touch. She ached for him to love her but was prepared to settle for less if only she could be with him.

Kane's hands tightened on her shoulders as he looked down at her. 'Deny what's between us, Bryony, but it won't go away. You can hate me all you like but you can't hide the fact that you want me just as much as I want you.'

She didn't bother denying it. Her body was already tingling with awareness, her breasts tight and her mouth swelling in anticipation of the pressure of his. She held her breath as he lowered his head, the warm dry brush of his lips on hers making her ache for more. When his kiss deepened she responded to it with the heated fervour of her desire for him. His tongue lit a flame inside her mouth, sending sharp arrows of need to the molten core of her where a pulse was already throbbing in preparation for the hard glide of his body.

Kane pressed her backwards against the sofa, his hands sliding down her body as he shaped her towards him. Bryony felt each hard contour of him against her, the heat and purpose of his body fuelling her need for even closer contact.

He slipped her dress and bra out of the way and his warm palm covered her breast in a gentle caress that made her feel totally feminine. His thumb rolled over the tight bud of her nipple and she arched her back in response, her senses teetering totally out of control when he replaced his thumb with his mouth, the shadowed skin of his jaw scraping her tender flesh as he moved to her other breast.

He moved from her breasts to her stomach, his tongue darting in and out of the tiny cave of her belly button before moving even lower in a slow tantalizing pathway to where her feminine pulse had become a dull, insistent ache.

She sucked in a prickly breath as he separated her, tasting her with such exquisite tenderness she felt herself melting, the dew of her desire anointing her in anticipation of his hard male presence.

She clutched at his shoulders as he deepened his caress, her head flinging back as the tiny tremors became earthquakes in her bloodstream. She shook against his mouth, her body racked with such intense pleasure she wondered if she would survive it.

Her eyes opened to see Kane looking down at her, his dark eyes smouldering as he took in her pleasure-slaked form underneath his.

She gave him a little shy smile, not trusting herself to speak after such a physically enthralling moment.

He gave her an answering smile, the tiny lines at the corners of his eyes softening his appearance.

She held her breath as his hand cupped the side of her face, his long fingers warm against her skin.

'No regrets this time?' he asked softly.

She gave a small heartfelt sigh. 'No.'

'So you won't call me every type of barbarian for making love to you?'

'I'm sorry...' She bit her lip, her cheeks firing. 'I shouldn't have said that...I was feeling out of my depth...'

'You are beautiful, do you know that?' Kane's voice was low and husky.

His words made her glow inside with liquid warmth. Bryony wondered if he could see the way he made her feel. Surely there was some sign of it on her skin, where his mouth and hands had touched, or in her eyes, which had been ensnared by the burning heat of his?

Kane touched a fingertip to the soft bow of her mouth as he held her clear blue gaze.

'What are you thinking, little one?'

She moistened her lips with her tongue, her stomach rolling over when she saw the way his eyes followed the movement.

'That you make me feel so…' She struggled to find adequate words but the task momentarily defeated her.

'I make you feel what, Bryony?' he asked.

She held his probing look. 'I…I feel alive when I'm with you.'

His dark gaze intensified as it dipped to the soft bow of her mouth before moving back to her shining eyes.

His continued silence made her reckless, her need for reassurance overriding her inbuilt sense of pride.

'What about you?' she asked. 'What do I make you feel?'

The thick, slightly rough pad of his thumb traced a pattern on her bottom lip, the gentle movement causing Bryony's breath to catch. When the seconds ticked by she wondered if he was going to ignore her question but then he smiled and tilted her head for his descending kiss, stopping just above her mouth to murmur softly, 'How about I show you what you make me feel?'

'Fine by me,' she whispered as his mouth came down over hers.

CHAPTER TWELVE

BRYONY spent the next few days in a haze of sensuality as Kane lavished her with his undivided attention. She kept nudging her mind away from thoughts of the future in order to concentrate more fully on the here and now, content to be in his arms under the brilliance of the warm summer sun.

The fringe of sand on the beach had been their bed so many times she lost count, the intense pleasure she felt each and every time making her love for Kane grow and grow until it seemed to fill every part of her.

As to his feelings, she was none the wiser. He was an ardent and attentive lover and, while he was free and easy with the use of affectionate endearments, no words of love ever escaped his lips, even in the throes of ecstasy. She tried not to be disappointed but his emotional aloofness was at times deeply unsettling. While his lovemaking more than made up for any other shortcomings, she couldn't help feeling as each day unfolded into the next that she was on the same downward spiral as her mother, loving her husband so desperately while he remained untouched.

Bryony propped her chin on her up-bent knees where she sat on the beach, her eyes following Kane as he swam along the shore just beyond the breakers. The sunlight dappled the water and with every strong stroke of his arms she could see the myriad water droplets shining like diamonds as he progressed. The lonely cry of a gull and the hiss and suck of water were the only sounds she could hear, the isolation and solitude so soothing she almost dreaded returning to the city the following day.

Kane had informed her the previous evening of his need to see to some business matters as well as a trip to Melbourne which he could no longer postpone.

'Why don't you come with me?' he'd suggested.

Bryony had so wanted to accompany him but as she'd already been away from the studio for over a week she knew Pauline would be feeling the burden of taking her classes as well as her own.

'I really have to get back to work,' she'd said, trailing her fingers down the length of his arm to soften the blow. 'Maybe some other time?'

Kane had eased himself out of her arms and, although he'd smiled down at her, she'd known that somehow her answer had annoyed him.

'I'll hold you to that,' he'd said, stepping back into his jeans.

She'd watched him leave the room, the words to call him back hovering on her lips but at the last minute her courage had deserted her, leaving the words unsaid.

He'd made love to her later that night with an edge of ruthlessness that had both thrilled and terrified her, her responses to him reaching new heights. She'd clung to him, her nails scoring his back as he brought her time and time again to the high pinnacle of pleasure, her body rocking with his until she felt totally spent. She'd lain in his arms for hours later, unable to sleep, wondering how he could possibly remain unmoved by what had passed between them.

Bryony watched as he came towards her after his swim, his body tall and strong and deeply tanned after days under the summer sun. His dark hair was wet and falling across his eyes and he brushed it back as he lowered himself on the sand beside her, some droplets of water from his skin falling on her, reminding her of all the physical intimacies they'd shared in the last few days.

She ran her fingertips along the length of his arm, the corded muscles never ceasing to amaze her, the masculine hairs springy but soft to touch. She became aware of his gaze, the way it lingered on her mouth before slowly dipping to where her bikini top cradled her already aching breasts.

'Kane...' She gasped his name as his head came down towards her mouth, his arms either side of her effectively trapping her.

'We have less than twenty-four hours before we leave.' He spoke against the soft surface of her lips. 'How do you suggest we spend them?'

She sucked in a breath as his fingers moved to unfasten her bikini top, freeing her breasts into his waiting hands. Speech was almost beyond her as his head came down, his tongue rolling over her engorged nipple.

'What did you have in mind?'

'I was thinking we could do this...' He sucked on her breast for a heart-stopping moment before releasing her to smile at her. 'And then this...' One of his hands slid down her body to the moist heat of her femininity, delving deeply before withdrawing with agonizing slowness. 'What do you think?'

'I stopped thinking about thirty seconds ago,' she breathed as his finger dipped again, this time lingering over the tiny pearl that triggered her release. She shuddered as he coaxed her into a response that surprised her yet again, the waves of pleasure so consuming she had trouble keeping her head.

He waited for her pleasure to subside before he took his own with a series of deep thrusts that spoke of his control finally reaching its limits. She held him as he convulsed through his release, glorying in the feel of him so vulnerable in her arms, his breathing laboured and his skin slick with sweat as it rubbed intimately against hers.

The sting of the afternoon sun drove them indoors into a cooling shower where Kane held her against him as the water anointed their bodies, the sensuous feeling of soapy skin heightening Bryony's awareness of his maleness where he pressed against her.

He kissed her lingeringly, his hands cupping her face so tenderly she felt the prickle of tears at the back of her eyes. He lifted his head to look down at her, his mouth tilting at one corner as he saw her struggle to regain her composure.

'I hope those are tears of happiness,' he remarked wryly.

She smiled a watery smile. 'I never thought I'd be saying this, but yes, I am happy.'

He stood under the rain of water without responding, his dark eyes holding hers in a silent embrace which communicated much more than words could ever do.

Bryony felt the squeezing of her heart as she looked up into his face and wondered, not for the first time, how she had ever thought she hated him.

He kissed her again, softly and slowly, before reaching behind her to turn off the flow of water, his hard wet body brushing hers awakening every nerve along the surface of her tingling skin.

He took a towel from the rack and began drying her, each soft press of the fabric like a caress on her damp flesh.

'You have such an amazing body,' he said, lingering over the proud mound of one breast. 'Perfect in every way.'

Bryony drew in a prickling little breath as his thumb rolled over her nipple, wondering if she would ever be able to resist his touch. She hadn't been able to stop herself from responding to him the first time he'd kissed her at the lake, and now he'd awakened such fervent need in her she knew it would be impossible to withstand the lure of satisfaction in his arms.

Kane placed the towel around her back and, tugging gently on both ends, brought her close to him, his aroused length probing her with male insistence.

It was difficult to think clearly with him so near to where she wanted him, the heat of his body scoring hers like a laser beam. She slid her arms up around his neck and rubbed herself against him, shivering in reaction when his body surged into her moistness, his hips pressing hard against hers, his hand on the wall of the cubicle to anchor them both.

Bryony felt each and every deep thrust, bringing her closer and closer to the summit of sensuality, no part of her untouched by the impact of his masterful lovemaking.

She felt him check himself, pausing in his urgent movements as if he was fighting to control his response. It made her feel so desirable and feminine, making her hope he cared for her other than in a physical sense.

Kane groaned against her mouth, his large body tensing all over.

His deep shudders of release triggered her own, the convulsions of his flesh against hers intensifying her response a hundredfold. She couldn't hold back her high gasps of pleasure as the tumultuous waves flowed through her with breath-locking power.

She felt herself sag against him, her legs shaking with reaction at the devastation of her senses. His arms came around her, holding her to his still heaving chest, his face burrowed in the soft skin of her neck, his warm breath a sweet caress.

'You're still wet,' she said, running her hands down the silky texture of his back, her fingers skating lightly over the sculptured muscles.

He lifted his head, grinning at her as he reached for the shower nozzle, releasing a torrent of water over both of them.

'So are you,' he said and, before she could get her startled gasp past her lips, he bent his head and claimed her mouth in another drugging kiss.

On the way back to the city the next day Bryony tried not to think too much about Kane leaving the next morning for Melbourne, but the closer they got to his house in Edgecliff the tighter her chest felt at the thought of the separation.

As if sensing her pensive mood he flicked a glance her way as he waited for the last set of traffic lights to change in his favour. 'Why the long face?'

She gave him a soulful look. 'Do you really have to go tomorrow?'

His eyes held hers for so long an impatient driver tooted him from behind. Glancing in the rear vision mirror, Kane lifted his hand and drove on, his expression thoughtful.

'I did ask you to come with me,' he reminded her.

'I know…but the dance studio—'

'Employ someone to take your place,' he suggested. 'You don't have to work full-time now, anyway.'

'But I like working,' she said.

'You don't need the money. I have enough for both of us.'

'It's not about the money.'

'What is it about?' he asked, looking at her briefly. 'Your independence?'

'Is the notion offensive to you?' she asked with an arch of one brow.

He turned back to the traffic. 'I told you the terms of our marriage. I want you to be available to me, not distracted by the demands of a career.'

She twisted in her seat to stare at him. 'You surely don't mean it?'

'I thought over the past few weeks I'd given you every possible reason to believe I mean exactly everything I say.'

Bryony sat back in her seat in a combination of shock and sinking despair. Surely he didn't mean to keep her chained to the kitchen sink like some poor housewife out of the nineteen-fifties?

'My business demands are exacting and tiring,' he went on. 'When I need to relax I don't want to have to be cooling my heels waiting for you to be free.'

'I'm not a plaything you can pick up and put down when you feel like it! I have responsibilities to my students, not to mention Pauline.'

'Those responsibilities will now have to take a second place to me,' he insisted. 'Besides, when we begin a family I want my child to have a proper mother.'

'You're very good at saying what you want and don't want but have you for once considered what I might want?' she asked. 'As far as I recall, I've never indicated to you a desire to have a child.'

'From what I've observed, you have a nasty habit of cutting off your nose to spite your face,' he said. 'If you were honest with yourself you'd admit you want the same things as me. You crave stability and security, not to mention genuine affection, which one must assume comes from the dearth of such from your father.'

Even though he was as close to the truth as anyone could be, Bryony wasn't going to give him the satisfaction of confirming it.

'Am I to suppose that what you feel for me is genuine affection or rather some sort of animalistic need to spread your genes into a more blue-blooded pool?' Her tone dripped with derision.

'How like you to throw a verbal punch when someone gets a little close to the bone,' he said with a curl of his lip.

She tossed her head to stare fixedly at the front, silently fuming as he drove into his driveway, counting the seconds before she could exit the car away from his hateful presence.

The car purred to a stop and she wrenched open the door, slamming it behind her as she stomped to the house, rummaging in her bag for the set of keys he'd given her earlier. She located them and stabbed the right key into the lock, ignoring his command from behind her to stop.

As soon as the door opened a thousand sirens went off, the cacophony of sound so piercing that she dropped her bag and clamped her hands over her ears.

Kane strode over with a glowering look at her from beneath his dark brows and, punching in a code into the security panel inside the front door, turned to face her. 'Happy now?'

On a childish impulse that hadn't surfaced in years she poked her tongue out at him and brushed past to enter the house, grinding her teeth as the sound of his mocking laughter followed her up the stairs.

Bryony locked herself in the spare room for the rest of the night, trying to ignore her sense of pique that not once did Kane come to summon her out. When the clock finally dragged around to midnight she flung herself on the bed, certain she'd never sleep for the anger coursing through her veins, but somehow as soon as her head found the comfort of the feather pillow her eyelids drifted shut and, with a soft sigh, she dragged the sheet across her body and snuggled into the cushioning of the mattress...

When she came downstairs the next morning she found a short note propped up on the breakfast counter indicating that Kane had already left. Calling herself every type of fool for feeling disappointed, she tossed the piece of paper aside and made her way back upstairs to get ready for the studio.

When Bryony arrived Pauline was doing paperwork, her glasses perched on the end of her nose.

'Well, hello there,' she drawled in her best Marlene Dietrich voice. 'So how was the life in your man?'

Bryony forced herself to smile even though behind it her tooth enamel was being pulverized. 'Fine.'

'Only fine?' Pauline gave a mock frown.

She could feel her cheeks heating and turned to inspect some papers on the desk. 'Great, then; it was great.'

'That's better.' Pauline rolled her chair back under the desk. 'You had me worried. Anyway, I thought you weren't coming back till next week?'

'Kane had to fly interstate this morning,' she explained.

'You should have gone with him.'

'I didn't think it was fair to leave you on your own so long.'

'I'm a big girl, more's the pity.' Pauline grinned ruefully and patted her thighs. 'Anyway, I could have asked Gemma to do some of your classes. You know how keen she is.'

Bryony wished she'd thought of it earlier. Gemma was one of their senior girls who had often expressed a desire to teach the younger students.

'I'll give her a call some time,' she said.

Pauline gave her an intent look. 'Is everything all right?'

Bryony re-pasted her overly bright smile. 'Of course it is.'

Pauline pursed her lips and tapped the pen she was holding against the back of her other hand. 'You're missing him, aren't you?'

Bryony was about to deny it when she remembered that Pauline assumed along with everyone else that her marriage was a normal one. 'Yes...I do miss him.' She sighed, realizing it was perfectly true.

'Poor darling,' Pauline soothed. Then, giving her a wicked smile, she added, 'Just think about the second honeymoon when he gets back. You probably won't be able to walk for days.'

She turned away so Pauline couldn't see the way her face was aflame. Even now she could still feel her internal muscles protesting when she moved in a certain way, reminding her of the hard male presence that had stretched her to accommodate him.

'Your mother just phoned, by the way.' Pauline reached for a memo note on the desk in front of her, handing it to Bryony. 'She left a number for you to call.'

Bryony looked down at the piece of paper, her forehead creasing into a small frown. 'I wonder why she didn't call me on my mobile.'

'Is it turned on?' Pauline asked.

Bryony rummaged in her purse and grimaced as she saw the blank screen. 'It must have gone flat while I was…'

'Please!' Pauline covered her ears theatrically. 'Spare me the details, I'm far too innocent.'

Bryony couldn't help a gurgle of laughter at her friend's playful attitude. Her light-heartedness was just the tonic she needed.

'I'd better call Mum. Will you excuse me for a minute?'

Pauline got up and pushed the chair towards her. 'Go for it. I'm going to warm up. The little darlings will be here any minute.'

Bryony waited until Pauline was out of earshot before she dialled the number her mother had left. She held the receiver to her ear as the international beeps sounded, unconsciously holding her breath as she waited for it to connect.

Her mother answered on the third ring, her voice sounding panicky and strained. 'Bryony? Oh, thank God you've finally called.'

'Mum?' Bryony gripped the receiver tightly. 'What's wrong?'

She heard the sound of her mother's choked sob. 'It's your father…he's had a stroke.'

A tremor of shock rumbled through her as her mother's announcement sank in. 'When? How is he? How are you coping?' Her questions spilled out haphazardly, her thoughts tumbling over themselves in an effort to gain control.

'Last night…darling, it looks serious.' Another gulping sob accompanied Glenys's words. 'I don't know what to do!'

'Where is he? In hospital?' Bryony asked.

'Yes, but it's all so primitive over here on this island! The doctor doesn't really speak English and no one seems to care that your father is in a ward with several others. I can't bear it. I think I'll go mad if someone doesn't do something.'

'We'll have to arrange to fly him home,' Bryony said, keeping her voice calm and even to soothe her mother's distraught emotions. 'Have you contacted the Australian embassy?'

'There isn't even a hairdresser let alone an embassy on this wretched island,' Glenys cried. 'Besides, I don't want to leave your father's side in case he wakes up.'

'He's unconscious?' Bryony asked.

'He hasn't woken since he collapsed,' her mother informed her brokenly.

'Don't worry. I'll make the necessary arrangements if you give me all the details. Which island are you on?' She jotted down the information as her mother delivered it to her in tearful bursts. 'Now, sit tight and I'll call you as soon as I know anything.'

Bryony put down the phone with a trembling hand, wondering who she should call first. Before she could decide the telephone rang and she snatched it up, her voice cracking as she answered. 'H-hello?'

'Bryony?' Kane's deep voice sounded from the other end and a huge wave of relief washed over her. 'You sound a little distracted, is everything OK?'

'M-my father has had a stroke,' she said. 'I need to get him back to Sydney. My mother is a mess and—'

'Leave it to me,' he said, interrupting her. 'I'll make the arrangements; you sit tight until they get home.'

'They don't have a home any more,' she cried as her emotions finally got the better of her.

There was a small pause before he spoke. 'Leave it to me, Bryony. Just stay calm until I get back. I'll be on the next available flight if all goes well. Do you think you can hang out that long?'

'I-I think so,' she said with a sniff.

'That's my girl.' There was a gruff softness to his tone that made her heart squeeze. 'See you soon.'

'See you.' She sighed as the connection ended.

She stared into space for several minutes, trying to get her head around the current crisis. Her father had always seemed so forceful and in control; it was hard to imagine him incapacitated by a stroke. She felt ill at the thought of what her mother would likely have to face if he didn't recover full mobility. He would make her life a living hell, no doubt taking out his frustration on her at every available opportunity.

'Oh, Austin!' she sobbed. 'Why did you have to die and leave me with all this?'

CHAPTER THIRTEEN

LATER Bryony had cause to wonder how she got through the first few days of her parents' return. Her concerns about her relationship with Kane had to take a back seat as she offered what support she could to her distraught mother.

Kane had arranged for Owen to be admitted to a private hospital where he began to make some small signs of progress. Once Owen was declared out of danger Kane suggested to Glenys and Bryony that he be transferred to Mercyfields with the support of a private nursing agency.

'Oh, Kane, that would be wonderful,' Glenys gushed gratefully, mopping at her eyes. 'I don't know how to thank you for all you've done.'

'It's no problem.'

Bryony was well aware of her parents' lack of finances and, once her mother had gone back in to be with her father in his plush single bed ward, she confronted Kane, her eyes flashing with brooding resentment. 'I'd like to know how my parents are expected to pay for months of private nursing when they no longer have a penny to their name!'

He gave her a long and thoughtful look. 'I don't expect them to pay for it.'

'Who do you expect to foot the bill—me?' she asked, her mouth twisting bitterly, hurt and anger coursing through her. 'No doubt with regular installments in the currency of the bedroom.'

He didn't answer, which annoyed her into throwing back, 'Or perhaps it's all part of the plan for revenge. You already have the business, Mercyfields and me and now apparently you have my parents' gratitude. Is that what you're after? Their pride on a platter?'

'You're upset and overwrought,' he said evenly. 'Let's go home so you can get some sleep.' He reached for her arm but she slapped his hand away.

'Don't touch me!' Her eyes grew wild with rage.

He shifted his tongue in his cheek as he looked down at her, making Bryony feel as if he were looking at a small recalcitrant child instead of a fully grown woman.

'Don't look at me like that.' She scowled at him.

'I will look at you any way I wish. Now, let's go home before I'm tempted to kiss you senseless right in front of those nurses who are showing an inordinate amount of interest in our conversation.'

Bryony flicked her gaze to the nurses' station where three nurses were standing, rather too obviously pretending to be engrossed in a patient's chart.

She drew in an angry breath and followed him as he shouldered open the double door leading to the exit.

She was determined she wouldn't utter a word to him on the way home and then when he seemed equally disinclined to talk felt her resentment towards him going up another notch.

'Aren't you going to say anything?' she asked as they turned into the driveway a short time later.

'Did you want me to say anything in particular?' He slanted a quick glance her way as he parked the car in the garage.

She pushed open her door without replying, slamming it behind her with unnecessary force. She wanted him to say many things, such as 'I love you,' but as far as she could tell he was more likely to tell her he had no further use for her. As he was footing her father's health bills she knew it would be impossible to convince him that her love for him was genuine for he would see it as nothing more than gratitude for how he'd come to the rescue. He hadn't touched her since he'd returned from Melbourne and, while she tried to convince herself he'd kept his distance due to the stress she was under with her father, another part of her wished he'd pulled her into his arms regardless.

Kane drew in a breath and followed her to the house, his brow furrowing at the difficulties that lay ahead for Bryony. He'd had a private discussion with Owen Mercer's specialist, who hadn't given a very promising recovery verdict. It was quite clear that Bryony's father was going to be an invalid, at least for the foreseeable future, and it worried him to think of her doing her level best to support her mother during what would prove to be an arduous time. Even in the best of health Owen wasn't a patient man; how much worse was he going to be, wheelchair bound and totally dependent on others?

Bryony deactivated the alarm and turned to look at him, her chin hitched up. 'See? I'm not as stupid as you thought.'

'I never said you were stupid.' He followed her inside, closing the door behind him. 'Stubborn maybe, bad-tempered and more than a little petulant but definitely not stupid.'

She bit her lip in such an endearingly childlike way he felt his gut clench painfully, making him want to enfold her in his arms and protect her from all of life's hurts.

'Would you like something to eat?' he asked. 'You've had a long day at the hospital and, as plush as Saint Honore's is, hospital food, in my opinion, is really only fit for the very ill.'

As much as Bryony felt in the mood to contradict everything he said, she reluctantly had to agree with him.

'I'm starving. The sandwich I had at lunchtime tasted like it came out of the bottom of someone's gym bag.'

He smiled as he loosened his tie. 'I'll fix us something. Why don't you go and have a shower or something while I fire up the kitchen?'

Bryony felt fired up physically by his disarming smile, all her earlier anger receding as if someone had turned a switch. She wanted food but much more than that she wanted to feel his arms around her, holding her close, telling her he would be there for her in the rough times ahead. Sudden tears pricked at the back of her eyes and she blinked to push them away.

'Why are you being so nice to me when I've been such a bitch to you all evening?'

He rolled up his tie and placed it on the nearest surface. 'You're not a bitch, *agape mou*. Annoying at times, intractable at others, but definitely not a bitch.'

His gentle teasing was her undoing. She blundered towards him, burying her head into his chest, sobbing openly and clutching at his shirt with her fingers.

'Hey, there…' He placed a warm protective hand on the back of her head. 'What did I say?'

'N-nothing…' She shook her head against his chest. 'I'm just feeling really emotional right now.'

'I understand.' He stroked her back with his free hand, his chin resting on the top of her silky head.

'I've been trying to be so strong for my mother but I can't do it,' she said.

'It's certainly been tough on you.'

'She needs me so much.' She gave a huge sniff and he handed her his clean handkerchief. She blew her nose and added, 'Ever since Austin died I've had to be strong for everyone. I didn't get time to grieve because I had to hold up everyone else. I just can't do it any more.'

'You don't have to do it alone,' he said.

She eased herself away from his chest to look up at him. 'Why should you help? You've always hated my family.'

He considered her words for a lengthy moment. 'Hate is a very strong word. I am wary around them but I no longer hate them.'

Bryony tried to make sense of his statement. If he no longer hated her parents was there a chance he could feel something more lasting for her? She stared at the open neck of his shirt, still in the circle of his strong arms, wishing she had the courage to tell him how much she loved him, how she believed him to be the most noble and caring person she'd ever met.

Kane released her gently, tapping her on the end of her nose with a long finger. 'Go and get into your most comfortable night gear and meet me in the kitchen in fifteen minutes. I promise you I'll have a veritable feast for you.'

She went upstairs and did as he'd said, somehow feeling better for the shower and a change of clothing. Deciding against her comfortable pyjamas, she put on one of his bathrobes instead, unable to stop herself from breathing in the lingering scent of his skin as she did so.

He was dishing up as she entered the kitchen, a tea towel tied around his waist.

'Grab yourself a glass of wine.' He pushed the open bottle towards her along with a glass. 'I won't be a minute.'

Bryony sniffed the air, her stomach instantly rumbling at the hint of garlic in the air. 'What have you made?'

'Garlic and pesto chicken,' he informed her.

'So soon?' She eyed the elaborate dish he set in front of her.

He tossed the tea towel to the bench and pulled out the stool opposite hers. 'This is the one I prepared earlier, just like all the celebrity chefs.'

She couldn't stop her smile in time.

He grinned back at her and charged his glass against hers. 'Eat, drink and be merry.'

She finished the quote with a grimace. 'For tomorrow someone may die.'

Kane put his glass down. 'He's not going to die, Bryony.'

She sighed and ran her fingertip around the rim of her glass rather than look up at him. 'I know it's awful of me, but sometimes I wish he had; that way my mother could finally be free.'

'She wouldn't want to be free in that way,' he said. 'I know you don't understand why she loves him, but it's quite clear she does and maybe this situation is exactly what Owen needs to show him what a loyal wife he's had all these years.'

Bryony considered his words as she sipped her wine. Her mother had certainly thrown herself into the primary carer role with gusto, taking charge of her husband's needs with authority and competence. Gone were the jittery nerves and endless tears; in their place were calming words and quiet and steady devotion as she saw to the many intimate details of her father's day.

'Maybe you're right…' She looked up at him. 'My father has always criticized my mother for fussing over silly little things, berating her for being too sensitive. But those are the very qualities he will need in her right now if he's to get through this.'

'Life has a habit of teaching us the lessons we need to learn,' he said. 'I'm a bit of a believer in what goes around comes around.'

'Karma.' She sighed as she cradled her glass in both hands and stared into the golden contents. 'My father is in for a rude shock, then.'

'Maybe.'

She lifted her gaze back to his. 'What did he do? I mean, what did he do that would incur a lengthy prison sentence? You've never told me.'

Kane drained the contents of his glass and set it back down. Bryony couldn't help thinking how loud the sound was in the sudden silence.

'It's irrelevant now,' he said, picking up his cutlery. 'I've sorted it all out.'

She frowned slightly. 'How?'

'The usual way.'

'Money?' she asked.

He dissected a piece of chicken and held it close to his mouth before he answered. 'It's the only language some of your father's disgruntled cronies speak. It was pay them off or stand by and watch them take him out.'

'He really had a contract on his head?'

'Not just one, I'm afraid. He'd certainly angered a few people but what do you expect? If you hang around the wrong sort of dogs, sooner or later you'll end up with fleas.'

Bryony toyed with her food, her appetite waning as she thought about what he'd said and also what he'd cleverly avoided telling her. She'd known her father wasn't father of the year material but neither had she thought he was an underworld criminal. Her mind scurried with horrible scenarios—contract killings, blackmail, grievous bodily harm…

'Quite frankly, I wasn't all that interested in protecting your father's back but word was going around that the people after him were going to issue a couple of serious warnings,' he continued. 'I couldn't ignore that, no matter how much I thought your father deserved what was coming to him.'

Bryony put her cutlery down, her desire for food totally disappearing. 'What sort of warnings?'

He refilled their glasses before he answered, his dark eyes coming back to hers, his expression serious. 'The sort of people your father put offside don't lie awake at night tortured by their conscience. They would think nothing of disposing of a wife and daughter to tighten the screws a bit.'

She stared at him as the sickening realisation dawned. 'They were going to come after my mother and me?' She shifted in her seat, knocking her cutlery to the floor with a jarring clatter.

'You first—your mother second.'

She swallowed the rising fear, her throat aching with the effort. 'How did you...how did you convince them not to do it?'

His eyes meshed with hers, their unreadable depths holding her captive for endless seconds before he finally spoke. 'I married you.'

She swallowed deeply, her eyes widening in incredulity. 'And that was enough to call them off?'

He picked up his glass and twirled the contents for a moment or two. 'I won't go into the details, but suffice it to say I was owed a favour or two. Once I made it clear you were to be my wife they had no choice but to back down. As soon as I released my grandfather's funds I paid them all that your father owed with interest.'

Bryony found it hard to get her head around this latest development. She'd thought he'd married her to get back at her father but if what he said was true...

She sat back in her seat, mentally backtracking to the afternoon he'd arrived at Mercyfields to announce his plans, informing her of his ownership of her father's business and assets. He'd made it clear she was part of the package for revenge, that if she didn't marry him he was going to feed her parents to the sharks already circling them looking for blood. She'd been convinced she had to marry him to save them, had only done it so that her mother wouldn't have to suffer. Why had he covered up his motives? Why hadn't he come right out and told her of his plan to protect her from harm?

She looked back at him, her expression clouded with uncertainty and confusion.

'Why didn't you tell me the truth? Why didn't you tell me you were marrying me to protect me? Why make me think the very worst of you?'

He pushed his chair back from the table and stood up, his height instantly shadowing her. 'I didn't make you think anything you didn't already feel. You hated me from the moment I walked into Mercyfields as a teenager. You looked down your nose at me from day one, as did your family. I was scum, remember? The bastard son of a lowly housekeeper who lifted her skirts for the man of the house in order to keep food on the table.'

She got to her feet, surprised to find they were still capable of supporting her. 'You should have told me. I had a right to know.'

'I wasn't prepared to risk it. Negotiations were tricky and I couldn't afford to waste valuable time trying to convince you to follow my plan. I decided to spin things so you had no choice but to marry me. I know it was blackmail, but as far as I was concerned it was a means to an end. The alternative was too frightening to think about.'

She watched as he ran a hand through his hair, making it stick up at odd angles, making him seem uncharacteristically vulnerable and unguarded.

'Why was it more frightening?' she asked, watching him closely.

He didn't answer. Instead, he gathered their half finished plates of food and disposed of the contents in the kitchen tidy, his actions effectively shutting her out.

'Why, Kane?' She approached him, touching him on the arm to make him look at her. 'Why did you find the alternative frightening?'

His dark eyes met hers briefly before he turned back to

the sink. 'Leave it, Bryony. You and your family are safe; that's all you need to know.'

She wanted to press him but could see by his taciturn manner that the subject was now closed. What secrets was he hiding about her father's dodgy dealings? Was he trying to spare her further pain or refusing to speak of it for his own reasons?

She wondered if her parents knew how much they now owed him. The irony of it was striking. He'd come charging back into their lives, taking everything out from under her father, issuing demands to be met, speaking of revenge for past wrongs, when in truth his motives had been anything but vengeful.

It was unthinkable that her life had been in such danger, that her father's underhand dealings had put both her mother and her at risk, but she'd read enough in the papers about how the underworld worked. It was definitely an eye for an eye out there, the law of the land holding no sway.

Kane switched the dishwasher on and, drying his hands on a tea towel, turned to leave the kitchen.

'I'm going to have a shower. I'll leave you to sleep in peace in the spare room.'

She hovered uncertainly, her expression falling at the thought of a long night alone.

'You don't want me to...?' She hesitated, not sure she could finish her sentence without betraying the real state of her feelings.

He came back towards her, tilting her chin up so she had to look into his eyes. 'You look done in, Bryony. There are shadows on top of shadows underneath your eyes.'

'I don't want to sleep alone.' There, she'd said it, admitted her need of him.

His hand moved from her chin to cup the side of her face, his thumb rolling across the smooth skin of her cheek in a softer than soft caress.

'Please…' She held his dark gaze, her tongue slipping out to moisten her dry lips. 'I don't want to be alone tonight.'

It seemed an age before he spoke.

'If I was truly a gentleman I'd put you from me right now and insist you get the good night's sleep you really need.' His hands went to her hips, bringing her closer to him, not quite touching but close enough for her to feel the heat of his body.

'I'm not tired.' She pressed even closer.

His eyes burned down into hers and she felt the unmistakable spring of his body against hers, making her own flesh leap into life with clawing need.

His mouth came down slowly, her eyes fluttering closed as his lips found hers, touching, pressing, lifting off briefly before coming back down with increasing pressure. She felt the gentle probe of his tongue and opened to it, circling its commanding presence with her own in soft, more hesitant movements. His arms tightened around her, his body hard and insistent against her softer yielding one.

He tore his mouth off hers to look down at her, his dark eyes glazed with desire. 'If we don't move right now this kitchen is going to see a little more heat than it's currently used to.'

She snaked her arms up around his neck and rubbed herself up against him enticingly, her blue eyes shining with passion. 'Just how hot does it get in here?'

He gave her a bone-melting sexy smile. 'Want to find out?'

'Why not?' She dimpled at him mischievously.

He walked her backwards, thigh upon thigh until she was up against the kitchen bench. He lifted her effortlessly so she was sitting, her legs either side of him, her head thrown back as he released the tie of the bathrobe.

What followed next both shocked and thrilled her. His

tongue left no part of her feminine form unexplored, drawing from her a response she hadn't thought possible. It was wild and unrestrained. It was heady and intoxicating; it was exhilarating and rapturous. She slumped when the tumult was over, her chest rising and falling as she struggled to restore some sort of normal breathing pattern.

He stood back from her, his eyes wild with unrelieved desire. 'Is that hot enough for you?'

She shimmied down off the bench and reached for the waistband of his trousers, sending him a sultry look from beneath her downcast lashes. 'Not quite. Why don't we see if this does the trick?'

He drew in a sharp breath as her searching fingers found and released him, her open mouth coming down, her warm breath feathering over his engorged length.

His hands went to her head to stabilize himself as her tongue ran in slow motion along the length of him, tasting him at the tip before going back in agonizingly slow movements, the slight abrasion of her tongue an exquisite torture in his heightened state of arousal.

He felt himself coming, unable to hold it back, the force of it rendering him helpless under the ministrations of her mouth. His scalp lifted as he braced himself for the final plunge, his voice hoarse as he tried to warn her, 'I can't hold it any longer.'

She drew on him even harder and he spilled, his body shuddering with the impact as she held him against her mouth, her hands tight on his hips.

After a few heart-thundering moments he eased himself away, his hands drawing her upwards until she was standing upright against him.

'You didn't have to do that.'

She ran her tongue across her lips, her bluer than blue gaze smouldering. 'I enjoyed it, didn't you?'

His breath snagged on her sexy smile. 'You know I did.'

She snuggled against him. 'Can we go to bed now?'

He drew her close, burying his head into the fragrant cloud of her hair. 'I can think of nothing better.'

A few minutes later Bryony lay back to receive him, his hard body pressing her into the mattress, his mouth on hers, his hands everywhere she wanted them.

No words were spoken, their bodies relaying the message of passion with fervent energy as each of them clamoured for their own release. Bryony distantly registered her sobbing cries against the hard muscles of his shoulder where her mouth was pressed and then, when his answering groan sounded as he emptied himself, her heart tightened in relief that she could have that effect on him.

She closed her eyes to the summon of sleep, her head on his chest, his heart thudding beneath her ear as his arms came around her like an embrace of velvet-covered steel.

She felt safe.

He was her protector.

She owed him her life...

Kane had left by the time she surfaced the next morning and, doing her best to squash her feelings of disappointment, she busied herself with getting ready to accompany her parents on the journey to Mercyfields.

When she arrived at the hospital her father was in a filthy mood but her mother was coping with uncharacteristic strength of spirit, issuing orders to the transporting staff as if she'd been doing it all her life.

Bryony stood back and watched as her father was wheeled into the back of the ambulance, his features distorted by a heavy scowl. In spite of her animosity she felt a faint trace of empathy for him. How the mighty are fallen, she thought as she followed the ambulance on the long drive to Mercyfields.

Not long after her father had been settled for an afternoon rest the front doorbell of Mercyfields sounded.

Bryony gave her mother a quick questioning glance but Glenys looked at her blankly.

'Who can that be? I'm not expecting anyone, are you? Kane said he was coming down tomorrow for the weekend, not today.'

Bryony got to her feet and made her way to the door, opening it to find an air courier standing there with a pet carrier in one hand.

'Delivery for Mrs Glenys Mercer,' he announced. 'I need a signature.'

Bryony turned to her mother, who was hovering in the background. 'Do you know anything about this?'

Glenys approached warily, her gaze going to the now wriggling carrier in the courier's hand.

'I'm not expecting any delivery,' she said, placing a nervous hand to her neck.

The courier gave them both a don't-tell-me-I've-driven-all-this-way-for-nothing look and handed Bryony the carrier. 'Sign here.' He thrust a pen into her hand. 'Pedigree puppy for Mrs Mercer, a gift from Mr Kane Kaproulias.'

Bryony scratched her signature and handed back the form to the courier, taking the carrier without demur. She waited until he'd gone before setting the crate down and opening the door.

A tiny Cavalier King Charles spaniel puppy came waddling out, his big bug eyes wide in both innocence and trepidation.

Bryony felt herself melting as the tiny body came towards her. 'Mum, look!' She picked up the tiny bundle and cuddled it closely, delighting in the lapping of the little enthusiastic tongue as it found her cheek. 'Look what Kane has sent you! A puppy to keep you company while you look after Dad.'

Glenys stared at the puppy in horror, her face crumpling as she clutched at the nearest surface for support.

'Oh, my God!' she gasped and sank to the bench seat in the foyer, looking up at Bryony in anguished despair. 'How could he have possibly known?'

CHAPTER FOURTEEN

BRYONY stared at her mother blankly. 'Mum? What's the matter? I thought you loved dogs. Here, look—isn't he gorgeous?' She held the squirming puppy in front of her mother but Glenys instantly shrank back, her face a deathly white.

'No, take it away...*please*.'

Bryony frowned as her mother got unsteadily to her feet, her high heels click-clacking agitatedly as she hurried off into the green sitting room, closing the door firmly behind her.

Bryony put the puppy back in the carrier and, leaving it out of harm's way, made her way to her mother, her puzzled frown even more entrenched on her brow.

When she'd seen the puppy she had been touched by Kane's thoughtfulness, knowing he had done it to help ease the burden her mother carried in looking after her father. Her mother's reaction was certainly confusing, considering how devoted she had been to Nero, the neighbour's dog, in the past. Bryony knew her mother had been very upset at Nero's death, but surely it wasn't still affecting her after all this time?

When Bryony opened the door Glenys was standing, staring out of the window overlooking the lake.

'Mum?'

Glenys turned around to face her and again Bryony was instantly struck by her ghostly pallor.

'Darling...I have something to tell you. I should have told you a long time ago but...' Glenys brushed at her leaking eyes and continued. 'Your father thought it best we

177

let things stand as they were. It was too late to change anything. Kane had been taken away and the chance to tell the truth had gone.'

Bryony felt her legs begin to tremble at the tortured expression on her mother's face.

'Go on.'

Glenys looked at her without wavering. 'It wasn't Kane who killed Nero. It was me.'

'*You?*' Bryony's eyes widened in shock.

Glenys gave her a pained look. 'I didn't mean to, of course...' She began to wring her thin hands. 'I overheard the argument between Kane and your father. Things were said...I don't want to distress you with the details—'

'I know about Dad's affair with Kane's mother.'

Her mother's face fell. 'I wish I could have spared you that.' She sat on the edge of the nearest sofa and continued, staring at her knotted hands as she did so. 'I was so angry and upset. I got in my car and bolted out the driveway...I didn't even see Nero until he was...under the front wheel. I didn't know what to do. I stopped and, wrapping him in the car blanket, took him back to the house, but when I came around the side I saw Kane driving the tractor through the rose garden. He'd already ruined the lawn...'

'Oh, Mum,' Bryony groaned.

Glenys met her daughter's agonized look. 'I'm so ashamed of what I did, but I was terribly upset. When I saw Kane I immediately thought of his mother and...and I wanted to get rid of both of them. I put Nero in the groove of one of the tractor tyre tracks on the lawn and went back into the house.'

'Did anyone see you?'

'No, but I told your father. I sometimes wish I hadn't. He's used it to keep me quiet about some of his...dealings. When Kane took over the company and Mercyfields I wanted to come clean but when he insisted on marrying you I thought better of it. I didn't want anything to jeopardize your future together.'

Bryony felt like screaming at her mother. The secrets and lies of the past had practically destroyed any chance of a happy future for herself and Kane. If only she had known! She cringed to think of how many times she'd accused him of killing that innocent dog! Would he ever forgive her for not believing in him?

Glenys was openly sobbing now. 'Kane must have known. Why else would he send me that puppy unless to show me he'd known all these years?'

Bryony came across and knelt down in front of her mother, taking her trembling hands in hers, stroking them soothingly.

'Mum? Listen to me. I know for a fact that Kane wouldn't be so cruel as to do something like that to you. Anyway, he told me ages ago he thought Austin was responsible.' She squeezed her mother's hand. 'Kane is the most caring person I know. I think I've always known deep down he couldn't possibly have killed Nero even in a fit of rage. I know he likes people to think he's ruthless and controlling but underneath he's a gentle humane person.'

Glenys lifted her head to look at her daughter through tear-washed eyes. 'You love him, don't you?'

Bryony felt her own tears sprouting. 'You have no idea how much.'

'Does he?' Glenys asked softly.

Bryony held her mother's questioning gaze. 'I think it's probably time I told him.' She got to her feet and smiled. 'Would you mind very much if I went back to town this evening?'

Glenys gave her a watery smile. 'Go, darling.'

*   *   *

Bryony pulled into the driveway of Kane's house three hours later, just as the puppy on the back seat started to whimper.

'Hang on, sweetie, won't be long now.' She lifted him out of the carrier and cuddled him close, loving the feel of his silky fur and fervent tongue as it rasped over the back of her hand.

She was bitterly disappointed to find that, although some lights were on, the house was empty. Her spirits plummeted at the thought of Kane out for the evening, her mind tortured with images of him escorting another woman on his arm, with the possible intention of bringing her back here to his house...

She sprang to her feet when she heard the front door open close to eleven, her heart thumping, her ears straining for the sound of a female voice.

She heard the firm tread of his footsteps approaching the sitting room and the door opening as his hand turned the knob.

'Bryony?' He came to a standstill and stared at her. 'What are you doing back here?'

Just then the puppy made a sound and waddled over towards him, stopping in the middle of the carpet to relieve itself.

'Oh, no!' Bryony scooped him up but only managed to spread the damage even further, including over the legs of her jeans.

Kane handed her his handkerchief and took the puppy from her, holding it against his chest where it gave his large hand three licks before nestling into the crook of his arm and shutting its eyes.

Bryony grimaced as she looked at the puddle seeping into the carpet.

'I can't believe he did that. I took him out half an hour ago.'

'Women.' Kane gave her a quick smile. 'They make your

life hell but you love them anyway.' He stroked the top of the puppy's silky head with one finger as he held her gaze. 'I take it your mother wasn't so keen on the idea of raising this little chap?'

Bryony worried her lip with her teeth for a moment. 'Would you mind very much if we were to keep him?'

His dark eyes were steady on hers. 'Aren't you afraid I might inflict some sort of intolerable cruelty on him some time in the future?'

'No, I'm not the least bit worried.'

'I see.' He placed the sleeping puppy on the sofa, tucking him behind the safety of a plump cushion. He turned back to face her, his expression still slightly guarded. 'May I ask what brought about this change of heart?'

'I know you didn't kill Nero,' she said. 'I knew it even before my mother told me this afternoon that she was responsible.'

A flicker of shock entered his dark gaze before he quickly covered it. 'So we were both wrong.'

'It wasn't Austin and it wasn't you,' she said. 'I'm sorry, Kane, can you ever forgive me for misjudging you? I know it's a lot to ask…I hate myself for being so blind for so long. I preferred you as the enemy because I thought I would be less vulnerable that way. I got it so wrong in so many ways.'

He stood so still before her that she wondered if he had taken anything she'd said in. His expression was mask-like—blank, almost, his dark mysterious eyes giving her no clue to what was going on in his head.

'Kane?' She approached him hesitantly. 'You said yesterday that you married me to protect me. I've been thinking about that…wondering why you would be motivated to do so when I have done nothing but demonstrate my dislike of you. Why did you do it?'

He had trouble holding her gaze, turning away to stare

out of the window to the leafy street outside. His voice when he spoke seemed to be coming from deep inside him, 'I've done some wrong things in my life. God knows I'd do differently if I had my time over, but I couldn't allow someone to hurt you, not without doing everything within my power to stop it.'

Hope exploded inside her, making her breathless and unsteady as if a powerful drug had been released into her system.

'Why?' she asked, her voice scratchy with emotion. 'Why did you want to protect me so much?'

His gravity was unsettling but she had come this far she couldn't bear to go on any longer without answers. She placed her hand on his arm, turning him to face her. She slid her hand down to curl around his stiff fingers, stroking them into life.

She drew in a breath as his fingers curled around hers, enclosing them in the warmth of his palm, his body moving closer so they were touching chest to thigh.

Kane touched her face with his other hand, tracing the soft curve of her cheek before running his thumb pad over her bottom lip in a gentle caress that released a host of feathery sensations up and down her spine.

'You can ask that?' His voice was strangely husky. 'You mean you haven't already guessed?'

'Guessed what?' she asked, a tentative smile hovering about her mouth. 'You're like a closed book most of the time. How can I possibly guess what you're thinking?'

'I suppose you're right.' He gave a short rueful sigh. 'For most of my life I've had to pretend to be invulnerable. One sign of weakness and others take advantage of it. I've learned that the hard way.'

Bryony was sure he was referring to her father and brother. She bit her lip, her expression clouding with guilt and shame.

He smiled down at her, his dark eyes warm as they rested on her up-tilted face. 'What's with the long face? I'm about to tell you I love you, so an encouraging smile would be really good right now.'

She stared at him in wonder, her stomach somersaulting, her heart tight with its own burden of love just waiting to be shared. A slow smile gradually spread across her face, her eyes becoming luminous with joy.

'That's better.' He gently tapped the end of her nose in approval. 'Now listen up because I've never said this to a woman before, unless you count my mother, but I guess that's different.' He paused, taking in her shining eyes and jubilant smile. 'Bryony, I love you. I think I've always loved you, although I've probably done far too good a job of hiding it. I love the way you care for your mother, I love the way you're so loyal to your brother's memory, I love the way you smile and laugh, I love the way you respond to me and I love the fact that you stand up to me, which makes me realise your father hasn't totally crushed your spirit.'

'Oh, Kane...' She breathed at last. 'I've been hiding something from you too. I love you. I don't know when I started to love you...I think it was when you kissed me at the lake, although you'd never think it by the way I reacted...' She gave him a strained look, her eyes going to his scar. 'How can you love me? How can you be so forgiving when my family caused you so much suffering?'

'Do you think it wasn't worth it to have you here with me now?' he asked. 'I would do it all again, even do double the time to hold you in my arms.'

'I never dreamed you felt anything for me but hate. You seemed so intent on revenge, insisting I give up work to run your house. You didn't mean a word of it, did you?'

He gave her a sheepish look. 'As much as I like the idea of you pregnant and barefoot in my kitchen, I can assure you I was only needling you to stop you guessing what I really felt. I had my pride to maintain.'

She gave herself up to his firm hug, burying her head into his neck, breathing in his scent, marvelling at the way life had turned ten years of bitterness into love.

'I don't deserve you,' she said. 'I'll never be able to make it up to you.'

He held her from him to smile down at her. 'Then perhaps we need to instigate some sort of instalment plan to even the score a bit.'

'What do you suggest?' She looped her arms around his neck, her eyes alight with adoration.

'I think it might be best to show you what I want.' He scooped her up in his arms and began to carry her towards the door, but just as he went to shoulder it open there was a whimper from behind the cushion on the sofa.

'Damn!' he swore softly.

Bryony giggled. 'I think our baby needs us. Can you wait until I do what needs to be done?'

He gave her a quick hard kiss and growled playfully, 'Whose idea was it to start a family so soon?'

'Not mine but I'm delighted, aren't you?'

He set her back down on her feet, holding her in the circle of his arms as if he found the task of letting her go impossible.

'I love you, Bryony,' he said. 'Do you have any idea how much?'

'No, but I'm hoping you might show me in a few minutes.'

He stepped away from her and picked up the puppy, addressing it in an affectionate but firm voice. 'Listen, kid, your mother and I need some time together so be a good baby and go back to sleep so I can show her how much she means to me.'

The puppy blinked at him engagingly before giving his knuckle another enthusiastic lick.

'Did you see that, Bryony?' Kane asked, turning to her. 'He loves me already.'

Bryony slid her arms around his waist and tilted her head to look up at him, her face radiant with love.

'I wonder what took him so long?'

* * * *

Melanie Milburne brings you more
Mediterranean passion in
Bound by the Marcolini Diamonds
available in August from
Mills & Boon® Modern˙.

The Billionaire Bodyguard

SHARON KENDRICK

Sharon Kendrick started story-telling at the age of eleven and has never really stopped. She likes to write fast-paced, feel-good romances with heroes who are so sexy they'll make your toes curl! Born in west London, she now lives in the beautiful city of Winchester – where she can see the cathedral from her window (but only if she stands on tip-toe). She has two children, Celia and Patrick, and her passions include music, books, cooking and eating – and drifting off into wonderful daydreams while she works out new plots!

CHAPTER ONE

HE DIDN'T say much, but maybe that was best. There was nothing worse than a driver who talked.

Keri settled back in the soft leather seat of the luxury car and stared at the back of the man in the driving seat in front of her. No, definitely no talker he—more the strong, silent type. Very strong—judging by the broad set of those shoulders—and very definitely silent. There had been little more than a nod when he had picked her up from her London flat early that morning, and very little since.

Keri shivered. Outside the snowflakes continued to flurry down—big, fat, splodgy things which melted on your cheeks and clung like stubborn confetti to your hair.

She pulled her sheepskin coat tighter and huddled into it. 'Brrr! Could you turn the heater up a little? I'm absolutely freezing.'

His eyes intently fixed on the road ahead, Jay flicked a switch. 'Can do.'

'And would you mind putting your foot down? I want to get back to London some time tonight.'

'I'll do my best,' he said equably.

He would drive only as fast as conditions demanded, no more and no less. Jay's face was hidden, but he flicked a glance at the rearview mirror to see the model sliding a pair of fur-lined gloves over her long fingers. If she *had* been able to see him she would have seen the unmistakable look of irritation on his face. Not that his irritation would have bothered her, of course—even if she had picked it up. He was simply the driver—employed to cater to her every whim and keep close watch on the priceless chandelier of a necklace which had been dripping exquisite diamonds from her long, pale neck during one of the coldest afternoons of the year.

He had watched while the stylists and the photographers and all their assistants had fussed round her, and had observed her blank, almost bored look of compliance as she had let them. He had been pretty bored himself, if the truth were known. Watching a magazine-shoot seemed to involve one hell of a lot of waiting around. The waiting he could deal with, if there was a good reason for it, but this had seemed like a complete waste of time.

To Jay, it had seemed crazy that a woman would agree to wear a flimsy evening dress outdoors on a bitterly icy day. Surely they could have recreated a winter scene inside the warmth and comfort of a studio, and made his job easier?

And then he had seen the Polaroids, and suddenly he had understood. Before the camera she had come alive—and how. He had given a long, low whistle and the photographer's assistant had flashed him a conspiratorial smile.

'Gorgeous, isn't she?'

Jay had studied them. Sure, she was exquisite—just like the diamonds themselves, if you liked diamonds, which personally he didn't. Framed by the sooty fall of her loose hair, her face was pale as a dusting of frost, her eyes as dark as the bare charcoal branches of the trees. Her lips were full and red—painted crimson, like rich ruby wine—and they parted into a shape of sheer, moist provocation. The thin silver gown had added to the wintry feel of the photograph, and it had clung like sparkling hoar-frost to her body, to the firm, high breasts and the curving bottom.

But she'd looked as if she had been made from ice, or wax—too perfect to be true and not real at all. If you pricked a woman like that, would she bleed? he wondered. If you made love to her, would she cry out in wild, uninhibited passion—or would she just smooth down that perfect hair and flick it back over her shoulders?

'She's okay,' he had drawled, and the assistant had given him another understanding smile.

'I know what you mean.' He'd shrugged. 'Not just a case of out of our league—she's probably never even heard of our league!'

Jay had nodded and turned away, not bothering to correct him—the day he decided a woman was out of his league would be the day he failed to draw breath. He was here to do a job and get away as soon as possible. He shouldn't even have been there in the first place, and he had a date that night with a cool dream of a blonde he had been fighting off without quite knowing why—only tonight he had decided that maybe it was time to throw in the towel.

A slow smile of anticipation curved his mouth.

'How long, do you think?'

The model's voice cut into thoughts which were just

threatening to get erotic, and her question didn't really help.

'How long is what?' he questioned.

Keri sighed. It had been a long, long day and, if the truth were known, she would have liked nothing more than to go home to a hot bath and then curl herself up with a good book instead of go out on a dinner date. Not that dinner with David would be anything other than enjoyable—it always was. True, he didn't set her pulses on fire, but he knew that and he didn't mind a bit. Well, that was what he said—but Keri couldn't help wondering if, deep down, he was quietly working on a campaign to make her change her mind. And she wouldn't, of course. David fell firmly into the category of friend and was stuck there, and that was probably best. Lovers—at least in Keri's limited experience—tended to be bad news.

'I was asking how long it will take us to get back to London.'

Jay narrowed his eyes at the road ahead. The snow was getting heavier now. The skies were pale grey, so pale that it was impossible to see where the falling, swirling snow ended and the sky began. Trees loomed up as they passed—skeletal brooms so inhospitable that you could not imagine them ever bearing fruit or leaves or blossoms.

It was tempting to say that if she hadn't wasted so much time then they would be well on their way now, but he didn't. It wasn't the job of the driver to offer anything in the way of opinions, which took more than a little self-restraint on his part.

'Difficult to say,' he murmured. 'Depends.'

'On what?' Something about that lazy, drawled air of assurance was making her prickly. What kind of driver was he, anyway, if he couldn't throw in a rough estimate of their time of arrival?

He heard the faintly impatient note in her voice and hid a smile. He had forgotten what it was like to be subordinate—to have people tell you what to do and to ask you questions and expect you to answer, just as if you were some kind of machine.

'On how bad this snow gets,' he said, frowning suddenly as he felt the treacherous slide of the front wheels. He slowed right down.

Keri stared out of the window. 'It doesn't look that bad to me.'

'You think so?' he murmured. 'Well, that's okay, then.'

He had a faint, almost American drawl, and for a moment she thought she detected a mocking note of humour underpinning it. Suspiciously, Keri stared at the unmoving set of his broad shoulders. Was he making fun of her?

Through a gap in the thick curtain of dark fringe which flopped into her eyes Jay could see the tiny frown which pleated the smooth, pale perfection of her forehead. 'Would you like the radio on?' he questioned, as soothingly as he would to a maiden aunt who was in danger of becoming fractious.

He was making her feel…uncomfortable, and she couldn't quite put her finger on why. 'Actually,' said Keri, very deliberately, 'what I would really like is to get some sleep, so if you wouldn't mind…?'

'Sure. No problem.' Jay hid a smile which vanished

as he drove further into the winter dusk. The flakes of snow had changed from being the innocent ones of storybook pictures—now they were small, and he knew that they would have the bite of ice behind them. The wind was gusting them into bitter white flurries so that they looked like swarms of white bees.

He glanced in the mirror again. She had fallen asleep. Her head had fallen back and her hair was spread out behind it, like a shiny black pillow. The blanket had slipped down and the slit in her skirt meant that her long legs were sprawled out—pretty much the longest legs he had ever seen on a woman. Legs like that could wrap themselves round a man's neck like a deadly snake. Deliberately, Jay averted his eyes from their coltish display and from the tantalising glimpse of lacy stocking-top. This drive was going to take longer than he had anticipated—far better she slept than distract him.

But the weather was distraction enough. The narrow lanes became more precarious by the second, with the snow falling heavier and heavier, and as night closed in the darkness hid the fall from sight and the car began to slow as it encountered the first drifts.

He knew way before it happened that things were going to get bad—really bad. Instinct told him that, coupled with the experience of having lived in some of the most God-awful conditions known to man.

His windscreen wipers were flicking dementedly, but still it was like gazing into an icy abyss. The road dipped slightly, and he eased his foot back. A dip was good. Slopes ran down into hollows and hollows were where you found people, and they built houses which equalled shelter, and he suspected that they very soon they might need shelter... Except that this was pretty desolate countryside. Unspoiled, he guessed. Chosen for its beauty and its very isolation.

He flicked the light on briefly, to glance down at the map, and then squinted his eyes as the car passed the darkened bulk of a building. Some way after that, Jay realised that he no longer had a choice, and braked. Hard.

The jerk of the car woke her, and Keri opened her eyes, caught in that warm half-world between waking and sleeping. She yawned. 'Where are we?' she questioned sleepily.

'In the middle of nowhere,' he answered succinctly. 'Take a look for yourself.'

The sound of the low, tough masculine voice shook her right out of her reverie, and for a moment it startled her, until she realised where she was. She looked out of the window, and then blinked. He wasn't joking.

While she had been sleeping the snowy landscape had been transformed into one which was now unrecognisable. Night had closed in, and with it the snow. Everything was black and white, like a photographic negative, and it would have been beautiful if it didn't look so...*forbidding*. And they were in the middle of it. Of nowhere, as he had said. 'Why have you stopped?' she asked.

Why do you think I've stopped? 'Because the fall is heavy here.'

'Well, how long is it going to take us to get back now?'

Jay shot another glance out, and then looked in the mirror at her beautiful perplexed face. It was clear from her question that she had no idea how bad it was, and he was going to have to break it to her. Gently.

'If it carries on like this there's no way we're going to make it back at all, at least not tonight—we'll be lucky if we make it as far as the nearest village.'

This was sounding like something out of a bad movie. 'But I don't want to go to a village!' she exclaimed. 'I want to go to home!'

I want. I want. He supposed a woman like that spent all her time getting exactly what it was she wanted. Well, not tonight. 'You and me both, sweetheart,' he said grimly. 'But I'll settle for what I can take.'

She let the sweetheart bit go. Now was not the time to get frosty because he was being over-familiar. 'Can't you just drive on?'

He pressed cautiously on the accelerator, then eased his foot off. 'Nope. We're stuck.'

Keri sat bolt upright. 'What do you mean?'

What the hell do you think I mean? 'Like I said, we're stuck. There are drifts in the road. Snowdrifts. And they're underpacked with ice. It's a potentially lethal situation.'

Keri briefly shut her eyes. *Please tell me this isn't happening.* She opened them again. 'Couldn't you have predicted this might happen and taken a different route?'

He might have let it go, but something in her accusation made his blood simmer. 'There *is* no alternative route—not out of that God-forsaken field they chose for the shoot—and, if you recall, I asked you three times to hurry up. I said that I didn't like the look of the sky. But you were too busy being fawned over by a load of luvvies to pay much attention to what I was saying.'

Was he *criticising* her? 'I was just doing my job!'

'And I'm *trying* to do mine,' he said darkly. 'Which is dealing with the situation as it is, not wasting time by casting around for recriminations!'

Keri stared at the back of his dark head, feeling like a tennis-player who had been wrong-footed. And the most annoying thing of all was that he was right. He might have an arrogant, almost insolent way of expressing himself, but she could see his logic. 'So what do you suggest we do?' she questioned coolly.

By *we* he guessed she meant *him*. 'I guess we find some shelter.'

'No.' Keri shook her head. What did he think—that she was going to book into a hotel for the night? With *him*? 'I don't think you understand—I have to be back in London. Tonight.' She eyed his muscular frame hopefully. 'Can't you dig us out?'

'With a spare snow-plough?' Jay smiled. 'I don't think *you* understand, sweetheart—even if I dug us out, it would only be a temporary measure. This road is impassable.'

She felt a momentary flare of panic, until reason reasserted itself. 'You can't know that!'

He wasn't about to start explaining that he had seen snow and ice in pretty much all its guises. The empty bleached horizons of arctic wastes which made this particular snow scene look like a benign Christmas card. Or swimming beneath polar ice-caps and wondering if your blood had frozen solid in your veins, wetsuit or no wetsuit. Men trapped…lost…never to be heard of again.

A hard note entered his voice. 'Oh, but I can—it's my job to know.' He turned off the ignition, and turned round and shrugged. 'Sorry, but that's the way it is.'

She opened her mouth to reply, but the words froze on her lips as she met his eyes for the first time—hard, glittering eyes which took her breath away, and it was a long time since a man had done that. It was the first time she had looked at him properly, but then you never really looked at a driver, did you? They were part of the fixtures and fittings, part of the car itself— or at least they were supposed to be. She sucked in a dry gulp of air, confused by the sudden pounding of her heart, as if it was trying to remind her that it still existed. Lord alive, what was a man like this doing driving a car for a living?

His face was chiselled—all hard and lean angles— which seemed at odds with the lush, sensual curve of his upper lip. In the low light she couldn't make out the colour of his slanting eyes, but she could appreciate the feathery forest of lashes which gave them such an enigmatic look, and she had been modelling for long enough to know that cheekbones like that were rare.

He was, quite simply, *gorgeous*.

Jay noted the dilation of her eyes with something approaching wry amusement and then put it out of his mind. This was business, not pleasure—and even if it had been he wasn't into spoiled, pretty girls who expected everyone to jump when they spoke.

'So we could stay here all night,' he said pleasantly. 'Keep the engine running and wait until morning and hope it gets better.'

Spend the night in the car? 'Are you *serious*?'

'Completely.' He would keep awake quite easily—he had had a lifetime's experience of waiting for the first faint glow of a winter dawn.

There was something so unequivocal about that one clipped-out word that Keri began to realise that he meant it. But surely there was something they could do? This was England, for heaven's sake—not the Rocky Mountains!

'We must be able to phone for help.' She began to fish around in her handbag. 'I have a mobile here somewhere.'

His own was snug in his pocket—did she really think he hadn't thought of that? 'Sure, go ahead,' he murmured. 'Call the emergency services and tell them we're in trouble.'

She knew just from the tone of his voice that there would be no signal, but stubborn pride made her jab at the buttons with frustration coupled with rising panic.

'No luck?' he questioned sardonically.

Her hand was shaking, but she put the phone back in her handbag with as much dignity as possible. 'So we really are stuck,' she said flatly.

'Looks like it.' Her eyes looked huge and dark, all wide and appealing in her pale, heart-shaped face—designed by nature to provoke protectiveness in a man.

And nature was a funny thing, he mused—a nose, two eyes and a mouth could be arranged in such a way to transform a face from the ordinary into the exquisite. Luck of the draw, like so much else in life. 'Listen,' he drawled, 'I thought I could make out a building a little way back. It makes far more sense to head for that. I'll go and investigate.'

The thought of being left here all alone made her feel even worse. What if he disappeared into the cold and snowy night and never came back again? What if someone came along? It wasn't much of a contest, but on balance she'd probably be much safer with him than staying here without him. He might be a little lacking in the respect department, but at least he seemed to know what he was doing. 'No, I don't want you leaving me here,' she said. 'I'm coming with you.'

His eyes flickered over her leather boots. They were good, soft, waterproof leather, but heels like that weren't made for walking. And neither, by the look of it, was she. He raised his eyebrows. 'Not exactly dressed for it, are you?'

'Well, I wasn't expecting to have to go for a *hike*!'

His eyes narrowed. 'Ever skied?'

Keri laughed. 'With my job? You're kidding—skiing is classified as a dangerous sport and therefore frowned on.'

Pretty restrictive job, he thought. 'Well, you're sure you're up to it?'

'I can manage,' she said stubbornly.

He supposed that there was no choice but to let her try. 'You'll have to—because there's no way I'm carrying you.' His eyes mocked her again as he saw her lips part, and he realised that he was lying. Of course he would carry her, just the way he had been conditioned to do. Men would walk miles across any terrain for a woman who looked like that. 'Button up your coat,' he said roughly. 'And put your gloves back on.'

She opened her mouth to ask him to please stop addressing her as he would an idiot, but something about the set of his mouth told her that the dynamics had subtly changed and he was no longer *just* the driver. It was indefinable but unmistakable from his body language that suddenly he was in charge. And she wasn't used to that either.

'Hat?' he drawled.

She shook her head and he reached in the glove compartment for a beanie and handed it to her.

'Put your hair up,' he instructed. 'And then put this on.'

'Won't you need it yourself?'

'You need it more,' he stated. 'You're a woman.'

She thought about making some clever remark about equality, but something cool and implacable in his eyes told her not to bother, as if he didn't really care *what* she thought. For a woman used to men hanging on her every word, it was certainly a change.

He got out and came round and opened the door for her, pulling it back with difficulty, for snow was piled up against it.

'Be careful,' he warned. 'It's cold and it's deep. Just follow me, okay? Close as you can and quickly as you can. And do exactly as I tell you.'

It was most definitely an order.

He seemed to know exactly where he was going,

even though Keri could barely make out what was lane or field or sky or hedge. She panted slightly as she stumbled into the blinding whiteness. It was an effort to keep up with him and he kept having to stop, turning to look at her, the slanting eyes narrowing.

'You okay?'

She nodded. 'I'm being slow, aren't I?'

You're a woman, and you aren't trained up for this kind of stuff. 'Don't worry about it. Fingers not freezing too badly?'

'Wh-what fingers are they?' She shivered.

He laughed then, an unexpected and oddly musical sound, and his breath made frozen clouds in the air. 'Not long now,' he promised softly.

As she teetered behind him she wondered how he could be so sure. Swirling flakes of snow flew against her face, shooting into her eyes and melting on her lips. The boots she had thought comfortable were only so in the context of a short stroll down a London street. Her feet felt as if they had been jammed into sardine cans and her toes were beginning to ache and to burn. And her fingers *were* freezing—so cold that she couldn't feel them any more.

She had never been so aware of her body in such an aching and uncomfortable way, and with the unfamiliar feelings of physical discomfort came an equally unfamiliar fear. What if they *couldn't* find the place he had claimed he had seen? Hadn't she read newspaper reports of people freezing to death, or getting lost in conditions not unlike this?

A shiver quite unconnected to the cold ran through her. Why hadn't they just waited in the car and sat it out until morning? At least they would have been easily found there. She bit her lip hard, but scarcely felt it, then he stopped suddenly.

'Here!' he said, and a note of satisfaction deepened his voice into a throaty growl. 'I knew it!'

Keri peered ahead, her breath a painful, icy gasp which shot from her lungs. 'What is it?' she questioned weakly.

'Shelter!'

As she came alongside it, it loomed up before her like a spectre. It didn't look either warm or welcoming. It was a very tall building—almost like a small church—and the path leading up to it was banked high with snow. There was no light whatsoever, and the high windows were uncurtained, but at least it was shelter.

And Keri did what any woman would do under the circumstances.

She burst into tears.

CHAPTER TWO

JAY narrowed his eyes and gave her a quick, assessing look. How like a woman! The Canadians had at least five different descriptions for snow; the Icelanders countless more—and so it was with women and their tears. They cried at the drop of a hat, for all kind of reasons, and it rarely meant anything serious. And these, he surmised, were simply tears of relief.

He ignored them.

'There's nobody home,' he said, half to himself. If indeed it *was* somebody's home.

The tears had taken her off guard. She couldn't remember the last time she had cried, for that was one thing her job *had* given her, in spades—the ability to hide her feelings behind a bright, professional smile. She supposed she should be grateful that he hadn't drawn attention to them, yet perversely she felt short-changed because he hadn't attempted to comfort her— even in a small way—and she scrubbed at the corners of her eyes rather defensively, with a frozen fist. 'How can you tell?' she sniffed.

Explaining would take longer than going through the motions, and so he began to pound at the door with a loud fist. He waited, but, as he had known, the place was empty.

'Stand back,' he said tersely.

'Why?'

'Because I'm going to have to get us inside.'

Keri eyed the door, which was made of strong, heavy oak. 'You're planning to kick the door in, are you?' she asked disbelievingly.

He shook his head, half tempted to give a macho display of strength just to show her. 'No, I'll jimmy the lock instead.'

'*J-jimmy the lock?*' It wasn't an expression she was familiar with, but she could work out what he meant. Alarmed, Keri took a step back and very nearly lost her balance, but he didn't appear to have noticed that either. 'You can't do that! That's called breaking and entering!'

He shot her one impatient glance. 'And what do you suggest?' he questioned coolly. 'That we stand here all night and freeze to death just to have our good citizen medals awarded to us?

'No, of course I—'

'Then just shut up for a minute and let me concentrate, will you?'

This was an order verging on the simply rude, but Keri didn't have time to be indignant, because, to her astonishment, he produced what looked like a screwdriver from the pocket of his flying jacket, leaving her wondering slightly hysterically if it was a necessary job requirement for all drivers to have house-breaking skills. She dug her gloved hands deep into the pockets of her coat, and with chattering teeth prepared for a long wait.

But with astonishing speed he was soon opening the front door, a small smile playing at the corners of his mouth as he saw her look of horror.

'You look surprised,' he commented.

'Surprise isn't quite the right word—how the hell did you manage to do it so quickly?' she demanded as she stepped inside and he shut the door firmly behind her.

'You don't want to know,' he drawled. 'Just put it down as one of many skills I have.'

Oh, great! What kind of a maniac had she found herself marooned with? A thief? Or worse?

She eyed him with apprehension, but he was looking around him, his face raised slightly, almost like an animal which had found itself in a new and potentially hostile terrain, his hard body tensed and watchful.

Jay was enjoying himself, he realised. He had forgotten what it was like to live on his wits, to cope with the unexpected, to use his instincts and his strength again. It had been a long time. Too long. 'Nobody lives here,' he said softly. 'At least, not all the time.'

'How can you tell?'

'Because it's cold—really cold. And there's no smell—when a place is inhabited people always leave a scent around.' He stared down at the floor, where the shadowed outline of untouched post lay. 'But it's more than that—it's a feeling. A place that isn't lived in feels lonely.'

Lonely...yes—quite apart from its geographical isolation, the house had a lonely feel. And Keri knew exactly what that meant—you could have the busiest life in the world, but inside you could sometimes feel achingly lonely.

'So here we are,' he said softly. Alone and stranded

in a beautiful house with a beautiful woman. An un-expected perk.'

His voice had dipped, and deepened, and Keri stared at him, the reality of their situation suddenly hitting her for the first time. It was just her and him. As her eyes became more accustomed to the gloom she started to become aware of him in a way which was too vivid and confusing. Not as someone employed by the company who had commissioned the photo-shoot, but as something quite different.

As a man.

The first impression she had had in the car had been the correct one—he was spectacular. Very tall—taller than she was, and that didn't happen too often either, because Keri was tall for a woman—models usually were. But it wasn't just his height which she was in-explicably finding so intimidating, it was something much more subtle, more dangerous, and it was all to do with the almost tangible masculinity radiating off him, and the raw, feral heat which seemed to make a mockery of the weather outside.

Keri swallowed, and inside her gloves the palms of her hands began to grow clammy, and maybe the place had just telescoped in on itself, because right now it felt small and claustrophobic, even though the hall was high and spacious. And perhaps he felt it too, because he reached out a hand towards the light switch.

'Let's see if we can throw a little light on the… damn!'

'What's the matter?'

'Should have guessed. No power.' He swore quietly underneath his breath and pulled a lighter out of his pocket, flicking the lid off and sliding his thumb down over the wheel. His face was startlingly illuminated by the bright flare.

'You don't happen to have a white rabbit in your pocket, too?' she questioned, but she noticed that her voice sounded high and rather wobbly.

He looked her up and down. 'You okay?'

Well, up until he had produced the lighter she had been fine, under the circumstances. Tearstained, cold and slightly shell-shocked, true, but more than a little relieved to be inside—if not exactly in the warm, then at least in the dry. But the more she saw of him, the more she realised that the first impression she had got of him in the shadowed recess of the car wasn't strictly accurate.

She had thought that he was good-looking, but she had been wrong. Good-looking implied something that was attractive on the surface but with little real depth to it, like lots of the male models she knew. Whereas this man...

Her breath suddenly caught in her throat.

The flare from the lighter threw deep shadows beneath the high cheekbones and his eyes glittered with a cold, intelligent gleam. She became aware of a strength that came from within, as well as from the deeply defined muscular build. He looked confident and unshakable, while she, on the other hand, was left feeling slightly dazed.

'I'm...I'm fine,' she managed, thinking that she had to pull herself together. It looked as if they might be here for some time—and if that were the case then she quickly needed to establish some kind of neutral relationship between them. So that they both knew where they were. They needed boundaries so that they wouldn't step over them. She mustn't think of him as a man. He's the driver of your car, for heaven's sake, Keri! And a burly security guard who has been employed to…to…

'Oh, my God!' she exclaimed.

He frowned. 'What is it?'

'The necklace! You're supposed to be guarding the necklace!'

His mouth curved into a disapproving line. 'Well, isn't that just like a woman? Save them from the extremes, find them shelter and safety, and all they can think of is damned diamonds!'

He dug his other hand in his pocket and indolently pulled out the gems so that they fell sinuously over his hand, where they glittered and sparkled with pure ice-fire against the tanned dark skin of his hand. 'There?' He sent her a mocking look. 'Happy now?'

Keri felt anything but. She was used to deference and adoration—she certainly wasn't used to men who behaved with such unashamed masculine *swagger*. Who clipped out orders and broke into strange houses with ease and didn't seem a bit bothered by it. 'You must be the happy one,' she observed. 'Happy you didn't lose them—after all, it's more than your job's worth!'

Jay smiled. It was a remark designed to put him firmly in his place, but Miss Beauty would soon discover that he was a man who did not fit into traditional slots. He slid the gems back negligently into his pocket. 'That's right,' he agreed innocently. 'Can't have them thinking I've skipped to pawn them on the black market, can we? Now, let's see if we can find a candle somewhere. We need to get a fire lit, but first I guess we'd better check out the rest of the house.'

Her teeth were chattering. 'With a view to finding— what, exactly?'

A dark sense of humour made him consider making a joke about corpses, but in view of the tears he thought he'd better not try. The trouble with women was that they always let their imaginations run away with them.

'With a view, sweetheart, to seeing what luxuries this place has to offer.'

There—he was doing it again. 'I am *not* your sweet-heart.'

Touchy. 'Well, then, I guess we'd better introduce ourselves,' he drawled. 'Since I don't even know your name.'

How bizarre it seemed, to be introducing themselves like this. As if all the normal rules of social intercourse had been turned upside down and re-invented. Into what? 'Keri.' She hesitated. 'And I, er, I don't know yours either.'

He could hear her skating round the edges of asking him, unsure whether or not it was 'appropriate' to be on first-name terms with him. She didn't know how to react to the situation, he thought with wry amuse-ment. Or to him. Take her out of her gilded cage and she probably didn't know how to fly properly! Maybe his first impression of a woman who would not bleed or love with vigour and passion had been the right one all along. 'It's Linur,' he said sardonically. 'Jay Linur.'

It was an unusual name, maybe that was why it suited him. Again, she felt the need to re-establish boundaries. 'Are you…American?'

He knew exactly what she was trying to do. That vaguely interested, vaguely patronising tone. His eyes sparked. 'Fascinating as my name must be to you,' he drawled, 'I'm freezing my bones off—so why don't we postpone the discussion until we've had a look around? Want to go and explore?'

'Do I have a choice?'

'Well, I guess we *could* stand around here and make polite conversation.'

'I'd hate to put you under any pressure,' she said sweetly. 'The strain of that might prove too much for you.'

He gave a brief smile. 'It just might,' he agreed silkily, but the subtle taunt set his pulse racing almost as much as the rose-petalled pout of her lips.

He seemed to show no fear, and she tried not to feel any either—yet who knew what they might find in this strange, empty place? Keri stayed as close to him as was possible without actually touching.

Illuminated only by the small flicker from the lighter, he led the way to what was obviously a kitchen—although by no stretch of the imagination did it resemble any kitchen Keri had ever seen before.

From the doorway, she surveyed the faint shape of ancient-looking appliances.

'I'm going to hunt around for some candles,' he said softly. 'Wait here.'

I'm not going anywhere because I can't, she thought rather desperately, as she watched him disappear into the gloom. He doesn't need me at all, but I need him. She could hear him opening drawers and cupboards, and the clatter of china as he hunted around. He suddenly made a small yelp of satisfaction, and when he reappeared it was with two lit candles waxed to saucers. He handed her one, the reflection of the flame flickering in his eyes.

'Hold it steady,' he instructed.

'I'm just about capable of carrying a candle!'

His mocking eyes seemed to doubt her, but he didn't retaliate.

'Come on—we'll look upstairs first.'

There were three bedrooms, but they looked ghostly and unreal, for the beds were stripped bare of all linen and there was no sign that they had been slept in.

'I feel like Goldilocks,' whispered Keri in a hollow voice. 'Any minute now and we'll bump into one of the three bears.'

'I've never been particularly fond of porridge,' he murmured. 'Come on, there's no point hanging around here.'

There was an archaic-looking bathroom, with a huge free standing bath.

Jay went over to the cistern and flushed the lavatory, and a great whooshing sound made Keri start.

'Well, that's something,' he said drily.

Thank God it was dark or he might have seen her blush—but Keri had never lived with anyone except for her family, and this was one more thing which felt too uncomfortably intimate.

They went back downstairs and moved in the op-

posite direction from the kitchen. Jay opened a door
and looked down into pitch blackness.

'Cellar,' he said succinctly. 'Want to explore?'

'I think I'll pass on that.'

On the other side of the hall was a heavy oak, door
and Jay pushed it open, waiting for a moment while
the candle flame stopped guttering.

'Come over here, Keri,' he said softly, his words
edged with an odd, almost excited note. 'And look at
this.'

Keri went down the step and followed the direction
of his gaze. 'Oh, my word,' she breathed. 'I feel like
Aladdin.'

'Yeah.' His voice was thoughtful. 'I know what you
mean.'

It was like stumbling unawares upon a treasure
trove—a gloriously old and elegant room which
looked as though it belonged to another age. Jay held
the candle aloft and Keri could see that it was as high
as four men—with a pointed raftered ceiling made out
of dark, wooden beams—and the room itself was so
big that she could not see the edges.

'Where are we?' she said. 'What is this place?'

He was busy taking more candles from his pocket
and lighting them, placing one on the mantelpiece and
one on a low table in front of the empty grate. 'I don't
know, and right at this moment I really don't care.'

It was amazing what a little light did, and as more
of it appeared so did the room, and the dark, threatening shadows were banished and forgotten as she
looked around. It was beautiful.

There were high, arched windows and a mighty fireplace, with two enormously long sofas sprawled at right-angles beside it. In one corner stood a piano, and there were books crammed into shelves on one wall and pictures on the walls.

'It looks almost like a church,' she whispered.

'Why are you whispering?' he asked, in a normal voice, and the sound seemed to shatter through the air.

'I don't know. Anyway, you were whispering too!' Keri's teeth began to chatter as the icy temperature began to register on her already chilled skin. 'B-but wh-wherever or whatever this place is, it's even c-colder here than it is outside.'

'Yeah.' He crouched down beside the fireplace, an old-fashioned type he had never seen before and big enough to roast an ox in. 'So why don't I light this, and you go and have a scout about—see what kind of supplies there are?' She was looking at him blankly, and he let out an impatient sigh as he began to pull some kindling towards him. 'Sustenance,' he explained. 'Food, drink, coffee, a spare suckling pig—anything.'

Keri eyed the darkness warily. 'On my own?'

He glanced up. Clearly she was a woman to whom the word 'initiative' was a stranger. 'You mean you want me to come and hold your hand for you?'

'No, of course not,' she said stiffly.

'There's nothing to be afraid of.' His voice softened by a fraction. 'Here, take a candle with you.'

'Well, I'm hardly going to feel my way out there in the dark!' She lifted her hand to her head. 'But before I do anything, I'm getting rid of this hat.'

His eyes narrowed as she pulled the snow-damp

beanie off, shaking her hair out so that it fell and splayed in night-dark glossy tendrils before falling down over the soft curves of her breasts. It was a captivating movement, as elegant as a dancer, and he wondered whether it just came naturally or if she'd learnt it from her modelling career. Keep your mind on the job, he told himself.

Except that the job he had set out to do was turning into something quite different. He sat back on his haunches and his eyes travelled up the endless length of her legs. He felt a pulse beat deep in his groin—an instinctive reaction to a beautiful woman. God, it had been a long time. 'Run along now,' he said softly. 'My throat is parched.'

Run along? *Run along?* 'Don't talk to me that way,' she said in a low voice.

He looked up. 'What way is that?'

As though he were some kind of caveman and she was the little woman, scurrying away with whatever he'd successfully hunted that day. Though when she stopped to think about it there was something pretty primitive about the deft way he seemed to be constructing the fire.

'You know *exactly* what way I'm talking about!'

'You mean you just can't cope with a man unless he's paying homage to you, is that it?'

'Don't put words into my mouth!'

If her feet hadn't been hurting so much, and if she hadn't been afraid that the candle might go out, then Keri might have flounced out of the room. But Jay Linur didn't seem like the kind of man who would be impressed by any kind of flouncing, and so she made do with walking, her back perfectly straight, her head held very high.

She made her way back to the kitchen and looked around. It didn't look very hopeful. An ancient old oven which looked as though it had seen better days. A big, scrubbed wooden table. And that was about it. A cupboard yielded little more than a couple of tins, and a box of dusty old teabags which had clearly seen better days.

She filled the kettle with water, but the kettle wouldn't work, and she remembered why and went back into the huge room, where he had managed to coax a tiny flame from the fire.

He looked up. 'What is it?'

'The kettle won't work! There's no electricity—remember?'

He stared at her consideringly. 'How about gas?' He raised his eyebrows questioningly and then shook his head. 'I don't believe it—you haven't even bothered to check, have you?'

She felt like telling him that she was a model, not a girl guide. And that she didn't even *want* a hot drink, and that if he *did* then he could jolly well go and make it himself. But there was something so forbidding about the expression on his face that she decided against it. Being stuck here with him was like a nightmare come true, but Keri suspected that it would be even more of a nightmare if he *wasn't* here.

'No,' she admitted reluctantly.

'Then I suggest you go and try again.'

He was doing it again—dismissing her as if she was a schoolgirl. This had to be addressed some time, and maybe it was best she did it now. 'Did anyone ever tell you that you are distinctly lacking in the charm department?'

'Oh.' There was a pause. 'Is it charm you want you want from me, then, Keri?'

The question threw her as much as the smoky look of challenge in his eyes and the silky note of caress in his voice, and suddenly she became aware of a whispering of unwelcome sensation, too nebulous to define. Almost as if... She shook her head to deny it and gave him her coolest smile, the kind which could intimidate most men—a frosty and distancing kind of smile. 'Not at all—but if you could hold back on the arrogant, macho, bossing-me-around kind of behaviour, I'd be very grateful.'

He raised his eyebrows laconically. 'You don't like it?'

'Show me a woman who does!'

'I could show you legions,' he observed softly, thinking of two in particular.

'Not *this* woman!'

He watched her wiggle out of the room in that sinful leather skirt, imagining its softness as it swished against her thighs.

In the kitchen, Keri gingerly scouted around, trying to rid herself of that strange, tingly sensation which was making her feel almost light-headed—as if her blood had suddenly come to life in her veins, making her acutely aware of the way it pulsed around her body. Here to her temple. There to her wrist. And there. *There*.

Her cheeks burned uncomfortably. Somehow *he* had

done this to her—brought to life in her something unknown and unwanted, with his silky taunts and that lazy way he had of looking at her. And he was so damned *blatant* about it, too!

Had she perhaps imagined that he would feel almost shy in her company, the way men so often did? Dazzled and slightly bemused by the impact of her looks and the status of her job? Especially someone who drove cars for a living, no matter how blessed he had been in the looks and body department.

She held her hands up to her hot cheeks, angry with herself for a physical reaction which seemed to be beyond her control. So it was time to take control. The important thing to remember was that if she *didn't* react to him then he wouldn't behave so provocatively. If she smiled serenely at his attempts to get under her skin then he would soon grow bored and stop it.

She found a battered-looking saucepan in one of the cupboards, and broke a fingernail into the bargain, and she was fractious and flustered by the time she returned, carrying two steaming mugs of black tea. But at least he had managed to get the fire going properly, and tentative flames were licking at one of the logs, bathing the room in soft, comforting shades of scarlet and orange.

She took her coat off and crept towards the fire's warmth. She handed him a mug, then crouched down on the floor, wishing she were wearing something warmer and more practical than a leather skirt and wondering why on earth she had, on such a cold day. Because it's fashionable, she reminded herself, and because the designer begged you to take it as a gift.

Jay Linur had removed his rather battered flying jacket too, but, unlike her, he had obviously made no concessions to sartorial elegance. His outfit was tough and practical. Faded jeans hugged his long, lean legs and he wore a warm dark sweater which softly clung to his torso. Firelight danced flames across the ruffled black hair, which was thick and slightly too long— giving him a buccaneer air which seemed to blend in well with the ancient fireplace.

He looked, she realised, completely at home as he lounged rather indolently along the rug, watching the progress of the fire—all rugged and arrogant confidence as he gazed into the flames, his thick lashes hooding his eyes. He turned his head to study her with lazy interest.

Keri put her mug down and winced as the ragged nail scratched against the palm of her hand.

'Hurt yourself?' he questioned softly.

'Not really, but I've broken my nail—and I can't even file it down—I left my make-up bag in the car!'

He gave a short laugh. 'Outside it's sub-zero, the snow is still coming down with no sign of a let-up, we're stranded God knows where, and all you can worry about is your damned fingernail!'

Keri was stung into defence. 'It isn't just vanity, if that's what you're implying—my job happens to depend on the state of my hands, among other things, and I was supposed to be doing a magazine-shoot for nail varnish next week!' It was, she realised, the first time in her life that she had ever felt the need to justify her job to anyone. So why—especially now, and to him of all people?

Jay took a mug of tea, sipped it and grimaced, wondering what type of world it was where a broken fingernail could mean anything at all other than just that. Not a world he could ever inhabit, that was for sure. Different strokes for different folks, he supposed.

He put the drink down in disgust. 'What the hell did you put in this? Arsenic?'

'Oh, please don't tempt me! I just used what was available,' she said crossly. 'Which were teabags which looked like they belonged in the Dark Ages!'

'Don't believe they had teabags in the Dark Ages,' he responded drily.

Keri almost laughed. Almost. Boundaries, she reminded herself. 'Do you have an answer for everything, Mr Linur?'

He looked at her. *Oh, yes.* The answer was staring him right in the face right now. Her lips were parted, so soft and so gleaming that they were practically begging to be kissed. He didn't have to approve of an icy beauty whose whole livelihood depended on the random paintbox of looks which nature had thrown together, but it didn't stop him wanting her.

'Try me,' he murmured. 'Ask me any question you like.'

There it was again—that tingy feeling, that sense of being out of control, as if she had drunk too much champagne too quickly. Keri swallowed. 'Okay. How's this for starters—just how are you proposing to get us out of here?'

CHAPTER THREE

JAY shrugged. 'I'm not,' he said flatly.

Keri raised her eyebrows. 'You mean that we're going to have to stay here for ever?'

He smiled at her sarcasm. Don't worry, sweetheart, he thought acidly—the idea appalls me just as much as it clearly does you. 'It's an intriguing prospect, but no. There's not a lot we can do, at least until the snow stops. Until then we'll just have to sit it out.'

The thought of that was making her more than uneasy. 'For how long?'

'Who knows? Until the thaw starts, or until someone finds us.'

And who knew how long that would be? 'You haven't even tried telephoning for help!' she accused.

'That's because there isn't a phone. I checked.'

'How can a place not have a telephone in this day and age?'

He shrugged his broad shoulders. It sounded like bliss to him. 'For the same reason that there's no television.' He shifted his legs slightly. 'I suspect that this is a holiday home and that the people who own it have deliberately decided to do away with all modern comforts.'

'Why would they do something like that?'

'The usual reasons. Televisions and telephones create stress, and some people don't like that stress. It's why they sail. Or climb mountains. Why they buy places like this—to escape.'

His voice had taken on a hard note, the tone of someone who was familiar with the word 'escape', and suddenly Keri longed for the safe and predictable. The sanctuary of her London flat—a clean and modernistic haven, as far removed from this big barn of a place as it was possible to imagine. Where heating was instantly produced by the touch of a button and cars and taxis moved comfortingly outside.

A world where men wore linen and silk and paid you clever compliments—not criticising you and then eyeing you with a kind of lazy watchfulness which had the ability to make you feel as flustered as a gauche young girl, and moving their legs as if to draw attention to their hard, muscular definition.

Quickly, she looked into the fire instead. 'Ironic, really,' she said, and thought how loud her voice sounded in the big, echoing room. 'A house designed for people to escape to, and we can't get out of it!'

'It could be a lot worse,' he said grimly. 'At least we're inside.'

Yes, they were. Alone. And Keri had been right— there were no rules in situation like this; they had to make them up as they went along. 'So what are we going to do?'

He sat up. 'Well, first we need to eat.'

'Eat?' she echoed blankly.

'You *do* eat, I suppose?' He watched her in the firelight. She was all bones, he thought—angles and shadows and long, slender legs, like a highly strung racehorse. The leather skirt clung to hips which were as narrow as a boy's, and although she did have breasts, they were tiny, like a young girl's. Jay liked his women curvy, with firm flesh that you could mould beneath the palms of your hands and soft hips that you could hold onto as you drove into them and catapulted them to pleasure. 'Though not a lot, by the look of you.'

'Oddly enough, the well-fed look isn't in vogue at the moment,' she said drily.

'I've never really understood why.'

'Because clothes look better on slender figures and that's a fact.'

Jay gave a half-smile. 'But nakedness looks better on a curvy figure, and *that's* a fact!'

'Well, thanks for bringing the conversation down-market!'

He shrugged. She thought that nakedness was down-market? 'That wasn't my intention.'

'You're saying you don't like thin women?'

His eyes narrowed. 'Careful, Keri,' he said softly. 'That sounds awfully like you're fishing for a compliment, and I'd guess you get more than the average quota of those.'

Yes, she did. It was part of the whole package which came with the way she looked. Men liked to look at her and to be seen with her—from her teen years she had been familiar with the phrase 'trophy girlfriend'. Yet beauty could be a double-edged sword. She had learned that, too. She earned her living through capitalising on her looks, then sometimes found herself wishing that people would see through

to the person beneath—a person with all the insecur-
ities of the next woman.

Defensively, she raked her hand back through her
hair. 'Not a lot of danger of that at the moment, I
imagine. I must look like I've been dragged through
several hedges backwards.'

Her hair had been rumpled by the beanie and she
hadn't brushed it, so it fell in ebony disarray over the
pale silky sweater she wore. Her pale cheeks were
tinged with roses, a combination of heat from the fire
and the exertion of her walk through the snow. Yet
she looked far more touchable and desirable than the
ice princess in the diamonds and silver gown, who had
pouted and swirled for the camera earlier.

'If you must know, you look a little…wild,' he said
softly. 'Like a wood nymph who has just been woken
out of a long sleep.'

Keri had never in her life been called 'wild', neither
had she been compared to a wood nymph, and the
poetic imagery of his words was so seductively powerful that for a moment she felt a slow, pulsing glow
of pleasure. Until she reminded herself that this was
madness.

Complete and utter madness.

Models had notoriously fragile egos—inevitable in
a job in which you were judged so critically on physical attributes alone—but surely hers wasn't so bad
that she needed praise from a house-breaking driver
with a dark and dangerous air about him?

Suddenly she felt like a baby fish, swimming around
in uncharted waters. 'Didn't you say something about
food?'

'Sure.' He rose to his feet and wondered if she knew how cute she looked when she lost the frost princess look and let her lips soften like that. 'How about a fair division of labour? I'll go and see if I can find more fuel for the fire, and you can fix us a meal.'

'You'll be lucky!'

'Oh?'

'It's just that I don't cook. Can't cook,' she amended hurriedly as she saw him frown.

'I'm not expecting you to spit-roast a pig to impress me,' he bit back. 'Just rustle up any old thing.'

Impress him? *In your dreams.* 'There wasn't,' said Keri deliberately, 'anything much in the way of food, save for a few old tins.'

'Then get opening,' said Jay, and threw another log on the fire.

But Keri quickly discovered that this was easier said than done, because the tin-opener looked as though it should have been in a museum.

Jay walked out into the kitchen to find her slamming a tin frustratedly onto the table. Great, he thought! Have a tantrum, why don't you?

'Having problems?' he questioned laconically.

'*You* try using it!'

He picked up the tin and read the label. His voice was cool. 'Tinned peaches?'

'Well, obviously there's no *fresh* fruit—'

'That wasn't,' he exploded, 'what I meant!'

'Well, there was nothing much else to choose from.'

'If you think I'm existing on *tinned peaches*, then you are very much mistaken!'

'Well, would you mind opening them for *me*?'

He dealt with the can quickly, and thrust it away as if it had been contaminated, then bent to examine the contents of the cupboard, rummaging around until he produced a sealed pack of dried spaghetti and a solitary tin of meat sauce, which he slammed down onto the worktop. 'What's wrong with these?'

She suspected that it was going to be a mistake to try to explain her dietary requirements, but she forged ahead anyway. 'I don't eat wheat,' she said.

Jay shuddered. Bloody women and their food fads! Well, I *do*,' he said coolly. 'So would you mind heating these up?' He saw her open her mouth to protest. 'Unless you'd rather tend to the fire?'

She could see the mocking look of challenge in his eyes, as if he knew perfectly well that she had never 'tended' a fire in her life. Lots of people she knew hadn't—so why was he trying to make her feel as though she was in some way inadequate? Just because he was the original cave-dweller, that didn't mean the rest of the world had to follow suit. Very well, she would heat his revolting food for him. 'I'll cook.'

'Good.' And he turned and walked out of the kitchen without another word, thinking that she was undeniably beautiful but about as much use as an igloo in a heatwave. He cast an assessing eye over the fuel. There were a couple of cupboards he'd noticed upstairs; they might yield an armful of blankets which they would need to see the night through. The strain of spending a night closeted with her made a tiny muscle work at the side of his temple, and then he remembered the only room they hadn't explored. Maybe the cellar might come up trumps. Something to ease the tension.

When he returned to the kitchen it was with a look of triumph on his face and a bottle of dusty wine in his hand. He put it carefully on the table.

'Look at that! Would you believe it?'

Fractiously, Keri looked up from the steaming pot. Half the spaghetti had snapped on the way into it, and she had scalded her finger into the bargain. 'It's a bottle of wine—so what?'

'It is not any old bottle of wine,' he contradicted, running his thumb reverentially over the label, as if he was caressing a woman's skin. 'It just happens to be a bottle of St Julien du Beau Caillou.'

His voice had deepened with appreciation and his French accent was close to perfect. Keri couldn't have been more amazed if he had suddenly leapt up onto the table and started tap dancing.

'You know about wine, do you?'

Jay's eyes glittered. The tone of her question said it all. 'Surprising for a common-or-garden driver, is that what you mean?' he drawled. 'Thought I'd be a beer man, did you?'

'I hadn't given it much thought, actually.'

Liar, he thought. You'd placed me in the little box of your sterotypical expectations. Though, when he stopped to think about it, hadn't he done exactly the same to her? Except that she seemed to be living up to hers—with her faddy eating habits and general inability to cope with the practicalities which misfortune sometimes threw up at you. In fact, she seemed pretty good at looking beautiful and not a lot else, as far as he could make out.

He found a corkscrew and raised his dark eyebrows at her in question.

'So, will you be joining me, Keri?' he queried. 'Or holding out for a glass of water?'

She *would* normally have had water, yes—damn him—but tonight Keri had never felt more in need of a drink in her life. And at least it might make the time go a little faster. Might even calm her frayed nerves and help her to sleep. She gave the pot another stir. She didn't even want to *think* about the sleeping arrangements.

'Yes, I'll join you in a glass,' she said repressively.

'How very gracious of you,' he murmured. He eased the cork from the bottle with a satisfying pop and, as always, the sensual significance of that didn't escape him.

Keri looked down at the saucepan and grimaced. She had seen more appetising things served up in a dogbowl. 'Shall I dish this out?'

Hunting through a cupboard for glasses, Jay glanced over his shoulder. 'Can't wait,' he murmured.

He poured two glasses of wine and watched while she picked up the heavy saucepan with two hands and carried it over to the sink. Hell, her wrists were so thin they looked as if they might snap.

'I can't find a colander anywhere.'

'Give it to me,' he said tersely. He rolled the sleeves of his sweater up and took it from her before she could drop it, using the lid to drain it, shaking his dark head a little as he did so. 'I can't believe that you've got to…what age are you?'

She supposed it would be pointless to tell him that it was none of his business. 'Twenty-six.'

'Twenty-*six*!' He carried back the pot. 'And you can't even cope with spaghetti!'

'This is the twenty-first century!' she retorted. 'And it isn't written into the female contract that she needs to cook!'

'Then pity the poor man you marry,' he offered.

'Well, there's no need to worry on that score,' she answered, more testily than she had intended, because her attention had been caught by the sight of his arms—all tanned and muscular and sprinkled with hair as dark as his head. At his wrist was a slim plait of leather.

A stir of interest quickened his blood. 'You mean there's no likely candidate on the horizon?'

She heard the sultry change in his voice and her eyes met his in a long, unspoken moment across the table. Its impact was such that she felt as if he had turned her to stone. Or clay. Yes, clay—far more malleable than stone, and that was exactly what she felt like at that moment. Clay—all damp and squidgy. Malleable.

Keri was used to a man looking at her with interest—she had encountered it often enough in the past—but never, never with such devastating *effect*. The slanting eyes glittered only momentarily, and the hard smile was so brief it might almost have been an illusion, but it was enough.

Enough to what? To set her pulses racing with the

knowledge that this was a man quite unlike any other she had ever come into contact with. Steely-edged and strong and capable—and yet, inexplicably, one who could read a wine label in the most perfect accent.

She wanted to say *Don't look at me that way!* She wanted to tell him that he didn't have a hope in hell if *that* was what he was thinking—even while a Keri she didn't know or recognise was wondering what it would be liked to be imprisoned in the embrace of a man with arms as muscular and as powerful as his.

'Keri?' he said softly.

His voice seemed to come from a great distance away, and her own, in response, sounded low, husky— a world away from her usual cool tones. 'Y-yes?'

'Get a couple of plates down, would you?'

He saw the flustered look in her eyes as she quickly turned away. So she had felt it too—that indefinable chemistry which existed between the sexes and sometimes shimmered through the air when you were least expecting it.

No, that wasn't quite true. *He* had been expecting it. He was as hot-blooded as the next man. Mix up an attractive man and an attractive woman, stir in a little bit of circumstance, and usually the result would be fairly predictable. Jay had been used to women coming on to him since he was old enough to want them to.

But Miss Beauty was different. This was a woman who would put up defences—probably a necessity when you looked the way she did. She would be wary and on her guard against men who wanted her—and what man in his right mind wouldn't?

And you didn't get a woman like that to want you back-not unless you played her very carefully.

Keri put a plate down on the table with a hand which wasn't quite steady.

'You aren't eating?' he asked.

'I'm not eating that,' she said. 'I'll have the peaches.'

'You're kidding?'

'No, Jay, I am not. They will do just fine—and you should never eat a heavy meal before—I mean…after six,' she finished, licking at lips which were suddenly parched. She had been about to say *before bedtime*, but she'd bitten the words back in time.

'Suit yourself.' He shrugged his shoulders and began to ladle the food out, liking the way she'd said his name—real slow and sweet, as if she'd dipped the single syllable in honey.

She watched as he heaped on what seemed to be an enormous amount of food.

'You honestly aren't planning to eat all that yourself?'

He flicked her a glance. 'I have a big appetite,' he said gravely.

Keri felt her knees grow weak. This was awful. Or was it inevitable that once sensual awareness had shivered into the mind it was impossible to think straight, or to forget it? He's your *driver*, Keri, she reminded herself. 'Then you should be careful,' she said coolly as she dolloped peaches into a dish. 'Or one day that muscle will turn to fat.'

'I don't think so. If a man stays active he doesn't get fat, and I am *very* active.' He smiled. 'Now, let's take all these goodies next door. We can sit in front of the roaring fire and then…'

'Then what?' she questioned, her voice rising in alarm.

'Then you can tell me the story of your life.' His eyes gleamed with anticipation. 'So far.'

CHAPTER FOUR

SOMEWHERE between the kitchen and the cavernous sitting room Keri gave herself the kind of silent pep-talk that she hadn't really needed since she was in that hormonal state of mid-teen flux which made girls think their heads were composed of cotton wool.

There was no denying that he was a gorgeous man, nor that she seemed to be attracted to him, in a rather confusing, pulse-racing kind of way. But that was hardly surprising. You would need to have been made out of stone not to acknowledge his physical presence or his to-die-for face. And he had taken charge and got them here safely, and there was an unmistakable appeal about that too. A man who could protect definitely did appeal to an age-old and very feminine need which until this moment she hadn't realised she possessed.

Yet it was more than that. All her adult life she had mixed with men who were good-looking, who probably could match him muscle for muscle—though theirs was of the type which was honed at the gym, which she suspected Jay Linur's wasn't. He looked as if he had been born strong and capable.

But looks were just the exterior package—she of all people knew what they could hide—and the thing about Jay Linur which seemed to set him apart was a kind of inner confidence and ease. And, yes, it was

49

surprising for a driver, and particularly surprising that he didn't seem to be fazed by the fact that he found himself in these isolated surroundings with a woman who would usually have the most confident man slightly lost for words.

Perhaps it was because he had nothing to lose that he seemed to have the ability to treat her as she was so rarely treated—as if she was just another woman and he was just another man.

Which was all he was. A man who was capable in crisis, but ultimately a man she would never see again once that crisis was resolved. So she had better forget all about the hard, rugged profile and stop snatching surreptitious little looks at the hard-packed body.

The fire was roaring now—a glorious blaze of amber and crimson logs sending off the most delicious smell as they burned—and she saw that he had put a small pile of blankets down to warm, well out of spitting range.

Keri sniffed the air, her heart hammering, trying to draw her attention away from the heap of blankets and its implications. Where on earth where they going to *sleep* tonight? With an effort, she dragged her thoughts back to the fragrant smoke. 'Mmm.'

'Applewood,' he informed her as he put the tray down. 'And there was dried lavender scattered in the bottom of the basket. Good, isn't it?'

Keri nodded. He had parked his long-legged frame on the floor, and after a moment's indecision she joined him. Because it made sense. This was where the warmth was—as close to the fire as possible.

But it seemed too intimate—a feeling not helped by

the fire, nor by the fact that the candlelight created a romantic look to the room. Never before had she realised the seductive potential of candlelight even though she had sat in countless restaurants which used it. She told herself that the soft, flickering light was designed to create a romantic 'mood', and she must be sure and remember that the mood they were creating here was an illusion.

He poured her a glass of wine. When she was pensive like that she looked ridiculously young—softer and sweeter. But models were tough—they had to be. He'd known a few in his time—women who wore so many different masks that in the end you wondered whether there was any real substance beneath.

'Here,' he said.

'Thanks.' She turned her head to take it from him, startled by the cold, searching light in his eyes, as if he was examining her under a microscope, as a scientist would.

'Eat,' he said sardonically. 'Mmm—those peaches look so tempting!'

Keri had trained her appetite rigorously over the years. She had learnt to regard hunger as a normal state; you needed to if you were to fit into the clothes you were expected to wear on shoots or on the catwalk. Unlike most of her peers, she didn't smoke any more—and whenever she wanted more food than she knew was necessary to maintain her slender frame she usually went for a walk, or read a book, or arranged flowers. Displacement therapy—none of which were remotely possible here and now.

She ate a peach and took a large gulp of wine, trying

to ignore the smell of Jay's food wafting towards her and trying not to watch as he curled the spaghetti round his fork and ate it with a pleasure which was almost sensual. How could some meaty slush like that smell so...so tempting?

For a while he said nothing, just ate with slow and obvious enjoyment. Then he moved a forkful towards her. 'Here. Have some,' he coaxed softly.

The smell was tantalising. 'I don't eat wheat,' she said weakly. 'Remember? Or...or red meat... particularly out of a tin.' She screwed her nose up in an expression of disgust she didn't quite feel.

'Suit yourself.' He transferred the forkful back and ate it himself, and began to scoop up another.

On the one hand she knew exactly what he was doing—trying to tempt her into eating when he knew she didn't want to—and yet there was this unrecognisable Keri who didn't care, whose stomach was empty and rumbling.

'Go on,' he said. 'You know you want to.'

His eyes were brilliant, hard and gleaming like a diamond, and now another loaded fork was just inches away from her mouth. Keri responded instinctively, her mouth opening like a goldfish, and he ladled the food in before she had had time for second thoughts.

She closed her eyes and ate it, afraid to see the mocking look of triumph in his, but sheer greed—a new and rather frightening animal—took over and she gave an instinctive little moan of pleasure.

'Like it?' he murmured.

Her eyes snapped open, but it was not triumph she read in his eyes, but relish, as if he was pleased to see her discovering the delight of indulging her hunger and then satisfying it.

Keri shrugged and gave him a rueful look. 'It's delicious.'

He put some more on the fork and held it up to her. 'See what you've been missing?'

She shook her head. 'No, honestly, I couldn't...'

'Shut up,' he said, but gently. 'And eat.'

The second forkful went the way of the first, and two more followed. She shook her head. 'I mustn't have any more—really, Jay—I'm eating all your supper!'

He considered telling her that he had deliberately put enough food on the plate for two, but decided against it. If she thought it had been pre-planned then her defences might go up, and that he most definitely didn't want.

The heaped fork moved from where it hovered close to her mouth back to his, and his lips closed round it. Something about that gesture was deeply erotic. There was silence, save for the spitting of the fire, and her eyes were fixed to his, as if they had drawn her in by their sheer, mesmeric power, rendering her incapable of breaking the gaze.

He licked his lips and smiled. 'One for me, and one for...you.'

Keri opened her mouth like an obedient child, feeling both weak and strong as he fed her again. The food was filling her full of warmth and energy, but it was an odd, slumberous kind of energy, and with it came helplessness as she recognised that never before had she realised that eating in itself could be a very sexual act.

Very soon the plate was completely clean, and Jay surveyed it with satisfaction and then looked at her. 'What a pity it's all gone. I was enjoying that.' He meant the feeding, not the eating.

Another gulp of wine. 'Yes.'

He glanced down at the dish of peaches—all golden and glistening and slickly luscious—and the stealthy beat of desire grew even stronger. 'We've still got pudding,' he said softly, and his eyes gleamed out a silent challenge. 'Your turn now.'

But Keri couldn't. Just the thought of slipping the soft fruit into his mouth was enough to make her feel very churned up indeed. Her hand would shake—she just knew it would—and then he might get some inkling of what was going on inside her head.

And her body.

Her limbs felt weighted and deliciously lethargic, and yet there was the sensation of blood beating like thick syrup through her veins, of her fingers and toes inexorably unfurling, along with her senses.

She shook her head, grounded and yet unbearably dizzy. 'Not for me, thanks, I'm full—but help yourself.'

Jay didn't want the peaches, not unless she was going to feed them to him the way he had done to her, but his brief feeling of disappointment was replaced by an infinitely better one of expectation. He thought of the blonde who had been pursuing him these past months—she wouldn't have fed him the peaches either, but by now she probably would have had half his clothes off and be busy feeding herself on his body.

It had been a long time, he realised, since he had wanted something he wasn't sure he was going to get.

'I'll pass too,' he said idly, and leaned back against the sofa instead, cradling the claret in his hand and watching the living beauty of the fire. 'So, how long have you been a model?'

The question broke the mood she had longed to be broken, but Keri had to fight her unreasonable sense of dismay. Conversation like this was safer by far—and surely that was preferable?

The wine had made her garrulous. 'Since I left school—well, actually, that's not quite true—I was still *at* school.' She thought how at ease he looked, lying there, one leg bent at the knee as he balanced his weight negligently on his elbow, the wine sending out dappled ruby reflections over his strong fingers, and she found herself imagining those fingers running with instinctive mastery over her body. Oh, for heaven's *sake*, Keri, she chided herself—since when did you start having fantasies like that?

'Mmm?' He raised his dark eyebrows, as if to prompt her, trying to rid himself of the image of her in pigtails and a school uniform.

With an effort she dragged her mind back to the subject in question. 'I was visiting London with my sister—'

'Is she a model too?'

Keri shook her head. 'No, she's a mother.' And a widow. She rushed on, the thoughts of that too painful. 'We were just having a coffee at Waterloo Station when a woman came over and asked if I'd ever thought about modelling.'

'The way it happens in all the movies?'

'Sort of.'

'And had you thought about it before that?'

Keri shrugged. 'It had crossed my mind from time to time—other people were always telling me I should try—but...'

His eyes gleamed. 'But?'

'Well, what I really wanted to do was interior design. Added to that I was very tall and very skinny, and that makes you kind of self-conscious.'

'Not the best quality for someone hoping for a career in front of the cameras, I would have thought,' he observed thoughtfully.

She had thought that too, but had soon discovered that a skinny and insecure girl who towered over her peers could become someone else in front of the camera. When it was make-believe it was easy to pretend that you were supremely confident and at ease with yourself.

'I was lucky,' she said truthfully. 'All that self-consciousness just vanished in front of the lens—and my face is one of those which looks better in photographs than it does in real life.'

He didn't agree. He thought she looked softer and more touchable in real life—far more of a woman when she wasn't acting up for the lens. 'The camera loves you, you mean?'

She nodded. 'So far—touch wood.'

'And what happens when it no longer does?'

Keri frowned. With uncanny precision he had

alighted on every model's most abiding fear—of being last-year's face, the face the public have tired of. 'Some people go on for years,' she said defensively.

'That isn't what I asked,' he mused. 'I was asking *when*—because presumably few continue into old age?'

Keri sipped at her wine again, because that seemed easier than answering straight away. He really did seem uncomfortably good at asking the right sort of questions. Or the wrong. She couldn't think of an answer that would satisfy him—or herself. That occasionally she dreamed of a 'normal' life? If she said she wanted to get married and start a family it would sound needy, as if she was unfulfilled because she didn't have a man.

And that wasn't true—she couldn't even lose herself in the everywoman fantasy about one day falling in love with a man who matched her every emotional and physical need. The two seemed intertwined; you couldn't have one without the other—and when you had never had one in particular...

She was aware that he was still looking at her questioningly, and she hoped that those discerning eyes hadn't noticed the fact that her cheeks had grown warm—but even if they had she guessed she could always blame it on the fire.

She stared into the flickering flames. 'I've never really given much thought to the future.'

'So the interior design went by the wayside?'

'I guess it did.' She looked up at him and met the question in his eyes with a shrug. 'I've done a few

projects—just for fun, really—my own apartment and
my sister's house, and I loved doing those.'

'So why not switch careers?'

'Because I haven't quite reached the stage of ageing
has-been,' she remarked sardonically. 'And even if I
wanted to it's notoriously difficult to break into something like that unless you have experience, and to gain
experience you have to start at the bottom of the ladder.' She gave a grimace. 'And I'm not sure I'd want
to do that. Not now.'

'You could always branch out on your own,' he
suggested.

Keri frowned. Since when had *he* become an expert
on careers? He was hardly in a position to offer advice! She switched the interrogation from him to her.
'And what about you? I mean, do you plan to be a
driver for the rest of your life?'

Her subtle emphasis on the word *driver* didn't escape him, and Jay smiled as he refilled their glasses.
She wanted to put some distance between them, to tell
him that he was stepping out of line by asking such
searching questions, particularly given his lowly
status.

He sighed. People got so hung up on status—they
let it blind them to the things that really mattered and
they hid behind it, as if it could protect them from the
world.

'Well, that's the beauty of a job like this,' he said
expansively. 'Easy come, easy go.'

How casual he made it sound—and yet it was interesting, in a funny kind of way. She never mixed
with men who didn't put ambition at the top of their

list of desires. 'And have you always done it?' she asked curiously. 'Driving, I mean?'

Jay almost laughed aloud, and if he hadn't been so easy in his own skin he might have taken offence at her assumption. Did she *really* think that he would have been happy sitting behind the wheel of a car all these years, ferrying around people like her, who were so far removed from the real world as to be on another planet?

His expansive mood evaporated. He threw another log on the fire. He didn't broadcast his past; people—especially women—seemed to be fascinated to the point of intrusion by a life which had been composed largely of excitement and danger and deprivation and discipline. His mouth tightened.

'Not always, no.'

His evasion interested her too, because in her experience men were renowned for wanting to talk about themselves.

'Oh? What kind of things have you done?'

Now she was very definitely patronising him, and it had the effect of making him want to master and subdue her. He suppressed it. For the moment.

'I was in the US Navy,' he said shortly. 'A SEAL.'

Keri screwed her nose up, but he didn't appear to be joking. 'What's that, exactly? I mean, I've heard of Navy SEALs, but I don't know much about them.'

He relaxed a little. She didn't know much about them. This was one of the reasons he'd chosen to come back to England—over here there was none of the SEAL-as-hero stuff which he'd lived with since the age of eighteen.

'What is a SEAL?' He played it down, the way he always did. 'Well, we root and toot and parachute,' he murmured, his eyes glittering as he saw her look of utter incomprehension. 'We're a combination of frogman and paratrooper,' he explained. 'We blow things up, dive to the deepest depths and jump from insane heights.' *And we always get the pretty girl.*

'So, were you an officer?'

This time Jay did laugh. He guessed that type of differentiation would be *very* important to her. One of the ratings certainly wouldn't be good enough for Miss Beauty. 'Yes, Keri,' he answered gravely. 'I was an officer.'

That explained a lot. The strength, the resourcefulness, the cool confidence in a crisis. And the body, of course—hard, honed muscle like that was the result of years of training. She had been right—you didn't get to look like that if you just frequented the gym, no matter how often.

And the US bit explained the slight drawl, the accent she had never heard before—and it might also explain the ease with which he spoke to her, because weren't Americans better at breaking down class barriers than their English counterparts?

'So you *are* American?'

Her body language was relaxing into the conversation, her long, long legs as coltish as they'd looked in his driver's mirror. Jay remembered the brief, tantalising view of her lacy stocking-tops and he felt the deep beat of his pulse in response. Maybe he would talk all she liked, if that was what it took to loosen her up.

'Half and half,' he said. 'Or maybe neither. That happens sometimes when you're torn between two cultures.' He saw her interested, inquisitive gaze. In any other situation he would have changed the subject—moved it on or away—but this was not any other situation, it was this one, and its very isolation seemed designed to draw out confidences he would usually have kept locked away.

'I grew up in both countries after my parents divorced,' he said tightly. 'My father was American and my mother British—but I hold dual nationality and that's what qualified me to join.' Along with an endurance test designed purposely to weed out all but the very toughest of the tough.

Keri blinked in confusion. Surely being in the US Navy was a lot more preferable to *this*? 'And did you er, did you *have* to leave?'

'You mean, was I kicked out?'

'No, I didn't mean that—'

'Oh, yes, you did, and no, I wasn't—it was just time to leave.'

'You'd had enough?'

Yes, he'd had enough. Too many demonstrations of how ultimately frail man could be—too many reminders of the shortness of life and the inevitability of death. It was a young man's game—always had been and always would be—and it needed a young man's vigour and invincible belief in himself. Once that was gone you were no good to anyone—least of all yourself. Or to people who needed you...

'Something like that,' he said shortly, and this time he could do nothing to stop the memories which came back to haunt him—nothing like as powerful as they had been in those early days and nights, but still powerful enough to make him flinch. Memories of death and betrayal which were light-years away from most men's experiences. And honour. Always honour. Honour and service.

'That kind of job has its own limited life-span—a bit like yours, probably.'

A muscle was working in the strong face, and for the first time Keri noticed a tiny, tiny scar which tracked down it. She reached her hand out, as if to touch it, but she did not. 'How did you do that?'

His eyes grew cold and hard, like flint.

'Oh, just something,' he said dismissively.

Keri knew when not to probe any further, and she dragged her attention away from his face, feeling curiously disorientated. She was alone in a deserted place with a man she scarcely knew—a man with muscles which looked real and a scarred face. A real man, not a silk-clad concoction of the city.

She should be scared and on her guard, but she wasn't. Inside, she felt warm and replete from the unexpectedly delicious food, and lulled by the velvet glow of the rich wine. She stretched her legs out, as if testing how far they would reach, feeling at peace, something beyond her control subduing the knowledge that this was somehow *wrong*—how could it be?

All she was doing was making the best of a bad situation. Only she was fast coming to the conclusion that it wasn't so bad at all. Quite the contrary. The fact that he had been in the Navy gave him a life other than as a driver, and somehow it made her feel *safe*.

She felt her gaze drawn towards him again and found that his attention was on her. It was a curious yet assessing look, and maybe she should have looked away, but she didn't—didn't want to. His eyes were dark and glittering—she still couldn't make out what colour they were—and all she was aware of was that a ripple of awareness had begun to lick at her skin.

There was a sudden soft hush in the air. Jay saw her relax. Saw the reflex as her fingers lost the tension which had stiffened them, like the way a woman relaxed after orgasm, and he felt the irresistible kick of desire as he put his empty wine glass down in the grate.

There were times to move and times to stay, and he would have wagered every cent he had that she wanted him to move. And why not? They had a long night to get through.

Flopping into her dark eyes was her over-long fringe, and he reached out and touched it, as if to brush it away. But he didn't. The feel of her skin was so soft that he left the tip of his finger right there, began to curl one of the wayward strands around it.

It felt curiously and inexplicably right. She should have shaken her head away, or demanded to know just what he thought he was playing at. And what did she do? She said one little word.

'Jay…' The word came out as a murmured and breathy little sound; it didn't sound a bit like her.

'Mmm?' He heard the catch in her voice and felt the race of his heart. 'Don't you like me tidying up your hair for you, Keri? It's all mussed.'

But he wasn't tidying up her hair at all, she thought

wildly. The hair lay neglected as instead he stroked his fingertips down her face to the line of her jaw, and she shivered beneath what was outwardly such an innocent gesture but which felt like the most erotic thing she had ever felt before. And how ridiculous was that?

'Don't you?' he urged.

'It's okay,' she admitted.

'Only okay?' he purred. 'Then I must be losing my touch.'

The arrogant boast should have raised her defences, for it implied that he was a consummate expert where touching women was concerned, but all Keri felt was a debilitating curiosity to know whether he was.

Losing his touch? Like hell he was! Helplessly, her eyes fluttered to a close as he began to stroke her neck. She lifted her head so that more of it was available to him, and the ripple of sensation became a stronger swell which pulled her along with it.

Keri felt pure excitement and expectancy as his touch danced sweet, tantalising pathways over her skin, as if he was opening up sensitive nerve-endings for the first time. How could the simple brush of someone's fingers against someone else's neck be so...so *electric*?

'Sh-should we be doing this?' she questioned unsteadily.

CHAPTER FIVE

JAY nearly said that they weren't doing anything...not yet, but instead he smiled a brief smile. 'It isn't a capital crime, is it, sweetheart, for me to touch you?'

'That...that wasn't quite what I meant.'

'Oh, I get you.' The smile hardened into one of granite. 'You mean...that it's unprofessional?' he queried acidly. 'Because I'm just the driver and you're the...client?'

Her eyes flew open at the use of a word which was open to rampant misunderstanding, but he shushed her with a shake of his dark head and his smile became cajoling.

'But I'm not working now, Keri,' he said. 'Neither are you. And what we do in our own time is nobody's business but our own. Is it?'

Put that way, it seemed to make sense. 'No,' she agreed slowly. 'I guess not.' She couldn't think straight; she was lulled by his touch, by the blinding light in his eyes and the sensation of her blood growing thick and heated in her veins, wanting him to touch her some more. Somewhere that wasn't her neck.

'Such a beautiful neck,' he mused, his voice deepening like a connoisseur. 'Like a swan—so pale and pure—such beautiful lines.'

'Why, thank you,' she murmured, once again taken

aback by the elegance of his words, which seemed so at odds with his tough, no-nonsense exterior.

She smiled, and Jay smiled back, knowing what a woman wanted when she smiled at you like that. She was so accessible, so unexpectedly compliant, and he leaned forward and placed his mouth where before there had been only his fingers, opening his lips slightly as they touched against her neck, so that he breathed soft and warm against the silk of her skin. He felt her instinctive shivering response beneath him, and the biting of her fingernails into his shoulders as she reached up her hands to grip him.

'Oh!' she breathed.

He continued to graze his lips against her neck, sensing that she wanted him to kiss her properly, but he knew from experience that the best way to turn a woman on was to make her wait. The slow, slow burn. But he felt her distracted little movement, the restless shake of her head, and suddenly it wasn't so easy to do that.

He lifted his lips from her neck and took her face between the palms of his hands, giving her one hard look before he lowered his mouth to hers. He kissed her long and deep, and it was as if someone had just pressed a button marked 'sizzle'.

Her lips opened hungrily, greedily to his, and she swayed against him, making no protest when he pulled her to the floor and into his arms, and through the desire which was fast building in his groin he felt momentarily taken aback.

He had expected ice, not fire. He had expected to have to work a lot harder than this... His fingers moved experimentally to her thigh, waiting for her to sit up and tell him that this was outrageous, but she did no such thing, just made a little moan of encouragement. He smiled as his fingertips roved upwards, to find the lacy provocation of her stocking-top and the silky skin above it. So his first impression had been the wrong one; she was obviously a lot more physical than he had thought.

She wriggled with pleasure as she felt the splay of his fingers over her inner thigh. 'Jay!' she whispered.

'Mmm?' His mouth was on her breast now, suckling at her tiny breasts through the thin sweater she wore, and her fingers moved distractedly to thread themselves in his hair. That was when he moved over her and began to kiss her.

'Oh, God—Jay!' she moaned.

He raised his head and looked down at her, his eyes glittering and impenetrable as his fingers tiptoed over her cool yet heated flesh. 'What is it?' he questioned unsteadily.

'That's good,' she breathed, a note of wonder in her voice. 'So good.'

'Tell me about it,' he said, in an odd strained voice, as his hand moved further and alighted on the delicious moistness of her panties. She writhed and mouthed a husky little plea until he lowered his head and began to kiss her again, feeling like a man who had tried to light a match and then discovered he had dynamite in his hands.

Maybe it was because it was so unexpected that the desire he felt was close to explosion point already, and

Jay sucked in a dry, painful breath. Take it easy, he told himself. And take it slow.

But she didn't seem to want that. He knew enough about women to realise that she was pretty close to the top. Roughly, he slid the leather skirt up her thighs and her legs parted for him. She was so warm and so wet. With a little groan he reached up and slithered the panties down, noting the way that she lifted her feet to help him. Oh, yes—she wanted this—maybe even more than he did.

He pushed the skirt still further up. Leather wasn't the easiest material in the world to cope with, but there wasn't a skirt invented which couldn't be slid up, and soon he had it rucked up round her hips, leaving her deliciously accessible. And that was when he discovered that she was shaved completely bare, and the unexpected novelty of *that* made him want to take her there and then, but he held back. He was good at holding back—a lifetime of discipline and training paid dividends at times like this.

'Oh, my,' he murmured, on a low, sweet note of anticipation. 'Now, what shall we do next?'

'Anything,' she gasped. 'Everything.'

She was so eager! 'How could any man resist an invitation like that?' he murmured.

Keri experienced a mixture of disbelief and satisfaction as he moved downwards and she felt the tickle of his dark hair between her knees. Her head fell back—she had never liked this, never let... And then his lips were brushing up her thigh, his tongue slicking its way up and up until it found the most intimate part of her, and then her mouth parted and she gave a tiny scream of pleasure.

It was as if someone had catapulted her into another dimension, or as if someone else had suddenly started inhabiting her skin. She began to move her head from side to side—and surely those gasping little cries weren't *hers*?

'Oh, Jay,' she moaned softly. 'Jay, Jay, *Jay*!'

Through a sensation so intense that she thought she might pass out, some tiny voice in her head reached out to tell her that she shouldn't be letting this happen, that someone had to stop it and it had to be her.

But she couldn't.

Wouldn't.

Not now.

Especially not now, because something was happening to her and she wanted it so badly that she felt she would die if she didn't get it. Something which was filling her with a fast-building heat and an unbearable hunger, and she was terrified in case it would go away and she would fail to reach it.

'Jay!' she whispered, on a tiny, pleading note.

He didn't answer. He was too busy orchestrating her response with the seasoned flick of his tongue—tasting the sweetness of her unmistakable woman's taste, teasing her with a featherlight touch which soon had her sobbing.

Keri heard her own wild, uninhibited cries, but they seemed to come from a distant place—and maybe she'd invented them, because she never cried out like that before. As if she was desperate and yearning and scared and seeking all at the same time—like being on a runaway train which just wouldn't stop.

He felt her tense, and knew she was close, and he licked at her luxuriously until he felt her spasm against his mouth. He held onto her hips while she bucked against him, tasting her sweet surrender. It seemed to go on and on and on, and he remembered reading somewhere that when women shaved like that it made them more sensitive. Was that why she had done it? To increase the power of her orgasm? Then he really *had* misjudged her.

Keri's breath shuddered to a slower pace while she alternated between the drenching bask of pleasure and the shaken sensation that this was what had eluded her all along. So this was why sex turned people's lives upside down and inside out and back again.

And it had taken a virtual stranger to show her.

A great bursting ache of pleasure seeped its warmth through her body, and as he came to lie over her again she breathed one heartfelt word.

'Beautiful.'

He smiled, and touched his lips to her nose. 'Yes, you are.'

'That wasn't what I meant.'

'I know it wasn't.' He brushed a strand of hair away from her damp cheek. 'Now, look at me.'

Cautiously, she opened her eyes, terrified of what she would find written in his. What would he think of her now? So wild and so free and with such little provocation? But there was no censure on his face, though the shadows thrown up by the firelight onto those cheekbones made him look faintly formidable. And his mouth was as soft as his eyes—if only she knew what colour they were—as if he were about to enjoy a delicious feast, and she felt strangely shy, the power of what had just happened to her making her realise just how inexperienced she really was. Especially compared to him. And now? What now? Could there be more, and as good as that? Suddenly her starved body was greedy.

He touched his lips to hers. She could taste herself on his mouth, and that felt so unbelievably intimate that she sighed, snaking her arms around his neck to pull him closer. She could feel the hard, flat planes of his body, and the cradle of him, where he was harder still.

'That's *good*,' he murmured approvingly. He ran his hand over the skirt, which was rucked up almost to her waist. 'Is it warm enough to take this off, do you think?'

The fire was blazing, and her skin was still glowing in the aftermath, but it seemed that his question had not really required an answer. He was pulling off his sweater with a practised hand and tossing it aside.

Underneath, a slim-fitting dark T-shirt moulded itself to the muscled sinews of his chest and he peeled that off too. She saw the rich, tawny skin, the sprinkling of hair which arrowed down to the waistband of his jeans. Oh, but he was magnificent! The way she had always known that a real man should look.

She trickled her fingertips over the oiled silk of his torso. And he felt the way that a real man should feel too. 'You are so beautiful,' she said shyly.

He smiled as he observed her rapt preoccupation

with his skin. For a moment there he had thought she was going to be a selfish lover—taking, never giving. Wanting only pleasure for herself without wanting to give any back. And thank heavens he had been wrong.

She was coming back to life, and the contrast between this near shyness and how wild she'd been earlier was making him feel as weak as water. Then he glanced down and saw the clean lines of her slim body, reminded himself that she was shaved—and how many women did *that*? So it figured that the shyness was probably just a show, to salve her conscience, to make her feel less guilty about what she had just let him do to her.

'Want to take my jeans off for me, Keri?' He ran her hand down the shaft of his thigh and glittered her a provocative look. 'I'm just putty in your hands.'

Insecurity threatened to swamp her as she felt like a complete novice in the light of his obvious and breathtaking experience. She dared not say no, but her hands were trembling so much that she was afraid she might make a complete mess of such a simple act.

He saw the shaking fingers and smiled. 'Don't hurt me now, will you?' he drawled mockingly.

'I…I'll do my best.'

Jay gave a low laugh—weren't the English the masters, or the mistresses in this case, of understated irony? She had just had the most mind-blowing orgasm and now she was fumbling around like a sweet young virgin.

Somehow she managed to get his jeans off, and everything else too, her heart beginning to thunder again when he was finally naked, lazily and assuredly naked, save for the narrow plaited band at his wrist. But she didn't have time for second thoughts, because he was skimming the rest of her clothes off until she, too, was naked. He pulled her against him, wrapping his long, strong limbs around her, the sensation of his warmth and his strength driving every thought from her mind other than the realisation that she wanted—no, *needed* him to make love to her. Properly.

'Oh, Jay.'

'What is it?'

How had this happened, and when? Her head fell heavily to his shoulder as he began to stroke at her breasts, and wherever he touched her it was though he burned into her, making her nerve endings shriek aloud in recognition. 'You make me feel...' The words trailed off, for there were no words for the way he made her feel.

'Wanton?' he prompted, his words molten whispers against her cheek. 'Because that's the way I want you to feel, Keri. And now just feel me. Go on, sweetheart—feel how much I want you.'

She touched him, feeling him spring against her, so hard and so virile, and it was as though she had never been intimately acquainted with a man's body before.

And maybe she hadn't. Not like this. Filled with a sudden need to explore him. As if she wanted to touch and kiss and caress every single centimetre of his body. She reached down to encircle him in her hand, curling her fingers around the rocky shaft, and some instinct made her writhe her hips against him even while she bent her head to tease and graze at his nipple with her teeth.

Jay shuddered beneath her touch. God, she was passionate! Too passionate, because suddenly he knew that he could not wait, that this was good, but not good enough. He had never felt so full, so hard, so ready to burst, and he wanted more. Everything. The real thing.

Decisively and irrevocably he moved over her, and Keri's eyes snapped open in alarm. 'You will…you will use something, won't you?'

It was a sensible question, and one which did not need to be asked, since his hand was already reaching out for the pocket of his jeans—yet it irritated the hell out of him and he wasn't sure why.

But he found what he was looking for and gave up thinking, sliding the condom on and then sliding straight into her. He groaned because she was so tight—oh, so beautifully tight—that it was almost over before it had begun, until he reined right back.

As he moved he lost himself in her heat, hearing her gasp in time with each exquisite thrust, and he heard some deep, primeval sound dragged from deep within his own lungs. Maybe it was because it had been too long, or maybe because this was like an unexpected gift, but his senses seemed more highly tuned than normal. This was the closest you got to heaven, he decided through the achingly sweet mist. And the furthest place from hell. This, this, *this…*

She cried out just before he did, tightening her arms around his neck and pulling his head down to kiss him, so that at the moment of abandonment they were locked together in every way that counted. She revelled in the feel of him inside her, the sensation of someone so big and so strong being momentarily helpless, caught in the grip of passion which made his powerful body shudder, and she thought she had never known anything quite so heart-stoppingly beautiful.

Emotions were funny things—they pounced on you at unpredictable times—but a woman was especially vulnerable after lovemaking, and Keri especially so just then. She felt rocked in the aftermath of debilitating pleasure, and then in flooded doubt, insecurity and an aching wistfulness which began to gnaw away at her dreamy state. How heartbreaking that it should have taken her until now to experience something as beautiful as this. She bit her lip.

Jay drew his mouth away and dropped his head heavily onto her shoulder, feeling empty, sleepy. He yawned against her skin and closed his eyes.

Keri felt the steady slowing of his breathing and her heart sank. She wasn't holding out for comfort or reassurance—she just wanted him to say something—anything—even if it wasn't true. For what could *she* say to him, when what had just happened was completely outside her experience?

Encroaching sleep was stalled by the sudden tension in her body, and Jay stifled a sigh. Why could women never let you sleep? Didn't they know that a man was empty—literally empty—after orgasm? That he had lost part of his body during the act and needed to recoup his strength? But he guessed he owed her more than that…she had, after all, been so very, very sweet.

He raised his head, his eyes dazed and smoky, about to murmur his appreciation when he saw her look of utter confusion and he frowned. Please don't come the *we shouldn't have done that* trip on me, he prayed silently.

He stared down at her gravely, his fierce expression warning her not to go down the route of pointless regret.

'Do you always look so uptight afterwards?' he observed softly.

Something in his unspoken censure made her do what she hadn't planned without stopping to think about the consequences. And she told him.

'I'm not sure.' She saw his look of confusion, but it didn't come even close to her own. 'That was the…my…my first time,' she admitted shakenly.

Jay froze. Oh, dear God, no—not that. 'You sure didn't *act* like a virgin,' he stated disbelievingly.

If she had been watching a film the scene might almost have been funny. But it was real, and it was happening to her, and funny was the last thing it was.

She shook her damp hair. 'That wasn't what I meant—of course I'm not a virgin.' But she might as well have been, for all that the other times counted next to this. Her body felt as though it had been steeped in sweet, sticky syrup, but she felt totally defenceless—as though he had touched a part of her that had been a mystery until now.

His eyes narrowed. His thinking wasn't at its best at times like this. 'Your first time?' he repeated carefully. 'What was?'

'My first orgasm,' she said in a small voice. 'Or, rather, my second now.'

CHAPTER SIX

FOR a moment there was complete silence, save for the hissing and spitting of the fire and the thunder of Keri's heart—so loud that it deafened her and surely must him too, when they were still so close and he was still intimately joined to her.

'Say that again,' he instructed softly.

To admit it once had been bad enough, and twice would be toe-curlingly awful, but she guessed it was too late in the day to play coy.

She attempted a shrug, but the truth in this particular case was bald, and no words could infuse it with a soft glow. 'I've never had an orgasm before.'

He withdrew from her abruptly and reached over to haul some blankets from the heap, throwing one over both of them, but he didn't pull her back into his arms, just levered himself up onto his elbow and surveyed her with steady, unblinking eyes.

'You're kidding?'

'You think my sense of humour is that warped?'

'I guess not,' he said slowly.

He leaned over and caught a strand of her hair which was dangling over her cheek. He looped it behind her ear and, stupidly, her stomach went to mush. She was missing him touching her, she realised. Wanting all over again that closeness which had seemed closer than she had been to anyone else—but that was an illusion, brought about by pleasure. She had not been close to him, not really—only in the physical sense, and that wasn't the way which counted.

'How come?' he murmured, seeing the brief tremble which shivered her skin, and he took her into his arms again, sensing that this was more complicated than he had thought. Though when he stopped to think about it he hadn't exactly been doing much *thinking*—had he?

'I'm sure you don't want a catalogue of my disastrous love-life,' said Keri, resisting the urge to snuggle right into him, as though that was an intimacy too far.

'Well, not a blow-by-blow account, that's for sure!' But it was a mistimed attempt at humour. 'Hey,' he said, his voice softening, for her lips were a soft pucker that he found himself wanting to kiss all over again. 'Come here.'

For a moment she was rigid in his arms, like an ice-cube refusing to melt, but then reaction kicked in and she began to dissolve under his touch, and for the first time in her life she realised the true supremacy which could be wielded by a man who brought a woman such heart-stopping pleasure.

The last thing he wanted was some kind of heavy scene on his hands. He dropped a soft kiss on the top of her head. 'You don't have to say anything—not a thing—if you don't want to.'

He was lightly skating his fingertips over her back now, an almost innocent gesture which should not have aroused her, but Keri had tasted pleasure and she was greedy for more.

But that was crazy. Once in the heat of the moment could be understood—but doing it again would be a whole different ball-game. Wouldn't it?

Almost imperceptibly she shifted away from him, so her breasts were no longer pressing into his chest, and Jay felt the tug of desire subside.

'It's just never happened before,' she whispered.

'I find that hard to believe.' He traced the line of her lips with a thoughtful finger. 'Someone as gorgeous as you. I thought men would be busting with a kind of macho pride to show themselves as great lovers.'

Someone as gorgeous as you. Keri supposed that a lot of women might have preened at that, but she had spent her whole adult life having compliments paid about her looks. Overkill—which resulted in them meaning nothing.

And would someone like Jay even begin to understand that what was perceived as physical beauty often got in the way? Men often regarded her as a possession—like a piece of priceless porcelain which must be treated with reverence and respect. And porcelain was cold, whereas she was warm flesh and blood. Or so she had just discovered with him.

Maybe if she hadn't been lying naked with him in front of a fire she might have clammed up, closed the subject completely. But the sudden rattle of the wind against one of the windows reminded her that outside a storm was still blowing and they were completely cut off, blanketed against the outside world, cocooned against the snow in this fire-darkened room. Could anything touch her here except for pleasure itself?

'I think that men are intimidated by me,' she admitted, growing hot with remembered rapture. Her voice was suddenly breathless as she turned her head to look at him. *He* certainly hadn't been intimidated. 'Which makes what just happened all the more amazing.'

There was a long pause while the implications of *that* hit him like a sledgehammer. 'You mean the lowly driver and the beautiful model?' His tone was dry, mocking. 'Not so unusual, I think, Keri. Literature is full of examples of unsuitable couplings—the high with the low, the rough with the smooth.' He ran his fingers over her belly with masterly possession, feeling her shake beneath their practised touch.

'So what was it that really turned you on?' he drawled. 'Are you one of those women who like a bit of rough—with the kind of man you wouldn't normally meet? Or was it the Navy connection—maybe you dream about a man in uniform? A lot of women do, you know, and you may be one of them.'

How had she been so short-sighted as to imagine that she was cocooned from pain and hurt in this place when his words were as wounding as arrows? She tried to push his hand away. 'Stop it—how dare you say those things?'

But he gripped her fingers, curling his own around them in a sensual trap and bringing his face close up to hers, his breath warm and sweet and wine-scented.

'It wasn't meant to be an insult,' he amended on a murmur. 'Just a problem you might like to solve, and then hopefully it won't happen again.' He grinned. 'Or, rather, it will!'

That hurt even more, and for a moment she couldn't figure out why—and then she realised that she had given herself to him passionately and freely, and now here he was, helping her to work out where she had gone wrong before, talking already about a future which did not include him. But it couldn't—she knew that, and so did he. Their lifestyles were oceans apart, their interests probably similarly separate. All they had was a physical compatibility which was almost cruel in its random unsuitability.

'Hey,' he said softly. 'Problems always have solutions, you know—don't look so sombre.'

Her chin came up, suddenly strong, almost defiant. Surely a woman was allowed one indiscriminate love affair in her life? From her back-catalogue of practised smiles, she fished out an I-don't-care one.

'I didn't mean to.'

'Good.' He stroked her cheek and she kissed him, softly and sweetly, and then harder, and deeper.

He groaned. Closed his eyes and let the world dissolve away. He moved his head and heard her catch her breath as the rough rasp of his jaw skated over her breast.

She swallowed as he caught a nipple in between his teeth, nipping and licking at it until she gave a sharp little cry of pleasure.

'Like that?' he murmured.

'No, I hate it.'

He laughed. That was better—easier by far to make love to a woman when she wasn't coming over all helpless.

'Jay, do you...?'

'Do I what?' he questioned thickly, between licks.

She had almost forgotten what she was asking, but then his hand snaked between her thighs again and she knew she must not be led by feeling alone. But it was hard to think of anything other than this hot, dark mist of wanting.

'Do you often do this kind of thing?'

'Funnily enough...' The pad of his thumb circled cool, silky flesh, and he felt her sigh of pleasure against his neck. He smiled as he moved it to where it was more heated, so that her head fell back against the rug. 'I don't often find myself marooned in the snow with beautiful models.'

Which hadn't been what she had been asking at all.

He stopped what he was doing and raised his head to look at her. Her eyes were closed, her expression abandoned and her hair spread out behind her, like a glorious shiny black pillow, and he felt the unexpected leap of his heart. 'If you're asking whether I sleep around indiscriminately,' he said huskily, 'then the answer is no. If you're asking for numbers, then I'd say it was none of your business—just the same as I wouldn't dream of asking you. Is that fair, Keri?'

Fair? She couldn't say, and frankly didn't care, because by now all she wanted was for him to carry on with what he had been doing. She had succumbed to his lovemaking and it wasn't going to last beyond the thaw, when they found their way out or someone found them. He had her in his thrall, and to deny that would be stupid—so why not just lie back and make the most of it?

But it seemed that Jay had other ideas, for once he

had stroked on another condom he effortlessly lifted her up, bringing her right down on top of him, his eyes narrowing as he heard her startled gasp of delight as he filled her.

'Do it to me,' he murmured, on a note of sensual invitation. 'Will you, Keri?' She *was* shy, he saw that now, and he shook his head in a gesture which spoke of both despair and elation. What kind of men had she known in the past?

He smoothed the flat of his hand gently down the side of her hip and saw the look she gave him—a look full of tentative trust and yet fear—and silently he damned his own sex for the way they sometimes took pleasure and left a woman with none. His voice softened. 'Only if you want to.'

He felt so hard inside her, as though he had been made to impale her just like that—the key fitting the lock in a door which had finally swung open.

'Yes, I want to,' she whispered. 'More than anything.'

His laugh was low and full of delight, and he let out a slow breath. 'Oh, me, too,' he murmured. 'Me, too.'

It felt different. Strange but wonderful. And Keri was filled with a suffusing kind of warmth and power as she assumed the dominant position over such a dominating man. She began to move, tentatively at first, seeing what pleased him most and then finding out what pleased her too.

He whispered soft words of encouragement and enticement, and touched his fingers to her breasts, and somewhere along the way she lost her inhibitions completely—taking him with her—wild and free—exulting in the sweet, shared journey—only bending her head to kiss him once she saw the rapture take him over and then felt herself caught up in it too. It overcame her with a force which was unstoppable, and she gasped and gasped until there was no air left in her lungs, shuddering out his name in a shaking voice.

She looked down at him, and their eyes locked in a long and silent moment before he pulled her down into his arms.

For breathless minutes they lay there, his arms wrapped tightly around her damp back. Her skin felt like smooth satin against his fingertips and Jay felt an inexplicable sense of contentment creeping over him. As if he could sleep for a million years, maybe more. For once he didn't fight it, just rested his head against her neck and yawned.

'That's three,' he murmured lazily, and fell asleep.

CHAPTER SEVEN

KERI awoke, naked and aching and glowing beneath a blanket, and batted her eyelids hard in confusion, certain that she must still be sleeping. Cautiously she opened her eyes fully against the sharp light.

Where the hell was she?

Pale winter light filtered down through high stained-glass windows, and the blur of white outside the big picture window was a bank of snow. Snow. And then back forged the memories of the long, erotic night and she turned her head to find the space beside her empty.

Jay.

Gone.

She blinked her eyes against the sun dazzling off the snow, remembering the long, sweet night. He had made love to her over and over again—she had lost count of the times—and just as sleep had finally laid its claim on her she had been aware of him disentangling his arms and getting up. She had felt the warmth of blankets as he had floated them down over her—but their warmth in no way matched up to the heat generated by his body.

'Jay,' she had murmured, on a protest.

'Go to sleep,' he had commanded.

Automatically she smoothed down her hair, her hands drifting to breasts which still tingled from his touch, and she felt the slow creep of colour into her cheeks, uncertain whether it was caused by desire or remorse.

But she wasn't going to feel ashamed—most definitely not. What had happened between them had been beautiful—Jay had said so himself, over and over again through the exquisite night which had followed—and how could something so beautiful ever be wrong?

Because life isn't like that, jeered a little voice somewhere in her head. You can't just take pleasure and expect there to be no outcome; there is always a price to pay.

She sat up, her hair falling down all about her shoulders. Where *was* he? And why on earth should she feel shy about calling out his name when last night she had given herself to him completely? And called it more than once then.

'Jay!'

And suddenly there he was, standing in the doorway, leaning against the doorjamb and surveying her with thoughtful eyes. He was, she noted with a disappointing sinking of her heart, already dressed. The darkening of his jaw made him look even more elemental than he had done the night before, and he just stood there, watching her, a curious and unreadable half-smile on his lips.

She could see for the first time that his eyes were green-grey, the colour of sage—wise and all-knowing, all-seeing. Just what *did* they see? she wondered. *Say something, Jay,* she pleaded silently. *Just say something.*

'Good news,' he said, his mouth relaxing into a smile.

Her heart missed a beat. 'Oh?'

'The power's back on. See.' He lifted his hand and flicked a switch and electric light flooded the room, dazzling her even more than the sun outside, so that she blinked her eyes against the bright artificial light.

She knew she ought to be enthusiastic, but this wasn't the conversation she wanted to have. The power supply was about the last thing on her mind. 'That's good. But could you please turn it off—it's blinding me?' Her voice sounded flat as he did as she asked, and she turned her head to stare unseeingly at the bank of brilliant snow outside.

She had expected him to say…what? That last night had been wonderful? That he wanted to do it all over again? She felt a slow, melting ache as she looked at him, because heaven only knew—*she* did.

But she felt shy again, and unsure of herself—the wild, free woman of last night was now like a cold and distant memory. If he wasn't going to mention it, then should she? Could what have happened between them be classified as a one-night-stand? And, if so, was there some kind of etiquette as to how you behaved afterwards? Because she sure as hell didn't have a clue what it was. She felt like the new child in the playground, where everyone else knew how to play the game and wasn't going to tell her the rules.

He saw the look on her face and ran a few options over in his head. If he went over there and took her in his arms then one thing was certain to happen, and he wasn't sure if that was a good idea, for all kinds of reasons he didn't care to analyse. Because Jay had never been into analysing feelings and he wasn't about to start now.

'You want to wash up?' he suggested slowly.

Her body was slick and redolent of the scent of love, but there was some alien, sentimental part of her that wanted to stay that way—a million miles away from the woman who showered twice a day without fail.

'We have towels?' she asked, babbling the words out as if they mattered.

'We do,' he answered gravely.

She wrapped a blanket around her and rose to her feet—and she of catwalk fame, who could flounce and strut to the insistent beat of the music, now found herself as gangly and as awkward as a newborn foal. If this was what orgasm did for you then you could keep it.

But as she went to walk by him he reached out a hand to catch her waist, drawing her up close to his body, and he felt himself grow hard in an instant. He bent his head so that his breath was warm against her cheek.

'I'd like to do it again too,' he whispered.

Keri closed her eyes, revelling in the nearness of him which awoke every aching sense all over again. 'I never said I wanted to do anything,' she whispered back.

'You didn't have to.' His voice was as soft as butter at room temperature. 'It was written all over your face.'

She heard the arrogance in that statement and tried to pull away from him. Was she really that transpar-

ent? Or was that the way all women reacted to him?
'You aren't blaming me this morning for wanting what
you wanted so badly yourself last night?'

'Blaming you?' He frowned. 'Are you out of your
mind? Of course I'm not blaming you.' He held her
tight and she melted against him. 'It was a two-way
thing, Keri, and it was pretty amazing—' Which was
an outrageous understatement and he knew it. 'But it
would be nothing short of irresponsible to go back to
bed now.' He glanced over at the heap of rumpled
blankets and his eyes gleamed. 'Or at least go back to
the floor.'

She couldn't laugh, couldn't move. One word stuck
out like a razorblade, half concealed beneath the snow.
She looked up at him. 'Irresponsible?'

'Sure.' His eyes narrowed. 'You don't think people
are going to be worried? You said you had an appointment last night—who was that with?'

She stared at him blankly, as if he was speaking
about another universe entirely, and then she remembered. Oh, Lord! 'David,' she said dully.

David. Yeah, it figured. Jay's mouth flattened and
he dropped his arms and let her go, wondering why
he should have thought otherwise. 'Well, don't you
think that David might be worried?' he questioned
coolly.

The fact that he hadn't asked her any questions hurt
Keri more than she had expected. She wanted to say
David is just a friend, but the complete disinterest on
his face stopped her stone-dead. He could have asked
but he hadn't asked—and the reason for that was as
plain as the day.

He *didn't care.*

Jay's mouth thinned into an expression of distaste. So was this David a suitable partner? he wondered. Good for the glamour stuff but a wash-out in bed? His eyes were very clear and hard, and so was his voice.

'He'll have wondered why you didn't show,' he said. 'And presumably he might have heard about the weather conditions and put two and two together and reported you missing? Didn't that occur to you, Keri?'

Nothing had occurred to her at all, bar the touch of his flesh against hers and the kiss of his lips. The outside world might not have existed for all the thought she had given it, cocooned inside in the warm, giving circle of his arms.

Now she felt stupid. And uncomfortable—as if he was judging her.

Keri shrugged her bare shoulders. 'It sort of slipped my mind.'

But there was no complicit gleam of understanding in his eyes, just that same coolness which rivalled the snow outside.

'Then I suggest we make a move to get out of here. You'd better get washed and dressed. I'm going out to see what the roads are like—maybe see if I can dig the car free.'

'You want me to help?'

'No,' he said shortly. 'I work better on my own. Fix us both something to eat and I'll be back as soon as I can.'

Just that, and then he was gone. No long, smoochy kiss or smouldering look promising more passion. Keri shivered as he slammed out of the door and a gust of chill wind blasted its way over her skin.

She found a sliver of soap in the bathroom and washed as best she could, trying to keep her mind on the task in hand and not to let it wander in pursuit of questions which could not be answered. At least she must be grateful for the slow trickle of hot water, which right at that moment felt a million times better than her usual power-shower.

She dressed in yesterday's clothes and went back down to the kitchen, where the leftovers from last night's meal lay congealing in the saucepan. She shuddered and upended them into the bin, then boiled a kettle and made herself a cup of black tea, wondering how long Jay would take and whether he would be successful.

He was gone for the best part of two hours, during which time she washed the dishes and tidied away the blankets in the sitting room. She pulled a book down from the shelf and curled up on the sofa, but she didn't take in a single word of it.

And then she heard the sound of a car drawing to a halt, and moments later Jay came in. His skin was flushed with exertion, fine sweat sheening the strong face, and his eyes were glittering.

Keri sprang to her feet, her heart thundering, searching his face for something—*anything*—but his features were non-committal. She knew that it mocked common sense, but deep down she was praying that they would be stuck here for longer.

'You…freed the car?'

He nodded. 'I did. The sun had softened the snow—

it wasn't difficult. The roads look okay. I think we should make a move—at least to the nearest town.' He paused, having decided on his strategy while he was shovelling snow. 'You can catch a train there.'

She was already disappointed, but at these words her mouth suddenly dried. 'I don't mind travelling with you.'

'No,' he said flatly. 'I don't want to risk it happening again.'

What? she thought, slightly hysterically. The breakdown, or the lovemaking? She saw the quick glance he flicked at his watch. 'You mean you want to leave straight away?'

'In a minute. I'm starving. We'll eat first, and then we'll get going.'

'Eat what?' she questioned steadily. 'You saw what there was.'

There was a heartbeat of a pause. 'We can heat up what we didn't eat last night.' He saw the look on her face and his eyes grew flinty. 'Oh, no.'

Oh, yes. 'I threw it away. We can't eat spaghetti bolognese for breakfast!'

'Brunch.' His eyes were cold. 'So we eat nothing. Is that right, Keri?'

She could feel his rage bouncing off him in almost tangible waves. 'You're angry,' she said flatly.

'Well, what do you expect?' he demanded incredulously. 'I've just been out doing hard labour, which produces real hunger—not the automatic mood to eat at mealtimes which you get from hanging around an office all day. Or the self-imposed denial brought about from trying to maintain an unnaturally low body-weight! Can't you do *anything* practical?'

'I can paint walls,' she said, stung into self-defence.

'Yeah, very useful under the circumstances! Just give that ceiling a quick coat, will you, while we starve to death?'

His contempt was withering—and not, she realised, simply because she had thrown the food away. In a couple of sentences he had managed to dismiss her world, and the standards by which she lived. Well, that should take care of any foolish romantic dreams she might have been in danger of harbouring.

'I'm sorry.' She met his gaze squarely. 'There isn't really a lot else I can say—unless you want me to try to fish it out of the bin for you?'

He looked at her. Since when did missing a meal make him grouchy to the point of unreasonable? Surely not because she'd had a date with a man last night? If she chose to play away then that was up to her—he certainly wasn't into making moral judgements.

And there was no point in parting on bad terms. It had, after all, been pretty…well… He shook his head in slight disbelief. 'Come here,' he said softly, and held out his hand.

A stronger woman might not have taken it, but Keri was not feeling particularly strong right then. Was this the price that you paid for the beauty and the closeness which went with the kind of sex she had shared with Jay? The feeling that he was now somehow *part* of her? As though he had captured something of her and now she belonged to him, unable to shake free the invisible chains which bound them?

You're being fanciful, she told herself. But his mouth was in her hair, and on her neck, his breath hot and warm and rapid, and she felt an instant response, threading her fingers greedily into the tangled thickness of his dark hair.

In an instant he was aroused, but he forced reason to take over from sheer physical desire. He lifted his head and stared down at her, a diamond-hard smile angling his mouth. 'The sooner we get moving, the less chance there is of the police being alerted. Could waste a lot of money if they mount an abortive rescue campaign. Unless, of course, you have a secret fantasy about being winched to safety by a helicopter?'

Keri blinked rapidly. How could he remain so calm and so reasonable, be able to switch off so thoroughly while she was at the mercy of a swirl of emotions which left her reeling?

All she could hear was the pounding of her heart and the swishing rush of her blood. She didn't want to go, or move from this place, and yet clearly he did. And he was right. There were people waiting for them back home who would be beginning to worry—she couldn't just turn her back and pretend they didn't exist.

Yet surely a man of his calibre was wasted, just driving round the country like this? Couldn't his undoubted gifts of strength and resourcefulness be put to some better use? And couldn't she be the one to point him in the right direction? Broach it gently, carefully, she thought. Don't offend his pride or his masculinity.

'Jay?'

Something was coming, and she wasn't about to ask him what he thought the road conditions would be like.

He kept his voice neutral. 'Yes, Keri?'

'It's been…well…'

'Wonderful—yes, it has.' He kissed the tip of her nose.

'And…well, haven't you ever thought that you're—well, *wasted* doing this kind of thing?'

He raised his eyebrows. 'In what way, exactly?'

His face looked so forbidding that she regretted having started, but she couldn't really stop now. 'Well, driving for a living.'

'There's something wrong with driving?'

There was some undercurrent to his voice that she didn't quite understand. 'Oh, there's nothing actually *wrong* with it—'

'Well, thank heavens for that,' he murmured sardonically.

'It's just that you seem to have so much else to offer…' She saw the slight twist of his mouth and rushed on, terrified that he might think she was alluding to his prowess in the lovemaking department. 'I mean your SEAL background, your resourcefulness. The way you got us out of a jam and made the best of it—not a lot of men could do that.'

Which, translated, meant *I want to go to bed with you again.* He kept his gaze steady. 'Well, thanks,' he murmured.

'Someone like you could make a fortune,' she continued softly, 'if you really set your mind to it.'

As in-house stud to beautiful but unfulfilled women like you? he wondered. But he couldn't admit he wasn't tempted—what man wouldn't be? He looked down into the wide dark eyes and thought fleetingly of telling her, and seeing her reaction *then*. But it wouldn't work—it *couldn't* work.

Would he call her up and ask her to dinner? To talk about *what*, exactly? The fact that her mascara had run? That she'd gained a pound? In other words ruin it—and ruin the memory into the bargain. He had told her more than he had intended to, but he could blame the weather and the isolation on that false intimacy.

But women always misinterpreted confidences—which was why he didn't usually fall into the trap of allowing any. They read more into them than they ought to, started thinking things which made him want to run a mile.

He hadn't been lying when he'd told her that it had been wonderful, but it was nothing to do with her world. Or his. And he was pragmatic enough to walk away from something before reality ruined even the memory of it.

'Well, I'll bear that in mind,' he said evenly, and his eyes glittered. 'Any time I'm thinking about a career change.'

Her face had gone very pale, and he was reminded of that look of trust and fear when he had lifted her onto his lap in the middle of the night, and he relented, sliding his fingertips down over the silken skin of her cheek.

'Listen, Keri,' he said. 'What happened last night was great.' His voice became a silken caress. 'You've

proved to yourself that you can have satisfying sex—
you just have to find the right man.'

The words hung on the air as clearly as if he had
painted them on a banner in letters six feet high. *But
that man isn't me.*

She knew that anyway.

A shudder of distaste ran through her. He thought
all she was talking about was physical satisfaction. She
had wanted not to hurt *his* pride and now it seemed
that it was going to take a monumental effort to sal-
vage her own. She pretended that there was a camera
trained close up on her face, and smiled as coldly as
the air outside.

'Didn't you say something about dropping me at the
nearest train station?' she questioned.

He nodded. So she wasn't going to cling. Predict-
ably, he found himself a little disappointed—but
wasn't that just human nature for you? Contrary as
hell—just like he was.

He looked down at her, drinking in the perfection
of her one last time. She looked, he realised, the very
antithesis of the ice queen he had first met—warm and
sensual and alive. Had he done that to her? Brought
life to her sexual desert? He remembered the eagerness
with which she had opened her body to him during
that long, exquisite night and some primitive emotion
flitted across his soul. He wondered why he was feeling some kind of misplaced loyalty to this guy David
she had been due to meet. If a man couldn't bother to
learn how to give a woman pleasure, then surely he
got what he deserved.

And why not complete this assignment himself? 'I

guess I'll catch up with you at the launch,' he said casually.

She had been mentally resigning herself to the fact that this was the last time she would see him, and his words startled her. 'The l-launch?' she stumbled.

'Sure. For the diamond campaign,' he elaborated. 'If you're the face which is about to sell a thousand gems, then won't they expect you to be there?'

Yes, of course they would. A lavish party at one of London's top hotels, which normally she would have considered a necessary duty in the line of work. But now...Keri's heart leapt with excitement and there was nothing she could do to stop it—because she wanted to see this man again more than she could ever remember wanting anything in her life. 'You mean that you've been invited too?' she questioned, equally casually.

'Hardly, sweetheart.' His mouth twisted into an odd kind of smile as he heard the note of surprise in her voice. 'I'll be there guarding the jewellery.'

CHAPTER EIGHT

ARRIVING back in London was like being on a different planet; there had been no snow in the capital other than a brief flurry of flakes which had melted before they touched the pavements. And Keri felt like a different woman from the one who had left there the day before.

She let herself into her apartment to find the Ansaphone flashing. Five messages. But she didn't play them straight away—for once having other things on her mind. She wandered from room to room feeling displaced, as if she were seeing the gleaming apartment for the first time and comparing it to the very basic standard of the house where she had experienced such intense physical love.

Keri shivered.

It was as if Jay had pervaded her senses with a power which seemed to throw everything else into the shadows. Acutely, she could remember the magic of his touch, the hard brilliance of his eyes and the fleeting softness of his features relaxed in the act of love. And she knew she couldn't even think straight until she had washed every trace of him from her body.

She threw a huge handful of her most expensive bath-soak into the tub and submerged herself, right up to her nose, closing her eyes and breathing in the fragrant fumes as she prayed for the glowing ache to leave her.

The messages were from David, her model agency, her sister, her model agency again—yes, the driver had contacted them about the diamonds and would she please let them know she was back safely?—and David again—where the hell was she?

Her head was aching by the time she pressed the 'delete' button. With a slight sense of cowardice she left a message on David's home phone and told him she was safe and would call soon. Then she punched out her sister's number, and the connection was made on the second ring.

In the background, Keri could hear the sound of a toddler screaming. 'Erin?'

'Keri! Thank God! Are you okay?'

Tough call. 'Well, I'm back—safe and sound.'

'What happened? David's been ringing—he said you hadn't showed and that he couldn't get hold of you.'

'I didn't know he had your number.'

'Neither did I. Keri—what the hell has been going on?'

Her whole world had been turned upside down, that was what. 'Can I come over and see you?' she questioned slowly.

'Of course you can. When?'

'I'm on my way,' said Keri grimly.

Her sister lived in the same city, but a few miles away from the expensive centre which Keri inhabited. It was short on parks and green open spaces, and maybe not the ideal place to bring up a young child, but for now it was home. One day, her sister said, she might just do the sensible thing and move to a cheaper and far-flung place in the countryside, but not yet. Erin still had too many memories to be able to bear to tear herself away from them.

Her husband had been killed in a hit-and-run, his life snuffed out like a candle. He had never seen his unborn son, nor lived to achieve the success he had worked so hard for. For a while Keri had thought that Erin might crumble and go under, but she hadn't. Thank God she'd had the baby. Thank God.

The door opened and Erin stood there, her dark eyes narrowed as she stared at her twin.

Nature had given her exactly the same mix from the genetic paintbox as Keri—black eyes, black hair, tall, rangy build—yet the two sisters no longer looked like two peas in pod. Or maybe their experience of life had just made them different.

Erin's hair was tied back in a French plait—her face entirely free of make-up. She was slim, though slightly rounder than Keri, and she rarely wore anything other than her tough workaday uniform of jeans and a shirt.

Her eyes narrowed as she stared at her sister. 'What's happened?' she demanded.

It was that shorthand, that telepathy of someone knowing you so well and so instinctively, who could read your face in an instant. Erin had had it with her husband, but Keri had never had it except with her sister.

'Where's Will?'

'Asleep. Tantrummed-out. So let's make the most of the peace.'

Keri slumped into an armchair and sighed, and then it all came tumbling out. The snowstorm. The breakdown. The man with the grey-green eyes who had been so unfazed by her while she had been dazzled and captivated and infuriated by him in turn.

'And attracted?' questioned Erin shrewdly. 'I mean sexually?'

There was a pause. 'Oh, God, yes. Overwhelmingly.'

The silence spoke volumes.

'So you slept with him.'

It was a statement, not a question, and Keri's head shot up. 'You're shocked?'

'Utterly.' Erin laughed. 'And, no, before you ask—not because I'm making a judgement, but because it's so unlike you!'

'I know it is,' said Keri unhappily.

'And now you've fallen for him big time?'

'I hardly know him.' But something had been forged that night—something she couldn't even come close to explaining, not even to herself.

'So get to know him better! Are you seeing him again?'

'Sort of.' Keri met a pair of eyes identical to her own.

'What's that supposed to mean?'

'He'll be at the diamond launch—it's at the Granchester Hotel, on Saturday.'

Erin frowned. 'As your guest?'

Keri shook her head. 'No. He'll be guarding the jewellery.'

'So it's not a date?'

'Nowhere near a date.' Keri sighed. 'The point is that he didn't ask for one.' Even after everything that had happened between them. Or maybe, she thought, with a sudden painful sense of insight, *because* of what had happened between them.

'You could have asked *him*,' Erin pointed out. 'This is the twenty-first century.

'A woman shouldn't have to,' Keri said stubbornly.

'Oh, Keri!'

'Anyway, it wouldn't work. He's a driver.'

Erin assumed a look of disgust. 'You don't believe all that crap?'

'No,' said Keri slowly. 'But I suspect he does.'

'Maybe that's why he didn't ask,' said Erin. 'And you can't really blame him. Think about it—you're one of the country's top models and he sits behind the wheel of a car for a living! Of course he isn't going to ask you out, because he isn't going to risk what he sees as certain rejection!'

'Despite the fact that we made love?' But the words seemed wrong, as if she was using them to dress up the act, to give it more importance than it actually merited.

'Of course!' Erin scoffed. 'Having a physical compatability is one thing—but going out together throws up all kinds of problems! Maybe he'll be worried about using the wrong knife if he takes you out to eat!'

Keri wanted to tell her sister she'd got it all wrong, that Jay had qualities which superseded his lowly position. Indeed, she'd never met a man so comfortable in his own skin. 'No. He isn't like that,' she said slowly.

'Well, in that case, just wait to see what happens on Saturday.' Erin leaned forward. 'Forgive me for sounding prurient, and you certainly don't *have* to answer this, but some of us live in a sex-free zone these days. Was it...?' Her voice was tentative. 'I mean, was it...good?'

There wasn't possibly anyone else in the world she would have told—except Jay, of course—but her sister was her own flesh and blood, and closer than close.

'Oh, Erin, it was the best,' she said simply. 'The very best...ever.'

There was silence for a moment, and then Erin nodded. 'Then maybe he's liberated you at last, Keri,' she said gently. 'And now you're free to find yourself a real relationship with someone else.'

Without intending to her twin had made it all sound like a question of mechanics—as if fulfilment was what it was all about. So was it? When something like that happened—did it bind you close to a man, even if he was the wrong man? And wouldn't it sound crazy to admit to her sister that she didn't want anyone else other than a sloe-eyed stranger who had made her feel like a real woman?

She drank tea and helped her sister make cupcakes, and when Will woke up Keri went upstairs to him. His bedroom was a bright, colourful and adventurous room—she had decorated it herself, in blues and greens, and painted a mural of the seashore on one wall.

His sleepy eyes blinked open and he held his arms

up, and Keri snuggled her little nephew tightly to her, closing her eyes and breathing in the warm, clean, child-like scent of him. She loved him dearly, though often she looked at Erin's dark-ringed eyes and wished he wouldn't run her so ragged, and today it was as if all her senses were sharpened—as if someone had left them raw and open and she saw his innocence and beauty as never before.

It was dark by the time she arrived home, and she walked slowly into her bedroom. The flat was quiet and dimly lit, and she hugged her arms tightly around herself, closing her eyes and wishing that Jay was here and that they were his arms.

And wondering how she could bear to wait until Saturday to see him again.

CHAPTER NINE

JAY hadn't realised he was waiting. Waiting was not in his nature; he was a man of action, not contemplation. But the moment he saw her walk into the crowded ballroom, he expelled a soft breath of expectation.

The ice-queen was back. Big-time.

Had the agency told her what to wear? Or did she normally attend functions like this—dripping in diamonds with a satin dress so clinging that it looked like gleaming black skin?

Probably. The room was full of beautiful women, all dressed up to the nines, but he couldn't stop staring at Keri, and his appetite was sharpened by the fact that she did not look his way. Not once. Which whetted his appetite even more.

Was she regretting that long and beautiful night?

Jay watched from the perfect vantage point as she drifted into the room and assorted bigwigs and flunkies began to lavish attention on her. He watched while someone took her wrap and someone else handed her a glass of champagne. He stood as silent and as still as a statue beside the glass-fronted cases containing a king's ransom worth of jewels. His heart was beating hard and loud and steady. And then at last she turned her head and stared straight into his eyes.

Keri felt the breath catch at the back of her throat.

He was wearing black jeans, which clung almost indecently to the hard, muscular shafts of his thighs, and a black roll-neck sweater. His jaw was shadowed and dark and his sage eyes were hooded.

Compared to every other man there—all resplendent in their black ties and shockingly expensive suits—he looked about as basic as could be. If she'd needed the perfect illustration of how very different their two worlds were then it was right there, but somehow she didn't care. Because he looked all man—the only man in the room who looked capable of breaking a door down and rescuing a woman. And then making love to her in a way guaranteed to ensure that she would never forget him.

She did her best not to react, not outwardly in any case, but inside her heart was hammering away so violently at her ribcage that she was certain it would be seen through the slippery silk-satin of her gown.

He was looking right at her. The dress she wore was normal for this kind of function, and it moulded itself to her body as if it had been sprayed on. She wore no bra, just two strategically placed pieces of tape which made her small breasts seem to defy gravity, yet she was no more revealingly clothed than any other woman in the room.

So how come she felt completely naked under Jay's scrutiny?

Her cheeks flushing, she turned away to talk to someone before he could see them.

She moved around the room, being introduced to the movers and shakers by the managing director of the diamond firm. Her photo was everywhere—the isolated backdrop of snow had been stunning, as the art director had intended—but all Keri could think about was that a few hours after those photos had been taken she had been naked in Jay's arms, crying out with amazed pleasure.

He hadn't moved from the spot where he was standing, and after half an hour of looking everywhere but there she could stand it no longer. She grabbed a second glass of champagne and wandered over to him.

'Well, hello again,' she said, with a smile she hoped wasn't too unsure. She held the glass out towards him. 'Drink?'

He shook his head. 'No, thanks. I'm driving.'

'Oh.' Now she felt stupid, standing there with both hands full, and maybe he realised that, for he took the glasses from her and put them on the tray of a passing waitress. Did he have an uncanny knack, she wondered, of knowing exactly what a woman wanted at any given time?

'Better?' he murmured.

'Much,' she lied, because 'better' would be the ability to clear the room completely and have the two of them standing there alone. And then, because this situation was so bizarre and unsettling, she gave him a glassy kind of smile. 'Enjoying yourself?'

In a way. The situation was certainly better than before—but maybe that was because she was about as good to look at as he could imagine. 'I'm working. I'm not here to enjoy myself.'

'Shall I go away again, then?'

'No.' He gave a brief smile. 'Did you come alone?'

'I...well, yes.'

A dark brow was raised in question. 'David not here?'

She looked him straight in the eyes, mesmerised by the soft grey-green light. 'David's just a friend.'

'Is he, now?' he questioned softly. Poor David. But her answer changed things, and Jay gave the stealthy smile of a circling predator. 'Maybe we could go for coffee...or something, when it finishes?'

She would have been a liar if she hadn't admitted to being tempted, because she knew that coffee was the last thing he had in mind, and the sight of him was making all kinds of erotic possibilities lick into life. Her mind flicked through a possible scenario. Would he offer to take her back to some tiny flat on the outskirts of the city with only one thing in mind? Or maybe he would suggest going back to her place, where the differences between them would be so glaringly obvious that it might inhibit both of them? She tried to imagine him climbing into her bed, with its rose-scattered brocade counterpane, and that was when her imagination gave up on her.

Had she really thought that things could be as they had been in the cottage, when the reality of their normal lives was so different?

And Keri realised something else in that moment. That it might be the twenty-first century, and women were supposed to be equal to men, but in something they most definitely were not. She did not want a relationship that was based completely and solely on sex. Once had been spontaneous and gorgeous, but anything else on the same terms would be nothing short of seedy.

She gave him a cool look. 'Sorry. I'll be tired by then.'

He would have suggested a remedy for tiredness, but he could see from the chilly expression on her face that she was no longer the accessible woman he had seduced. He realised that she was about to walk away. So, was the sight of his tough, practical persona in a room full of the glitterati enough to have given her second thoughts?

He saw the faint colour which had washed over her high cheekbones and the hectic glitter of her eyes. No, it was not. 'How about lunch?' he suggested.

Keri blinked up at him in surprise. 'Lunch?'

'I think we've established the fact that you *can* eat, given the motivation.'

She felt the sudden quickening of her pulse. Had he deliberately said that to remind her of the sensual food-fest they had indulged in?

But lunch wasn't seedy—lunch was civilised—though he did somehow stretch the definition of the word civilised. And it was certainly safer than dinner.

'I can do lunch,' she agreed.

'Monday?'

'Why not?'

'I know a place in Docklands, overlooking the water. It's pretty, and it's close to where I work.'

So he was seeing her on his lunchbreak! Keri let out a small sigh of relief. An hour would mean lunch and only lunch, with no time for anything else. And most people were like Jay, she reminded herself. They worked normal hours with normal restraints. 'We

could just go for a sandwich, then,' she said under-
standingly.

He gave a small smile. 'There's a place called
Carter's on the river—do you know it?'

She shook her head. 'No, but I can find it.'

'Okay. I'll see you in there at one.' He slid his hand
into the back pocket of his jeans and withdrew a card.
'Here's my number—call me if you get held up.'

As she took the card from him their fingers brushed
and it was electric, her skin tingling with just that brief
contact. Her head jerked up and she saw the inky dilation of his eyes in silent response. Did this happen
for him with all women? she wondered desperately.
Could he make them melt with a single touch?

'I'll see you at one,' she agreed, and walked away
from him, back across the ballroom, her heart thundering with excitement as she asked herself if she was
walking straight into trouble.

It felt like the first date she had ever been out on. On
Sunday night Keri had slept badly and woke as soon
as it was light, and, terrified of going back to sleep
and not leaving herself enough time, she over-
compensated and arrived in Docklands with an hour
to spare.

The winter weather was unforgiving. A soft, cold
haze of rain ruled out a pre-lunch walk, she thought,
looking out at the troubled waters of the Thames.
There was no art gallery close enough to while away
the minutes and no shops to wander aimlessly around.
Maybe he could shift his lunchbreak around? Oh, what
the hell.

She pulled her mobile out of her pocket and tapped in his number. He picked it up on the second ring.

'Jay Linur.'

'Jay? It's Keri. The traffic was better than I thought and I'm here—is there any chance you could knock off a little early?'

There was a pause.

'Why don't you come up to the office?' he said at last. 'I have some paperwork which I must get done.'

'Okay,' she said, wondering if he had deliberately tried to make himself sound important. Paperwork! What paperwork did he have that couldn't wait—his timesheets? 'Tell me where to find you.'

Jay put the phone down and frowned.

'Andy!' he called. 'I'm expecting someone.'

Keri found the building easily and took the stairs rather than the elevator to find herself in a large office which was high-ceiled and wonderfully dimensioned. True, the walls were dull and dingy, but the reflected light from the river helped, and the view of the swirling waters from the windows was spectacular.

An enormous man with the widest pair of shoulders Keri had ever seen crinkled up his blue eyes as she walked in. 'Hi.' He smiled. 'Jay's expecting you.' He clicked an intercom button on his desk. 'She's here, boss!'

Jay silently cursed, and then said, 'Send her in.' How many times had he told Andy to lose the handle by which he had been known for years?

'Go right through.' Andy grinned, pointing to the door of an inner office.

Keri's forehead pleated in a small frown. Boss? 'Thanks.'

She walked into the inner sanctum and it was not what she was expecting—though, to be honest, what exactly *had* she been expecting?

Jay was seated behind an impressive wooden desk, the sleeves of his dark sweater rolled up and a computer quietly humming away. Behind him was a map of the world, and there were lots of different coloured pins stuck in it. It looked, she thought suddenly, like a powerhouse. As if this was a place which mattered and he was a person who mattered.

Something didn't add up.

She stared at him.

'Hello, Keri.' Her hair was tied back like a schoolgirl's and she wore a knee-length leather coat, with long boots to match. She was very fond of leather, he thought, and the hot kick of lust became as scorching as the desert.

She looked around the office again. 'Would you mind telling me what's going on? Why did that man call you boss?'

He guessed he could play the evasion game for as long as it took, but what would be the point?

'Because I am. It's my company. I own it. I supply the drivers, and the guards, and private investigators too.' He didn't mention his significant portfolio of property. That might have seemed like a little too much information all at once.

It was like having a gauze curtain whisked away from her eyes so that her vision suddenly became crystal-clear. Of course. Of *course*. It all began to make perfect sense now—why things had not quite added up.

The confident, almost arrogant way he had behaved towards her when most men were slightly intimidated. His knowledge of French wines. You didn't need to wear fancy clothes or splash money around to prove you were a rich man—sometimes success could just ooze from every pore—and, my God, it certainly oozed from him.

'You…you lease these offices?'

'Well, I own them, actually. There are a couple more on the floor beneath.'

Her eyes widened as the significance of *that* sank in. Offices in this part of London didn't come cheap. 'You aren't a driver at all, are you, Jay?' she said quietly.

He met the accusation full-on. He could see the sudden stiffening of her body, but worse than that was the fleeting look of hurt which clouded her big dark eyes. As if he'd betrayed her. Hell, one night in her arms and she was acting as if he owed her something! 'Well, that's not strictly true—'

The confusion began to evaporate and anger took over—and in a way that helped dissolve the feeling that he had left her looking like a fool. 'Oh, please don't play with words! I'm not doubting your ability to drive a car!' She drew in an angry little snort of breath. 'Did it amuse you to deliberately deceive me?'

'I did *not* deliberately do anything. Why would I want to deceive you? Don't read more into it than there was, Keri—one of my drivers went off sick at the last minute so I stood in for him.'

'Why didn't you tell me that at the time?'

'Why on earth should I?' He gave a slightly incredulous smile. 'Can you just see the scenario if I'd suddenly just announced it to a client? *Hi, my name is Jay, and actually what you see isn't really what you get. I'm not a driver; I own the company!* How crass would that have been?'

'You're missing the point!'

'Am I?' His gaze was very steady as he moved across the room towards her. 'I fail to see how. Would you have treated me differently if you'd known?' He gave a slow smile as he remembered the way she had treated him. 'Maybe that would have been something worth telling you for!'

'That is cheap!'

He shook his head as he allowed himself the rare luxury of recall. How long had it been since *that* had happened? A woman taking him on the most basic terms of all, without trappings or status? 'No, it's true,' he contradicted softly.

She backtracked through her memory. Maybe he hadn't actually told her any lies, but he must have been laughing fit to burst—especially when she had falteringly suggested that he was wasted as a driver and he might be able to find other work. 'Did it give you pleasure to masquerade as something you weren't?' she demanded bitterly.

'Of course it didn't give me pleasure!' He sighed, held the palms of his hands up in a gesture of peace. 'It just seemed irrelevant at the beginning, and if I'd told you during or afterwards then it might have seemed like boasting. As if I was trying to impress you with what I was rather than who I was.' And hadn't playing his wealth down become second nature?

She glared at him. 'Well, if you're so bloody rich then I suggest you do something about these offices—I've never seen anything so dingy in my life!'

He started laughing. 'Are we still on for lunch?'

'I've lost my appetite!'

'No change there, then.'

She didn't smile back. 'Very funny.'

He was aching to take her in his arms, but something in her eyes was warning him off—and in a way that excited him almost as much as it frustrated him. 'Have you any work lined up?' he asked suddenly.

Keri narrowed her eyes. 'Why?'

'Is that a yes or a no?'

'I have a...' She wasn't about to start telling him about the lingerie contract—she could just imagine his reaction to *that*. 'A job in a few weeks' time.' Other than that she was free—a welcome space in her workload after jobs being booked back-to-back for months.

'And in the meantime? What do you normally do in between jobs?'

She filled in her time as usefully as possible, that was what she did. She visited galleries and friends, and shopped and saw films. 'Depends.'

My, but she was paying him back for his supposed 'deception'. 'Do you want to do something for me?'

Her suspicious body-stance did not alter. 'Like what?'

'Why not paint my offices?' He saw her mystified look and it amused him. 'Is it such a crazy idea?' he mused. 'You told me that you're good at it. You told me that was what you originally wanted to do, and you've just torn the place to pieces. You're right— they are dingy.'

The suggestion pleased her more than it had any right to. It was, she realised, a way to maybe find out who the real Jay Linur was. And a chance to show him that she was not just some mindless clotheshorse who paraded in front of the camera. To show him what she could do—maybe more importantly to prove to *herself* what she could do.

She stared at him. 'Why, Jay?'

Because I want to make love to you again. Because you've left me with a fever in my blood and I need a little saturation therapy to make it go away. But maybe it was more than that. There had to be more to life than standing in a snowy field in the middle of winter wearing very little. Hadn't she said so herself?

He shrugged. 'You told me you sometimes were bored with standing in front of a camera, that interior design was what you planned before modelling came out and grabbed you—so why not explore it as an option? I can be your first legitimate assignment, if you like.'

Keri stared at him, at the grey-green eyes which were surveying her quizzically. He was offering her an opportunity to do something different, allowing her to indulge the creative side of her nature, but it wasn't that which was making her mouth dry with excitement.

She knew deep down that they would be lovers again—she wasn't that self-deluding. But this time she wasn't going to make it easy for him—not in any way. Sex wasn't supposed to be a battle, but even so she had given in too easily before. If Jay Linur wanted her then he was going to have to try a whole lot harder.

'So what's your answer?' he questioned softly.

'You'll give me a free hand?' she verified.

'Free as you like, sweetheart,' he agreed, but once again his body began to ache.

CHAPTER TEN

JAY'S motorbike zipped through the heavy late-morning traffic, the rain buffeting against him, the thunder-laden clouds matching his mood of expectation and anticipation.

She was there, in his office, putting into practice his crazy idea. He knew this because he had already received a phone call from Andy, asking did Jay know that the dishy broad had arrived bearing enough paint to cover the front of Buckingham Palace?

The unspoken question had been why Jay had not bothered mentioning it to his right-hand man. Maybe that was a classic case of denial—of not wanting to admit what he found hard to admit to himself.

He had let a woman onto *his territory*. Not just any woman, either, but a woman *he had had sex with*! For the first time in his life he had allowed desire to blind him to sense.

And he had no one to blame but himself.

He had done some work at home in order to be out of the way when she arrived—he hadn't felt quite ready to lay on the red carpet treatment for her himself—and by the time he'd parked the bike and removed his helmet and made his way upstairs he could hear Andy chatting.

Andy—*chatting*?

The two men had been SEALS together. They had

119

trained and fought side-by-side, seen the very worst of life and made light of it afterwards. They had wreaked havoc behind enemy lines and then left without a trace. Jay had spent much of his adult life with the tough ex-commando, but he had never once heard him *chatting* like that.

But then she was, he realised suddenly, very easy to talk to.

He walked into the office to be greeted by the sight of a pert bottom leaning over the desk and pointing out something on a chart to Andy, who had clearly never heard the expression eating-out-of-her-hand.

'Well, hello,' Jay said softly.

Andy stopped mid-sentence, and Keri stopped what she was doing, and they both turned round—Andy jumping back from the paint chart as if it had been alive. For a big man, he could certainly move fast!

Jay stood there, his helmet under one arm, the thumb of his other hand hooked into a loop on his trousers, his stance both watchful and territorial, like some latter-day cowboy. Did he do it *deliberately*? she wondered. Decide just what would be the number-one female fantasy and then become its very personification?

He was dressed completely in soft black leather. Leather trousers which clung to the long, lean shafts of his legs and a close-fitting leather jacket. With his black hair and shadowed jaw, the only colour relief came in the grey-green glitter of colour from between the thick forest of eyelashes.

'Good morning, Jay,' she said brightly. 'Though not a very nice one, is it?

He groaned. 'You're not going to be cheerful in the mornings, are you?'

'Probably by *your* standards, yes,' she said innocently, and saw Andy fail to hide a smile. 'I've tried a few patches of paint on the walls of your office—like to have a look at them?'

Surprisingly, his mood had started to lift by a fraction—but then she sure beat Andy on the decorative front. Paint-splattered baggy denim dungarees were proving far more appealing than they should have done—but then he knew only too well what lay beneath.

'I guess so,' he growled, and began to walk towards his office. 'Come on through. Coffee, please, Andy.'

'Sure.'

Keri dawdled for a minute, turned to Andy, and smiled. 'Thanks for all your help.'

His eyes crinkled at the corners. 'My pleasure, ma'am.'

Andy was very definitely American—where Jay only had the hint of a drawl, his was the real thing. They'd been in the SEALs together, so he'd told her. He had bright blue eyes and hair the colour of shadowed corn, and the oddly gentle manner which big men sometimes had.

'Keri!' called Jay's voice impatiently. 'Are you coming in here or not?'

'Demanding, isn't he?' she murmured, half to herself, as she went into the inner sanctum. She had been busy preparing the room before she started painting, though not as busy as she might have expected. Most rooms had some degree of clutter and personal effects, but Jay's had precisely none. No photos. No cute paperweights. No pictures on the walls. There wasn't even a dying pot plant as so often seen in the workplaces of lone men. Nothing. A functional room for a functional man.

Jay was standing in the middle of the room, staring incredulously at the wall next to the window which had a splodge of colour on it—a bright, vibrant red.

He turned around, seeing her dark eyes widened in expectation, like a little girl who had spent all night making a gift for the teacher.

'Is this some kind of joke?' he questioned, in a strangled kind of voice.

'You don't like red?'

'I don't like sitting in a room which looks like someone has been flinging ketchup at the walls.'

'It isn't finished yet,' she said helpfully.

Silently, he counted to ten. 'I may not be Van Gogh, Keri, but I'd kind of worked that out for myself. It's not the lack of application I'm objecting to—it's the damn colour!'

'What's wrong with red? The sky outside is blue, the paintwork white and, given your dual nationality, I thought it would conjure up images of both the British and American flags!'

He looked at her. 'Are you trying to be funny?'

'No.' She shook her head. 'Honestly, Jay—I think it will look stunning—and you *did* tell me I had a free hand!'

'That's because I thought you were just going to brighten it up with the same colour.'

'And what? Paint it *magnolia*? Although it was difficult to make out just what colour it was under the layers of grime—which I am going to have to scrub before I can start.' She gave an exaggerated shudder. 'Places of work should be inspirational, and you won't get much if you're sitting surrounded by a colour which looks like the inside of a milk bottle. Trust me—it will look fine by the time I've finished.'

There was silence for a moment. If he wanted inspiration he wasn't going to start looking for it in his office! Was now the time to enlighten her that places of work were supposed to be just that? And how come they sounded like a pair of newlyweds sparring over the décor for their first home?

'And if it doesn't?'

She heard the dangerous note in his voice. 'Then I'll paint it back exactly the colour it was!' And saw the dangerous look in his eyes. He really *could* be a Big, Bad Wolf.

While she had been chatting she had learnt just how successful the company was. It seemed that Jay was a very wealthy man. Yet, oddly enough, that didn't change her feelings for him one jot. She had been ensnared by him when she'd thought he had very little—so what difference did it make that he actually had a great deal?

He was still looking at her in a way designed to make the steadiest hand drip paint all over the floor, and that was hardly the best way to begin. 'Maybe I'd better begin on the outside office,' she said thoughtfully.

Jay didn't know which was more infuriating—the fact that Keri was innocently painting in the next door office, or the fact that Andy kept whistling. Tunelessly. He hadn't heard him whistle like that for a long time.

He kept out of the way until lunchtime and then stole silently into the outer office. To his surprise, almost one large wall had already been painted blue— the same colour as the sea when you started to go really deep. It was a beautiful colour, but not one he would have considered putting on a wall.

Keri was sitting perched on the desk, with a blob of paint on her nose and Andy looking up at her like a lost puppy dog who had just found its owner. A muscle flickered in Jay's cheek as some inexplicable irritation flared.

'Aren't you going out for sandwiches?' he questioned tersely.

Andy glanced at his watch in surprise and levered his long frame out of the chair. 'Is that the time?' He turned to Keri. 'And what would you like, princess?'

Jay gave a tight smile. *Princess?*

'Oh, don't bother about me,' said Keri quickly. 'I don't normally bother with lunch.'

'She'll have the same as me,' said Jay firmly, and met her eyes. 'There's no way you're starving yourself—understand? You're not standing around having your photo taken now, Keri—this is real work, and I certainly don't want you fainting on the job.'

She felt pretty faint as it was, and that had nothing to do with *real* work. Now that Jay had peeled off his leather jacket he was treating her to the sight of a black T-shirt clinging to all the right places. Keri swallowed. Maybe a sandwich wasn't such a bad idea after all.

Might send the blood rushing to her head and her stomach instead of all the wrong places. 'Thanks. Sounds good.'

The silence seemed immense while Andy grabbed his jacket and put it on, and after he had left it seemed even bigger. Keri seemed aware of every sound in the universe—the faint cry of seagulls outside, the occasional blast of a ship's horn. And her heartbeat. That was absolutely deafening, especially now, because he was strolling across the room towards her, a lazy smile on his lips.

'Do you realise we haven't said hello properly?' he questioned silkily, and pulled her into his arms.

She had been practising for just this moment, and had planned to resist, but now—faced with the reality—resistance flew straight out of the window.

'Hello, Jay,' she said pertly.

He allowed himself a small smile. 'Ah, Keri,' he murmured, brushing his mouth tantalisingly over hers. 'Haven't you been wanting to do that all morning?'

She had been trying her best not to think about it, with varying degrees of success. 'I've actually been concentrating on my painting,' she managed.

'And just how do you concentrate on painting?'

'I...oh, God...I don't *know*,' she gasped, as he flicked his tongue out and teased it against her lips, and she closed her eyes and gave in, wrapping her arms tightly around his neck and pressing her body to his.

He groaned, sliding his hand down over her dungarees and cupping her breast through the rough denim. 'I must have been out of my mind,' he whispered. 'Thinking that I could have you anywhere near me and even think straight, let alone do any work.'

She jerked her head back with a monumental effort. 'Well, you're going to have to try,' she said shakily. 'Otherwise your business will go bust and you'll blame me.'

'I want you.' He drifted his hand further down and heard her moan.

Someone had to stop this and it had better be her, since Jay's eyes were smoky with the kind of desire which was reminding her all too vividly of what he was like as a lover. Any minute now and she wouldn't be able to resist anything.

'The...the wanting has never been in any question,' she agreed firmly. 'But, Jay, we mustn't.'

'Mustn't what?' He dipped his head to trail a feather-light kiss along the line of her jaw. 'We aren't doing anything.' He nuzzled again. 'Just kissing.'

But it was more than that. At least for her it was. This warm sense of homecoming, as if no place in the world could be more perfect than in Jay's arms. And this kind of kisses could lead you to only one place if you weren't very careful. Look what had happened before.

'Andy will be back in a minute.'

'It's his lunch-hour. I'll tell him to go take a walk in the park.'

'It's the middle of winter!' she protested.

'Oh, Andy's tough,' he said easily. 'Like me. We're used to the elements, sweetheart. He'll understand.'

For one second she was tempted as she imagined an erotic way of spending the rest of the lunch-hour.

Jay had awoken in her a voraciously hungry sexual appetite and she would have liked nothing more than to feed it.

But then what? She would have to field Andy's curious and knowing stares all afternoon and live with the feeling that where Jay was concerned she was in danger of always selling herself short. She wasn't going to use sex as a weapon or a tool, but she needed her self-respect as well as his respect—and a quick bout of lovemaking in between coats of paint wasn't designed to help achieve that. Either they did things properly, or not at all.

She shook her head. 'No, Jay.'

He gave a faintly disbelieving moan. 'Are you trying to drive me out of my mind?'

'There wouldn't be a lot of point, would there? Not when you just told me you're already losing it!'

Reluctantly, he laughed and let her go, which made the aching slightly less intense, but his eyes glittered with curiosity. 'So what had you planned? To keep me at arm's length?'

'Certainly during working hours,' she said steadily.

He heard the underlying message. 'You want to go out later?'

It was unbelievable how he broke all the normal rules of conventional behaviour and managed to get away with it. She had heard invitations phrased far more elegantly, but she had never been so excited by one before.

Yet she had vowed not to make it too easy for him, and if she went out with him tonight would she honestly be able to resist him?

He observed her hesitation. 'Or are you "busy" to-night?' he suggested mockingly.

Determinedly, she made herself focus on a pile of bills waiting to be paid. 'I'm afraid I am.'

'Oh, I see.' Suddenly the air became full of tension. 'That's your plan, then, is it, Keri?' he questioned softly. 'To tempt and taunt me and ultimately to tease me, by saying no?'

His bad-tempered response made her realise that her instinctual refusal had been the right thing to do. She raised her eyebrows.

'My, my, my—is that always your reaction when a woman turns you down?'

He was frustrated, and temporarily wrong-footed, but not shortsighted enough to point out that it was the first time it had ever happened. 'So you aren't going to go out with me?'

She paused just long enough to give him doubts. 'Not tonight, no. Ask me again.'

So beautifully sure of herself. Had she read all those rulebooks which told you that to hook a man you had to play games—never be free and never return his calls? Because if she was holding out for commitment she was in for a disappointment.

'I'm not a man who likes waiting,' he warned her darkly.

His arrogance fuelled her indignation and she shrugged her shoulders. 'Then don't wait,' she answered coolly. 'Go ahead—ask someone else. And now, if that's everything—I'm going out.'

He watched her grab her coat from the hook, his

eyes drinking in her graceful beauty with admiration. She must have been reading some book—because if there was anything which made him want something it was being told that he might not be able to have it.

CHAPTER ELEVEN

KERI quickly learnt that she didn't like to be kept waiting either, and Jay made her wait three days before he asked her out again. Three days which were an agony of excitement and expectation and fear that he might have decided against it. Three days during which time she learnt that he liked his coffee black, his bread brown, that he worked non-stop and that he wouldn't take telephone calls from a woman called Candy.

'Who's Candy?' asked Keri casually, as she carefully tore off a piece of masking tape.

'Just some broad,' replied Andy. 'One of many.'

Maybe her face remained quizzical.

'Like moths to a flame,' he added with a rueful kind of look. 'But half the time he doesn't notice.'

Or doesn't care? she wondered.

When Andy went out to fetch sandwiches at lunchtime, Jay wandered through, rubbing his eyes and stifling a yawn.

'Late night?' murmured Keri, but she felt the powerful tug of jealousy.

'Late-night call to the States.' His eyes drifted over her. 'You have paint on your nose.'

'Paint everywhere,' she agreed steadily.

I'd like to see it. 'So, are we going out together tonight?'

'I thought you were tired.'

His eyes widened by a fraction. 'Suddenly I'm wide awake.'

She'd done the self-respect thing. Now surely she could relax a little. 'Okay, then.' She smiled up at him and suddenly ached to put her arms around him. 'What would you like to do?'

I think we both know the answer to that, sweetheart. 'You choose.'

She wanted something normal. Something which didn't involve her gazing into his eyes and thinking how bloody gorgeous he was. 'How about a film—we could grab a bite to eat afterwards?'

'A film?'

'You know. Man and woman go to into large, darkened room. Man and woman watch story told on big screen—popcorn optional.'

He gave a reluctant laugh. It wouldn't have been number one on *his* list. 'Okay—why not?'

'Anything in particular you'd like to see?'

He shook his head. 'You choose.

The door opened and Andy reappeared, carrying a brown bag full of food.

Jay's first thought was that this wasn't proving quite as simple as he had anticipated.

And his second was one of suspicion.

All he had wanted was to take her to bed—so how come he'd agreed to see a film with her? He hadn't been to the movies with a woman for years.

The night was dark, but there were no stars. That was the trouble with cities, thought Jay—too much man-made light which killed the natural beauty of the heavens. The neon lights of the cinema complex made Keri's face look ghostly and unreal.

'Did you enjoy it?' she asked.

'It was okay,' he said. 'Though I'm not crazy about subtitles.'

'Because you didn't need them, unlike me.' She looked up at him. 'It isn't just wine labels that you read, is it, Jay? You understood the entire dialogue of the film. You speak French.'

'People do, particularly in Paris,' he mocked.

'But you weren't raised in Paris,' she mocked back. 'So how come?'

'Because I spent the first few years of my life in New Orleans, and then whichever parent I happened to be with at the time insisted I keep my French—so I went to schools where the teaching was bilingual.' He flicked her a smile. 'Maybe we should go and eat now.'

It was a conversational cut-off, presumably as a way of avoiding elaborating on a childhood which sounded awfully disruptive. Maybe it was his way of saying that he had told her things about himself when they were marooned in the house, but now things were different. She wasn't hungry, but she wasn't risking any more barbs about her lack of appetite, so she nodded anyway. 'Sounds good.'

'Where do you want to go?'

'I suggested the film, why don't you decide the food?'

There was a pause, and he touched her cheek with the tip of his finger, snaking it down in a spine-tingling little spiral. 'But you might not like my suggestion, Keri.'

She shivered at his touch. 'Try me.'

'I don't want anything to eat,' he said evenly. 'At least, not yet. I want to take all your clothes off and run my hands over your body and make you gasp and cry again.'

He couldn't see the hot colour which had flushed into her cheeks, nor hear the frantic clamour of her heart. She could look outraged, shocked, appalled. She could refuse and hail a cab. All those choices available to her, and what did she do?

She smiled a slightly shaky smile. 'I have a fridge full of food.'

But he was already lifting his arm for a taxi.

The ride back to her apartment was conducted in a tense and expectant silence. He didn't touch her, nor did he say a word, and Keri's emotions felt as churned up as cake mix. Was it right that this should feel almost *clinical*? But that was down to Jay. Given the choice, she would be snuggled up in his arms, smothering his face with tiny little kisses. Not sitting at either end of the seat, as if they were on their way to a business conference.

She was barely aware of him paying the cab, or of their swift journey to her front door, only that once it was closed behind them they fell on each other with a wild kind of hunger.

He pushed her coat from her shoulders and it fell to the floor, and she found herself frantically unbuttoning his shirt, sliding her hands up underneath the

T-shirt he wore beneath and moaning when she made contact with the silken flesh.

Something hot exploded inside his head. It was all buttons and lace and hardness, and achingly moist softness too. With some last vestige of sanity he groped into his pocket for protection and stroked it on, then kicked his trousers off impatiently. Her panties were down by her ankles, and he pushed her up against the wall and parted her thighs, and her mouth sought his, sucked greedily on his lips as he lifted her up and drove into her with a low, exultant cry torn from his lips.

He tried to slow it down, but it was impossible— *she* was impossible, urging him on with little pleas and moans until she dragged her mouth away from his. He felt her tense, her back arching, and only when he felt her begin to shudder around him could he finally let go, in an orgasm which seemed to go on and on and on.

Through the slowing and muffled beat of her heart, Keri let her damp face fall heavily to his shoulder. 'Shouldn't I at least have offered you a drink first?' she questioned, her voice as sleepy as a well-fed cat.

Jay closed his eyes and locked his arms tightly around her waist. 'You are amazing,' he murmured. 'Completely and utterly and unbelievably amazing. Which way's the bedroom?'

'What bedroom's that?' she whispered. 'You've got me so I can't think straight.'

He tilted up her chin. 'How about a rough idea?' he drawled.

'Keep going, and I'll tell you when to stop.'

He picked her up, a smile playing at the corners of his mouth as he stared down into her eyes. 'Well, I guess there's a first time for everything!' he commented wryly.

He took her to bed, only this time he made love to her as if he had all the time in the world, slowly whispering his fingertips all over her skin, making her feel as if she had only ever been briefly acquainted with her body before, and now he was introducing her to it properly for the first time.

He teased and stroked, tipped her almost to the edge of desire, then drew her back again, time after time, the flow building towards some inexorable peak, frustration growing alongside excitement until finally she begged him not to stop. He gave a small, low laugh of pleasure, as though that had been what he had been waiting for all along. Through the tug of enchantment a vague disquiet touched her as she became aware of his sexual power over her, but by then it was too late to try to even the balance.

And what followed felt as though the world had ended and then begun all over again, only this time her senses were so heightened—so raw and so feeling and so acute—that she didn't know if she could bear to live with that kind of intensity.

When Keri finally drifted back to some kind of consciousness it was to find Jay dressed—well, half dressed. He was wearing his jeans, his torso bare, the hard, muscular body bathed in moonlight as he stared out of the uncurtained window. He looked like a warrior, she thought—tense, alert and watchful—though what was there to threaten him in the winter sky outside?

He must have sensed that she was awake, because he turned around.

'Hi.'

Did he sound cautious? 'You're dressed,' she observed, stifling a yawn and hoping that she sounded impartial, not needy.

'Yeah. Time I was getting back.' He looked at his watch, as if to illustrate the point. 'It's way past midnight.'

Keri sat up, her hair tumbling down over her naked breasts, seeing the fleeting light of reaction in his eyes—but it was only fleeting. 'But you haven't had anything to eat!'

'This from the woman who doesn't. Ever. Not unless coerced,' he teased. 'Actually, I'm not really hungry.'

But, oddly enough, Keri was—utterly ravenous. She would have liked for him to climb back into bed beside her and for her to go out to the kitchen and pile high a tray full of goodies. They could have eaten them together and he could have fed her again, as he had done so erotically at the house. But maybe that kind of love-play was only part of the wooing, and now that he had no need to woo her he had got straight out of bed and distanced himself. Jay didn't seem to do the cuddling-in-each-other's-arms bit afterwards.

'Could you pass me my robe?'

He pulled a silken-looking Chinese thing from the back of the door and handed it to her, his resolve momentarily wavering when he saw her long, pale limbs emerging from the rumpled sheets like a Venus.

'I'm expecting a call from the States,' he said, by way of explanation—except, of course, that was not the whole story. The kind of sex he'd just shared with Keri was... He shook his head. It took you too close to yourself. Made you feel things you didn't want to feel. If he'd given in to that kind of stuff he could never have done the job he'd been trained for. And he didn't do night-times either, for they brought with them their own particular problems. He felt as if he had strayed into some kind of unknown trap, and he knew he had to get the hell out of there.

She knotted the belt. 'Of course,' she said calmly—amazing, really, considering what was going on inside her head. The woman who had been so thoroughly pleasured now desperately needed to connect. She wanted to run to him, to have him pull her into his arms and show her that what had just taken place in some way mattered.

Wasn't it worth a try?

She walked towards him, leaned forward and kissed him softly, and as she deepened the kiss she felt him respond. But then he drew back, his eyes unreadable, the curve of his mouth regretful—but how true was that? she wondered.

'I have to go, Keri.'

He wanted to go; that was the bottom line. She gave a brittle smile. Sometimes you just had no control over what your face did. 'I'll see you out.'

In silence, they walked towards the hall, where he located his T-shirt and the shirt she had ripped from his back like a hungry animal. Keri as uninhibited predator. It was an image she wasn't used to, and one she wasn't sure she liked very much.

But his parting kiss was almost tender—unless that was hurt female pride searching for the most acceptable interpretation.

'That was incredible,' he said softly.

Mild hysteria made her think she was being marked out of ten. 'Yes, it was.'

'I'll see you tomorrow,' he said.

Somehow she managed the serene kind of grown-up look she knew was expected, even though inside was a little girl who wanted to cling onto his arm and beg him not to leave her. 'You certainly will—unless you can bear to live with only one and a half walls painted.'

Yet the painting seemed somehow irrelevant. Everything did. She bolted the door after he'd gone, with a hand which was trembling, realising that she might be able to lock out his physical presence but that somehow—had she been mad enough to think he wouldn't?—Jay Linur was creeping into her heart.

She slept better than she had anticipated, and by the time she was up and dressed she had talked herself back into a positive attitude. She had no right to blame him because he hadn't met her romantic expectations and spent the night cradled in her arms. If she wanted roses by candlelight then she had picked the wrong man.

She arrived soon after Andy and perched on his desk, sipping coffee.

'Good evening?' he asked casually.

Keri's face didn't react. 'Great,' she answered, non-committally.

The two men were close—had Jay said anything on the lines of *Hey, guess what I'm doing with Keri*? Was that what men did? Especially men who had been close, in an all-male environment where women had their place and not necessarily a very important one. 'How about you?'

'Pretty quiet.' He shrugged. 'Guess I need to get out there and network a little more.'

'Do you miss America?'

He stirred his coffee and shook his head. 'England's been pretty good to me. I like the fact that it's small, that it's surrounded by sea—you feel kind of safe here.'

'But it's not home?' she ventured.

He smiled. 'What's home? Wherever you lay your hat? Well, I must have laid mine in a hundred different places from the age of eighteen until I was almost thirty-two! My parents are dead—my sisters are married and scattered all over. So I guess home is here.'

It wasn't just an insight into Andy's life, but into Jay's as well. He had lived that same nomadic existence, and some people never tired of the excitement of the new and undiscovered. Not just with places, but with people too.

She heard Jay's footfall outside and she tensed. How would he be with her today? Cool? Non-committal? What if…? She felt tiny pinpricks of sweat beading her forehead… What if it was only ever intended to be a one-off? Or a second-off, she amended wryly.

He came in and put his helmet down, took the mail that Andy handed him and headed straight for his office, turning his head very slightly to call over his shoulder.

'Just come in here for a moment, would you, Keri?'

She was being summoned. Her heart racing, she rose to her feet with a certain reluctance, giving Andy what she hoped was a sunny, confident smile, and went towards the inner sanctum.

She stood framed in his doorway and Jay grew hard just thinking about last night.

'Come in,' he said quietly. 'And shut the door behind you.'

For a moment she couldn't move—she felt rooted to the spot, like a tree, and Jay had the power to fell her if he chose.

Keep it businesslike and take the lead from him, she told herself as she quietly closed the door and lifted her eyebrows politely. 'What can I do for you, Jay?'

'You can come right over here and kiss me.'

'I thought we tried that yesterday, and it didn't work.'

'That was before last night.'

'Which surely makes it even more of a bad idea?'

Jay studied her. He had half feared an over-the-top display of emotion—and hadn't a part of him wanted that? Wouldn't that have made it easier to categorise her as being like all the others?

'My, but you're grouchy this morning,' he accused softly.

'Not grouchy at all.'

'Stubborn, then.'

She smiled, feeling more powerful by the moment. 'Because I won't do exactly what you want?'

He laughed. 'I guess.' Deliberately, he ran his eyes slowly over her, from the top of her head to the tip of her toes, blatantly and arrogantly undressing her with his eyes, enjoying the rise of colour and the sudden darkening of her eyes. And enjoying just as much this silent battle of wills. 'Still don't want to kiss me?' he taunted.

'Wanting has nothing to do with it—we've already established that.' She frowned. 'Does Andy know?'

Jay stilled. 'Know *what*, exactly?'

She nearly said, about *us*, but in the nick of time she realised how needlessly possessive that would sound. So she made it as bald as possible—but still a few steps short of how she suspected a SEAL might describe it.

'Does he know we're sleeping together?' It was only after she'd said it that she realised it wasn't strictly accurate.

Jay raised his eyebrows. 'Well, I didn't get on the phone last night after I'd left you to call him, if that's what you mean. And unless you told him before I arrived, then, no.'

'So he doesn't know about the house?'

'You're kidding!' His eyes narrowed. 'How the hell can I expect to have standards about professionalism if I don't adhere to them myself?'

'You bastard,' she said, with feeling. 'I'm sorry I made you flout your higher-than-high standards!'

'Oh, Keri,' he remonstrated softly. 'That wasn't what I meant and you know it! I don't go around boasting about my conquests, if that's what you're asking.'

'I wasn't aware that I *was* a conquest,' she said stiffly.

Hell! 'You're twisting me up with words!' he complained.

'Shall we communicate by sign language then?'

'Or touch?' He rallied instantly, inordinately pleased when he saw a smile curve the corners of her mouth. 'How about we go to a show tonight?'

Keri blinked in surprise. 'What kind of show?'

'Do you like musicals? Because I have two tickets.'

'To what?'

Eyes glittering, he gave the name of a hit which had two Hollywood stars proving their stage credentials and was currently packing them in.

'You can't have tickets for that—they're like gold-dust!'

'Well, I have,' he responded, with cool arrogance. 'So shall I pick you up later? Say around seven? We could go for a drink first, if you like.'

And Keri smiled, something telling her that tonight it *was* safe to have him collect her. The frantic stuff was done—this really was a date.

'Love to,' she said, and hoped that her smile didn't look too soppy.

CHAPTER TWELVE

THE plane bumped down to the sound of spontaneous applause from the passengers and Jay gave a grim smile. It had been a bumpy ride, the aircraft buffeted by storms which had lit the skies with an eerie brilliance. Most people had been terrified, but not him—he'd been on tough flights before, and he knew that if a plane was going to crash then screaming about it wasn't going to stop it.

He'd paid a flying visit to Manchester, summoned there by one of his agents who had been staking out a house which had been sheltering an abducted child caught up in a particularly ugly divorce battle. The police had failed to find her, and in her desperation the mother had contact Linur's.

It had been a delicate and potentially explosive situation, and Jay had gone along to give his man assistance on the sort of case he had once thrived on. There had been both danger and excitement icing the dark, unforgiving night and the long, cold dawn which had followed before they had plucked the child to safety.

But Jay had been aware that his usually sharpened instincts seemed blunted. For once it had been hard to be impartial, to view the case through clear, cold eyes. Instead, he'd found himself identifying with the terror and bewilderment of the child. He'd gone through all the motions, but had felt as if he was only half there—nothing anyone else would have noticed, but he had.

Just as he had noticed Keri's fearful expression when he had told her he was flying north on business.

'What kind of business?' she had asked.

'That's none of *your* business, sweetheart.' He had seen the hurt and worry which had clouded her eyes but had steeled his heart to it. What did she expect? For him to give her a briefing of his case, chapter and verse? And it wasn't just the secrecy, which was vital to the operation, it was her expectation that somehow she had a right to know just because they had something going on between them. Was she planning to pack him sandwiches and tell him to be sure to ring her if he was delayed?

His mouth hardened. It was what women did. They built on relationships and then they worried and fretted about them. Put a woman on a ship full of men, and everything was altered. Inevitably. Women changed the dynamic, and it was both their weakness and their strength. Slowly but surely they sapped the strength of their men with the stealthy allure of domesticity.

Well, he didn't want it. He'd never wanted it. And the sooner she learnt that the better all round—and if she couldn't cope with the situation as it was, rather than how she wanted it to be, then she had better resign herself to the fact that it was over.

There was a text message from her awaiting him. It said. *Come straight round and I'll cook you dinner. K xxx*

His eyes narrowed. He knew what he wanted from her, and it wasn't any damned dinner—just to lose himself in her body and forget the memory of the human drama he had just dealt with.

When she answered the door, her hair was all over the place and she looked flustered, but he felt it all the same—that strong and overpowering need in him she always provoked.

Her eyes widened. 'Oh, God, is that the time?'

He pulled her into his arms. She smelt of warm milk and apples. 'Well, hello to you too!'

She gave him a brief, distracted kiss and pulled away, just as the sound of a child's wail came wafting through from the sitting room.

Jay froze, memories of the child he had just rescued playing tricks with his mind, taking him right back to the cold and the dark and the terror. 'What the hell is that?'

But she was already dashing along the corridor towards the sound of the wail, calling over her shoulder, 'It's—oh, come through, Jay—it's William.'

He followed her. The wail had become a noisy, gulping cry, and when he walked into her usually restful rose-pink room it was almost unrecognisable. Cushions and crayons littered the floor, the contents of a fruit dish were scattered all over the sofa, and in the midst of the general chaos a small child was sobbing against Keri's neck.

She met Jay's eyes over William's silky ebony hair and gave him a helpless expression. 'Shush, Will,' she crooned. 'It's all right. Look—here's Jay.'

William turned his head, looked at Jay, and then screamed even louder before burying his face again.

'He'll be all right in a minute, once he gets to

know you,' she said. 'He's always a bit funny with strangers.'

This must be her nephew, he surmised. Her sister's child. What was he doing here?

'Erin wanted to go for a pedicure,' she explained, as William drummed his feet against her hips.

This explanation fuelled his vague feeling of discontent, and he let it flood in with a sensation of relief. So her sister was getting her toenails painted while her child screamed. Were both of them hostages to beauty, then?

'Why don't you help yourself to a drink?' Keri asked, wondering why his face was looking so thunderous. Surely William's presence wasn't *that* bad? Or was anything bad in Jay's mind if it impeded their journey to the bedroom?

'I don't want a drink,' he said shortly. 'I've had a long night and I'm pretty bushed. Looks like you've got your hands tied here—I'll see you tomorrow.'

He saw her mouth open by a fraction. Her tousled hair fell and mingled with the dark hair of William, who seemed now to be more interested in Jay, for he kept darting him little looks from eyes as ebony-dark as hers. He saw the relaxed way she rested the child on her hip and it was light-years away from the frozen silver model. Her cheeks were all pink, and with the child clinging onto her she looked extremely sexy in a very wholesome way. Who would have dreamed she could do a very credible imitation of an earth mother?

It made him want her even more. But he wanted her to himself and *damn it*—he didn't want to want her this much at all!

'I'll let myself out.'

'Okay, then,' she said faintly, and watched him leave. She couldn't stop the dull sense of foreboding which began to gnaw away at her heart.

Something was happening—he was growing distant from her. But, come to think of it, hadn't there been more and more of that just lately?

She knew she was falling in deep—past the point of no return—but she couldn't seem to do anything about it. On a good day she told herself that there was no reason why she should.

But today was a bad day, for no reason she could think of, and when something was bad it made you dwell on the negative. She settled William on the sofa and he began eating one of the apples which was lying there. She began to pick up all the cushions, her mind fixing and staying on the things which caused her pain if she let them, so she didn't often let them.

Like the fact that Jay had never stayed the night with her. Not once. Even that first night at the house he had left her side while she'd been sleeping.

She hadn't remarked on it at first. Hadn't wanted to scare him or have him think she was getting needy or possessive, though in fact it was neither—she just wanted to hold his strong, warm body during the night and to wake up with him the next day. To touch his face, to outline the strong, firm line of his lips. To make him breakfast and to drink coffee together, just like a normal couple.

But one night, when she had lain back against the pillows with a lazy, satisfied grin just refusing to wipe itself from her face, she had risked it.

'Do you *have* to go, Jay?'

He didn't pause in the act of pulling a sweater over his head. 'I'm afraid so.' There was an odd, fraught kind of silence. 'I do work from home at all kinds of ungodly hours,' he explained tightly. 'The time difference means I can't deal with the States during the day.'

Slowly and deliberately, she sucked the end of her finger and saw his eyes darken.

'And what if I told you I didn't mind being woken up?' she questioned softly.

'I couldn't do it, Keri,' he murmured. 'Think of the trouble I'd be in with your agency if you started to get dark rings underneath your eyes.'

Which was a very neat and diplomatic way of getting out of it, but it hurt.

I'll never ask him again, she had vowed. Ever.

Nor did he ever take her to *his* apartment.

Now, why was that?

But her thoughts were broken by the arrival of Erin, minutes later, her face glowing. 'Oooh, I feel wonderful,' she confided. 'Haven't had that done since...' She bit her lip, but then smiled bravely. 'Well, not for ages, anyway.'

'Who knows?' Keri teased. 'We might even get you to the hairdresser's soon.'

'Steady on!' Erin paused in the middle of buttoning up William's coat and frowned at her twin. 'What's up?'

'Nothing.'

'Keri, it's me you're talking to—remember?'

Keri shrugged. 'Jay just came by.'

Erin looked around. 'So where is he now?'

'He went home.'

'In a grump?'

'What makes you say that?'

'Your face does. Did you have a row?'

'No. No, we haven't had a row.'

'Well, what *is* the matter, Keri?'

Was she fussing over something unnecessary? 'I was just thinking that I've never actually seen where he lives.'

Erin's eyebrows shot up. 'How very peculiar.'

'You think so?'

'Of course I do. Maybe he's shy about asking you.'

'Jay? Shy?' Keri gave a hollow laugh. 'I don't think so!'

'Look, you don't have to be so passive about this, you know. Why don't you call over there and surprise him?'

'No,' Keri said slowly. 'I couldn't.'

Erin looked cross. 'Oh, for goodness' sake, Keri— are you a grown woman or some kind of compliant mouse? What's the worst thing that could happen? He won't let you in?'

But that wasn't the worst thing that could happen. The worst thing was something which haunted her in darker moments, even when she tried not to let it. It all finishing. Jay no longer wanting or needing her. Could the world continue to turn if that should happen? She turned to stare out to where stars twinkled untouchably in the distance. Not her world, that was for sure.

And if it all hinged on whether or not she turned

up unexpectedly at his apartment, then wouldn't it be better to find out now?

She took a cab. He lived in Greenwich, close to the river and the park, and his motorbike stood out from all the expensive cars parked along his street.

Her fingers were trembling as she rang the bell, and when he answered he was wearing just jeans, his hair still damp from the shower, his feet bare, the expression on his face watchful and wary.

'Keri,' he said smoothly. 'What a surprise.'

She stood there and looked at him. She certainly wasn't going to force an entrance.

'Come in.'

'Thank you.'

She walked inside and looked around. The apartment was huge, and had spectacular views of the river, but it was so…so *bare* that it made his office look positively overcrowded. There was essential furniture only—a giant sofa in tough, masculine leather in the sitting room, and a bleached oak dining table with matching chairs in the dining section. There was a frighteningly modern kitchen, which looked like the inside of a spacecraft, and a superb sound system, and that, basically, was that.

It was like his office, only more so, because this was where he *lived*, for heaven's sake. But there was little in the way of decoration, only objects which were useful. It looked, she thought, like a temporary place. As if he was renting and about to leave at any time. Transitory and temporary. As if anyone at all could have been living there, for there was nothing of Jay within its four walls.

'Sit down,' he said. 'Can I get you a drink?'

Unlike him, she didn't refuse. 'Yes, please.'

She sat down on the sofa, leaning back and trying to relax, but feeling about as relaxed as someone on a job interview for a position they really wanted. 'Have you lived here long?'

'Just over a year.' He could see her frowning. 'You like it?'

'I...well, yes. Yes, I do—though it's pretty basic.'

'Well, that's how I like it,' he said.

My, but he was touchy! And she would have had to be the dumbest woman in the world not to read the not-so-subtle warning in *that*.

He opened a bottle of white burgundy, poured out two glasses and handed her one, his mouth softening in a smile. 'I'm cooking some Cajun food—ever tried it before?'

She shook her head and sipped at her wine, impressed yet not surprised at his self-sufficiency. No tin-opener and a can of beans for Jay. 'Never.'

'Then you haven't lived.'

The wine hit her stomach, and by the time he sat her up at the table she realised she was very hungry. He served up a concoction of okra and shrimps and rice, which he called Gumbo.

'Eat,' he said.

She did. It was delicious, and she gave a little moan of greed as she tucked in.

He watched her for a while. 'You're really enjoying it, aren't you?' he observed.

She looked up. 'Don't sound so surprised!'

'But I am. When I first met you, you seemed to have made food your enemy.'

'Well, not any longer! Dinner every night and sandwiches for lunch most days!'

His eyes roved over her. 'You're looking well.'

'If by that you mean I've put on weight, then, yes, I have. I could hardly do up the zip of my jeans this morning.' She put her fork down and recklessly drank another mouthful of wine. 'God only knows what's going to happen when I have to go for my next modelling job!'

The statement hung in the air like a bubble waiting to burst.

'You'll have finished the painting soon,' said Jay carefully.

'That's right.' She certainly couldn't drag it out much longer.

'But you'll carry on modelling?'

He was talking about the future, and suddenly she was scared, but she hid her fear in bravado. 'Of course I will—that's what I do! What did you imagine? That I would set myself up as an interior designer?'

'Why not? You're good.'

'Well, for a start I have no qualifications and very little experience.'

'So what?'

'Because things don't work that way, Jay, that's why not!'

She felt frustrated now, the warmth of the wine evaporating with his words. She was terrified of the job ending, because she didn't know whether she would see him again. He hadn't said, and she was afraid to ask...afraid of what the answer might be.

'You've stopped eating,' he said softly.

Well, damn him! Damn him for his indifference and his stubborn determination not to let her spend the night with him!

Keri pushed the plate away, stretched her arms high above her head and yawned. 'I'm tired too,' she confessed.

He watched while the T-shirt spread tightly across her breasts, their tips outlined in provocative display with the dark glossy hair spilling down all over them. He knew what she was doing. It was a blatant demonstration of her physical power over him. For a few moments he had a silent tussle with himself. So, did he give in? Sometimes he liked to deny himself, just to feel fully in control. To prove he could. And it would certainly make it easier. If he made love to her now, he could hardly ask her to leave...

But if she stayed, then where was that going to lead? To more nights, and then still more? Soon she would be cluttering up his very masculine bathroom with all kinds of feminine junk and leaving drifts of lace underwear everywhere. Then she would start asking him what time he was coming home and keeping tabs on him. Very soon after that they would be shopping at the supermarket together—dithering over which brand of juice to buy—and wouldn't that be a kind of living hell?

'Come here,' he instructed silkily.

There was something in his expression which made it impossible to disobey him, even if she had wanted to. And some new, hard light in his eyes, both cautioning and yet inviting.

Like a robot she got up and went to sink onto his lap, but he shook his head.

'No. Not yet.' His eyes glittered. 'First of all, take your clothes off.'

Keri blinked. 'Just like that?'

'Wouldn't you like to strip for me, Keri?' His voice hardened. 'I thought that was what you were working up to.'

Some feeling like fear tiptoed down her spine. He was making her feel like... Like what? Like a live exhibit? A good-time girl? She looked at him, shaken. 'Oddly enough, no. I wouldn't.'

He raised his eyebrows, but in his heart he knew he had been testing her. Now she was hurt; that much was plain. And it told him something that maybe he had been blind to, or had maybe simply chosen not to see. That she saw more in what they had than just a very enjoyable affair. And, if they continued it, wouldn't she get hurt even more? That was his track record, after all—causing pain to women because he couldn't give them what they really wanted.

But he saw the tremble of her lips and something inside him melted. If fighting it didn't seem to work, he found he didn't even want to. He reached out to pull her down onto his lap, because the physical act was easy—he could lose himself in that and forget all the troublesome questions which nagged at his mind.

'Kiss me,' he whispered.

For a moment she resisted, was ice in his arms, but

he drifted his mouth to her neck and the thaw began and there was nothing she could do to stop it.

Her eyes fluttered to a close. 'Oh, Jay,' she said weakly, hating that weakness even while his hands began to stroke her into molten submission.

He took her to his bedroom and took her clothes off himself, slowly—agonisingly slowly—kissing her flesh as he laid it bare.

And she tiptoed her fingers down over his torso, down over his hips, and down further still...

'Keri,' he groaned.

'What?' This was better. The cold-eyed man had gone, and in his place was someone who could be as weak as she was. He loved to control—well, now let *him* be controlled.

She wriggled from beneath him and slithered down his body, her tongue sliding its way to his belly, loving the way he squirmed, holding himself tense, as if he couldn't quite believe that she was going to...

'Oh, God—yes!' he moaned.

She had never done it to a man before, not even with Jay, but she just followed her instincts, her mouth gentle, caressing, teasing and inciting. She found what he liked and then she did it some more. And then some more.

And when at last he moved to push her head away she wouldn't let him. She wanted to possess that most essential part of him in a way which made her feel almost primitive as she tasted the salt which was present in blood and sweat and tears, too.

He shuddered, lost in the mists of pleasure and, for a moment, totally vulnerable.

He lifted her off him and flipped her over onto her back, moving to lie above her, his eyes glittering with a hectic green-grey light, his expression unreadable. She was going to stay in his bed all night, he realised.

'Your turn now,' he said, in an odd kind of voice.

CHAPTER THIRTEEN

JAY seemed edgy and distracted when they showered
and dressed to go to work the following morning, and
it was obvious that he felt relieved when she went off
to find a cab on her own, though he did his best to
hide it.

And while Keri floated around in a dream, because
they'd finally spent the night together, Jay remained
on edge for the rest of the day. When he told her that
he needed to 'catch up' that evening, she wasn't really
surprised. Hurt, yes, but not surprised. But neither of
them had slept much the night before, and things
would be back to normal tomorrow.

But next morning it looked particularly bleak, with
a dank drizzle leaking down from dark and heavy
clouds.

The rain was seeping into Keri's face as she pulled
her bag over her shoulder and ran up the steps, and
once inside she looked around, as if recognising for
the first time that the end of the job really was in sight.

It was amazing the difference she had made—trans-
forming the place into somewhere unrecognisable
from the bland and dingy building it had been. The
strong, vibrant colours had worked out even better
than she had anticipated. The rich sapphire hue em-
phasised and reflected the living water outside, and the

157

dimensions of the rooms were dramatic enough to take it.

Even Jay had said so.

'Some people lack the ability to see what possibilities a place can have,' he had murmured. 'And you have that ability. It's a gift, Keri. It looks so different.'

Maybe he would let her buy a few more prints. She could find a few posters of New Orleans, maybe. He had spent his first few years there and he liked cooking Cajun food—what could be better?

Perhaps she could even get away with a large, leafy plant in the corner—weren't all places supposed to have living things in them? He might like living in a place which resembled an interrogation cell, but that didn't mean he had to work in one.

Andy was on the phone, and she was just hanging up her dripping raincoat and wondering what Jay's reaction would be to a soothing and therapeutic fish tank, when he hung up and looked at her.

'Hi, Keri,' he said, just a little too casually.

Something told her something was wrong.

'Has something happened?'

'Depends what you mean by happened,' answered Andy carefully.

Keri had grown to like Andy. He had a relaxed and uncomplicated nature—so why was he looking as though he had sat down in a nest of ants?

'Where's Jay?'

He took a deep breath, like someone who had been rehearsing how to say something. Or maybe how he had been told to say it.

'He's gone.'

'Gone? Gone where?'

'He had to fly out to New York this morning.'

'How long for?'

'He didn't say.' He must have seen something stricken in her face, because he added, 'It wasn't planned, Keri.'

Keri stared sightlessly at the ground. Maybe it hadn't been—but there were phones, weren't there? And texts. Why, you could even send an e-mail from an airport these days. But Jay hadn't, and it wasn't difficult to work out why.

And there was that soft, underlying note of something approaching sympathy in Andy's voice too.

She looked up. 'You know, don't you, that I've been seeing him? Did he tell you?'

He shook his head. 'He never discusses his personal life with me—ever. I worked it out for myself.' He gave her a sweet smile. 'When a couple go to such a lot of trouble to avoid being together then there's usually a reason why.'

Yes, they had avoided each other as much as possible at work—at *Jay's* instigation—but when she stopped to think about it he had managed to avoid too much contact all round, hadn't he? Never sleeping with her apart from that one reluctant night.

Had Keri committed the cardinal female crime of wishing for something and then imagining that it was coming true? She had wanted him to feel something deeper for her, as she had for him, but it was patently obvious that he didn't.

Andy patted her hand, like a man making peace and

offering comfort. 'It isn't personal, you know. It's just the way he is.'

Her eyes were very clear and bright. 'And what way is that?'

He took a deep breath, as if weighing up whether or not to tell her, but maybe something resolute and determined in her eyes made him decide. 'This is what he does, Keri. He won't be owned or possessed or constrained. He's a free spirit, and the moment he thinks he's in danger of being tied down, or tying *himself* down,' he amended hastily, 'then he just cuts and runs.'

'Runs from what?' she asked tonelessly. 'Himself?'

'Who knows? Maybe.' He was quiet for a moment. 'Let me tell you something about him. I've known him a long time, and he was the best damn commander I ever had, but even I sometimes feel I don't really know him. He's tough and cold and emotionally detached, and needed to be. Those kind of men make the best leaders.'

He glanced up at her. 'When I left the SEALs I sort of…well, I went off the rails. A lot of the guys can't cope with the reality of the real world, and I was one of them. I started drinking—big-time—and then… well, someone thought that it might be a good idea to introduce an already screwed-up guy to drugs.'

His eyes narrowed, and Keri saw the pain in them.

'When Jay found me again I was pretty much dead—I sure wasn't living. He picked me up and cleaned me up and told me that if I ever so much as looked at a chemical substance again he would deal with me himself, and I believed him.'

His voice changed and his eyes looked startlingly blue as he looked into hers. 'I never looked back,' he said. 'He gave me a job—and then somehow he swung it for me to come and work over here when he was starting up. And I worked my butt off, because I wanted to show him just how much I owed him. My life, really,' he added simply.

Keri nodded, for a moment her sense of admiration for her lover eclipsing her bitterness that he had gone away so abruptly.

'He *rescues* people, Keri,' said Andy. 'That's what he does. He sees what they need and he gives it to them, and then he moves on.'

It was like being given the answer to a conundrum which had been puzzling you for ages.

He rescued people.

Yes, of course he did.

He had swept in and rescued Keri, first from the snow and then from her sexual desert, topping it all off by encouraging her to start using her own creative talents instead of just being the blank canvas a model invariably was.

That he had failed to complete the fantasy by galloping off on his charger with her firmly in the saddle didn't mean that *he* had failed, only that she had failed to understand him. Or refused to.

She nodded, like someone who had just been given a piece of bad news but who was determined not to go to pieces over it.

'Well, I guess I'd better finish what I'm being paid for.' Her smile was as bright as anything she had ever flashed on camera. 'And don't I get any coffee this morning, Andy Baxter?'

She told Erin about it between tears and sips of wine. 'God, I could do with a cigarette!' she wailed.

'Well, you can't have one,' said Erin firmly. 'You gave up years ago and you're not starting again now.' She tipped some more wine into her glass. 'Maybe it's not over,' she said hopefully.

But, in a way, wasn't that the worst possible scenario? Nothing would change except for her feelings. Jay wouldn't—why should he? He was happy with his life the way it was. Being a free spirit was probably very enjoyable.

But Keri's feelings would grow—she just knew they would—and where would that get her?

'It has to be over,' she said, putting the glass down with a bump. 'I need it to be, for my peace of mind.'

'And if he calls—you're going to tell him that?'

There was a pause. Keri looked at her twin. 'Well, I was actually hoping that *you* might do that.'

There was a short, disbelieving pause and then Erin shook her head. 'Oh, no, Keri—you have to be out of your mind!'

'Please, Erin, please—we used to do it for each other when we were younger, so what's the difference?'

'Are you serious? The difference is time, and maturity. For a start, I'm ten pounds heavier.'

'I wouldn't count on that at the moment,' Keri answered wryly. 'And you could wear a big sweater!'

Erin looked furious. 'For God's sake, Keri—you've

had a sexual relationship with this man! What am I supposed to do when he starts coming on to me? I presume he knows you have a twin?'

Keri nodded.

'Well, how long do you think it will take him to guess it isn't you at all? About a second?'

Keri frowned. Maybe she was right. Jay might be insensitive to a woman's needs, but he certainly wasn't insensitive to her desires—not only would he guess, but he would be furious!

Did she care about his rage?

No, she did not.

'We could set a meeting up in a restaurant,' she said pleadingly. 'A busy restaurant, where there's no chance of him so much as touching you—he hates public displays of affection anyway. You can tell him over the first course, then walk out and leave him to pay the bill—it will be so short and businesslike that he won't have time to guess it isn't me.'

'Tell him *what*, exactly?'

'That you don't want to see him again. You don't even have to explain yourself, Erin—he certainly didn't offer me any explanation about why he left without so much as a goodbye. And it's only *if* he rings,' she added. 'Which he may not even do. I'm out of his office now, so probably out of his life. This may be the way he's using to break it off without having to go through the discomfort of telling me.'

There was silence for a moment, and when Erin spoke her face was very serious.

'Why can't you just do that yourself—tell him?'

Admission time—time to tell the truth, even though

it damned her. 'Because I don't think I can resist him,' she confessed in a hollow whisper. 'Maybe I won't even want to resist him. But I have to—I need to. If he makes love to me and persuades me to stay it's only putting off the inevitable and increasing the likelihood of more pain. Erin, please. Please.'

There was another pause.

'My hair is different from yours.'

Keri smiled, and the look she gave her sister was tender. 'I think you've done all your mourning now, don't you, kiddo?' she said softly. 'And I know that my hairdresser would be over the moon if you let him style your hair. A present from me to you—as a kind of thank-you for doing something I'm too cowardly to do myself. Think how great you felt when I persuaded you to get your toes done!'

Anticipation gleamed from her eyes and Erin's mouth twitched into an answering smile. 'A baggy jumper, you say? It'll have to be a pretty downmarket restaurant!'

Jay put his helmet down and looked around his office, surveying the bright prints, the warm and vibrant walls, and some tall, fleshy plant which made the room seem somehow alive. He frowned. He didn't remember there being a plant there.

He walked over to the window and stared out at where the sunlight was dancing over the water. His business in New York had been necessary, but not urgent, but he had needed to get away. A change of scene, a change of people—he had never known it not to work before, but this time it hadn't.

So what had gone wrong?

New York had been buzzing, and it was a city he knew well—yet the refuge he had sought had seemed somehow empty.

He had been haunted by Keri, picturing her wide, dark eyes last thing at night, and every morning he had woken aching, unable to dispel the feeling that maybe this time he had cut and run too soon, that he had let go of something which was precious, only he had failed to see it at the time.

'Where is she?' he demanded.

Andy handed him a coffee. 'Who?' he questioned innocently.

'Who? Keri, of course,' Jay growled.

'The job's finished, boss. She's gone.'

'Gone?' he echoed blankly.

So they had got the place back to themselves at last. By rights, he should be pleased. He could work in peace now, and not be distracted by a foxy woman in paint-splattered overalls. He frowned. 'What did she say?'

'Not a lot. She's billed you for the work owing—you'll find it on your desk.'

Jay walked into his office, found the envelope sitting on his desk and slit it open.

But inside was a bill—just that, nothing more. No little note saying, Hope you like it. No kisses. Nothing.

What the hell did you expect?

He picked up the phone and rang her, and it rang for such a long time that he was waiting for it to go through to the machine when she answered at last.

'Hello?'

'Keri?'

Her heart pounded. Keep calm, she told herself. 'Jay?'

'Yes.' He smiled. 'Missed me?'

She quashed the desire to say *Why did you leave without telling me?* She wasn't going to show her hurt, or show she cared. She had no right to say that, in any case—he had never promised her anything. 'I've been busy,' she prevaricated. 'Doing some magazine work.'

'Oh? Anything interesting?'

'Advertising stockings, actually,' she said matter-of-factly.

Stockings? He very nearly dropped the phone. 'So when am I going to see you?'

He had gone away without telling her, and now he was back and clearly feeling rampant. This could obviously be a sexual relationship made in heaven—but was that enough? No, it was not.

Her nerve nearly failed her, but she told herself that it was better this way. Better to suffer the ache of missing him now instead of rekindling the embers of something which was dying.

When something came to an end there had to be some kind of closure—she just didn't trust herself to go through with it on her own.

She looked down at her diary; he wasn't to know that the pages were blank. 'How about lunch? Tomorrow?'

'Lunch?' he echoed, surprised.

'You don't have a problem with lunch, do you?' Of course he did. He probably wanted to carry her straight off to bed, and if he was only just back then he would be needed in the office.

Jay shook his head. He wanted to see her now. Or tonight. And he knew he had no right to ask. He could hear the slight coolness in her voice and knew that he deserved it.

'I can do lunch,' he agreed. 'Where?'

She closed her eyes as she gave him the name of the restaurant. God forgive me, she thought, but I have to do it this way.

CHAPTER FOURTEEN

THERE was a slight murmur in the restaurant, and Jay's eyes moved in her direction as she walked in.

His weren't the only ones, but that shouldn't have surprised him. She really was very, very beautiful, but it was rare for him to observe her from afar like this. He watched her weave her way through the busy room. And his eyes narrowed.

She walked over towards his table, her fingers gripping onto her clutch-bag. 'Hi.'

'Hi,' he said softly.

She sat down. Her hands were trembling, he noticed, and he scanned her eyes, but it was difficult to read anything in them—she'd gone overboard on the make-up and that damned fringe was flopping about all over the place.

She cleared her throat. 'Before we go any further, there's something I need to say to you, Jay.'

He had been watchful before, but now an extra sense of perception crept in and his thumb moved thoughtfully to rub at the faint rasp of shadow at his jaw. 'You don't want to order a drink first?'

'No.' She shook her head, the dark hair spilling like ebony satin all over her shoulders. 'I haven't come here for a drink. Not even for lunch—not really.'

'How very intriguing. What have you come for, then?'

He could see the nervous flutter of her lashes.

'It's not easy to say...'

'Oh, do try,' he coaxed, an odd kind of note in his voice. 'I'm fascinated.'

'I...I just wanted to tell you how much I enjoyed what we had. But I've been doing a lot of thinking—and, well, I think it's best if we don't see one another again.' She gave a brittle smile. 'That's it, really.' And pushed her chair back. 'I shouldn't think you'll be *too* broken-hearted.'

He waited until she was standing, and then he smiled.

'Will you do me a favour before you go?' he asked quietly.

She looked startled. 'What is it?'

His voice became edged with a certain hardness. 'Just tell Keri I'll be in touch.'

Keri had thought of leaving the Ansaphone on. Of vacating her apartment for a week or two. Even of ringing her agency up and asking if they had any lengthy shoots in exotic locations.

But what would be the point? If Jay wanted to see her, then see her he would—she didn't doubt that for a moment. And, though her courage had failed her before, surely she could grasp it with two hands now? He knew what she wanted—or, rather, what she *needed* to do, and he was man enough to accept that.

When the doorbell rang, loudly and angrily, she didn't need to check in the peephole to see who it was. She just opened the door to him, thinking how tight his features looked. He was dressed in his habitual black, but today he looked as menacing as she had ever seen him.

'You'd better come in.'

He was silent as he stepped inside, silent as he closed the door behind him. His eyes were hot and angry, and when he spoke his voice was as tight as a coiled spring.

'Do you take me for a complete fool, Keri?'

She was taken aback by the depth of his venom. 'How did you guess?'

'How did I guess?' he exploded. 'That you'd sent your twin to try to do your dirty work for you? Do you think I'm completely lacking in comprehension?'

'But we're identical!' she blurted out.

'No, you look nearly the same,' he corrected grimly. 'But you are *not* identical. No two human beings are— nor ever could be. For a start you're a model, and you have a way of moving which is both studied and nat- ural—your sister doesn't. She talks differently. She clearly *thinks* differently too. I've never seen a woman look more uncomfortable—tell me, did you have to twist her arm to get her to agree?'

Keri turned and began walking away, but Jay fol- lowed her, and once they had reached the sitting room there was no escape left to her. He caught her, turned her round to face him, the grey-green eyes blazing.

'Did you?'

'Yes,' she admitted, in a whisper.

'Why, Keri? Just tell me why! If you want it to be over, then why the hell didn't you tell me so yourself? You're a strong woman—an independent woman—

surely you must have had to say that to men plenty of times during your life?'

She bit her lip. In this he was wrong. She wasn't strong—not around him. She was all open and raw and hurting, weak and wounded from the pain of wanting him.

'Don't make me say it, Jay!'

'Say what? That you've had enough? That your rough-tough man was good for a while but now he's shown you that you're a normal woman who can experience pleasure it's time to move on to someone more suited to a high-class model?'

The way he said *high-class* made it sound like something else altogether.

'Don't be so dense!' she snapped. 'It isn't like that, and you bloody well know it!'

Jay expelled a breath. His heart was pounding like a piston and he wanted to shake her and kiss her all at the same time. What the *hell* was she doing to him? 'Then tell me what it *is* like, Keri?' he demanded silkily.

'*You're* the one who just upped and went off without even telling me you were going! You're the cautious, wary man who goes on about your independence and the way you like *your* flat to look. As if I'm trying to ensnare you and get you to march me down the aisle!'

'This is all to do with the fact that I went away on business without first asking your permission?'

'That's got nothing to do with it! You were running away!'

He froze and stared at her incredulously. 'I was *what*? And just what, pray, was I running away from?'

'From me! From the relationship! Just the way you always do. Andy told me.'

'Oh, did he?' he questioned dangerously. 'Well, I'll just have to have a word with Andy—he works with me, for God's sake, he's not my damned analyst!'

'Oh, don't shoot the messenger!' she declared furiously. 'I didn't actually need Andy to tell me, if you must know. I'd worked it out for myself and he just confirmed it. Well, I've made it easy for you. I'm giving you the let-out clause. It's over! That's what you want, isn't it?'

There was silence for a moment, and when he looked at her his eyes were bright and piercing. 'Is that what you want?'

Of course it wasn't what she wanted! She glared at him. 'I asked first!'

He felt a pain so fierce he couldn't believe that it wasn't physical. 'Oh, Keri,' he groaned. 'Of course it isn't what I want.'

She didn't care if it scared him away; she just knew that she could not exist in this curious half-life of not knowing. 'Then just what *do* you want, Jay?' she asked pointedly.

He knew he owed her this, but it was difficult to find the words to describe the way he felt—he'd never had to do it before. Not even to himself. Yet he looked into her dark eyes and knew he had to. No, he wanted to. He just wasn't sure he knew how.

Just when had this all happened? he asked himself dazedly. This connection to another person which seemed to have reached out and captured him? In his time he had triumphed in hostage rescue and guerrilla warfare, but this was completely unknown territory.

'I want you,' he said at last.

There should have been joy, but all she felt was suspicion. And feelings which she had been flattening down, as you would a sandcastle, suddenly erupted out in a storm.

'Sure you do, Jay—that's why you ran away. Because I had the temerity to turn up uninvited at your apartment and end up staying the night with you! My God, you couldn't have given me a clearer message if you'd tried!'

He sighed. 'I know.'

It was the first chink she had ever seen in his armour. A fleeting moment of something which, if it were any other man than Jay, might almost be described as vulnerability. And all her anger left her. She felt as cautious as someone trying to offer food to a wild, starving animal.

Her voice softened. 'So why? What's changed?'

'I have,' he said slowly. 'I've changed—or, rather, you've made me want to change. I've never wanted to settle down before, and I always ran away from commitment because...'

He could blame a lot of things; that was what people did. His parents' divorce and the subsequent transatlantic ping-pong. Or his choice of a male-dominated career and his need for the emotional detachment which that career demanded.

Or he could say it how it was. Incredibly and unbelievably how it was. So simple, really, like all the very best things in life.

He looked at her, and she had never seen his eyes look so bright. 'Because I never found the right woman before, and now I have.'

For a moment she didn't believe him. Didn't dare to for fear that she was dreaming it and in a moment she would wake up to the bleak reality of a life without Jay. But the message burning from his eyes told her that he spoke the truth, plain and simple. He cared for her. Deeply. Deeper than deep. He hadn't yet used the conventional vocabulary for saying so, but then Jay was not a conventional man. And love didn't always have to be spoken out loud.

Some women might have wanted more than that, but she took the words at more than their face value. He was breaking what for him was a taboo. He had started searching beneath what was happening on the surface of his life, and for a man like Jay that was something pretty big.

Those other words might follow, but she wanted to savour this—the look in his eyes which was reaching out to her, telling her that this strong, experienced man could be vulnerable too.

Come to think of it, she felt a bit that way herself. As if she was standing on the brink of a great big sea, and was about to dabble her toe in and get it wet.

'Oh, Jay,' she whispered.

Some day he would tell her about the bitter trans-atlantic custody battle which had dominated his growing up. And of the fear of making any place too permanent, knowing that the courts could snatch him away at any time. Through all his childhood he had never trusted in the word 'home'.

He held his arms out and she went into them, as if she had found her safe harbour too, and they stood there together for a long, long time.

CHAPTER FIFTEEN

THE light had that bright, almost bleached quality which was particular to the Caribbean. Huge, fleshy palm trees fringed the dancing aquamarine of the sea and provided welcome shade from the dazzling sun overhead.

The photo-shoot was finished, and the other models and stylists and photographers were paying serious attention to the cocktails on offer at the beach bar, but Keri felt light-headed after one and a half Cosmopolitans. It was really too hot to drink alcohol, and she wished she could just find herself on a plane heading back to England.

And Jay.

'Think I'll head back to the hotel.' She yawned. 'Maybe have a sleep and then go for a swim.'

No one could persuade her to change her mind, and she didn't think they'd miss her much. Something happened to a woman when she was in love and the object of her affections was several thousand miles away. It meant she was there only in body and not in spirit, no matter how much she tried.

Over the months something had changed in her too, because time changed everything. Her feelings for Jay had grown deeper and stronger—the tiny pebble on which their relationship had started had become a firm bedrock. They lived their lives in parallel harmony—

each with their successful career, spending nights and weekends together in his flat or hers.

She glanced out at the pale blue water. Was there something inherent in human nature that made you always long for what you didn't have? She had the relationship she had always longed for—one that fulfilled her in every way which mattered—and yet somehow she wanted more. She wanted marriage, she realised—and babies too. And, while he showed her that he adored her in every way that counted, she sensed that the whole family package would be a commitment too far.

So stop yearning for the impossible, she told herself—just enjoy what you have.

She saw a figure in the far distance, heading her way, and her idle glance became a double-take as her heart suddenly missed a beat. She shook her head slightly. For a minute there she had imagined she'd seen Jay, walking across the beach towards her.

Yeah, sure. He had secretly taken a flight out to join her the day before she was due to fly home—in your dreams, Keri!

She continued to walk towards the approaching man, waiting for confirmation that it was just another tall, dark stranger enjoying the delights of a Caribbean holiday.

It was difficult to say at what point she realised that she had not been mistaken. She was too far away to see the expression on the beautiful scarred face, and his eyes were shielded by a pair of wraparound shades, but some sense which transcended sight told her without a doubt that it was Jay.

She was so taken aback that her footsteps faltered to a halt. Funny how reality never quite fitted the dream. She should be flinging her arms out and running towards him, and he should catch her in his arms and whirl her round and round and round. But...

Why was he here?

She looked, he thought, like the stuff that dreams were made of, sillhouetted against the blinding light in some pale, floaty dress with a flower-laden straw hat shielding her face from the blazing sun.

He moved towards her slowly, wanting to enjoy the moment, his heart beating loud and strong in his chest, his head feeling curiously light. Now he could see the pale heart-shaped face, and the look of bewilderment and anxiety in the dark eyes, and he felt a rush of something deeper than desire.

'What's happened?' Keri demanded, her heart beating with fear. 'What are you doing here?'

He smiled. 'What kind of a greeting is that for your lover?'

Briefly, she thought how modern, how *temporary* that sounded. She looked up at him questioningly, but she could not read the expression behind the shades he wore and it was too blindingly bright to ask him to take them off. 'Jay?'

He reached his hand out, brushing the fringe from her eyes as he had once done a lifetime ago. 'Aren't you pleased to see me?' he asked softly.

'Of course I am,' she answered breathlessly, but she didn't fall into his arms, and neither did he pull her into them. 'Nothing's wrong, is it?'

'Well, that depends on your definition of wrong.'

'*Jay!*' Her voice was shaking, remonstrating, breathless. 'I'm due home tomorrow—why are you here?'

'Because I've missed you.'

'Well, that's…'

'That's what?'

'Surprising,' she admitted.

'Yeah,' he agreed, with a rueful smile. 'Thought I'd be crazy about a woman who gave me plenty of space.'

She opened her eyes very wide. She had clung on to her independence like a lifeline, because an independent woman was the one he had been attracted to.

'And aren't you?'

'Completely and utterly crazy,' he said gravely.

'It doesn't happen very often,' she pointed out. 'The trips, I mean.'

'No.'

'And you spent your whole life travelling all over the place.'

'I know I did.' And he hoped to God that she wasn't living the kind of life he had lived when he was in the SEALs! No, he knew she wasn't—she was sweet and loyal and true—but when she was away he found himself aching for her in a way which was quite alien to him. But if that was the way she wanted it, then that was the way it had to be. He bent and touched her lips with his. 'Do you like being away for weeks at a time, sweetheart?'

Keri hesitated. 'Well, actually, no—not really.'

He frowned. 'Then why do you do it?'

'Because it's my job! Because the best shoots are

ones like these—they pay well and keep my profile high. And, oddly enough, I seem to have got more work since I developed a few curves—and that's all down to you, Jay!'

'But what happened to the interior design?' he questioned. 'I thought my offices were supposed to be your starting block for a whole new change of direction?'

'That was more *your* dream, not mine!'

'I thought for a while it was yours, too, Keri. Did exposure to it put you off it?'

She bit her lip. Oh, what the hell? Just tell him— *tell him.* 'I decided not to start something else because my relationship with you was too new and too important, and I wanted to concentrate on that. I didn't want to make any big career changes because I didn't...' Her voice faltered and her words trailed away as she stared down at the sand.

'Didn't what?' he prompted softly. 'Look at me, Keri.'

This was the crunch moment. Did she have the courage to say it and risk the consequences?

'I can't see your eyes,' she whispered.

He took the shades off. 'How's that?' he questioned steadily.

Better—and worse. She had never seen him look more intent or serious, and she knew then that she had no choice, that the crunch time really *had* come.

'I didn't know if we were going to last. Or if you would change your mind about commitment,' she admitted. 'And I wasn't sure that I could cope with all that if I'd made a huge life-change.'

He nodded, recognising that insecurity still dogged

her. She hadn't rushed him, or pushed him or hinted or cajoled—and hadn't part of him perhaps been waiting for her to do that, wondering if then he truly would feel trapped? But this relationship was no trap. He had found a place he wanted to stay and he wanted to secure that place, to make it permanent and to make it home. To anchor down. And he needed to tell her.

'I love you, Keri,' he said simply, wondering why it had taken so long for him to get around to saying it. He felt as if someone had lit a fire inside him. It had started out as just a tiny flicker, the kind of flame you had to cherish and to nurture, and now it was blazing within him. And feelings, he was discovering, like fires, couldn't be hurried. 'I love you,' he said again, and his smile was blinding.

'Oh, Jay!' She began to cry, and he pulled her into his arms and held onto her as if he would never let her go. After a while she was through, and he kissed the tip of her nose.

'What the hell are you crying about?' he questioned tenderly.

'I love you too, so much!'

By now he had learnt that women *always* cried for a reason, and if Keri was crying her heart out because she loved him, then that was just fine with him.

Everything seemed to happen in a bit of a blur after that. They kissed for a while, and quite passionately too—but they were on a Caribbean beach where that kind of behaviour was seen as perfectly respectable, so nobody gave them a second glance.

Until eventually Keri just wanted some privacy.

'Shall we go back to the hotel?'

He smiled and felt the pump of his heart. 'I guess we'd better.'

They walked hand in hand along the sand, but as they approached the hotel they heard the jubilant beat of steel drums and saw a couple barefoot in the sea, the woman dressed in white with a garland of flowers in her hair and the man in a white tuxedo.

'Oh, Jay, look,' she breathed. 'It's a wedding!'

He thought fleetingly that it was easier to get behind enemy lines than to understand what was going on inside the head of a woman. 'You want to get married?' he questioned casually. 'Here?'

She stopped, dead. 'Oh, my God! You want to marry me?'

'Of course I do,' he answered steadily. 'What do you think I came out here for? Do you want to marry me?'

'You know I do! But not here,' she said firmly. 'I mean, I know it's beautiful and romantic and everything, but...' She looked up at him and her eyes were suddenly anxious. 'I'd really like my parents there. And Erin—she'd never forgive me if I did it without telling her. Would you mind, darling?'

He thought of Keri's twin—of her courage and her strength and the little boy she was raising just fine.

His face softened as he tilted up her chin to look at him. 'Tell you what—how do you suppose your family would like a holiday in the Caribbean?'

And in that moment she loved him so much she felt her heart would burst. 'Oh, Jay! Can't you just imagine William playing on that beautiful sand?'

He nodded and drew a deep breath, knowing that

he couldn't put this off any longer. 'There's something else, Keri.'

Some unrecognisable quality in his voice made her look at him very hard.

'You see, my name isn't Jay Linur at all.'

EPILOGUE

KERI gave the ribbon around the ceramic pot holding a bay tree a last tweak, and stood back for an overall view of the newly painted shop-front. The opening of Linur Lifestyles was due to take place in a couple of hours' time. There were bottles of champagne chilling, and soon caterers would be arriving with bite-sized hamburgers and mini fish and chips housed in tiny little cornets of newspaper. 'A celebration of the best of both English and American cuisine,' Keri had announced, and Jay had laughed.

'What do you think?' she asked now, anxiously.

He looked down at her. 'Honestly?'

'Honestly.'

He smiled. 'I think it looks absolutely incredible. And so, incidentally, do you. But then, you always do.'

She smiled back as she touched his face, remembering the bombshell he had dropped just before their wedding. About his father, heir to one of America's biggest fortunes, which Jay had inherited. 'Just too much money,' he had said bitterly. 'And that kind of wealth taints things.' He had wanted good to come of it, not corruption, and had set up a charitable foundation to help children who were underprivileged in all senses of the word. And he had adopted his mother's surname to distance himself from all of the expectation which his father's carried.

184

Had she been shocked by the revelation? Not really, no. Nothing Jay did could surprise her—only delight her. She had thought right at the beginning that learning to know him was like peeling away all the layers of an onion, and in that she had been uncannily right.

Oh, he could still be autocratic, and stubborn, and high-handed, but these days she found that a bit of a turn-on. Well, more than a bit.

He lifted her hand from where it was still tweaking unnecessarily at the ribbon and lifted it to his lips. It was a sweet and romantic gesture, but then he captured her gaze as he slowly licked his way along one of the fingers and Keri coloured with pleasure. Gone was the man who had only shown affection in bed—but then, so much had changed.

With Jay. With her. With them both. Love was a liberating thing, she decided—it made you free to say what was really in your heart, instead of worrying whether or not it was the right thing to say. And the astonishing thing was that their wants and their needs seemed to coincide perfectly.

It had all started with a remark he had made while they were waiting for the papers to come through for their Caribbean wedding. They had been strolling along a moon-washed beach, with the stars as bright as diamonds in the sky above them.

'The stars are so clear here,' Jay had said, almost wistfully, and she'd remembered him saying something similar before—that city lights meant you couldn't really see the stars properly.

And so she had hatched a plan. They would move to the country and he could work from an office there, leaving Andy in charge of the London office.

'I really think he's ready for promotion,' she had

said seriously, 'Ready to move out from underneath your wing. And I think it's time you stopped doing such dangerous missions.'

'Oh, do you?' He laughed, thinking that once he would have been outraged if anyone had suggested that. But now he was ready. More than ready.

'Yes. And I can quit modelling—I *want* to, Jay— and I can start up the design business. I can afford to.'

'*We* can afford to,' he said possessively.

Keri nodded, growing warm with pleasure because it all seemed to make such perfect sense.

'And I can give my apartment to Erin, and I'm not going to take no for an answer. She can live there or she can sell it, if that's what she wants.'

Erin had agreed to accept the gift, bowing under the gentle pressure from both Keri and Jay. In the end she had opted to sell, and to move to the country not far from them.

'There's not a lot of point me being in London if you're not there, Keri,' she'd said. 'That's if you don't mind, Jay?'

He'd shaken his head. 'I don't mind a bit.'

Jay had grown to understand the intense bond between the twins, to cherish it and not to be threatened by it, as some men might have been. And he liked Erin—she was a lot like his wife, but she was different. As he'd said—no two people were the same, even though a lot of people seemed to have difficulty telling them apart. But he would have known Keri in the dark from a hundred paces, and that was just instinct.

No, maybe not just instinct. It was something else— something much stronger than instinct.

He smiled down at his wife.

It was love.

THE ROYAL HOUSE OF KAREDES

Two crowns, two islands, one legacy

Volume 1 – April 2009
BILLIONAIRE PRINCE, PREGNANT MISTRESS
by Sandra Marton

Volume 2 – May 2009
THE SHEIKH'S VIRGIN STABLE-GIRL
by Sharon Kendrick

Volume 3 – June 2009
THE PRINCE'S CAPTIVE WIFE
by Marion Lennox

Volume 4 – July 2009
THE SHEIKH'S FORBIDDEN VIRGIN
by Kate Hewitt

8 VOLUMES IN ALL TO COLLECT!